The Love of a Good Woman

The Love of a Good Woman

Alice Munro

W F HOWES LTD

This large print edition published 2002 by
W F Howes Ltd
Units 6/7, Victoria Mills, Fowke Street
Rothley, Leicester LE7 7PJ

1 3 5 7 9 10 8 6 4 2

First published in the United Kingdom in 1998 by
Chatto & Windus Ltd

A CIP catalogue record for this book is available
from the British Library

ISBN 1 84197 513 3

Typeset by Palimpsest Book Production Limited,
Polmont, Stirlingshire
Printed and bound in Great Britain
by Antony Rowe Ltd, Chippenham, Wilts.

For Ann Close

My valued editor and constant friend

AUTHOR'S NOTE

For certain expert information essential to these stories, my thanks to Ruth Roy, Mary Carr, and D. C. Coleman. And for his inspired and ingenious research on many occasions, I thank Reg Thompson.

Stories included in this collection that were previously published in *The New Yorker* appeared there in very different form.

CONTENTS

The Love of a Good Woman

THE LOVE OF A GOOD WOMAN

For the last couple of decades, there has been a museum in Walley, dedicated to preserving photos and butter churns and horse harnesses and an old dentist's chair and a cumbersome apple peeler and such curiosities as the pretty little porcelain-and-glass insulators that were used on telegraph poles.

Also there is a red box, which has the letters D. M. WILLENS, OPTOMETRIST printed on it, and a note beside it, saying, 'This box of optometrist's instruments though not very old has considerable local significance, since it belonged to Mr D. M. Willens, who drowned in the Peregrine River, 1951. It escaped the catastrophe and was found, presumably by the anonymous donor, who dispatched it to be a feature of our collection.'

The ophthalmoscope could make you think of a snowman. The top part, that is – the part that's fastened onto the hollow handle. A large disk, with a smaller disk on top. In the large disk a hole to look through, as the various lenses are moved. The handle is heavy because the batteries are still inside. If you took the batteries out and put in the rod that

1

is provided, with a disk on either end, you could plug in an electric cord. But it might have been necessary to use the instrument in places where there wasn't any electricity.

The retinoscope looks more complicated. Underneath the round forehead clamp is something like an elf's head, with a round flat face and a pointed metal cap. This is tilted at a forty-five-degree angle to a slim column, and out of the top of the column a tiny light is supposed to shine. The flat face is made of glass and is a dark sort of mirror.

Everything is black, but that is only paint. In some places where the optometrist's hand must have rubbed most often, the paint has disappeared and you can see a patch of shiny silver metal.

I. JUTLAND

This place was called Jutland. There had been a mill once, and some kind of small settlement, but that had all gone by the end of the last century, and the place had never amounted to much at any time. Many people believed that it had been named in honor of the famous sea battle fought during the First World War, but actually everything had been in ruins years before that battle ever took place.

The three boys who came out here on a Saturday morning early in the spring of 1951 believed, as most children did, that the name came from the old wooden planks that jutted out of the earth of the riverbank and from the other straight thick boards that stood up in the nearby water, making an uneven palisade. (These were in fact the remains of a dam, built before the days of cement.) The planks and a heap of foundation stones and a lilac bush and some huge apple trees deformed by black knot and the shallow ditch of the millrace that filled up with nettles every summer were the only other signs of what had been here before.

There was a road, or a track, coming back from the township road, but it had never been gravelled, and appeared on the maps only as a dotted line, a road allowance. It was used quite a bit in the summer by people driving to the river to swim or at night by couples looking for a place to park. The turnaround spot came before you got to the ditch, but the whole area was so overrun by nettles, and cow parsnip, and woody wild hemlock in a wet year, that cars would sometimes have to back out all the way to the proper road.

The car tracks to the water's edge on that spring morning were easy to spot but were not taken notice of by these boys, who were thinking only about swimming. At least, they would call it swimming; they would go back to town and say that they had been swimming at Jutland before the snow was off the ground.

It was colder here upstream than on the river flats close to the town. There was not a leaf out yet on the riverbank trees – the only green you saw was from patches of leeks on the ground and marsh

3

marigolds fresh as spinach, spread along any little stream that gullied its way down to the river. And on the opposite bank under some cedars they saw what they were especially looking for – a long, low, stubborn snowbank, gray as stones.

Not off the ground.

So they would jump into the water and feel the cold hit them like ice daggers. Ice daggers shooting up behind their eyes and jabbing the tops of their skulls from the inside. Then they would move their arms and legs a few times and haul themselves out, quaking and letting their teeth rattle; they would push their numb limbs into their clothes and feel the painful recapture of their bodies by their startled blood and the relief of making their brag true.

The tracks that they didn't notice came right through the ditch – in which there was nothing growing now, there was only the flat dead straw-colored grass of the year before. Through the ditch and into the river without trying to turn around. The boys tramped over them. But by this time they were close enough to the water to have had their attention caught by something more extraordinary than car tracks.

There was a pale-blue shine to the water that was not a reflection of sky. It was a whole car, down in the pond on a slant, the front wheels and the nose of it poking into the mud on the bottom, and the bump of the trunk nearly breaking the surface. Light blue was in those days an unusual

4

color for a car, and its bulgy shape was unusual, too. They knew it right away. The little English car, the Austin, the only one of its kind surely in the whole county. It belonged to Mr Willens, the optometrist. He looked like a cartoon character when he drove it, because he was a short but thick man, with heavy shoulders and a large head. He always seemed to be crammed into his little car as if it was a bursting suit of clothes.

The car had a panel in its roof, which Mr Willens opened in warm weather. It was open now. They could not see very well what was inside. The color of the car made its shape plain in the water, but the water was really not very clear, and it obscured what was not so bright. The boys squatted down on the bank, then lay on their stomachs and pushed their heads out like turtles, trying to see. There was something dark and furry, something like a big animal tail, pushed up through the hole in the roof and moving idly in the water. This was shortly seen to be an arm, covered by the sleeve of a dark jacket of some heavy and hairy material. It seemed that inside the car a man's body – it had to be the body of Mr Willens – had got into a peculiar position. The force of the water – for even in the millpond there was a good deal of force in the water at this time of year – must have somehow lifted him from the seat and pushed him about, so that one shoulder was up near the car roof and one arm had got free. His head must have been shoved down against the driver's door and window. One front wheel was stuck deeper in the river bottom than the other, which meant that the car was on a slant from side to side as well as back to front. The window in fact must have been open and the head sticking out for the body to be lodged in that position. But they could not get to see that. They could picture Mr Willens's face as they knew it – a big square face, which often wore a theatrical sort of frown but was never seriously intimidating. His thin crinkly hair was reddish or brassy on top, and combed diagonally over his forehead. His eyebrows were darker than his hair, thick and fuzzy like caterpillars stuck above his eyes. This was a face already grotesque to them, in the way that many adult faces were, and they were not afraid to see it drowned. But all they got to see was that arm and his pale hand. They could see the hand quite plain once they got used to looking through the water. It rode there tremulously and irresolutely, like a feather, though it looked as solid as dough. And as ordinary, once you got used to its being there at all. The fingernails were all like neat little faces, with their intelligent everyday look of greeting, their sensible disowning of their circumstances.

'Son of a gun,' these boys said. With gathering energy and a tone of deepening respect, even of gratitude. *Son of a gun.*

It was their first time out this year. They had come across the bridge over the Peregrine River, the single-lane double-span bridge known locally as Hell's Gate or the Death Trap – though the danger had really more to do with the sharp turn the road took at the south end of it than with the bridge itself.

There was a regular walkway for pedestrians, but they didn't use it. They never remembered using it. Perhaps years ago, when they were so young as to be held by the hand. But that time had vanished for them; they refused to recognize it even if they were shown the evidence in snapshots or forced to listen to it in family conversation.

They walked now along the iron shelf that ran on the opposite side of the bridge from the walkway. It was about eight inches wide and a foot or so above the bridge floor. The Peregrine River was rushing the winter load of ice and snow, now melted, out into Lake Huron. It was barely back within its banks after the yearly flood that turned the flats into a lake and tore out the young trees and bashed any boat or hut within its reach. With the runoff from the fields muddying the water and the pale sunlight on its surface, the water looked like butterscotch pudding on the boil. But if you fell into it, it would freeze your blood and fling you out into the lake, if it didn't brain you against the buttresses first.

Cars honked at them – a warning or a reproof – but they paid no attention. They proceeded single file, as self-possessed as sleepwalkers. Then, at the north end of the bridge, they cut down to the flats, locating the paths they remembered from the year before. The flood had been so recent that these paths were not easy to follow. You had to kick your way through beaten-down brush and jump from one hummock of mud-plastered grass to another. Sometimes they jumped carelessly and landed in mud or pools of leftover floodwater, and once their feet were wet they gave up caring where they landed. They squelched through the mud and splashed in the pools so that the water came in over the tops of their rubber boots. The wind was warm; it was pulling the clouds apart into threads of old wool, and the gulls and crows were quarrelling and diving over the river. Buzzards were circling over them, on the high lookout; the robins had just returned, and the red-winged blackbirds were darting in pairs, striking bright on your eyes as if they had been dipped in paint.

'Should've brought a twenty-two.'

'Should've brought a twelve-gauge.'

They were too old to raise sticks and make shooting noises. They spoke with casual regret, as if guns were readily available to them.

They climbed up the north banks to a place where there was bare sand. Turtles were supposed to lay their eggs in this sand. It was too early yet for that to happen, and in fact the story of turtle eggs dated from years back – none of these boys had ever seen any. But they kicked and stomped the sand, just in case. Then they looked around for the place where last year one of them, in company with another boy, had found a cow's hipbone, carried off by the flood from some slaughter pile. The river could be counted on every year to sweep off and deposit elsewhere a good number of surprising or cumbersome or bizarre or homely objects. Rolls of wire, an intact set of steps, a bent shovel, a corn kettle. The hip-bone had been found caught on the branch of a sumac – which seemed proper, because all those smooth branches were like cow horns or deer antlers, some with rusty cone tips.

They crashed around for some time – Cece Ferns showed them the exact branch – but they found nothing.

It was Cece Ferns and Ralph Diller who had made that find, and when asked where it was at present Cece Ferns said, 'Ralph took it.' The two boys who were with him now – Jimmy Box and Bud Salter – knew why that would have to be. Cece could never take anything home unless it was of a size to be easily concealed from his father.

They talked of more useful finds that might be made or had been made in past years. Fence rails could be used to build a raft, pieces of stray lumber could be collected for a planned shack or boat. Real luck would be to get hold of some loose muskrat traps. Then you could go into business. You could pick up enough lumber for stretching boards and steal the knives for skinning. They spoke of taking over an empty shed they knew of, in the blind alley behind what used to be the livery barn. There was a padlock on it, but you could probably get in through the window, taking the boards off it at night and replacing them at daybreak. You could take a flashlight to work by. No – a lantern. You could skin the muskrats and stretch the pelts and sell them for a lot of money.

This project became so real to them that they started to worry about leaving valuable pelts in the shed all day. One of them would have to stand watch while the others went out on the traplines. (Nobody mentioned school.)

This was the way they talked when they got clear of town. They talked as if they were free – or almost free – agents, as if they didn't go to school or live with families or suffer any of the indignities put on them because of their age. Also, as if the countryside and other people's establishments would provide them with all they needed for their undertakings and adventures, with only the smallest risk and effort on their part.

Another change in their conversation out here was that they practically gave up using names. They didn't use each other's real names much anyway – not even family nicknames such as Bud. But at school nearly everyone had another name, some of these having to do with the way people looked or talked, like Goggle or Jabber, and some, like Sore-arse and Chickenfucker, having to do with incidents real or fabulous in the lives of those named, or in the lives – such names were handed down for decades – of their brothers, fathers, or uncles. These were the names they let go of when they were out in the bush or on the river flats. If they had to get one another's attention, all they said was 'Hey.' Even the use of names that were outrageous and obscene and that grown-ups supposedly never heard would have spoiled a sense they had at these times, of taking each other's looks, habits, family, and personal history entirely for granted.

And yet they hardly thought of each other as friends. They would never have designated someone as a best friend or a next-best friend, or joggled people around in these positions, the way girls did. Any one of at least a dozen boys could have been substituted for any one of these three, and accepted by the others in exactly the same way. Most members of that company were between nine and twelve years old, too old to be bound by yards and neighborhoods but too young to have jobs – even jobs sweeping the sidewalk in front of stores or delivering groceries by bicycle. Most of them lived in the north end of town, which meant that they would be expected to get a job of that sort as soon as they were old enough, and that none of them would ever be sent away to Appleby or to Upper Canada College. And none of them lived in a shack or had a relative in jail. Just the same, there were notable differences as to how they lived at home and what was expected of them in life. But these differences dropped away as soon as they were out of sight of the county jail and the grain elevator and the church steeples and out of range of the chimes of the courthouse clock.

⋆   ⋆   ⋆

On their way back they walked fast. Sometimes they trotted but did not run. Jumping, dallying, splashing, were all abandoned, and the noises they'd made on their way out, the hoots and howls, were put aside as well. Any windfall of the flood was taken note of but passed by. In fact they made their way as adults would do, at a fairly steady speed and by the most reasonable route, with the weight on them of where they had to go and what had to be done next. They had something close in front of them, a picture in front of their eyes that came between them and the world, which was the thing most adults seemed to have. The pond, the car, the arm, the hand. They had some idea that when they got to a certain spot they would start to shout. They would come into town yelling and waving their news around them and everybody would be stockstill, taking it in.

They crossed the bridge the same way as always, on the shelf. But they had no sense of risk or courage or nonchalance. They might as well have taken the walkway.

Instead of following the sharp-turning road from which you could reach both the harbor and the square, they climbed straight up the bank on a path that came out near the railway sheds. The clock played its quarter-after chimes. A quarter after twelve.

This was the time when people were walking home for dinner. People from offices had the afternoon

12

off. But people who worked in stores were getting only their customary hour – the stores stayed open till ten or eleven o'clock on Saturday night.

Most people were going home to a hot, filling meal. Pork chops, or sausages, or boiled beef, or cottage roll. Potatoes for certain, mashed or fried; winter-stored root vegetables or cabbage or creamed onions. (A few housewives, richer or more feckless, might have opened a tin of peas or butter beans.) Bread, muffins, preserves, pie. Even those people who didn't have a home to go to, or who for some reason didn't want to go there, would be sitting down to much the same sort of food at the Duke of Cumberland, or the Merchants' Hotel, or for less money behind the foggy windows of Shervill's Dairy Bar.

Those walking home were mostly men. The women were already there – they were there all the time. But some women of middle age who worked in stores or offices for a reason that was not their fault – dead husbands or sick husbands or never any husband at all – were friends of the boys' mothers, and they called out greetings even across the street (it was worst for Bud Salter, whom they called Buddy) in a certain amused or sprightly way that brought to mind all they knew of family matters, or distant infancies.

Men didn't bother greeting boys by name, even if they knew them well. They called them 'boys' or 'young fellows' or, occasionally, 'sirs.'

'Good day to you, sirs.'

'You boys going straight home now?'

'What monkey business you young fellows been up to this morning?'

All these greetings had a degree of jocularity, but there were differences. The men who said 'young fellows' were better disposed – or wished to seem better disposed – than the ones who said 'boys.' 'Boys' could be the signal that a telling off was to follow, for offenses that could be either vague or specific. 'Young fellows' indicated that the speaker had once been young himself. 'Sirs' was outright mockery and disparagement but didn't open the way to any scolding, because the person who said that could not be bothered.

When answering, the boys didn't look up past any lady's purse or any man's Adam's apple. They said 'Hullo' clearly, because there might be some kind of trouble if you didn't, and in answer to queries they said 'Yessir' and 'Nosir' and 'Nothing much.' Even on this day, such voices speaking to them caused some alarm and confusion, and they replied with the usual reticence.

At a certain corner they had to separate. Cece Ferns, always the most anxious about getting home, pulled away first. He said, 'See you after dinner.'

Bud Salter said, 'Yeah. We got to go downtown then.'

This meant, as they all understood, 'downtown to the Police Office.' It seemed that without needing to consult each other they had taken up a new plan of operation, a soberer way of telling their

14

news. But it wasn't clearly said that they wouldn't be telling anything at home. There wasn't any good reason why Bud Salter or Jimmy Box couldn't have done that.

Cece Ferns never told anything at home.

Cece Ferns was an only child. His parents were older than most boys' parents, or perhaps they only seemed older, because of the disabling life they lived together. When he got away from the other boys, Cece started to trot, as he usually did for the last block home. This was not because he was eager to get there or because he thought he could make anything better when he did. It may have been to make the time pass quickly, because the last block had to be full of apprehension.

His mother was in the kitchen. Good. She was out of bed though still in her wrapper. His father wasn't there, and that was good, too. His father worked at the grain elevator and got Saturday afternoon off, and if he wasn't home by now it was likely that he had gone straight to the Cumberland. That meant it would be late in the day before they had to deal with him.

Cece's father's name was Cece Ferns, too. It was a well-known and generally an affectionately known name in Walley, and somebody telling a story even thirty or forty years later would take it for granted that everybody would know it was the father who was being talked about, not the son. If a person relatively new in town said, 'That doesn't sound like Cece,' he would be told that nobody meant *that* Cece.

'Not him, we're talking about his old man.'

They talked about the time Cece Ferns went to the hospital – or was taken there – with pneumonia, or some other desperate thing, and the nurses wrapped him in wet towels or sheets to get the fever down. The fever sweated out of him, and all the towels and sheets turned brown. It was the nicotine in him. The nurses had never seen anything like it. Cece was delighted. He claimed to have been smoking tobacco and drinking alcohol since he was ten years old.

And the time he went to church. It was hard to imagine why, but it was the Baptist church, and his wife was a Baptist, so perhaps he went to please her, though that was even harder to imagine. They were serving Communion the Sunday he went, and in the Baptist church the bread is bread but the wine is grape juice. 'What's this?' cried Cece Ferns aloud. 'If this is the blood of the Lamb then he must've been pretty damn anemic.'

Preparations for the noon meal were under way in the Fernses' kitchen. A loaf of sliced bread was sitting on the table and a can of diced beets had been opened. A few slices of bologna had been fried – before the eggs, though they should have been done after – and were being kept slightly warm on top of the stove. And now Cece's mother had started the eggs. She was bending over the stove with the egg lifter in one hand and the other hand pressed to her stomach, cradling a pain.

Cece took the egg lifter out of her hand and turned down the electric heat, which was way too high. He had to hold the pan off the burner while the burner cooled down, in order to keep the egg whites from getting too tough or burning at the edges. He hadn't been in time to wipe out the old grease and plop a bit of fresh lard in the pan. His mother never wiped out the old grease, just let it sit from one meal to the next and put in a bit of lard when she had to.

When the heat was more to his liking, he put the pan down and coaxed the lacy edges of the eggs into tidy circles. He found a clean spoon and dribbled a little hot fat over the yokes to set them. He and his mother liked their eggs cooked this way, but his mother often couldn't manage it right. His father liked his eggs turned over and flattened out like pancakes, cooked hard as shoe leather and blackened with pepper. Cece could cook them the way he wanted, too.

None of the other boys knew how practiced he was in the kitchen – just as none of them knew about the hiding place he had made outside the house in the blind corner past the dining-room window, behind the Japanese barberry.

His mother sat in the chair by the window while he was finishing up the eggs. She kept an eye on the street. There was still a chance that his father would come home for something to eat. He might not be drunk yet. But the way he behaved didn't always depend on how drunk he was. If he came into the kitchen now he might tell Cece to make him some eggs, too. Then he might ask him where his apron was and say that he would make some fellow a dandy wife. That would be how he'd behave if he was in a good mood. In another sort of mood he would start off by staring at Cece in a certain way – that is, with an exaggerated, absurdly threatening expression – and telling him he better watch out.

'Smart bugger, aren't you? Well, all I got to say to you is better watch out.'

Then if Cece looked back at him, or maybe if he didn't look back, or if he dropped the egg lifter or set it down with a clatter – or even if he was sliding around being extra cautious about not dropping anything and not making a noise – his father was apt to start showing his teeth and snarling like a dog. It would have been ridiculous – it was ridiculous – except that he meant business. A minute later the food and the dishes might be on the floor, and the chairs or the table overturned, and he might be chasing Cece around the room yelling how he was going to get him this time, flatten his face on the hot burner, how would he like that? You would be certain he'd gone crazy. But if at this moment a knock came at the door – if a friend of his arrived, say, to pick him up – his face would reassemble itself in no time and he would open the door and call out the friend's name in a loud bantering voice.

'I'll be with you in two shakes. I'd ask you in, but the wife's been pitching the dishes around again.'

He didn't intend this to be believed. He said such things in order to turn whatever happened in his house into a joke.

Cece's mother asked him if the weather was warming up and where he had been that morning.

'Yeah,' he said, and, 'Out on the flats.'

She said that she'd thought she could smell the wind on him.

'You know what I'm going to do right after we eat?' she said. 'I'm going to take a hot-water bottle and go right back to bed and maybe I'll get my strength back and feel like doing something.'

That was what she nearly always said she was going to do, but she always announced it as if it was an idea that had just occurred to her, a hopeful decision.

Bud Salter had two older sisters who never did anything useful unless his mother made them. And they never confined their hair arranging, nail polishing, shoe cleaning, making up, or even dressing activities to their bedrooms or the bathroom. They spread their combs and curlers and face powder and nail polish and shoe polish all over the house. Also they loaded every chair back with their newly ironed dresses and blouses and spread out their drying sweaters on towels on every clear space of floor. (Then they screamed at you if you walked near them.) They stationed themselves in front of various mirrors – the mirror in the hall coat stand, the mirror in the dining-room buffet, and the mirror beside the kitchen door with the shelf underneath always loaded with safety pins, bobby pins, pennies, buttons, bits of pencils. Sometimes one of them would stand in front of a mirror for twenty minutes or so, checking herself from various angles, inspecting her teeth and pulling her hair back then shaking it forward. Then she would walk away apparently satisfied or at least finished – but only as far as the next room, the next mirror, where she would begin all over again just as if she had been delivered a new head.

Right now his older sister, the one who was supposed to be good-looking, was taking the pins out of her hair in front of the kitchen mirror. Her head was covered with shiny curls like snails. His other sister, on orders from his mother, was mashing the potatoes. His five-year-old brother was sitting in place at the table, banging his knife and fork up and down and yelling, 'Want some service. Want some service.'

He got that from their father, who did it for a joke.

Bud passed by his brother's chair and said quietly, 'Look. She's putting lumps in the mashed potatoes again.'

He had his brother convinced that lumps were something you added, like raisins to rice pudding, from a supply in the cupboard.

His brother stopped chanting and began complaining.

'I won't eat none if she puts in lumps. Mama, I won't eat none if she puts lumps.'

'Oh, don't be silly,' Bud's mother said. She was frying apple slices and onion rings with the pork chops. 'Quit whining like a baby.'

'It was Bud got him started,' the older sister said. 'Bud went and told him she was putting lumps in. Bud always tells him that and he doesn't know any better.'

'Bud ought to get his face smashed,' said Doris, the sister who was mashing the potatoes. She didn't always say such things idly – she had once left a claw scar down the side of Bud's cheek.

Bud went over to the dresser, where there was a rhubarb pie cooling. He took a fork and began carefully, secretly prying at it, letting out delicious steam, a delicate smell of cinnamon. He was trying to open one of the vents in the top of it so that he could get a taste of the filling. His brother saw what he was doing but was too scared to say anything. His brother was spoiled and was defended by his sisters all the time – Bud was the only person in the house he respected.

'Want some service,' he repeated, speaking now in a thoughtful undertone.

Doris came over to the dresser to get the bowl for the mashed potatoes. Bud made an incautious movement, and part of the top crust caved in.

21

'So now he's wrecking the pie,' Doris said. 'Mama – he's wrecking your pie.'

'Shut your damn mouth,' Bud said.

'Leave that pie alone,' said Bud's mother with a practiced, almost serene severity. 'Stop swearing. Stop tattle-telling. Grow up.'

Jimmy Box sat down to dinner at a crowded table. He and his father and his mother and his four-year-old and six-year-old sisters lived in his grand-mother's house with his grandmother and his great-aunt Mary and his bachelor uncle. His father had a bicycle-repair shop in the shed behind the house, and his mother worked in Honeker's Department Store.

Jimmy's father was crippled – the result of a polio attack when he was twenty-two years old. He walked bent forward from the hips, using a cane. This didn't show so much when he was working in the shop, because such work often means being bent over anyway. When he walked along the street he did look very strange, but nobody called him names or did an imitation of him. He had once been a notable hockey player and baseball player for the town, and some of the grace and valor of the past still hung around him, putting his present state into perspective, so that it could be seen as a phase (though a final one). He helped this perception along by cracking silly jokes and taking an optimistic tone, denying the pain that showed in his sunken eyes and kept him awake many nights.

And, unlike Cece Ferns's father, he didn't change his tune when he came into his own house.

But, of course, it wasn't his own house. His wife had married him after he was crippled, though she had got engaged to him before, and it seemed the natural thing to do to move in with her mother, so that the mother could look after any children who came along while the wife went on working at her job. It seemed the natural thing to the wife's mother as well, to take on another family – just as it seemed natural that her sister Mary should move in with the rest of them when her eyesight failed, and that her son Fred, who was extraordinarily shy, should continue to live at home unless he found some place he liked better. This was a family who accepted burdens of one kind or another with even less fuss than they accepted the weather. In fact, nobody in that house would have spoken of Jimmy's father's condition or Aunt Mary's eyesight as burdens or problems, any more than they would of Fred's shyness. Drawbacks and adversity were not to be noticed, not to be distinguished from their opposites.

There was a traditional belief in the family that Jimmy's grandmother was an excellent cook, and this might have been true at one time, but in recent years there had been a falling off. Economies were practiced beyond what there was any need for now. Jimmy's mother and his uncle made decent wages and his aunt Mary got a pension and the bicycle shop was fairly busy, but one egg was used instead

23

of three and the meat loaf got an extra cup of oatmeal. There was an attempt to compensate by overdoing the Worcestershire sauce or sprinkling too much nutmeg on the custard. But nobody complained. Everybody praised. Complaints were as rare as lightning balls in that house. And everybody said 'Excuse me,' even the little girls said 'Excuse me,' when they bumped into each other. Everybody passed and pleased and thank-you'd at the table as if there was company every day. This was the way they managed, all of them crammed so tight in the house, with clothes piled on every hook, coats hung over the banister, and cots set up permanently in the dining room for Jimmy and his uncle Fred, and the buffet hidden under a load of clothing waiting to be ironed or mended. Nobody pounded on the stairsteps or shut doors hard or turned the radio up loud or said anything disagreeable.

Did this explain why Jimmy kept his mouth shut that Saturday at dinnertime? They all kept their mouths shut, all three of them. In Cece's case it was easy to understand. His father would never have stood for Cece's claiming so important a discovery. He would have called him a liar as a matter of course. And Cece's mother, judging everything by the effect it would have on his father, would have understood – correctly – that even his going to the Police Office with his story would cause disruption at home, so she would have told him to please just keep quiet. But the two other boys lived in quite reasonable homes and they could have spoken. In Jimmy's house there would have been consternation and some disapproval, but soon enough they would have admitted that it was not Jimmy's fault.

Bud's sisters would have asked if he was crazy. They might even have twisted things around to imply that it was just like him, with his unpleasant habits, to come upon a dead body. His father, however, was a sensible, patient man, used to listening to many strange rigmaroles in his job as a freight agent at the railway station. He would have made Bud's sisters shut up, and after some serious talk to make sure Bud was telling the truth and not exaggerating he would have phoned the Police Office.

It was just that their houses seemed too full. Too much was going on already. This was true in Cece's house just as much as in the others, because even in his father's absence there was the threat and memory all the time of his haywire presence.

'Did you tell?'
  'Did you?'
  'Me neither.'
They walked downtown, not thinking about the way they were going. They turned onto Shipka Street and found themselves going past the stucco bungalow where Mr and Mrs Willens lived. They were right in front of it before they recognized it. It had a small bay window on either side of the front

door and a top step wide enough for two chairs, not there at present but occupied on summer evenings by Mr Willens and his wife. There was a flat-roofed addition to one side of the house, with another door opening toward the street and a separate walk leading up to it. A sign beside that door said D. M. WILLENS, OPTOMETRIST. None of the boys themselves had visited that office, but Jimmy's aunt Mary went there regularly for her eyedrops, and his grandmother got her glasses there. So did Bud Salter's mother.

The stucco was a muddy pink color and the doors and window frames were painted brown. The storm windows had not been taken off yet, as they hadn't from most of the houses in town. There was nothing special at all about the house, but the front yard was famous for its flowers. Mrs Willens was a renowned gardener who didn't grow her flowers in long rows beside the vegetable garden, as Jimmy's grandmother and Bud's mother grew theirs. She had them in round beds and crescent beds and all over, and in circles under the trees. In a couple of weeks daffodils would fill this lawn. But at present the only thing in bloom was a forsythia bush at the corner of the house. It was nearly as high as the eaves and it sprayed yellow into the air the way a fountain shoots water.

The forsythia shook, not with the wind, and out came a stooped brown figure. It was Mrs Willens in her old gardening clothes, a lumpy little woman in baggy slacks and a ripped jacket and a peaked cap that might have been her husband's – it slipped down too low and almost hid her eyes. She was carrying a pair of shears.

They slowed right down – it was either that or run. Maybe they thought that she wouldn't notice them, that they could turn themselves into posts. But she had seen them already; that was why she came hastening through.

'I see you're gawking at my forsythia,' said Mrs Willens. 'Would you like some to take home?'

What they had been gawking at was not the forsythia but the whole scene – the house looking just as usual, the sign by the office door, the curtains letting light in. Nothing hollow or ominous, nothing that said that Mr Willens was not inside and that his car was not in the garage behind his office but in Jutland Pond. And Mrs Willens out working in her yard, where anybody would expect her to be – everybody in town said so – the minute the snow was melted. And calling out in her familiar tobacco-roughened voice, abrupt and challenging but not unfriendly – a voice identifiable half a block away or coming from the back of any store.

'Wait,' she said. 'Wait, now, I'll get you some.'

She began smartly, selectively snapping off the bright-yellow branches, and when she had all she wanted she came towards them behind a screen of flowers.

'Here you are,' she said. 'Take these home to your mothers. It's always good to see the forsythia, it's the very first thing in the spring.' She was

27

dividing the branches among them. 'Like all Gaul,' she said. 'All Gaul is divided into three parts. You must know about that if you take Latin.'

'We aren't in high school yet,' said Jimmy, whose life at home had readied him, better than the others, for talking to ladies.

'Aren't you?' she said. 'Well, you've got all sorts of things to look forward to. Tell your mothers to put them in lukewarm water. Oh, I'm sure they already know that. I've given you branches that aren't all the way out yet, so they should last and last.'

They said thank you – Jimmy first and the others picking it up from him. They walked toward downtown with their arms loaded. They had no intention of turning back and taking the flowers home, and they counted on her not having any good idea of where their homes were. Half a block on, they sneaked looks back to see if she was watching.

She wasn't. The big house near the sidewalk blocked the view in any case.

The forsythia gave them something to think about. The embarrassment of carrying it, the problem of getting rid of it. Otherwise, they would have to think about Mr Willens and Mrs Willens. How she could be busy in her yard and he could be drowned in his car. Did she know where he was or did she not? It seemed that she couldn't. Did she even know that he was gone? She had acted as if there was nothing wrong, nothing at all, and when they were standing in front of her this had seemed to be the truth. What they knew, what they had seen, seemed actually to be pushed back, to be defeated, by her not knowing it.

Two girls on bicycles came wheeling around the corner. One was Bud's sister Doris. At once these girls began to hoot and yell.

'Oh, look at the flowers,' they shouted. 'Where's the wedding? Look at the beautiful bridesmaids.'

Bud yelled back the worst thing he could think of.

'You got blood all over your arse.'

Of course she didn't, but there had been an occasion when this had really been so – she had come home from school with blood on her skirt. Everybody had seen it, and it would never be forgotten.

He was sure she would tell on him at home, but she never did. Her shame about that other time was so great that she could not refer to it even to get him in trouble.

They realized then that they had to dump the flowers at once, so they simply threw the branches under a parked car. They brushed a few stray petals off their clothes as they turned onto the square.

Saturdays were still important then; they brought the country people into town. Cars were already parked around the square and on the side streets. Big country boys and girls and smaller children from the town and the country were heading for the movie matinee.

It was necessary to pass Honeker's in the first block. And there, in full view in one of the windows, Jimmy saw his mother. Back at work already, she was putting the hat straight on a female dummy, adjusting the veil, then fiddling with the shoulders of the dress. She was a short woman and she had to stand on tiptoe to do this properly. She had taken off her shoes to walk on the window carpet. You could see the rosy plump cushions of her heels through her stockings, and when she stretched you saw the back of her knee through the slit in her skirt. Above that was a wide but shapely behind and the line of her panties or girdle. Jimmy could hear in his mind the little grunts she would be making; also he could smell the stockings that she sometimes took off as soon as she got home, to save them from runs. Stockings and underwear, even clean female underwear, had a faint, private smell that was both appealing and disgusting.

He hoped two things. That the others hadn't noticed her (they had, but the idea of a mother dressed up every day and out in the public world of town was so strange to them that they couldn't comment, could only dismiss it) and that she would not, please not, turn around and spot him. She was capable, if she did that, of rapping on the glass and mouthing hello. At work she lost the hushed discretion, the studied gentleness, of home. Her obligingness turned from meek to pert.

He used to be delighted by this other side of her, this friskiness, just as he was by Honeker's, with its extensive counters of glass and varnished wood, its big mirrors at the top of the staircase, in which he could see himself climbing up to Ladies' Wear, on the second floor.

'Here's my young mischief,' his mother would say, and sometimes slip him a dime. He could never stay more than a minute; Mr or Mrs Honeker might be watching.

Young mischief.

Words that were once as pleasant to hear as the tinkle of dimes and nickels had now turned slyly shaming.

They were safely past.

In the next block they had to pass the Duke of Cumberland, but Cece had no worries. If his father had not come home at dinner-time, it meant he would be in there for hours yet. But the word 'Cumberland' always fell across his mind heavily. From the days when he hadn't even known what it meant, he got a sense of sorrowful plummeting. A weight hitting dark water, far down.

Between the Cumberland and the Town Hall was an unpaved alley, and at the back of the Town Hall was the Police Office. They turned into this alley and soon a lot of new noise reached them, opposing the street noise. It was not from the Cumberland – the noise in there was all muffled up, the beer parlor having only small, high windows like a public toilet. It was coming from the Police

31

Office. The door to that office was open on account of the mild weather, and even out in the alley you could smell the pipe tobacco and cigars. It wasn't just the policemen who sat in there, especially on Saturday afternoons, with the stove going in winter and the fan in summer and the door open to let in the pleasant air on an in-between day like today. Colonel Box would be there – in fact, they could already hear the wheeze he made, the long-drawn-out aftereffects of his asthmatic laughter. He was a relative of Jimmy's, but there was a coolness in the family because he did not approve of Jimmy's father's marriage. He spoke to Jimmy, when he recognized him, in a surprised, ironic tone of voice. 'If he ever offers you a quarter or anything, you say you don't need it,' Jimmy's mother had told him. But Colonel Box had never made such an offer.

Also, Mr Pollock would be there, who had retired from the drugstore, and Fergus Solley, who was not a half-wit but looked like one, because he had been gassed in the First World War. All day these men and others played cards, smoked, told stories, and drank coffee at the town's expense (as Bud's father said). Anybody wanting to make a complaint or a report had to do it within sight of them and probably within earshot.

Run the gauntlet.

They came almost to a stop outside the open door. Nobody had noticed them. Colonel Box said, 'I'm not dead yet,' repeating the final line of some story. They began to walk past slowly with their heads down, kicking at the gravel. Round the corner of the building they picked up speed. By the entry to the men's public toilet there was a recent streak of lumpy vomit on the wall and a couple of empty bottles on the gravel. They had to walk between the refuse bins and the high watchful windows of the town clerk's office, and then they were off the gravel, back on the square.

'I got money,' Cece said. This matter-of-fact announcement brought them all relief. Cece jingled change in his pocket. It was the money his mother had given him after he washed up the dishes, when he went into the front bedroom to tell her he was going out. 'Help yourself to fifty cents off the dresser,' she had said. Sometimes she had money, though he never saw his father give her any. And whenever she said 'Help yourself' or gave him a few coins, Cece understood that she was ashamed of their life, ashamed for him and in front of him, and these were the times when he hated the sight of her (though he was glad of the money). Especially if she said that he was a good boy and he was not to think she wasn't grateful for all he did.

They took the street that led down to the harbor. At the side of Paquette's Service Station there was a booth from which Mrs Paquette sold hot dogs, ice cream, candy, and cigarettes. She had refused to sell them cigarettes even when Jimmy said they were for his uncle Fred. But she didn't hold it against them that they'd tried. She was a fat, pretty woman, a French Canadian.

They bought some licorice whips, black and red. They meant to buy some ice cream later when they weren't so full from dinner. They went over to where there were two old car seats set up by the fence under a tree that gave shade in summer. They shared out the licorice whips.

Captain Tervitt was sitting on the other seat.

Captain Tervitt had been a real captain, for many years, on the lake boats. Now he had a job as a special constable. He stopped the cars to let the children cross the street in front of the school and kept them from sledding down the side street in winter. He blew his whistle and held up one big hand, which looked like a clown's hand, in a white glove. He was still tall and straight and broad-shouldered, though old and white-haired. Cars would do what he said, and children, too.

At night he went around checking the doors of all the stores to see that they were locked and to make sure that there was nobody inside committing a burglary. During the day he often slept in public. When the weather was bad he slept in the library and when it was good he chose some seat out-of-doors. He didn't spend much time in the Police Office, probably because he was too deaf to follow the conversation without his hearing aid in, and like many deaf people he hated his hearing aid. And he was used to being solitary, surely, staring out over the bow of the lake boats.

His eyes were closed and his head tilted back so that he could get the sun in his face. When they went over to talk to him (and the decision to do this was made without any consultation, beyond one resigned and dubious look) they had to wake him from his doze. His face took a moment to register – where and when and who. Then he took a large old-fashioned watch out of his pocket, as if he counted on children always wanting to be told the time. But they went on talking to him, with their expressions agitated and slightly shamed. They were saying, 'Mr Willens is out in Jutland Pond,' and 'We seen the car,' and 'Drownded.' He had to hold up his hand and make shushing motions while the other hand went rooting around in his pants pocket and came up with his hearing aid. He nodded his head seriously, encouragingly, as if to say, Patience, patience, while he got the device settled in his ear. Then both hands up – Be still, be still – while he was testing. Finally another nod, of a brisker sort, and in a stern voice – but making a joke to some extent of his sternness – he said, 'Proceed.'

Cece, who was the quietest of the three – as Jimmy was the politest and Bud the mouthiest – was the one who turned everything around.

'Your fly's undone,' he said.

Then they all whooped and ran away.

Their elation did not vanish right away. But it was not something that could be shared or spoken about: they had to pull apart.

Cece went home to work on his hideaway. The

cardboard floor, which had been frozen through the winter, was sodden now and needed to be replaced. Jimmy climbed into the loft of the garage, where he had recently discovered a box of old Doc Savage magazines that had once belonged to his uncle Fred. Bud went home and found nobody there but his mother, who was waxing the dining-room floor. He looked at comic books for an hour or so and then he told her. He believed that his mother had no experience or authority outside their house and that she would not make up her mind about what to do until she had phoned his father. To his surprise, she immediately phoned the police. Then she phoned his father. And somebody went to round up Cece and Jimmy.

A police car drove into Jutland from the township road, and all was confirmed. A policeman and the Anglican minister went to see Mrs Willens.

'I didn't want to bother you,' Mrs Willens was reported to have said. 'I was going to give him till dark.'

She told them that Mr. Willens had driven out to the country yesterday afternoon to take some drops to an old blind man. Sometimes he got held up, she said. He visited people, or the car got stuck.

Was he downhearted or anything like that? the policeman asked her.

'Oh, surely not,' the minister said. 'He was the bulwark of the choir.'

'The word was not in his vocabulary,' said Mrs. Willens.

Something was made of the boys' sitting down and eating their dinners and never saying a word. And then buying a bunch of licorice whips. A new nickname – Deadman – was found and settled on each of them. Jimmy and Bud bore it till they left town, and Cece – who married young and went to work in the elevator – saw it passed on to his two sons. By that time nobody thought of what it referred to.

The insult to Captain Tervitt remained a secret.

Each of them expected some reminder, some lofty look of injury or judgment, the next time they had to pass under his uplifted arm, crossing the street to the school. But he held up his gloved hand, his noble and clownish white hand, with his usual benevolent composure. He gave consent.

Proceed.

II. HEART FAILURE

'Glomerulonephritis,' Enid wrote in her notebook. It was the first case that she had ever seen. The fact was that Mrs Quinn's kidneys were failing, and nothing could be done about it. Her kidneys were drying up and turning into hard and useless granular lumps. Her urine at present was scanty and had a smoky look, and the smell that came out on her breath and through her skin was acrid and ominous. And there was another, fainter smell, like rotted fruit, that seemed to Enid related to the

37

pale-lavender-brown stains appearing on her body. Her legs twitched in spasms of sudden pain and her skin was subject to a violent itching, so that Enid had to rub her with ice. She wrapped the ice in towels and pressed the packs to the spots in torment.

'How do you contract that kind of a disease anyhow?' said Mrs Quinn's sister-in-law. Her name was Mrs. Green. Olive Green. (It had never occurred to her how that would sound, she said, until she got married and all of a sudden everybody was laughing at it.) She lived on a farm a few miles away, out on the highway, and every few days she came and took the sheets and towels and nightdresses home to wash. She did the children's washing as well, brought everything back freshly ironed and folded. She even ironed the ribbons on the nightdresses. Enid was grateful to her – she had been on jobs where she had to do the laundry herself, or, worse still, load it onto her mother, who would pay to have it done in town. Not wanting to offend but seeing which way the questions were tending, she said, 'It's hard to tell.'

'Because you hear one thing and another,' Mrs Green said. 'You hear that sometimes a woman might take some pills. They get these pills to take for when their period is late and if they take them just like the doctor says and for a good purpose that's fine, but if they take too many and for a bad purpose their kidneys are wrecked. Am I right?'

'I've never come in contact with a case like that,' Enid said.

Mrs Green was a tall, stout woman. Like her brother Rupert, who was Mrs Quinn's husband, she had a round, snub-nosed, agreeably wrinkled face – the kind that Enid's mother called 'potato Irish.' But behind Rupert's good-humored expression there was wariness and withholding. And behind Mrs Green's there was yearning. Enid did not know for what. To the simplest conversation Mrs Green brought a huge demand. Maybe it was just a yearning for news. News of something momentous. An event.

Of course, an event was coming, something momentous at least in this family. Mrs Quinn was going to die, at the age of twenty-seven. (That was the age she gave herself – Enid would have put some years on it, but once an illness had progressed this far age was hard to guess.) When her kidneys stopped working altogether, her heart would give out and she would die. The doctor had said to Enid, 'This'll take you into the summer, but the chances are you'll get some kind of a holiday before the hot weather's over.'

'Rupert met her when he went up north,' Mrs Green said. 'He went off by himself, he worked in the bush up there. She had some kind of a job in a hotel. I'm not sure what. Chambermaid job. She wasn't raised up there, though – she says she was raised in an orphanage in Montreal. She can't help that. You'd expect her to speak French, but if she does she don't let on.'

Enid said, 'An interesting life.'

'You can say that again.'

'An interesting life,' said Enid. Sometimes she couldn't help it – she tried a joke where it had hardly a hope of working. She raised her eyebrows encouragingly, and Mrs Green did smile.

But was she hurt? That was just the way Rupert would smile, in high school, warding off some possible mockery.

'He never had any kind of a girlfriend before that,' said Mrs Green.

Enid had been in the same class as Rupert, though she did not mention that to Mrs Green. She felt some embarrassment now because he was one of the boys – in fact, the main one – that she and her girlfriends had teased and tormented. 'Picked on,' as they used to say. They had picked on Rupert, following him up the street calling out, 'Hello, Rupert. Hello, Ru-pert,' putting him into a state of agony, watching his neck go red. 'Rupert's got scarlet fever,' they would say. 'Rupert, you should be quarantined.' And they would pretend that one of them – Enid, Joan McAuliffe, Marian Denny – had a case on him. 'She wants to speak to you, Rupert. Why don't you ever ask her out? You could phone her up at least. She's dying to talk to you.'

They did not really expect him to respond to these pleading overtures. But what joy if he had. He would have been rejected in short order and the story broadcast all over the school. Why? Why did they treat him this way, long to humiliate him? Simply because they could.

40

Impossible that he would have forgotten. But he treated Enid as if she were a new acquaintance, his wife's nurse, come into his house from anywhere at all. And Enid took her cue from him.

Things had been unusually well arranged here, to spare her extra work. Rupert slept at Mrs Green's house, and ate his meals there. The two little girls could have been there as well, but it would have meant putting them into another school – there was nearly a month to go before school was out for the summer.

Rupert came into the house in the evenings and spoke to his children.

'Are you being good girls?' he said.

'Show Daddy what you made with your blocks,' said Enid. 'Show Daddy your pictures in the coloring book.'

The blocks, the crayons, the coloring books, were all provided by Enid. She had phoned her mother and asked her to see what things she could find in the old trunks. Her mother had done that, and brought along as well an old book of cutout dolls which she had collected from someone – Princesses Elizabeth and Margaret Rose and their many outfits. Enid hadn't been able to get the little girls to say thank you until she put all these things on a high shelf and announced that they would stay there till thank you was said. Lois and Sylvie were seven and six years old, and as wild as little barn cats.

Rupert didn't ask where the playthings came

from. He told his daughters to be good girls and asked Enid if there was anything she needed from town. Once she told him that she had replaced the lightbulb in the cellarway and that he could get her some spare bulbs.

'I could have done that,' he said.

'I don't have any trouble with lightbulbs,' said Enid. 'Or fuses or knocking in nails. My mother and I have done without a man around the house for a long time now.' She meant to tease a little, to be friendly, but it didn't work.

Finally Rupert would ask about his wife, and Enid would say that her blood pressure was down slightly, or that she had eaten and kept down part of an omelette for supper, or that the ice packs seemed to ease her itchy skin and she was sleeping better. And Rupert would say that if she was sleeping he'd better not go in.

Enid said, 'Nonsense.' To see her husband would do a woman more good than to have a little doze. She took the children up to bed then, to give man and wife a time of privacy. But Rupert never stayed more than a few minutes. And when Enid came back down-stairs and went into the front room – now the sickroom – to ready the patient for the night, Mrs Quinn would be lying back against the pillows, looking agitated but not dissatisfied.

'Doesn't hang around here very long, does he?' Mrs Quinn would say. 'Makes me laugh. Ha-ha-ha, how-are-you? Ha-ha-ha, off-we-go. Why don't we take her out and throw her on the manure pile?

42

Why don't we just dump her out like a dead cat? That's what he's thinking. Isn't he?'

'I doubt it,' said Enid, bringing the basin and towels, the rubbing alcohol and the baby powder.

'I doubt it,' said Mrs Quinn quite viciously, but she submitted readily enough to having her nightgown removed, her hair smoothed back from her face, a towel slid under her hips. Enid was used to people making a fuss about being naked, even when they were very old or very ill. Sometimes she would have to tease them or badger them into common sense. 'Do you think I haven't seen any bottom parts before?' she would say. 'Bottom parts, top parts, it's pretty boring after a while. You know, there's just the two ways we're made.' But Mrs Quinn was without shame, opening her legs and raising herself a bit to make the job easier. She was a little bird-boned woman, queerly shaped now, with her swollen abdomen and limbs and her breasts shrunk to tiny pouches with dried-currant nipples.

'Swole up like some kind of pig,' Mrs Quinn said. 'Except for my tits, and they always were kind of useless. I never had no big udders on me, like you. Don't you get sick of the sight of me? Won't you be glad when I'm dead?'

'If I felt like that I wouldn't be here,' said Enid.

'Good riddance to bad rubbish,' said Mrs Quinn. 'That's what you'll all say. Good riddance to bad rubbish. I'm no use to him anymore, am I? I'm no use to any man. He goes out of here every night and he goes to pick up women, doesn't he?'

'As far as I know, he goes to his sister's house.'

'As far as you know. But you don't know much.'

Enid thought she knew what this meant, this spite and venom, the energy saved for ranting. Mrs Quinn was flailing about for an enemy. Sick people grew to resent well people, and sometimes that was true of husbands and wives, or even of mothers and their children. Both husband and children in Mrs Quinn's case. On a Saturday morning, Enid called Lois and Sylvie from their games under the porch, to come and see their mother looking pretty. Mrs Quinn had just had her morning wash, and was in a clean night-gown, with her fine, sparse, fair hair brushed and held back by a blue ribbon. (Enid took a supply of these ribbons with her when she went to nurse a female patient – also a bottle of cologne and a cake of scented soap.) She did look pretty – or you could see at least that she had once been pretty, with her wide forehead and cheekbones (they almost punched the skin now, like china door-knobs) and her large greenish eyes and childish translucent teeth and small stubborn chin.

The children came into the room obediently if unenthusiastically.

Mrs Quinn said, 'Keep them off of my bed, they're filthy.'

'They just want to see you,' said Enid.

'Well, now they've seen me,' said Mrs Quinn. 'Now they can go.'

This behavior didn't seem to surprise or disappoint the children. They looked at Enid, and Enid said, 'All right, now, your mother better have a rest,' and they ran out and slammed the kitchen door.

'Can't you get them to quit doing that?' Mrs Quinn said. 'Every time they do it, it's like a brick hits me in my chest.'

You would think these two daughters of hers were a pair of rowdy orphans, wished on her for an indefinite visit. But that was the way some people were, before they settled down to their dying and sometimes even up to the event itself. People of a gentler nature – it would seem – than Mrs Quinn might say that they knew how much their brothers, sisters, husbands, wives, and children had always hated them, how much of a disappointment they had been to others and others had been to them, and how glad they knew everybody would be to see them gone. They might say this at the end of peaceful, useful lives in the midst of loving families, where there was no explanation at all for such fits. And usually the fits passed. But often, too, in the last weeks or even days of life there was mulling over of old feuds and slights or whimpering about some unjust punishment suffered seventy years earlier. Once a woman had asked Enid to bring her a willow platter from the cupboard and Enid had thought that she wanted the comfort of looking at this one pretty possession for the last time. But it turned out that she wanted to use her last, surprising strength to smash it against the bedpost.

'Now I know my sister's never going to get her hands on that,' she said.

And often people remarked that their visitors were only coming to gloat and that the doctor was responsible for their sufferings. They detested the sight of Enid herself, for her sleepless strength and patient hands and the way the juices of life were so admirably balanced and flowing in her. Enid was used to that, and she was able to understand the trouble they were in, the trouble of dying and also the trouble of their lives that sometimes overshadowed that.

But with Mrs Quinn she was at a loss.

It was not just that she couldn't supply comfort here. It was that she couldn't want to. She could not conquer her dislike of this doomed, miserable young woman. She disliked this body that she had to wash and powder and placate with ice and alcohol rubs. She understood now what people meant when they said that they hated sickness and sick bodies; she understood the women who had said to her, I don't know how you do it, I could never be a nurse, that's the one thing I could never be. She disliked this particular body, all the particular signs of its disease. The smell of it and the discoloration, the malignant-looking little nipples and the pathetic ferretlike teeth. She saw all this as the sign of a willed corruption. She was as bad as Mrs Green, sniffing out rampant impurity.

In spite of being a nurse who knew better, and in spite of its being her job – and surely her nature – to be compassionate. She didn't know why this was happening. Mrs Quinn reminded her somewhat of girls she had known in high school – cheaply dressed, sickly looking girls with dreary futures, who still displayed a hardfaced satisfaction with themselves. They lasted only a year or two – they got pregnant, most of them got married. Enid had nursed some of them in later years, in home childbirth, and found their confidence exhausted and their bold streak turned into meekness, or even piety. She was sorry for them, even when she remembered how determined they had been to get what they had got.

Mrs Quinn was a harder case. Mrs Quinn might crack and crack, but there would be nothing but sullen mischief, nothing but rot inside her.

Worse even than the fact that Enid should feel this revulsion was the fact that Mrs Quinn knew it. No patience or gentleness or cheerfulness that Enid could summon would keep Mrs Quinn from knowing. And Mrs Quinn made knowing it her triumph.

Good riddance to bad rubbish.

When Enid was twenty years old, and had almost finished her nurse's training, her father was dying in the Walley hospital. That was when he said to her, 'I don't know as I care for this career of yours. I don't want you working in a place like this.'

Enid bent over him and asked what sort of place he thought he was in. 'It's only the Walley hospital,' she said.

'I know that,' said her father, sounding as calm and reasonable as he had always done (he was an insurance and real-estate agent). 'I know what I'm talking about. Promise me you won't.'

'Promise you what?' said Enid.

'You won't do this kind of work,' her father said. She could not get any further explanation out of him. He tightened up his mouth as if her questioning disgusted him. All he would say was 'Promise.'

'What is all this about?' Enid asked her mother, and her mother said, 'Oh, go ahead. Go ahead and promise him. What difference is it going to make?'

Enid thought this a shocking thing to say, but made no comment. It was consistent with her mother's way of looking at a lot of things.

'I'm not going to promise anything I don't understand,' she said. 'I'm probably not going to promise anything anyway. But if you know what he's talking about you ought to tell me.'

'It's just this idea he's got now,' her mother said. 'He's got an idea that nursing makes a woman coarse.'

Enid said, 'Coarse.'

Her mother said that the part of nursing her father objected to was the familiarity nurses had with men's bodies. Her father thought – he had

48

decided – that such familiarity would change a girl, and furthermore that it would change the way men thought about that girl. It would spoil her good chances and give her a lot of other chances that were not so good. Some men would lose interest and others would become interested in the wrong way.

'I suppose it's all mixed up with wanting you to get married,' her mother said.

'Too bad if it is,' said Enid.

But she ended up promising. And her mother said, 'Well, I hope that makes you happy.' Not 'makes him happy.' 'Makes *you*.' It seemed that her mother had known before Enid did just how tempting this promise would be. The deathbed promise, the self-denial, the wholesale sacrifice. And the more absurd the better. This was what she had given in to. And not for love of her father, either (her mother implied), but for the thrill of it. Sheer noble perversity.

'If he'd asked you to give up something you didn't care one way or the other about, you'd probably have told him nothing doing,' her mother said. 'If for instance he'd asked you to give up wearing lipstick. You'd still be wearing it.'

Enid listened to this with a patient expression.

'Did you pray about it?' said her mother sharply.

Enid said yes.

She withdrew from nursing school; she stayed at home and kept busy. There was enough money that she did not have to work. In fact, her mother had not wanted Enid to go into nursing in the first place, claiming that it was something poor girls did, it was a way out for girls whose parents couldn't keep them or send them to college. Enid did not remind her of this inconsistency. She painted a fence, she tied up the rosebushes for winter. She learned to bake and she learned to play bridge, taking her father's place in the weekly games her mother played with Mr and Mrs Willens from next door. In no time at all she became – as Mr Willens said – a scandalously good player. He took to turning up with chocolates or a pink rose for her, to make up for his own inadequacies as a partner.

She went skating in the winter evenings. She played badminton.

She had never lacked friends, and she didn't now. Most of the people who had been in the last year of high school with her were finishing college now, or were already working at a distance, as teachers or nurses or chartered accountants. But she made friends with others who had dropped out before senior year to work in banks or stores or offices, to become plumbers or milliners. The girls in this group were dropping like flies, as they said of each other – they were dropping into matrimony. Enid was an organizer of bridal showers and a help at trousseau teas. In a couple of years would come the christenings, where she could expect to be a favorite godmother. Children not related to her would grow up calling her Aunt. And she was already a sort of honorary daughter to women of her mother's age and older, the only young woman who had time for the Book Club and the Horticultural Society. So, quickly and easily, still in her youth, she was slipping into this essential, central, yet isolated role.

But in fact it had been her role all along. In high school she was always the class secretary or class social convener. She was well liked and high-spirited and well dressed and good-looking, but she was slightly set apart. She had friends who were boys but never a boyfriend. She did not seem to have made a choice this way, but she was not worried about it, either. She had been preoccupied with her ambition – to be a missionary, at one embarrassing stage, and then to be a nurse. She had never thought of nursing as just something to do until she got married. Her hope was to be good, and do good, and not necessarily in the orderly, customary, wifely way.

At New Year's she went to the dance in the Town Hall. The man who danced with her most often, and escorted her home, and pressed her hand good night, was the manager of the creamery – a man in his forties, never married, an excellent dancer, an avuncular friend to girls unlikely to find partners. No woman ever took him seriously.

'Maybe you should take a business course,' her mother said. 'Or why shouldn't you go to college?'

51

Where the men might be more appreciative, she was surely thinking.

'I'm too old,' said Enid.

Her mother laughed. 'That only shows how young you are,' she said. She seemed relieved to discover that her daughter had a touch of folly natural to her age – that she could think twenty-one was at a vast distance from eighteen.

'I'm not going to troop in with kids out of high school,' Enid said. 'I mean it. What do you want to get rid of me for anyway? I'm fine here.' This sulkiness or sharpness also seemed to please and reassure her mother. But after a moment she sighed, and said, 'You'll be surprised how fast the years go by.'

That August there were a lot of cases of measles and a few of polio at the same time. The doctor who had looked after Enid's father, and had observed her competence around the hospital, asked her if she would be willing to help out for a while, nursing people at home. She said that she would think about it.

'You mean pray?' her mother said, and Enid's face took on a stubborn, secretive expression that in another girl's case might have had to do with meeting her boyfriend.

'That promise,' she said to her mother the next day. 'That was about working in a hospital, wasn't it?'

Her mother said that she had understood it that way, yes.

'And with graduating and being a registered nurse?'

Yes, yes.

So if there were people who needed nursing at home, who couldn't afford to go to the hospital or did not want to go, and if Enid went into their houses to nurse them, not as a registered nurse but as what they called a practical nurse, she would hardly be breaking her promise, would she? And since most of those needing her care would be children or women having babies, or old people dying, there would not be much danger of the coarsening effect, would there?

'If the only men you get to see are men who are never going to get out of bed again, you have a point,' said her mother.

But she could not keep from adding that what all this meant was that Enid had decided to give up the possibility of a decent job in a hospital in order to do miserable backbreaking work in miserable primitive houses for next to no money. Enid would find herself pumping water from contaminated wells and breaking ice in winter washbasins and battling flies in summer and using an outdoor toilet. Scrub boards and coal-oil lamps instead of washing machines and electricity. Trying to look after sick people in those conditions and cope with housework and poor weaselly children as well.

'But if that is your object in life,' she said, 'I can see that the worse I make it sound the more determined you get to do it. The only thing is,

53

I'm going to ask for a couple of promises myself. Promise me you'll boil the water you drink. And you won't marry a farmer.'

Enid said, 'Of all the crazy ideas.'

That was sixteen years ago. During the first of those years people got poorer and poorer. There were more and more of them who could not afford to go to the hospital, and the houses where Enid worked had often deteriorated almost to the state that her mother had described. Sheets and diapers had to be washed by hand in houses where the washing machine had broken down and could not be repaired, or the electricity had been turned off, or where there had never been any electricity in the first place. Enid did not work without pay, because that would not have been fair to the other women who did the same kind of nursing, and who did not have the same options as she did. But she gave most of the money back, in the form of children's shoes and winter coats and trips to the dentist and Christmas toys.

Her mother went around canvassing her friends for old baby cots, and high chairs and blankets, and worn-out sheets, which she herself ripped up and hemmed to make diapers. Everybody said how proud she must be of Enid, and she said yes, she surely was.

'But sometimes it's a devil of a lot of work,' she said. 'This being the mother of a saint.'

Then came the war, and the great shortage of

doctors and nurses, and Enid was more welcome than ever. As she was for a while after the war, with so many babies being born. It was only now, with the hospitals being enlarged and many farms getting prosperous, that it looked as if her responsibilities might dwindle away to the care of those who had bizarre and hopeless afflictions, or were so irredeemably cranky that hospitals had thrown them out.

This summer there was a great downpour of rain every few days, and then the sun came out very hot, glittering off the drenched leaves and grass. Early mornings were full of mist – they were so close, here, to the river – and even when the mist cleared off you could not see very far in any direction, because of the overflow and density of summer. The heavy trees, the bushes all bound up with wild grapevines and Virginia creeper, the crops of corn and barley and wheat and hay. Everything was ahead of itself, as people said. The hay was ready to cut in June, and Rupert had to rush to get it into the barn before a rain spoiled it.

He came into the house later and later in the evenings, having worked as long as the light lasted. One night when he came the house was in darkness, except for a candle burning on the kitchen table.

Enid hurried to unhook the screen door.

'Power out?' said Rupert.

Enid said, 'Shhh.' She whispered to him that she was letting the children sleep downstairs, because the upstairs rooms were so hot. She had pushed the chairs together and made beds on them with quilts and pillows. And of course she had had to turn the lights out so that they could get to sleep. She had found a candle in one of the drawers, and that was all she needed, to see to write by, in her notebook.

'They'll always remember sleeping here,' she said. 'You always remember the times when you were a child and you slept somewhere different.'

He set down a box that contained a ceiling fan for the sickroom. He had been into Walley to buy it. He had also bought a newspaper, which he handed to Enid.

'Thought you might like to know what's going on in the world,' he said.

She spread the paper out beside her notebook, on the table. There was a picture of a couple of dogs playing in a fountain.

'It says there's a heat wave,' she said. 'Isn't it nice to find out about it?'

Rupert was carefully lifting the fan out of its box.

'That'll be wonderful,' she said. 'It's cooled off in there now, but it'll be such a comfort to her tomorrow.'

'I'll be over early to put it up,' he said. Then he asked how his wife had been that day.

Enid said that the pains in her legs had been easing off, and the new pills the doctor had her on seemed to be letting her get some rest.

'The only thing is, she goes to sleep so soon,' she said. 'It makes it hard for you to get a visit.'

'Better she gets the rest,' Rupert said.

This whispered conversation reminded Enid of conversations in high school, when they were both in their senior year and that earlier teasing, or cruel flirtation, or whatever it was, had long been abandoned. All that last year Rupert had sat in the seat behind hers, and they had often spoken to each other briefly, always to some immediate purpose. Have you got an ink eraser? How do you spell 'incriminate'? Where is the Tyrrhenian Sea? Usually it was Enid, half turning in her seat and able only to sense, not see, how close Rupert was, who started these conversations. She did want to borrow an eraser, she was in need of information, but also she wanted to be sociable. And she wanted to make amends – she felt ashamed of the way she and her friends had treated him. It would do no good to apologize – that would just embarrass him all over again. He was only at ease when he sat behind her, and knew that she could not look him in the face. If they met on the street he would look away until the last minute, then mutter the faintest greeting while she sang out 'Hello, Rupert,' and heard an echo of the old tormenting tones she wanted to banish.

But when he actually laid a finger on her shoulder, tapping for attention, when he bent forward, almost touching or maybe really touching – she could not tell for sure – her thick hair that was wild even in a bob, then she felt forgiven. In a way, she felt honored. Restored to seriousness and to respect.

Where, where exactly, is the Tyrrhenian Sea?

She wondered if he remembered anything at all of that now.

She separated the back and front parts of the paper. Margaret Truman was visiting England, and had curtsied to the royal family. The King's doctors were trying to cure his Buerger's disease with vitamin E.

She offered the front part to Rupert. 'I'm going to look at the crossword,' she said. 'I like to do the crossword – it relaxes me at the end of the day.'

Rupert sat down and began to read the paper, and she asked him if he would like a cup of tea. Of course he said not to bother, and she went ahead and made it anyway, understanding that this reply might as well be yes in country speech.

'It's a South American theme,' she said, looking at the crossword. 'Latin American theme. First across is a musical . . . *garment*. A musical garment? Garment. A lot of letters. Oh. Oh. I'm lucky tonight. Cape Horn!

'You see how silly they are, these things,' she said, and rose and poured the tea.

If he did remember, did he hold anything against her? Maybe her blithe friendliness in their senior year had been as unwelcome, as superior-seeming to him, as that early taunting?

When she first saw him in this house, she thought that he had not changed much. He had been a tall, solid, round-faced boy, and he was a tall, heavy, round-faced man. He had worn his hair cut so short, always, that it didn't make much difference that there was less of it now and that it had turned from light brown to gray-brown. A permanent sunburn had taken the place of his blushes. And whatever troubled him and showed in his face might have been just the same old trouble – the problem of occupying space in the world and having a name that people could call you by, being somebody they thought they could know.

She thought of them sitting in the senior class. A small class, by that time – in five years the unstudious, the carefree, and the indifferent had been weeded out, leaving these overgrown, grave, and docile children learning trigonometry, learning Latin. What kind of life did they think they were preparing for? What kind of people did they think they were going to be?

She could see the dark-green, softened cover of a book called *History of the Renaissance and Reformation*. It was secondhand, or tenthhand – nobody ever bought a new textbook. Inside were written all the names of the previous owners, some of whom were middle-aged housewives or merchants around the town. You could not imagine them learning these things, or underlining 'Edict of Nantes' with red ink and writing 'N.B.' in the margin.

Edict of Nantes. The very uselessness, the exotic nature, of the things in those books and in those students' heads, in her own head then and Rupert's, made Enid feel a tenderness and wonder. It wasn't that they had meant to be something that they hadn't become. Nothing like that. Rupert couldn't have imagined anything but farming this farm. It was a good farm, and he was an only son. And she herself had ended up doing exactly what she must have wanted to do. You couldn't say that they had chosen the wrong lives or chosen against their will or not understood their choices. Just that they had not understood how time would pass and leave them not more but maybe a little less than what they used to be.

'"Bread of the Amazon,"' she said. '"Bread of the Amazon"?'

Rupert said, 'Manioc?'

Enid counted. 'Seven letters,' she said. 'Seven.'

He said, 'Cassava?'

'Cassava? That's a double *s*? Cassava.'

Mrs Quinn became more capricious daily about her food. Sometimes she said she wanted toast, or bananas with milk on them. One day she said peanut-butter cookies. Enid prepared all these things – the children could eat them anyway – and when they were ready Mrs Quinn could not stand the look or the smell of them. Even Jell-O had a smell she could not stand.

Some days she hated all noise; she would not even have the fan going. Other days she wanted the radio on, she wanted the station that played requests for birthdays and anniversaries and called people up to ask them questions. If you got the answer right you won a trip to Niagara Falls, a tankful of gas, or a load of groceries or tickets to a movie.

'It's all fixed,' Mrs Quinn said. 'They just pretend to call somebody up – they're in the next room and already got the answer told to them. I used to know somebody that worked for a radio, that's the truth.'

On these days her pulse was rapid. She talked very fast in a light, breathless voice. 'What kind of car is that your mother's got?' she said.

'It's a maroon-colored car,' said Enid.

'What *make*?' said Mrs Quinn.

Enid said she did not know, which was the truth. She had known, but she had forgotten.

'Was it new when she got it?'

'Yes,' said Enid. 'Yes. But that was three or four years ago.'

'She lives in that big rock house next door to Willenses?'

Yes, said Enid.

'How many rooms it got? Sixteen?'

'Too many.'

'Did you go to Mr Willens's funeral when he got drownded?' Enid said no. 'I'm not much for funerals.'

'I was supposed to go. I wasn't awfully sick then, I was going with Herveys up the highway, they said I could get a ride with them and then her mother and her sister wanted to go and there

61

wasn't enough room in back. Then Clive and Olive went in the truck and I could've scrunched up in their front seat but they never thought to ask me. Do you think he drownded himself?'

Enid thought of Mr Willens handing her a rose. His jokey gallantry that made the nerves of her teeth ache, as from too much sugar.

'I don't know. I wouldn't think so.'

'Did him and Mrs Willens get along all right?'

'As far as I know, they got along beautifully.'

'Oh, is that so?' said Mrs Quinn, trying to imitate Enid's reserved tone. 'Bee-you-tif-ley.'

Enid slept on the couch in Mrs Quinn's room. Mrs Quinn's devastating itch had almost disappeared, as had her need to urinate. She slept through most of the night, though she would have spells of harsh and angry breathing. What woke Enid up and kept her awake was a trouble of her own. She had begun to have ugly dreams. These were unlike any dreams she had ever had before. She used to think that a bad dream was one of finding herself in an unfamiliar house where the rooms kept changing and there was always more work to do than she could handle, work undone that she thought she had done, innumerable distractions. And then, of course, she had what she thought of as romantic dreams, in which some man would have his arm around her or even be embracing her. It might be a stranger or a man she knew – sometimes a man whom it was quite a joke to think of in that way. These dreams made her thoughtful or a little sad but relieved in some way to know that such feelings were possible for her. They could be embarrassing, but were nothing, nothing at all compared with the dreams that she was having now. In the dreams that came to her now she would be copulating or trying to copulate (sometimes she was prevented by intruders or shifts of circumstances) with utterly forbidden and unthinkable partners. With fat squirmy babies or patients in bandages or her own mother. She would be slick with lust, hollow and groaning with it, and she would set to work with roughness and an attitude of evil pragmatism. 'Yes, this will have to do,' she would say to herself. 'This will do if nothing better comes along.' And this coldness of heart, this matter-of-fact depravity, simply drove her lust along. She woke up unrepentant, sweaty and exhausted, and lay like a carcass until her own self, her shame and disbelief, came pouring back into her. The sweat went cold on her skin. She lay there shivering in the warm night, with disgust and humiliation. She did not dare go back to sleep. She got used to the dark and the long rectangles of the net-curtained windows filled with a faint light. And the sick woman's breath grating and scolding and then almost disappearing.

If she were a Catholic, she thought, was this the sort of thing that could come out at confession? It didn't seem like the sort of thing she could even bring out in a private prayer. She didn't pray much anymore, except formally, and to bring the experiences she had just been through to the attention of God seemed absolutely useless, disrespectful. He would be insulted. She was insulted, by her own mind. Her religion was hopeful and sensible and there was no room in it for any sort of rubbishy drama, such as the invasion of the devil into her sleep. The filth in her mind was in her, and there was no point in dramatizing it and making it seem important. Surely not. It was nothing, just the mind's garbage.

In the little meadow between the house and the riverbank there were cows. She could hear them munching and jostling, feeding at night. She thought of their large gentle shapes in there with the money musk and chicory, the flowering grasses, and she thought, They have a lovely life, cows.

It ends, of course, in the slaughterhouse. The end is disaster.

For everybody, though, the same thing. Evil grabs us when we are sleeping; pain and disintegration lie in wait. Animal horrors, all worse than you can imagine beforehand. The comforts of bed and the cows' breath, the pattern of the stars at night – all that can get turned on its head in an instant. And here she was, here was Enid, working her life away pretending it wasn't so. Trying to ease people. Trying to be good. An angel of mercy, as her mother had said, with less and less irony as time went on. Patients and doctors, too, had said it.

And all the time how many thought that she was

64

a fool? The people she spent her labors on might secretly despise her. Thinking they'd never do the same in her place. Never be fool enough. No.

Miserable offenders, came into her head. *Miserable offenders.*

Restore them that are penitent.

So she got up and went to work; as far as she was concerned, that was the best way to be penitent. She worked very quietly but steadily through the night, washing the cloudy glasses and sticky plates that were in the cupboards and establishing order where there was none before. None. Teacups had sat between the ketchup and the mustard and toilet paper on top of a pail of honey. There was no waxed paper or even newspaper laid out on the shelves. Brown sugar in the bag was as hard as rock. It was understandable that things should have gone downhill in the last few months, but it looked as if there had been no care, no organization here, ever. All the net curtains were gray with smoke and the windowpanes were greasy. The last bit of jam had been left to grow fuzz in the jar, and vile-smelling water that had held some ancient bouquet had never been dumped out of its jug. But this was a good house still, that scrubbing and painting could restore.

Though what could you do about the ugly brown paint that had been recently and sloppily applied to the front-room floor?

When she had a moment later in the day she pulled the weeds out of Rupert's mother's flower beds, dug up the burdocks and twitch grass that were smothering the valiant perennials.

She taught the children to hold their spoons properly and to say grace.

> *Thank you for the world so sweet,*
> *Thank you for the food we eat . . .*

She taught them to brush their teeth and after that to say their prayers.

'God bless Mama and Daddy and Enid and Aunt Olive and Uncle Clive and Princess Elizabeth and Margaret Rose.' After that each added the name of the other. They had been doing it for quite a while when Sylvie said, 'What does it mean?'

Enid said, 'What does what mean?'

'What does it mean "God bless"?'

Enid made eggnogs, not flavoring them even with vanilla, and fed them to Mrs Quinn from a spoon. She fed her a little of the rich liquid at a time, and Mrs Quinn was able to hold down what was given to her in small amounts. If she could not do that, Enid spooned out flat, lukewarm ginger ale.

The sunlight, or any light, was as hateful as noise to Mrs Quinn by now. Enid had to hang thick quilts over the windows, even when the blinds were pulled down. With the fan shut off, as Mrs Quinn demanded, the room became very hot, and sweat dripped from Enid's forehead as she bent over the bed attending to the patient. Mrs Quinn went into fits of shivering; she could never be warm enough.

'This is dragging out,' the doctor said. 'It must be those milk-shakes you're giving her, keeping her going.'

'Eggnogs,' said Enid, as if it mattered.

Mrs Quinn was often now too tired or weak to talk. Sometimes she lay in a stupor, with her breathing so faint and her pulse so lost and wandering that a person less experienced than Enid would have taken her for dead. But at other times she rallied, wanted the radio on, then wanted it off. She knew perfectly well who she was still, and who Enid was, and she sometimes seemed to be watching Enid with a speculative or inquiring look in her eyes. Color was long gone from her face and even from her lips, but her eyes looked greener than they had in the past – a milky, cloudy green. Enid tried to answer the look that was bent on her.

'Would you like me to get a priest to talk to you?'

Mrs Quinn looked as if she wanted to spit.

'Do I look like a Mick?' she said.

'A minister?' said Enid. She knew this was the right thing to ask, but the spirit in which she asked it was not right – it was cold and faintly malicious.

No. This was not what Mrs Quinn wanted. She grunted with displeasure. There was some energy in her still, and Enid had the feeling that she was building it up for a purpose. 'Do you want to talk to your children?' she said, making herself speak compassionately and encouragingly. 'Is that what you want?'

No.

'Your husband? Your husband will be here in a little while.'

Enid didn't know that for sure. Rupert arrived so late some nights, after Mrs Quinn had taken the final pills and gone to sleep. Then he sat with Enid. He always brought her the newspaper. He asked what she wrote in her notebooks – he noticed that there were two – and she told him. One for the doctor, with a record of blood pressure and pulse and temperature, a record of what was eaten, vomited, excreted, medicines taken, some general summing up of the patient's condition. In the other notebook, for herself, she wrote many of the same things, though perhaps not so exactly, but she added details about the weather and what was happening all around. And things to remember.

'For instance, I wrote something down the other day,' she said. 'Something that Lois said. Lois and Sylvie came in when Mrs Green was here and Mrs Green was mentioning how the berry bushes were growing along the lane and stretching across the road, and Lois said, "It's like in 'Sleeping Beauty.'" Because I'd read them the story. I made a note of that.'

Rupert said, 'I'll have to get after those berry canes and cut them back.'

Enid got the impression that he was pleased by what Lois had said and by the fact that she had written it down, but it wasn't possible for him to say so.

One night he told her that he would be away for a couple of days, at a stock auction. He had asked the doctor if it was all right, and the doctor had said to go ahead.

That night he had come before the last pills were given, and Enid supposed that he was making a point of seeing his wife awake before that little time away. She told him to go right into Mrs Quinn's room, and he did, and shut the door after him. Enid picked up the paper and thought of going upstairs to read it, but the children probably weren't asleep yet; they would find excuses for calling her in. She could go out on the porch, but there were mosquitoes at this time of day, especially after a rain like the afternoon's.

She was afraid of overhearing some intimacy or perhaps the suggestion of a fight, then having to face him when he came out. Mrs Quinn was building up to a display – of that Enid felt sure. And before she made up her mind where to go she did overhear something. Not the recriminations or (if it was possible) the endearments, or perhaps even weeping, that she had been half expecting, but a laugh. She heard Mrs Quinn weakly laughing, and the laughter had the mockery and satisfaction in it that Enid had heard before but also something she hadn't heard before, not in her life – something deliberately vile. She didn't move, though she should have, and she was at the table still, she was still there staring at the door of the room, when he came out a moment later. He didn't avoid her eyes – or she his. She couldn't. Yet she couldn't have said for sure that he saw her. He just looked at her and went on outside. He looked as if he had caught hold of an electric wire and begged pardon – who of? – that his body was given over to this stupid catastrophe.

The next day Mrs Quinn's strength came flooding back, in that unnatural and deceptive way that Enid had seen once or twice in others. Mrs Quinn wanted to sit up against the pillows. She wanted the fan turned on.

Enid said, 'What a good idea.'

'I could tell you something you wouldn't believe,' Mrs Quinn said.

'People tell me lots of things,' said Enid.

'Sure. Lies,' Mrs Quinn said. 'I bet it's all lies. You know Mr Willens was right here in this room?'

III. MISTAKE

Mrs Quinn had been sitting in the rocker getting her eyes examined and Mr Willens had been close up in front of her with the thing up to her eyes, and neither one of them heard Rupert come in, because he was supposed to be cutting wood down by the river. But he had sneaked back. He sneaked back through the kitchen not making any noise – he must have seen Mr Willens's car outside before he did that – then he opened the door to this room just easy, till he saw Mr Willens there on his knees holding the thing up to her eye and he had the other hand on her leg to keep his balance. He had grabbed her leg to keep his balance and her skirt got scrunched up and her leg showed bare, but that was all there was to it and she couldn't do a thing about it, she had to concentrate on keeping still.

So Rupert got in the room without either of them hearing him come in and then he just gave one jump and landed on Mr Willens like a bolt of lightning and Mr Willens couldn't get up or turn around, he was down before he knew it. Rupert banged his head up and down on the floor, Rupert banged the life out of him, and she jumped up so fast the chair went over and Mr Willens's box where he kept his eye things got knocked over and all the things flew out of it. Rupert just walloped him, and maybe he hit the leg of the stove, she didn't know what. She thought, It's me next. But she couldn't get round them to run out of the room. And then she saw Rupert wasn't going to go for her after all. He was out of wind and he just set the chair up and sat down in it. She went to Mr Willens then and hauled him around, as heavy as he was, to get him right side up. His eyes were not quite open, not shut either, and there was dribble coming out of his mouth. But no skin broke on his face or bruise you could see – maybe it wouldn't have come up yet. The stuff coming out of his mouth didn't even look like blood. It was pink stuff, and if you wanted to know what it looked like it looked exactly like when the froth comes up when you're boiling the strawberries to make jam. Bright pink. It was smeared over his face from when Rupert had him facedown. He made a sound, too, when she was turning him over. *Glug-glug*. That was all there was to it. *Glug-glug* and he was laid out like a stone.

Rupert jumped out of the chair so it was still rocking, and he started picking up all the things and putting each one back where it went in Mr Willens's box. Getting everything fitted in the way it should go. Wasting the time that way. It was a special box lined with red plush and a place in it for each one of his things that he used and you had to get everything in right or the top wouldn't go down. Rupert got it so the top went on and then he just sat down in the chair again and started pounding on his knees.

On the table there was one of those good-for-nothing cloths, it was a souvenir of when Rupert's mother and father went up north to see the Dionne Quintuplets. She took it off the table and wrapped it around Mr Willens's head to soak up the pink stuff and so they wouldn't have to keep on looking at him.

Rupert kept banging his big flat hands. She said, Rupert, we got to bury him somewhere.

Rupert just looked at her, like to say, Why?

She said they could bury him down in the cellar, which had a dirt floor.

'That's right,' said Rupert. 'Where are we going to bury his car?'

She said they could put it in the barn and cover it up with hay.

He said too many people came poking around the barn.

Then she thought, Put him in the river. She thought of him sitting in his car right under the water. It came to her like a picture. Rupert didn't say anything at first, so she went into the kitchen and got some water and cleaned Mr Willens up so he wouldn't dribble on anything. The goo was not coming up in his mouth anymore. She got his keys, which were in his pocket. She could feel, through the cloth of his pants, the fat of his leg still warm.

She said to Rupert, Get moving.

He took the keys.

They hoisted Mr Willens up, she by the feet and Rupert by the head, and he weighed a ton. He was like lead. But as she carried him one of his shoes kind of kicked her between the legs, and she thought, There you are, you're still at it, you horny old devil. Even his dead old foot giving her the nudge. Not that she ever let him do anything, but he was always ready to get a grab if he could. Like grabbing her leg up under her skirt when he had the thing to her eye and she couldn't stop him and Rupert had to come sneaking in and get the wrong idea.

Over the doorsill and through the kitchen and

across the porch and down the porch steps. All clear. But it was a windy day, and, first thing, the wind blew away the cloth she had wrapped over Mr Willens's face.

Their yard couldn't be seen from the road, that was lucky. Just the peak of the roof and the upstairs window. Mr Willens's car couldn't be seen.

Rupert had thought up the rest of what to do. Take him to Jutland, where it was deep water and the track going all the way back and it could look like he just drove in from the road and mistook his way. Like he turned off on the Jutland road, maybe it was dark and he just drove into the water before he knew where he was at. Like he just made a mistake.

He did. Mr Willens certainly did make a mistake.

The trouble was it meant driving out their lane and along the road to the Jutland turn. But nobody lived down there and it was a dead end after the Jutland turn, so just the half mile or so to pray you never met anybody. Then Rupert would get Mr Willens over in the driver's seat and push the car right off down the bank into the water. Push the whole works down into the pond. It was going to be a job to do that, but Rupert at least was a strong bugger. If he hadn't been so strong they wouldn't have been in this mess in the first place.

Rupert had a little trouble getting the car started because he had never driven one like that, but he did, and got turned around and drove off down the lane with Mr Willens kind of bumping over against him. He had put Mr Willens's hat on his head – the hat that had been sitting on the seat of the car.

Why take his hat off before he came into the house? Not just to be polite but so he could easier get a clutch on her and kiss her. If you could call that kissing, all that pushing up against her with the box still in one hand and the other grabbing on, and sucking away at her with his dribbly old mouth. Sucking and chewing away at her lips and her tongue and pushing himself up at her and the corner of the box sticking into her and digging her behind. She was so surprised and he got such a hold she didn't know how to get out of it. Pushing and sucking and dribbling and digging into her and hurting her all at the same time. He was a dirty old brute.

She went and got the Quintuplets cloth where it had blown onto the fence. She looked hard for blood on the steps or any mess on the porch or through the kitchen, but all she found was in the front room, also some on her shoes. She scrubbed up what was on the floor and scrubbed her shoes, which she took off, and not till she had all that done did she see a smear right down her front. How did she come by that? And the same time she saw it she heard a noise that turned her to stone. She heard a car and it was a car she didn't know and it was coming down the lane.

She looked through the net curtain and sure

enough. A new-looking car and dark green. Her smeared-down front and shoes off and the floor wet. She moved back where she couldn't be seen, but she couldn't think of where to hide. The car stopped and a car door opened, but the engine didn't cut off. She heard the door shut and then the car turned around and she heard the sound of it driving back up the lane. And she heard Lois and Sylvie on the porch.

It was the teacher's boyfriend's car. He picked up the teacher every Friday afternoon, and this was a Friday. So the teacher said to him, Why don't we give these ones a lift home, they're the littlest and they got the farthest to go and it looks like it's going to rain.

It did rain, too. It had started by the time Rupert got back, walking home along the riverbank. She said, A good thing, it'll muddy up your tracks where you went to push it over. He said he'd took his shoes off and worked in his sock feet. So you must have got your brains going again, she said.

Instead of trying to soak the stuff out of that souvenir cloth or the blouse she had on, she decided to burn the both of them in the stove. They made a horrible smell and the smell made her sick. That was the whole beginning of her being sick. That and the paint. After she cleaned up the floor, she could still see where she thought there was a stain, so she got the brown paint left over from when Rupert painted the steps and she painted over the whole floor. That started her throwing up, leaning

76

over and breathing in that paint. And the pains in her back – that was the start of them, too.

After she got the floor painted she just about quit going into the front room. But one day she thought she had better put some other cloth on that table. It would make things look more normal. If she didn't, then her sister-in-law was sure to come nosing around and say, Where's that cloth Mom and Dad brought back the time they went to see the Quints? If she had a different cloth on she could say, Oh, I just felt like a change. But no cloth would look funny.

So she got a cloth Rupert's mother had embroidered with flower baskets and took it in there and she could still smell the smell. And there on the table was sitting the dark-red box with Mr Willen's things in it and his name on it and it had been sitting there all the time. She didn't even remember putting it there or seeing Rupert put it there. She had forgot all about it.

She took that box and hid it in one place and then she hid it in another. She never told where she did it and she wasn't going to. She would have smashed it up, but how do you smash all those things in it? Examining things. Oh, Missus, would you like me to examine your eyes for you, just sit down here and just you relax and you just shut the one eye and keep the other one wide open. Wide open, now. It was like the same game every time, and she wasn't supposed to suspect what was going on, and when he had the thing out looking in her eye he wanted her to keep her panties on, him the dirty old cuss puffing away getting his fingers slicked in and puffing away. Her not supposed to say anything till he stops and gets the looker thing packed up in his box and all and then she's supposed to say, 'Oh, Mr Willens, now, how much do I owe you for today?'

And that was the signal for him to get her down and thump her like an old billy goat. Right on the bare floor to knock her up and down and try to bash her into pieces. Dingey on him like a blowtorch.

How'd you've liked that?

Then it was in the papers. Mr Willens found drowned.

They said his head got bunged up knocking against the steering wheel. They said he was alive when he went in the water. What a laugh.

IV. LIES

Enid stayed awake all night – she didn't even try to sleep. She could not lie down in Mrs Quinn's room. She sat in the kitchen for hours. It was an effort for her to move, even to make a cup of tea or go to the bathroom. Moving her body shook up the information that she was trying to arrange in her head and get used to. She had not undressed, or unrolled her hair, and when she brushed her teeth she seemed to be doing something laborious and unfamiliar. The moonlight came through the

78

kitchen window – she was sitting in the dark – and she watched a patch of light shift through the night, on the linoleum, and disappear. She was surprised by its disappearance and then by the birds waking up, the new day starting. The night had seemed so long and then too short, because nothing had been decided.

She got up stiffly and unlocked the door and sat on the porch in the beginning light. Even that move jammed her thoughts together. She had to sort through them again and set them on two sides. What had happened – or what she had been told had happened – on one side. What to do about it on the other. What to do about it – that was what would not come clear to her.

The cows had been moved out of the little meadow between the house and the riverbank. She could open the gate if she wanted to and go in that direction. She knew that she should go back, instead, and check on Mrs Quinn. But she found herself pulling open the gate bolt.

The cows hadn't cropped all the weeds. Sopping wet, they brushed against her stockings. The path was clear, though, under the riverbank trees, those big willows with the wild grape hanging on to them like monkeys' shaggy arms. Mist was rising so that you could hardly see the river. You had to fix your eyes, concentrate, and then a spot of water would show through, quiet as water in a pot. There must be a moving current, but she could not find it.

Then she saw a movement, and it wasn't in

the water. There was a boat moving. Tied to a branch, a plain old rowboat was being lifted very slightly, lifted and let fall. Now that she had found it, she kept watching it, as if it could say something to her. And it did. It said something gentle and final.

You know. You know.

When the children woke up they found her in bountiful good spirits, freshly washed and dressed and with her hair loose. She had already made the Jell-O crammed with fruit that would be ready for them to eat at noon. And she was mixing batter for cookies that could be baked before it got too hot to use the oven.

'Is that your father's boat?' she said. 'Down on the river?'

Lois said yes. 'But we're not supposed to play in it.' Then she said, 'If you went down with us we could.' They had caught on at once to the day's air of privilege, its holiday possibilities, Enid's unusual mix of languor and excitement.

'We'll see,' said Enid. She wanted to make the day a special one for them, special aside from the fact – which she was already almost certain of – that it would be the day of their mother's death. She wanted them to hold something in their minds that could throw a redeeming light on whatever came later. On herself, that is, and whatever way she would affect their lives later.

That morning Mrs Quinn's pulse had been hard

to find and she had not been able, apparently, to raise her head or open her eyes. A great change from yesterday, but Enid was not surprised. She had thought that great spurt of energy, that wicked outpouring talk, would be the last. She held a spoon with water in it to Mrs Quinn's lips, and Mrs Quinn drew a little of the water in. She made a mewing sound – the last trace, surely, of all her complaints. Enid did not call the doctor, because he was due to visit anyway later that day, probably early in the afternoon.

She shook up soapsuds in a jar and bent a piece of wire, and then another piece, to make bubble wands. She showed the children how to make bubbles, blowing steadily and carefully until as large a shining bladder as possible trembled on the wire, then shaking it delicately free. They chased the bubbles around the yard and kept them afloat till breezes caught them and hung them in the trees or on the eaves of the porch. What kept them alive then seemed to be the cries of admiration, screams of joy, rising up from below. Enid put no restriction on the noise they could make, and when the soapsud mixture was all used up she made more.

The doctor phoned when she was giving the children their lunch – Jell-O and a plate of cookies sprinkled with colored sugar and glasses of milk into which she had stirred chocolate syrup. He said he had been held up by a child's falling out of a tree and he would probably not be out before suppertime. Enid said softly, 'I think she may be going.'

'Well, keep her comfortable if you can,' the doctor said. 'You know how as well as I do.'

Enid didn't phone Mrs Green. She knew that Rupert would not be back yet from the auction and she didn't think that Mrs Quinn, if she ever had another moment of consciousness, would want to see or hear her sister-in-law in the room. Nor did it seem likely that she would want to see her children. And there would be nothing good about seeing her for them to remember.

She didn't bother trying to take Mrs Quinn's blood pressure anymore, or her temperature – just sponged off her face and arms and offered the water, which was no longer noticed. She turned on the fan, whose noise Mrs Quinn had so often objected to. The smell rising from the body seemed to be changing, losing its ammoniac sharpness. Changing into the common odor of death.

She went out and sat on the steps. She took off her shoes and stockings and stretched out her legs in the sun. The children began cautiously to pester her, asking if she would take them down to the river, if they could sit in the boat, or if they found the oars could she take them rowing. She knew enough not to go that far in the way of desertion, but she asked them, Would they like to have a swimming pool? Two swimming pools? And she brought out the two laundry tubs, set them on the grass, and filled them with water from the cistern pump. They stripped to their underpants and lolled in the water, becoming Princess Elizabeth and Princess Margaret Rose.

'What do you think,' said Enid, sitting on the grass with her head back and her eyes shut, 'what do you think, if a person does something very bad, do they have to be punished?'

'Yes,' said Lois immediately. 'They have to get a licking.'

'Who did it?' said Sylvie.

'Just thinking of anybody,' said Enid. 'Now, what if it was a very bad thing but nobody knew they did it? Should they tell that they did and be punished?'

Sylvie said, 'I would know they did it.'

'You would not,' said Lois. 'How would you know?'

'I would've seed them.'

'You would not.'

'You know the reason I think they should be punished?' Enid said. 'It's because of how bad they are going to feel, in themselves. Even if nobody did see them and nobody ever knew. If you do something very bad and you are not punished you feel worse, and feel far worse, than if you are.'

'Lois stold a green comb,' Sylvie said.

'I did not,' said Lois.

'I want you to remember that,' Enid said.

Lois said, 'It was just laying the side the road.'

Enid went into the sickroom every half hour or so to wipe Mrs Quinn's face and hands with a damp cloth. She never spoke to her and never touched her hand, except with the cloth. She had never absented herself like this before with anybody who was dying. When she opened the door at around half past five she knew there was nobody alive in the room. The sheet was pulled out and Mrs Quinn's head was hanging over the side of the bed, a fact that Enid did not record or mention to anybody. She had the body straightened out and cleaned and the bed put to rights before the doctor came. The children were still playing in the yard.

'July 5. Rain early a.m. L. and S. playing under porch. Fan off and on, complains noise. Half cup eggnog spoon at a time. B.P. up, pulse rapid, no complaints pain. Rain didn't cool off much. R.Q. in evening. Hay finished.

'July 6. Hot day, vy. close. Try fan but no. Sponge often. R.Q. in evening. Start to cut wheat tomorrow. Everything 1 or 2 wks ahead due to heat, rain.

'July 7. Cont'd heat. Won't take eggnog. Ginger ale from spoon. Vy. weak. Heavy rain last night, wind. R.Q. not able to cut, grain lodged some places.

'July 8. No eggnog. Ginger ale. Vomiting a.m. More alert. R.Q. to go to calf auction, gone 2 days. Dr says go ahead.

'July 9. Vy. agitated. Terrible talk.

'July 10. Patient Mrs Rupert (Jeanette) Quinn

84

died today approx 5 p.m. Heart failure due to uremia. (Glomerulonephritis.)'

Enid never made a practice of waiting around for the funerals of people she had nursed. It seemed to her a good idea to get out of the house as soon as she decently could. Her presence could not help being a reminder of the time just before the death, which might have been dreary and full of physical disaster, and was now going to be glossed over with ceremony and hospitality and flowers and cakes.

Also, there was usually some female relative who would be in place to take over the household completely, putting Enid suddenly in the position of unwanted guest.

Mrs Green, in fact, arrived at the Quinns' house before the undertaker did. Rupert was not back yet. The doctor was in the kitchen drinking a cup of tea and talking to Enid about another case that she could take up now that this was finished. Enid was hedging, saying that she had thought of taking some time off. The children were upstairs. They had been told that their mother had gone to heaven, which for them had put the cap on this rare and eventful day.

Mrs Green was shy until the doctor left. She stood at the window to see him turn his car around and drive away. Then she said, 'Maybe I shouldn't say it right now, but I will. I'm glad it happened now and not later when the summer was over and they were started back to school. Now I'll have time to get them used to living at our place and used to the idea of the new school they'll be going to. Rupert, he'll have to get used to it, too.'

This was the first time that Enid had realized that Mrs Green meant to take the children to live with her, not just to stay for a while. Mrs Green was eager to manage the move, had been looking forward to it, probably, for some time. Very likely she had the children's rooms ready and material bought to make them new clothes. She had a large house and no children of her own.

'You must be wanting to get off home yourself,' she said to Enid. As long as there was another woman in the house it might look like a rival home, and it might be harder for her brother to see the necessity of moving the children out for good. 'Rupert can run you in when he gets here.'

Enid said that it was all right, her mother was coming out to pick her up.

'Oh, I forgot your mother,' said Mrs Green. 'Her and her snappy little car.'

She brightened up and began to open the cupboard doors, checking on the glasses and the tea-cups – were they clean for the funeral?

'Somebody's been busy,' she said, quite relieved about Enid now and ready to be complimentary.

Mr Green was waiting outside, in the truck, with the Greens' dog, General. Mrs Green called upstairs for Lois and Sylvie, and they came running down with some clothes in brown paper bags. They ran through the kitchen and slammed the door, without taking any notice of Enid.

'That's something that's going to have to change,' said Mrs Green, meaning the door slamming. Enid could hear the children shouting their greetings to General and General barking excitedly in return.

Two days later Enid was back, driving her mother's car herself. She came late in the afternoon, when the funeral would have been well over. There were no extra cars parked outside, which meant that the women who had helped in the kitchen had all gone home, taking with them the extra chairs and teacups and the large coffeepot that belonged to their church. The grass was marked with car tracks and some dropped crushed flowers.

She had to knock on the door now. She had to wait to be asked in.

She heard Rupert's heavy, steady footsteps. She spoke some greeting to him when he stood in front of her on the other side of the screen door, but she didn't look into his face. He was in his shirtsleeves, but was wearing his suit trousers. He undid the hook of the door.

'I wasn't sure anybody would be here,' Enid said. 'I thought you might still be at the barn.'

Rupert said, 'They all pitched in with the chores.'

She could smell whiskey when he spoke, but he didn't sound drunk.

'I thought you were one of the women come back to collect something you forgot,' he said.

Enid said, 'I didn't forget anything. I was just wondering, how are the children?'

'They're fine. They're at Olive's.'

It seemed uncertain whether he was going to ask her in. It was bewilderment that stopped him, not hostility. She had not prepared herself for this first awkward part of the conversation. So that she wouldn't have to look at him, she looked around at the sky.

'You can feel the evenings getting shorter,' she said. 'Even if it isn't a month since the longest day.'

'That's true,' said Rupert. Now he opened the door and stood aside and she went in. On the table was a cup without a saucer. She sat down at the opposite side of the table from where he had been sitting. She was wearing a dark-green silk-crepe dress and suede shoes to match. When she put these things on she had thought how this might be the last time that she would dress herself and the last clothes she would ever wear. She had done her hair up in a French braid and powdered her face. Her care, her vanity, seemed foolish but were necessary to her. She had been awake now three nights in a row, awake every minute, and she had not been able to eat, even to fool her mother.

'Was it specially difficult this time?' her mother had said. She hated discussion of illness or deathbeds, and the fact that she had brought herself to ask this meant that Enid's upset was obvious.

'Was it the children you'd got fond of?' she said. 'The poor little monkeys.'

Enid said it was just the problem of settling down after a long case, and a hopeless case of course had its own strain. She did not go out of her mother's house in the daytime, but she did go for walks at night, when she could be sure of not meeting anybody and having to talk. She had found herself walking past the walls of the county jail. She knew there was a prison yard behind those walls where hangings had once taken place. But not for years and years. They must do it in some large central prison now, when they had to do it. And it was a long time since anybody from this community had committed a sufficiently serious crime.

Sitting across the table from Rupert, facing the door of Mrs Quinn's room, she had almost forgotten her excuse, lost track of the way things were to go. She felt her purse in her lap, the weight of her camera in it – that reminded her.

'There is one thing I'd like to ask you,' she said. 'I thought I might as well now, because I wouldn't get another chance.'

Rupert said, 'What's that?'

'I know you've got a rowboat. So I wanted to ask you to row me out to the middle of the river. And I could get a picture. I'd like to get a picture of the riverbank. It's beautiful there, the willow trees along the bank.'

'All right,' said Rupert, with the careful lack of

surprise that country people will show, regarding the frivolity – the rudeness, even – of visitors.

That was what she was now – a visitor.

Her plan was to wait until they got out to the middle of the river, then to tell him that she could not swim. First ask him how deep he thought the water would be there – and he would surely say, after all the rain they had been having, that it might be seven or eight, or even ten, feet. Then tell him that she could not swim. And that would not be a lie. She had grown up in Walley, on the lake, she had played on the beach every summer of her childhood, she was a strong girl and good at games, but she was frightened of the water, and no coaxing or demonstrating or shaming had ever worked with her – she had not learned to swim.

He would only have to give her a shove with one of the oars and topple her into the water and let her sink. Then leave the boat out on the water and swim to shore, change his clothes, and say that he had come in from the barn or from a walk and found the car there, and where was she? Even the camera if found would make it more plausible. She had taken the boat out to get a picture, then somehow fallen into the river.

Once he understood his advantage, she would tell him. She would ask, Is it true?

If it was not true, he would hate her for asking. If it was true – and didn't she believe all the time that it was true? – he would hate her in another, more dangerous way. Even if she said at once –

and meant it, she would mean it – that she was never going to tell.

She would speak very quietly all the time, remembering how voices carry out on the water on a summer evening.

I am not going to tell, but you are. You can't live on with that kind of secret.

You cannot live in the world with such a burden. You will not be able to stand your life.

If she had got so far, and he had neither denied what she said nor pushed her into the river, Enid would know that she had won the gamble. It would take some more talking, more absolutely firm but quiet persuasion, to bring him to the point where he would start to row back to shore.

Or, lost, he would say, What will I do? and she would take him one step at a time, saying first, Row back.

The first step in a long, dreadful journey. She would tell him every step and she would stay with him for as many of them as she could. Tie up the boat now. Walk up the bank. Walk through the meadow. Open the gate. She would walk behind him or in front, whichever seemed better to him. Across the yard and up the porch and into the kitchen.

They will say goodbye and get into their separate cars and then it will be his business where he goes. And she will not phone the Police Office the next day. She will wait and they will phone her and she will go to see him in jail. Every day, or as often as they will let her, she will sit and talk to him in jail, and she will write him letters as well. If they take him to another jail she will go there; even if she is allowed to see him only once a month she will be close by. And in court – yes, every day in court, she will be sitting where he can see her.

She does not think anyone would get a death sentence for this sort of murder, which was in a way accidental, and was surely a crime of passion, but the shadow is there, to sober her when she feels that these pictures of devotion, of a bond that is like love but beyond love, are becoming indecent.

Now it has started. With her asking to be taken on the river, her excuse of the picture. Both she and Rupert are standing up, and she is facing the door of the sickroom – now again the front room – which is shut.

She says a foolish thing.

'Are the quilts taken down off the windows?'

He doesn't seem to know for a minute what she is talking about. Then he says, 'The quilts. Yes. I think it was Olive took them down. In there was where we had the funeral.'

'I was only thinking. The sun would fade them.'

He opens the door and she comes around the table and they stand looking into the room. He says, 'You can go in if you like. It's all right. Come in.'

The bed is gone, of course. The furniture is pushed back against the walls. The middle of the room, where they would have set up the chairs for the funeral, is bare. So is the space in between the north windows – that must have been where they put the coffin. The table where Enid was used to setting the basin, and laying out cloths, cotton wool, spoons, medicine, is jammed into a corner and has a bouquet of delphiniums sitting on it. The tall windows still hold plenty of daylight.

'Lies' is the word that Enid can hear now, out of all the words that Mrs Quinn said in that room. *Lies. I bet it's all lies.*

Could a person make up something so detailed and diabolical? The answer is yes. A sick person's mind, a dying person's mind, could fill up with all kinds of trash and organize that trash in a most convincing way. Enid's own mind, when she was asleep in this room, had filled up with the most disgusting inventions, with filth. Lies of that nature could be waiting around in the corners of a person's mind, hanging like bats in the corners, waiting to take advantage of any kind of darkness. You can never say, Nobody could make that up. Look how elaborate dreams are, layer over layer in them, so that the part you can remember and put into words is just the bit you can scratch off the top.

When Enid was four or five years old she had told her mother that she had gone into her father's office and that she had seen him sitting behind his desk with a woman on his knee. All she could remember about this woman, then and now, was that she wore a hat with a great many flowers on it and a veil (a hat quite out of fashion even at that time), and that her blouse or dress was unbuttoned and there was one bare breast sticking out, the tip of it disappearing into Enid's father's mouth. She had told her mother about this in perfect certainty that she had seen it. She said, 'One of her fronts was stuck in Daddy's mouth.' She did not know the word for breasts, though she did know they came in pairs.

Her mother said, 'Now, Enid. What are you talking about? What on earth is a front?'

'Like an ice-cream cone,' Enid said.

And she saw it that way, exactly. She could see it that way still. The biscuit-colored cone with its mound of vanilla ice cream squashed against the woman's chest and the wrong end sticking into her father's mouth.

Her mother then did a very unexpected thing. She undid her own dress and took out a dull-skinned object that flopped over her hand. 'Like this?' she said.

Enid said no. 'An ice-cream cone,' she said.

'Then that was a dream,' her mother said. 'Dreams are sometimes downright silly. Don't tell Daddy about it. It's too silly.'

Enid did not believe her mother right away, but in a year or so she saw that such an explanation had to be right, because ice-cream cones did not ever arrange themselves in that way on ladies' chests and they were never so big. When she was older still she realized that the hat must have come from some picture.

Lies.

She hadn't asked him yet, she hadn't spoken. Nothing yet committed her to asking. It was still *before*. Mr Willens had still driven himself into Jutland Pond, on purpose or by accident. Everybody still believed that, and as far as Rupert was concerned Enid believed it, too. And as long as that was so, this room and this house and her life held a different possibility, an entirely different possibility from the one she had been living with (or glorying in – however you wanted to put it) for the last few days. The different possibility was coming closer to her, and all she needed to do was to keep quiet and let it come. Through her silence, her collaboration in a silence, what benefits could bloom. For others, and for herself.

This was what most people knew. A simple thing that it had taken her so long to understand. This was how to keep the world habitable.

She had started to weep. Not with grief but with an onslaught of relief that she had not known she was looking for. Now she looked into Rupert's face and saw that his eyes were bloodshot and the skin around them puckered and dried out, as if he had been weeping, too.

He said, 'She wasn't lucky in her life.'

Enid excused herself and went to get her handkerchief, which was in her purse on the table. She was embarrassed now that she had dressed herself up in readiness for such a melodramatic fate.

'I don't know what I was thinking of,' she said. 'I can't walk down to the river in these shoes.'

Rupert shut the door of the front room.

'If you want to go we can still go,' he said. 'There ought to be a pair of rubber boots would fit you somewhere.'

Not hers, Enid hoped. No. Hers would be too small.

Rupert opened a bin in the woodshed, just outside the kitchen door. Enid had never looked into that bin. She had thought it contained firewood, which she had certainly had no need of that summer. Rupert lifted out several single rubber boots and even snow boots, trying to find a pair.

'These look like they might do,' he said. 'They maybe were Mother's. Or even mine before my feet got full size.'

He pulled out something that looked like a piece of a tent, then, by a broken strap, an old school satchel.

'Forgot all the stuff that was in here,' he said, letting these things fall back and throwing the unusable boots on top of them. He dropped the lid and gave a private, grieved, and formal-sounding sigh.

A house like this, lived in by one family for so long a time, and neglected for the past several years, would have plenty of bins, drawers, shelves, suitcases, trunks, crawl spaces full of things that it would be up to Enid to sort out, saving and labelling some, restoring some to use, sending others by the boxload to the dump. When she got that chance she wouldn't balk at it. She would make this house into a place that had no secrets from her and where all order was as she had decreed.

He set the boots down in front of her while she was bent over unbuckling her shoes. She smelled under the whiskey the bitter breath that came after a sleepless night and a long harsh day; she smelled the deeply sweat-soaked skin of a hardworked man that no washing – at least the washing he did – could get quite fresh. No bodily smell – even the smell of semen – was unfamiliar to her, but there was something new and invasive about the smell of a body so distinctly not in her power or under her care.

That was welcome.

'See can you walk,' he said.

She could walk. She walked in front of him to the gate. He bent over her shoulder to swing it open for her. She waited while he bolted it, then stood aside to let him walk ahead, because he had brought a little hatchet from the woodshed, to clear their path.

'The cows were supposed to keep the growth down,' he said. 'But there's things cows won't eat.'

She said, 'I was only down here once. Early in the morning.'

The desperation of her frame of mind then had to seem childish to her now.

Rupert went along chopping at the big fleshy thistles. The sun cast a level, dusty light on the bulk of the trees ahead. The air was clear in some places, then suddenly you would enter a cloud of tiny bugs. Bugs no bigger than specks of dust that were constantly in motion yet kept themselves together in the shape of a pillar or a cloud. How did they manage to do that? And how did they choose one spot over another to do it in? It must have something to do with feeding. But they never seemed to be still enough to feed.

When she and Rupert went underneath the roof of summer leaves it was dusk, it was almost night. You had to watch that you didn't trip over roots that swelled up out of the path, or hit your head on the dangling, surprisingly tough-stemmed vines. Then a flash of water came through the black branches. The lit-up water near the opposite bank of the river, the trees over there still decked out in light. On this side – they were going down the bank now, through the willows – the water was tea-colored but clear.

And the boat waiting, riding in the shadows, just the same.

'The oars are hid,' said Rupert. He went into the willows to locate them. In a moment she lost sight of him. She went closer to the water's edge, where her boots sank into the mud a little and held her. If she tried to, she could still hear Rupert's movements in the bushes. But if she concentrated on the motion of the boat, a slight and secretive motion, she could feel as if everything for a long way around had gone quiet.

JAKARTA

Kath and Sonje have a place of their own on the beach, behind some large logs. They have chosen this not only for shelter from the occasional sharp wind – they've got Kath's baby with them – but because they want to be out of sight of a group of women who use the beach every day. They call these women the Monicas.

The Monicas have two or three or four children apiece. They are all under the leadership of the real Monica, who walked down the beach and introduced herself when she first spotted Kath and Sonje and the baby. She invited them to join the gang.

They followed her, lugging the carry-cot between them. What else could they do? But since then they lurk behind the logs.

The Monicas' encampment is made up of beach umbrellas, towels, diaper bags, picnic hampers, inflatable rafts and whales, toys, lotions, extra clothing, sun hats, thermos bottles of coffee, paper cups and plates, and thermos tubs in which they carry homemade fruit-juice Popsicles.

They are either frankly pregnant or look as if they

might be pregnant, because they have lost their figures. They trudge down to the water's edge, hollering out the names of their children who are riding and falling off logs or the inflatable whales.

'Where's your hat? Where's your ball? You've been on that thing long enough now, let Sandy have a turn.'

Even when they talk to each other their voices have to be raised high, over the shouts and squalls of their children.

'You can get ground round as cheap as hamburger if you go to Woodward's.'

'I tried zinc ointment but it didn't work.'

'Now he's got an abscess in the groin.'

'You can't use baking powder, you have to use soda.'

These women aren't so much older than Kath and Sonje. But they've reached a stage in life that Kath and Sonje dread. They turn the whole beach into a platform. Their burdens, their strung-out progeny and maternal poundage, their authority, can annihilate the bright water, the perfect small cove with the red-limbed arbutus trees, the cedars, growing crookedly out of the high rocks. Kath feels their threat particularly, since she's a mother now herself. When she nurses her baby she often reads a book, sometimes smokes a cigarette, so as not to sink into a sludge of animal function. And she's nursing so that she can shrink her uterus and flatten her stomach, not just provide the baby – Noelle – with precious maternal antibodies.

Kath and Sonje have their own thermos of coffee and their extra towels, with which they've rigged up a shelter for Noelle. They have their cigarettes and their books. Sonje has a book by Howard Fast. Her husband has told her that if she has to read fiction that's who she should be reading. Kath is reading the short stories of Katherine Mansfield and the short stories of D. H. Lawrence. Sonje has got into the habit of putting down her own book and picking up whichever book of Kath's that Kath is not reading at the moment. She limits herself to one story and then goes back to Howard Fast.

When they get hungry one of them makes the trek up a long flight of wooden steps. Houses ring this cove, up on the rocks under the pine and cedar trees. They are all former summer cottages, from the days before the Lions Gate Bridge was built, when people from Vancouver would come across the water for their vacations. Some cottages – like Kath's and Sonje's – are still quite primitive and cheap to rent. Others, like the real Monica's, are much improved. But nobody intends to stay here; everybody's planning to move on to a proper house. Except for Sonje and her husband, whose plans seem more mysterious than anybody else's.

There is an unpaved crescent road serving the houses, and joined at either end to Marine Drive. The enclosed semicircle is full of tall trees and an undergrowth of ferns and salmonberry bushes, and various intersecting paths, by which you can take a shortcut out to the store on Marine Drive. At the store Kath and Sonje will buy takeout French fries for lunch. More often it's Kath who makes this expedition, because it's a treat for her to walk under the trees – something she can't do anymore with the baby carriage.

When she first came here to live, before Noelle was born, she would cut through the trees nearly every day, never thinking of her freedom. One day she met Sonje. They had both worked at the Vancouver Public Library a little while before this, though they had not been in the same department and had never talked to each other. Kath had quit in the sixth month of pregnancy as you were required to do, lest the sight of you should disturb the patrons, and Sonje had quit because of a scandal.

Or, at least, because of a story that had got into the newspapers. Her husband, Cottar, who was a journalist working for a magazine that Kath had never heard of, had made a trip to Red China. He was referred to in the paper as a left-wing writer. Sonje's picture appeared beside his, along with the information that she worked in the library. There was concern that in her job she might be promoting Communist books and influencing children who used the library, so that they might become Communists. Nobody said that she had done this – just that it was a danger. Nor was it against the law for somebody from Canada to visit China. But it turned out that Cottar and Sonje were both Americans, which made their behavior more alarming, perhaps more purposeful.

'I know that girl,' Kath had said to her husband, Kent, when she saw Sonje's picture. 'At least I know her to see her. She always seems kind of shy. She'll be embarrassed about this.'

'No she won't,' said Kent. 'Those types love to feel persecuted, it's what they live for.'

The head librarian was reported as saying that Sonje had nothing to do with choosing books or influencing young people – she spent most of her time typing out lists.

'Which was funny,' Sonje said to Kath, after they had recognized each other, and spoken and spent about half an hour talking on the path. The funny thing was that she did not know how to type.

She wasn't fired, but she had quit anyway. She thought she might as well, because she and Cottar had some changes coming up in their future.

Kath wondered if one change might be a baby. It seemed to her that life went on, after you finished school, as a series of further examinations to be passed. The first one was getting married. If you hadn't done that by the time you were twenty-five, that examination had to all intents and purposes been failed. (She always signed her name 'Mrs Kent Mayberry' with a sense of relief and mild elation.) Then you thought about having the first baby. Waiting a year before you got pregnant was a good idea. Waiting two years was a little more prudent than necessary. And three years started

104

people wondering. Then down the road somewhere was the second baby. After that the progression got dimmer and it was hard to be sure just when you had arrived at wherever it was you were going.

Sonje was not the sort of friend who would tell you that she was trying to have a baby and how long she'd been trying and what techniques she was using. She never talked about sex in that way, or about her periods or any behavior of her body – though she soon told Kath things that most people would consider much more shocking. She had a graceful dignity – she had wanted to be a ballet dancer until she got too tall, and she didn't stop regretting that until she met Cottar, who said, 'Oh, another little bourgeois girl hoping she'll turn into a dying swan.' Her face was broad, calm, pink skinned – she never wore any makeup, Cottar was against makeup – and her thick fair hair was pinned up in a bushy chignon. Kath thought she was wonderful looking – both seraphic and intelligent.

Eating their French fries on the beach, Kath and Sonje discuss characters in the stories they've been reading. How is it that no woman could love Stanley Burnell? What is it about Stanley? He is such a boy, with his pushy love, his greed at the table, his self-satisfaction. Whereas Jonathan Trout – oh, Stanley's wife, Linda, should have married Jonathan Trout, Jonathan who glided through the water while Stanley splashed and snorted. 'Greetings, my celestial peach blossom,' says Jonathan in his velvety bass voice. He is full of irony, he is subtle and weary. 'The shortness of life, the shortness of life,' he says. And Stanley's brash world crumbles, discredited.

Something bothers Kath. She can't mention it or think about it. Is Kent something like Stanley?

One day they have an argument. Kath and Sonje have an unexpected and disturbing argument about a story by D. H. Lawrence. The story is called 'The Fox.'

At the end of that story the lovers – a soldier and a woman named March – are sitting on the sea cliffs looking out on the Atlantic, towards their future home in Canada. They are going to leave England, to start a new life. They are committed to each other, but they are not truly happy. Not yet.

The soldier knows that they will not be truly happy until the woman gives her life over to him, in a way that she has not done so far. March is still struggling against him, to hold herself separate from him, she is making them both obscurely miserable by her efforts to hang on to her woman's soul, her woman's mind. She must stop this – she must stop thinking and stop wanting and let her consciousness go under, until it is submerged in his. Like the reeds that wave below the surface of the water. Look down, look down – see how the reeds wave in the water, they are alive but they never break the surface. And that is how her female nature must live within his male nature. Then she will be happy and he will be strong

106

and content. Then they will have achieved a true marriage.

Kath says that she thinks this is stupid.

She begins to make her case. 'He's talking about sex, right?'

'Not just,' says Sonje. 'About their whole life.'

'Yes, but sex. Sex leads to getting pregnant. I mean in the normal course of events. So March has a baby. She probably has more than one. And she has to look after them. How can you do that if your mind is waving around under the surface of the sea?'

'That's taking it very literally,' says Sonje in a slightly superior tone.

'You can either have thoughts and make decisions or you can't,' says Kath. 'For instance – the baby is going to pick up a razor blade. What do you do? Do you just say, Oh, I think I'll just float around here till my husband comes home and he can make up his mind, that is our mind, about whether this is a good idea?'

Sonje said, 'That's taking it to extremes.'

Each of their voices has hardened. Kath is brisk and scornful, Sonje grave and stubborn.

'Lawrence didn't want to have children,' Kath says. 'He was jealous of the ones Frieda had from being married before.'

Sonje is looking down between her knees, letting sand fall through her fingers.

'I just think it would be beautiful,' she says. 'I think it would be beautiful, if a woman could.'

Kath knows that something has gone wrong. Something is wrong with her own argument. Why is she so angry and excited? And why did she shift over to talking about babies, about children? Because she has a baby and Sonje doesn't? Did she say that about Lawrence and Frieda because she suspects that it is partly the same story with Cottar and Sonje?

When you make the argument on the basis of the children, about the woman having to look after the children, you're in the clear. You can't be blamed. But when Kath does that she is covering up. She can't stand that part about the reeds and the water, she feels bloated and suffocated with incoherent protest. So it is herself she is thinking of, not of any children. She herself is the very woman that Lawrence is railing about. And she can't reveal that straight out because it might make Sonje suspect – it might make Kath herself suspect – an impoverishment in Kath's life.

Sonje who has said, during another alarming conversation, 'My happiness depends on Cottar.'

My happiness depends on Cottar.

That statement shook Kath. She would never have said it about Kent. She didn't want it to be true of herself.

But she didn't want Sonje to think that she was a woman who had missed out on love. Who had not considered, who had not been offered, the prostration of love.

II

Kent remembered the name of the town in Oregon to which Cottar and Sonje had moved. Or to which Sonje had moved, at the end of the summer. She had gone there to look after Cottar's mother while Cottar took off on another journalistic junket to the Far East. There was some problem real or imagined about Cottar's getting back into the United States after his trip to China. When he came back the next time he and Sonje planned to meet in Canada, maybe move the mother up there too.

There wasn't much chance that Sonje would be living in the town now. There was just a slight chance that the mother might be. Kent said that it wasn't worth stopping for, but Deborah said, Why not, wouldn't it be interesting to find out? And an inquiry at the Post Office brought directions.

Kent and Deborah drove out of town through the sand dunes – Deborah doing the driving as she had done for most of this long leisurely trip. They had visited Kent's daughter Noelle, who was living in Toronto, and his two sons by his second wife, Pat – one of them in Montreal and the other in Maryland. They had stayed with some old friends of Kent's and Pat's who now lived in a gated community in Arizona, and with Deborah's parents – who were around Kent's age – in Santa Barbara. Now they were headed up the West Coast, home to Vancouver, but taking it easy every day, so as not to tire Kent out.

The dunes were covered with grass. They looked like ordinary hills, except where a naked sandy shoulder was revealed, to make the landscape look playful. A child's construction, swollen out of scale.

The road ended at the house they'd been told to look for. It couldn't be mistaken. There was the sign – PACIFIC SCHOOL OF DANCE. And Sonje's name, and a FOR SALE sign underneath. There was an old woman using shears on one of the bushes in the garden.

So Cottar's mother was still alive. But Kent remembered now that Cottar's mother was blind. That was why somebody had to go and live with her, after Cottar's father died.

What was she doing hacking away with those shears if she was blind?

He had made the usual mistake, of not realizing how many years – decades – had gone by. And how truly ancient the mother would have to be by now. How old Sonje would be, how old he was himself. For it was Sonje, and at first she did not know him either. She bent over to stick the shears into the ground, she wiped her hands on her jeans. He felt the stiffness of her movements in his own joints. Her hair was white and skimpy, blowing in the light ocean breeze that had found its way in here among the dunes. Some firm covering of flesh had gone from her bones. She had always been rather flat chested but not so thin in the waist. A broad-backed, broad-faced, Nordic sort of girl. Though her name didn't come from that ancestry

– he remembered a story of her being named Sonje because her mother loved Sonja Henie's movies. She changed the spelling herself and scorned her mother's frivolity. They all scorned their parents then, for something.

He couldn't see her face very well in the bright sun. But he saw a couple of shining silver-white spots where skin cancers, probably, had been cut away.

'Well Kent,' she said. 'How ridiculous. I thought you were somebody come to buy my house. And is this Noelle?'

So she had made her mistake too.

Deborah was in fact a year younger than Noelle. But there was nothing of the toy wife about her. Kent had met her after his first operation. She was a physiotherapist, never married, and he a widower. A serene, steady woman who distrusted fashion and irony – she wore her hair in a braid down her back. She had introduced him to yoga, as well as the prescribed exercises, and now she had him taking vitamins and ginseng as well. She was tactful and incurious almost to the point of indifference. Perhaps a woman of her generation took it for granted that everybody had a well-peopled and untranslatable past.

Sonje invited them into the house. Deborah said that she would leave them to have their visit – she wanted to find a health-food store (Sonje told her where one was) and to take a walk on the beach.

The first thing Kent noticed about the house

was that it was chilly. On a bright summer day. But houses in the Pacific Northwest are seldom as warm as they look – move out of the sun and you feel at once a clammy breath. Fogs and rainy winter cold must have entered this house for a long time almost without opposition. It was a large wooden bungalow, ramshackle though not austere, with its veranda and dormers. There used to be a lot of houses like this in West Vancouver, where Kent still lived. But most of them had been sold as teardowns.

The two large connected front rooms were bare, except for an upright piano. The floor was scuffed gray in the middle, darkly waxed at the corners. There was a railing along one wall and opposite that a dusty mirror in which he saw two lean white-haired figures pass. Sonje said that she was trying to sell the place – well, he could see that by the sign – and that since this part was set up as a dance studio she thought she might as well leave it that way.

'Somebody could still make an okay thing out of it,' she said. She said that they had started the school around 1960, soon after they heard that Cottar was dead. Cottar's mother – Delia – played the piano. She played it until she was nearly ninety years old and lost her marbles. ('Excuse me,' said Sonje, 'but you do get rather nonchalant about things.') Sonje had to put her in a nursing home where she went every day to feed her, though Delia didn't know her anymore. And she hired new people to play the piano, but things didn't work out. Also she was getting so that she couldn't show the pupils anything, just tell them. So she saw that it was time to give up.

She used to be such a stately girl, not very forthcoming. In fact not very friendly, or so he had thought. And now she was scurrying and chattering in the way of people who were too much alone.

'It did well when we started, little girls were all excited then about ballet, and then all that sort of thing went out, you know, it was too formal. But never completely, and then in the eighties people came moving in here with young families and it seemed they had lots of money, how did they get so much money? And it could have been successful again but I couldn't quite manage it.'

She said that perhaps the spirit went out of it or the need went out of it when her mother-in-law died.

'We were the best of friends,' she said. 'Always.'

The kitchen was another big room, which the cupboards and appliances didn't properly fill. The floor was gray and black tiles – or perhaps black and white tiles, the white made gray by dirty scrub water. They passed along a hallway lined with shelves, shelves right up to the ceiling crammed with books and tattered magazines, possibly even newspapers. A smell of the brittle old paper. Here the floor had a covering of sisal matting, and that continued into a side porch, where at last he had a chance to sit down. Rattan chairs and settee, the genuine article, that might be worth some money if they hadn't been falling apart. Bamboo blinds also not in the best condition, rolled up or half lowered, and outside some overgrown bushes pressing against the windows. Kent didn't know many names of plants, but he recognized these bushes as the sort that grow where the soil is sandy. Their leaves were tough and shiny – the greens looking as if dipped in oil.

As they passed through the kitchen Sonje had put the kettle on for tea. Now she sank down in one of the chairs as if she too was glad to settle. She held up her grubby big-knuckled hands.

'I'll clean up in a minute,' she said. 'I didn't ask you if you wanted tea. I could make coffee. Or if you like I could skip them both and make us a gin and tonic. Why don't I do that? It sounds like a good idea to me.'

The telephone was ringing. A disturbing, loud, old-fashioned ring. It sounded as if it was just outside in the hall, but Sonje hurried back to the kitchen.

She talked for some time, stopping to take the kettle off when it whistled. He heard her say 'visitor right now' and hoped she wasn't putting off someone who wanted to look at the house. Her nervy tone made him think this wasn't just a social call, and that it perhaps had something to do with money. He made an effort not to hear any more.

The books and papers stacked in the hall had reminded him of the house that Sonje and Cottar lived in above the beach. In fact the whole sense of discomfort, of disregard, reminded him. That living room had been heated by a stone fireplace at one end, and though a fire was going – the only time he had been there – old ashes were spilling out of it and bits of charred orange peel, bits of garbage. And there were books, pamphlets, everywhere. Instead of a sofa there was a cot – you had to sit with your feet on the floor and nothing at your back, or else crawl back and lean against the wall with your feet drawn up under you. That was how Kath and Sonje sat. They pretty well stayed out of the conversation. Kent sat in a chair, from which he had removed a dull-covered book with the title *The Civil War in France*. Is that what they're calling the French Revolution now? he thought. Then he saw the author's name, Karl Marx. And even before that he felt the hostility, the judgment, in the room. Just as you'd feel in a room full of gospel tracts and pictures of Jesus on a donkey, Jesus on the Sea of Galilee, a judgment passed down on you. Not just from the books and papers – it was in the fireplace mess and the rug with its pattern worn away and the burlap curtains. Kent's shirt and tie were wrong. He had suspected that by the way Kath looked at them, but once he put them on he was going to wear them anyway. She was wearing one of his old shirts over jeans fastened with a string of safety pins. He had thought that a sloppy outfit to go out to dinner in, but concluded that maybe it was all she could get into.

115

That was right before Noelle was born.

Cottar was cooking the meal. It was a curry, and turned out to be very good. They drank beer. Cottar was in his thirties, older than Sonje and Kath and Kent. Tall, narrow shouldered, with a high bald forehead and wispy sideburns. A rushed, hushed, confidential way of talking.

There was also an older couple, a woman with low-slung breasts and graying hair rolled up at the back of her neck and a short straight man rather scruffy in his clothes but with something dapper about his manner, his precise and edgy voice and habit of making tidy box shapes with his hands. And there was a young man, a redhead, with puffy watery eyes and speckled skin. He was a part-time student who supported himself by driving the truck that dropped off newspapers for the delivery boys to pick up. Evidently he had just started this job, and the older man, who knew him, began to tease him about the shame of delivering such a paper. Tool of the capitalist classes, mouthpiece of the elite.

Even though this was said in a partly joking way, Kent couldn't let it pass. He thought he might as well jump in then as later. He said he didn't see much wrong with that paper.

They were just waiting for something like that. The older man had already drawn out the information that Kent was a pharmacist and worked for one of the chain drugstores. And the young man had already said, 'Are you on the management track?' in a way that suggested the others would

116

see this as a joke but Kent wouldn't. Kent had said he hoped so.

The curry was served, and they ate it, and drank more beer, and the fire was replenished and the spring sky went dark and the lights of Point Grey showed up across Burrard Inlet, and Kent took it upon himself to defend capitalism, the Korean War, nuclear weapons, John Foster Dulles, the execution of the Rosenbergs – whatever the others threw at him. He scoffed at the idea that American companies were persuading African mothers to buy formula and not to nurse their babies, and that the Royal Canadian Mounted Police were behaving brutally to Indians, and above all at the notion that Cottar's phone might be tapped. He quoted *Time* magazine and announced that he was doing so.

The younger man clapped his knees and wagged his head from side to side and manufactured an incredulous laugh.

'I can't believe this guy. Can you believe this guy? I can't.'

Cottar kept mobilizing arguments and tried to keep a rein on exasperation, because he saw himself as a reasoning man. The older man went off on professorial tangents and the low-slung woman made interjections in a tone of poisonous civility.

'Why are you in such a hurry to defend authority wherever it rears its delightful head?'

Kent didn't know. He didn't know what propelled him. He didn't even take these people seriously, as the enemy. They hung around on the fringes of real life, haranguing and thinking themselves important, the way fanatics of any sort did. They had no solidity, when you compared them with the men Kent worked with. In the work Kent did, mistakes mattered, responsibility was constant, you did not have time to fool around with ideas about whether chain drugstores were a bad idea or indulge in some paranoia about drug companies. That was the real world and he went out into it every day with the weight of his future and Kath's on his shoulders. He accepted that, he was even proud of it, he was not going to apologize to a roomful of groaners.

'Life is getting better in spite of what you say,' he had told them. 'All you have to do is look around you.'

He did not disagree with his younger self now. He thought he had been brash maybe, but not wrong. But he wondered about the anger in that room, all the bruising energy, what had become of it.

Sonje was off the phone. She called to him from the kitchen, 'I am definitely going to skip the tea and get to that gin and tonic.'

When she brought the drinks he asked her how long Cottar had been dead, and she told him more than thirty years. He drew his breath in, and shook his head. That long?

'He died very quickly of some tropical bug,' Sonje said. 'It happened in Jakarta. He was buried before I even knew he was sick. Jakarta used to be called Batavia, did you know that?'

Kent said, 'Vaguely.'

'I remember your house,' she said. 'The living room was really a porch, it was all the way across the front, like ours. There were blinds made of awning material, green and brown stripes. Kath liked the light coming through them, she said it was jungly light. You called it a glorified shack. Every time you mentioned it. The Glorified Shack.'

'It was on posts stuck in cement,' Kent said. 'They were rotting. It was a wonder it didn't fall down.'

'You and Kath used to go out looking at houses,' said Sonje. 'On your day off you'd walk around some subdivision or other with Noelle in the baby carriage. You'd look at all the new houses. You know what those subdivisions were like then. There were never any sidewalks because people weren't supposed to walk anymore and they'd taken down all the trees and the houses were just stuck together staring at each other through the picture windows.'

Kent said, 'What else could anybody afford, for a start?'

'I know, I know. But you'd say, "Which one do you like?" and Kath would never answer. So finally you got exasperated and said, well, what sort of house did she like, anywhere, and she said, "The Glorified Shack."'

Kent could not remember that happening. But he supposed it had. Anyway it was what Kath had told Sonje.

III

Cottar and Sonje were having a farewell party, before Cottar went off to the Philippines or Indonesia or wherever he was going, and Sonje went to Oregon to stay with his mother. Everybody who lived along the beach was asked – since the party was going to be held out-of-doors, that was the only sensible policy. And some people Sonje and Cottar had lived with in a communal house, before they moved to the beach, were asked, and journalists Cottar knew, and people Sonje had worked with in the library.

'Just everybody,' Kath said, and Kent said cheerfully, 'More pinkos?' She said she didn't know, just everybody.

The real Monica had hired her regular babysitter, and all the children were to be brought to her house, the parents chipping in on the cost. Kath brought Noelle along in her carry-cot just as it was beginning to get dark. She told the sitter that she'd come back before midnight, when Noelle would probably wake up for a feed. She could have brought the supplemental bottle which was made up at home, but she hadn't. She was uncertain about the party and thought she might welcome a chance to get away.

She and Sonje had never talked about the dinner at Sonje's house when Kent got into the fight with everybody. It was the first time Sonje had met Kent and all she said afterwards was that he was really quite good-looking. Kath felt as if the good looks were being thought of as a banal consolation prize.

She had sat that evening with her back against the wall and a cushion hugged against her stomach. She had got into the habit of holding a cushion against the spot where the baby kicked. The cushion was faded and dusty, like everything in Sonje's house (she and Cottar had rented it ready-furnished). Its pattern of blue flowers and leaves had gone silvery. Kath fastened her eyes on these, while they tied Kent up in knots and he didn't even realize it. The young man talked to him with the theatrical rage of a son talking to his father, and Cottar spoke with the worn patience of a teacher to a pupil. The older man was bitterly amused, and the woman was full of moral repugnance, as if she held Kent personally responsible for Hiroshima, Asian girls burned to death in locked factories, for all foul lies and trumpeted hypocrisy. And Kent was asking for most of this, as far as Kath could see. She had dreaded something of the sort, when she saw his shirt and tie and decided to put on jeans instead of her decent maternity skirt. And once she was there she had to sit through it, twisting the cushion this way and that to catch the silver gleam.

Everybody in the room was so certain of everything. When they paused for breath it was just to draw on an everlasting stream of pure virtue, pure certainty.

Except perhaps for Sonje. Sonje didn't say any-thing. But Sonje drew on Cottar; he was her cer-tainty. She got up to offer more curry, she spoke into one of the brief angry silences.

'It looks as if nobody wanted any coconut.'

'Oh, Sonje, are you going to be the tactful host-ess?' the older woman said. 'Like somebody in Virginia Woolf?'

So it seemed Virginia Woolf was at a discount too. There was so much Kath didn't understand. But at least she knew it was there; she wasn't prepared to say it was nonsense.

Nevertheless she wished her water would break. Anything to deliver her. If she scrambled up and puddled the floor in front of them, they would have to stop.

Afterwards Kent did not seem perturbed about the way the evening had gone. For one thing, he thought he had won. 'They're all pinkos, they have to talk that way,' he said. 'It's the only thing they can do.'

Kath was anxious not to talk anymore about politics so she changed the subject, telling him that the older couple had lived with Sonje and Cottar in the communal house. There was also another couple who had since moved away. And there had been an orderly exchange of sexual partners. The older man had an outside mistress and she was in on the exchange part of the time.

Kent said, 'You mean young guys would go to bed with that old woman? She's got to be fifty.'

Kath said, 'Cottar's thirty-eight.'

'Even so,' said Kent. 'It's disgusting.'

But Kath found the idea of those stipulated and obligatory copulations exciting as well as disgusting. To pass yourself around obediently and blamelessly, to whoever came up on the list – it was like temple prostitution. Lust served as your duty. It gave her a deep obscene thrill, to think of that.

It hadn't thrilled Sonje. She had not experienced sexual release. Cottar would ask her if she had, when she came back to him, and she had to say no. He was disappointed and she was disappointed for his sake. He explained to her that she was too exclusive and too much tied up in the idea of sexual property and she knew he was right.

'I know he thinks that if I loved him enough I'd be better at it,' she said. 'But I do love him, agonizingly.'

For all the tempting thoughts that came into her mind, Kath believed that she could only, ever, sleep with Kent. Sex was like something they had invented between them. Trying it with somebody else would mean a change of circuits – all of her life would blow up in her face. Yet she could not say she loved Kent agonizingly.

As she walked along the beach from Monica's house to Sonje's, she saw people waiting for the party. They stood around in small groups or sat on logs watching the last of the sunset. They drank beer. Cottar and another man were washing out a garbage tin in which they would make the punch. Miss Campo, the head librarian, was sitting alone on a log. Kath waved to her vivaciously but didn't go over to join her. If you joined somebody at this stage, you were caught. Then there were two of you alone. The thing to do was to join a group of three or four, even if you found the conversation – that had looked lively from a distance – to be quite desperate. But she could hardly do that, after waving at Miss Campo. She had to be on her way somewhere. So she went on, past Kent talking to Monica's husband about how long it took to saw up one of the logs on the beach, she went up the steps to Sonje's house and into the kitchen.

Sonje was stirring a big pot of chili, and the older woman from the communal house was setting out slices of rye bread and salami and cheese on a platter. She was dressed just as she had been for the curry dinner – in a baggy skirt and a drab but clinging sweater, the breasts it clung to sloping down to her waist. This had something to do with Marxism, Kath thought – Cottar liked Sonje to go without a brassiere, as well as without stockings or lipstick. Also it had to do with unfettered unjealous sex, the generous uncorrupted appetite that did not balk at a woman of fifty.

A girl from the library was there too, cutting up green peppers and tomatoes. And a woman Kath didn't know was sitting on the kitchen stool, smoking a cigarette.

'Have we ever got a bone to pick with you,' the girl from the library said to Kath. 'All of us at work. We hear you've got the darlingest baby and you haven't brought her in to show us. Where is she now?'

Kath said, 'Asleep I hope.'

This girl's name was Lorraine, but Sonje and Kath, recalling their days at the library, had given her the name Debbie Reynolds. She was full of bounce.

'Aww,' she said.

The low-slung woman gave her, and Kath, a look of thoughtful distaste.

Kath opened a bottle of beer and handed it to Sonje, who said, 'Oh, thanks, I was so concentrated on the chili I forgot I could have a drink.' She worried because her cooking wasn't as good as Cottar's.

'Good thing you weren't going to drink that yourself,' the girl from the library said to Kath. 'It's a no-no if you're nursing.'

'I guzzled beer all the time when I was nursing,' the woman on the stool said. 'I think it was recommended. You piss most of it away anyhow.'

This woman's eyes were lined with black pencil, extended at the corners, and her eyelids were painted a purplish blue right up to her sleek black brows. The rest of her face was very pale, or made up to look so, and her lips were so pale a pink that they seemed almost white. Kath had seen faces like this before, but only in magazines.

'This is Amy,' said Sonje. 'Amy this is Kath. I'm sorry, I didn't introduce you.'

'Sonje, you're always sorry,' the older woman said.

Amy took up a piece of cheese that had just been cut, and ate it.

Amy was the name of the mistress. The older woman's husband's mistress. She was a person Kath suddenly wanted to know, to be friends with, just as she had once longed to be friends with Sonje.

The evening had changed into night, and the knots of people on the beach had become less distinct; they showed more disposition to flow together. Down at the edge of the water women had taken off their shoes, reached up and pulled off their stockings if they were wearing any, touched their toes to the water. Most people had given up drinking beer and were drinking punch, and the punch had already begun to change its character. At first it had been mostly rum and pineapple juice, but by now other kinds of fruit juice, and soda water, and vodka and wine had been added.

Those who were taking off their shoes were being encouraged to take off more. Some ran into the water with most of their clothes on, then stripped and tossed the clothes to catchers on shore. Others stripped where they were, encouraging each other by saying it was too dark to see anything. But actually you could see bare bodies splashing and

126

running and falling into the dark water. Monica had brought a great pile of towels down from her house, and was calling out to everyone to wrap themselves up when they came out, so they wouldn't catch their death of cold.

The moon came up through the black trees on top of the rocks, and looked so huge, so solemn and thrilling, that there were cries of amazement. What's that? And even when it had climbed higher in the sky and shrunk to a more normal size people acknowledged it from time to time, saying 'The harvest moon' or 'Did you see it when it first came up?'

'I actually thought it was a great big balloon.'

'I couldn't imagine what it was. I didn't think the moon could be that size, ever.'

Kath was down by the water, talking to the man whose wife and mistress she had seen in Sonje's kitchen earlier. His wife was swimming now, a little apart from the shriekers and splashers. In another life, the man said, he had been a minister.

'"The sea of faith was once too at the full,"' he said humorously. '"And round earth's shore, lay like the folds of a bright girdle furled" – I was married to a completely different woman then.'

He sighed, and Kath thought he was searching for the rest of the verse.

'"But now I only hear,"' she said, '"its melancholy long with-drawing roar, down the vast edges drear and naked shingles of the world."' Then she stopped, because it seemed too much to go on with 'Oh love let us be true—'

His wife swam towards them, and heaved herself up where the water was only as deep as her knees. Her breasts swung sideways and flung drops of water round her as she waded in.

Her husband opened his arms. He called, 'Europa,' in a voice of comradely welcome.

'That makes you Zeus,' said Kath boldly. She wanted right then to have a man like this kiss her. A man she hardly knew, and cared nothing about. And he did kiss her, he waggled his cool tongue inside her mouth.

'Imagine a continent named after a cow,' he said. His wife stood close in front of them, breathing gratefully after the exertion of her swim. She was so close that Kath was afraid of being grazed by her long dark nipples or her mop of black pubic hair.

Somebody had got a fire going, and those who had been in the water were out now, wrapped up in blankets or towels, or crouched behind logs struggling into their clothes.

And there was music playing. The people who lived next door to Monica had a dock and a boat-house. A record player had been brought down, and people were starting to dance. On the dock and with more difficulty on the sand. Even along the top of a log somebody would do a dance step or two, before stumbling and falling or jumping off. Women who had got dressed again, or never got undressed, women who were feeling too restless to stay in one place – as Kath was – went walking along the edge of the water (nobody was swimming anymore, swimming was utterly past and forgotten) and they walked in a different way because of the music. Swaying rather self-consciously, jokingly, then more insolently, like beautiful women in a movie.

Miss Campo was still sitting in the same place, smiling.

The girl Kath and Sonje called Debbie Reynolds was sitting in the sand with her back against a log, crying. She smiled at Kath, she said, 'Don't think I'm sad.'

Her husband was a college football player who now ran a bodyrepair shop. When he came into the library to pick up his wife he always looked like a proper football player, faintly disgusted with the rest of the world. But now he knelt beside her and played with her hair.

'It's okay,' he said. 'It's the way it always takes her. Isn't it, honey?'

'Yes it is,' she said.

Kath found Sonje wandering around the fire circle, doling out marshmallows. Some people were able to fit them on sticks and toast them; others tossed them back and forth and lost them in the sand.

'Debbie Reynolds is crying,' Kath said. 'But it's all right. She's happy.'

They began to laugh, and hugged each other,

squashing the bag of marshmallows between them.

'Oh I will miss you,' Sonje said. 'Oh, I will miss our friendship.'

'Yes. Yes,' Kath said. Each of them took a cold marshmallow and ate it, laughing and looking at each other, full of sweet and forlorn feeling.

'This do in remembrance of me,' Kath said. 'You are my realest truest friend.'

'You are mine,' said Sonje. 'Realest truest. Cottar says he wants to sleep with Amy tonight.'

'Don't let him,' said Kath. 'Don't let him if it makes you feel awful.'

'Oh, it isn't a question of let,' Sonje said valiantly. She called out, 'Who wants some chili? Cottar's dishing out the chili over there. Chili? Chili?'

Cottar had brought the kettle of chili down the steps and set it in the sand.

'Mind the kettle,' he kept saying in a fatherly voice. 'Mind the kettle, it's hot.'

He squatted to serve people, clad only in a towel that was flapping open. Amy was beside him, giving out bowls.

Kath cupped her hands in front of Cottar.

'Please Your Grace,' she said. 'I am not worthy of a bowl.'

Cottar sprang up, letting go of the ladle, and placed his hands on her head.

'Bless you, my child, the last shall be first.' He kissed her bent neck.

'Ahh,' said Amy, as if she was getting or giving this kiss herself.

Kath raised her head and looked past Cottar.

'I'd love to wear that kind of lipstick,' she said.

Amy said, 'Come along.' She set down the bowls and took Kath lightly by the waist and propelled her to the steps.

'Up here,' she said. 'We'll do the whole job on you.'

In the tiny bathroom behind Cottar and Sonje's bedroom Amy spread out little jars and tubes and pencils. She had nowhere to spread them but on the toilet seat. Kath had to sit on the rim of the bathtub, her face almost brushing Amy's stomach. Amy smoothed a liquid over her cheeks and rubbed a paste into her eyelids. Then she brushed on a powder. She brushed and glossed Kath's eyebrows and put three separate coats of mascara on her lashes. She outlined and painted her lips and blotted them and painted them again. She held Kath's face up in her hands and tilted it towards the light.

Someone knocked on the door and then shook it.

'Hang on,' Amy called out. Then, 'What's the matter with you, can't you go and take a leak behind a log?'

She wouldn't let Kath look in the mirror until it was all done.

'And don't smile,' she said. 'It spoils the effect.'

Kath let her mouth droop, stared sullenly at

131

her reflection. Her lips were like fleshy petals, lily petals. Amy pulled her away. 'I didn't mean like that,' she said. 'Better not look at yourself at all, don't try to look any way, you'll look fine.

'Hold on to your precious bladder, we're getting out,' she shouted at the new person or maybe the same person pounding on the door. She scooped her supplies into their bag and shoved it under the bathtub. She said to Kath, 'Come on, beautiful.'

On the dock Amy and Kath danced, laughing and challenging each other. Men tried to get in between them, but for a while they managed not to let this happen. Then they gave up, they were separated, making faces of dismay and flapping their arms like grounded birds as they found themselves blocked off, each of them pulled away into the orbit of a partner.

Kath danced with a man she did not remember seeing before during the whole evening. He seemed to be around Cottar's age. He was tall, with a thickened, softened waistline, a mat of dull curly hair, and a spoiled, bruised look around the eyes.

'I may fall off,' Kath said. 'I'm dizzy. I may fall overboard.'

He said, 'I'll catch you.'

'I'm dizzy but I'm not drunk,' she said.

He smiled, and she thought, That's what drunk people always say.

'Really,' she said, and it was true because she had

132

not finished even one bottle of beer, or touched the punch.

'Unless I got it through my skin,' she said. 'Osmosis.'

He didn't answer, but pulled her close then released her, holding her eyes.

The sex Kath had with Kent was eager and strenuous, but at the same time reticent. They had not seduced each other but more or less stumbled into intimacy, or what they believed to be intimacy, and stayed there. If there is only to be the one partner in your life nothing has to be made special – it already is so. They had looked at each other naked, but at those times they had not except by chance looked into each other's eyes.

That was what Kath was doing now, all the time, with her unknown partner. They advanced and retreated and circled and dodged, putting on a show for each other, and looking into each other's eyes. Their eyes declared that this show was nothing, nothing compared to the raw tussle they could manage when they chose.

Yet it was all a joke. As soon as they touched they let go again. Close up, they opened their mouths and teased their tongues across their lips and at once drew back, pretending languor.

Kath was wearing a short-sleeved brushed-wool sweater, convenient for nursing because it had a low V neck and was buttoned down the front.

The next time they came close her partner raised his arm as if to protect himself and moved the back of his hand, his bare wrist and forearm across her stiff breasts under their electric wool. That made them stagger, they almost broke their dance. But continued – Kath weak and faltering.

She heard her name being called.

Mrs Mayberry. Mrs Mayberry.

It was the baby-sitter, calling from halfway down Monica's steps.

'Your baby. Your baby's awake. Can you come and feed her?'

Kath stopped. She worked her way shakily through the other dancers. Out of the light, she jumped down, and stumbled in the sand. She knew her partner was behind her, she heard him jump behind her. She was ready to offer her mouth or her throat to him. But he caught her hips, turned her around, dropped to his knees, and kissed her crotch through her cotton pants. Then he rose up lightly for such a large man, they turned away from each other at the same moment. Kath hurried into the light and climbed the steps to Monica's house. Panting, and pulling herself up by the railing, like an old woman.

The baby-sitter was in the kitchen.

'Oh, your husband,' she said. 'Your husband just came in with the bottle. I didn't know what the arrangement was or I could have saved myself yelling.'

Kath went on into Monica's living room. The only light there came from the hall and the kitchen, but she could see that it was a real living room, not a modified porch like hers and Sonje's. There was a Danish modern coffee table and upholstered furniture and draw drapes.

Kent was sitting in an armchair, feeding Noelle from her supplemental bottle.

'Hi,' he said, speaking quietly though Noelle was sucking too vigorously to be even half asleep.

'Hi,' said Kath, and sat down on the sofa.

'I just thought this would be a good idea,' he said. 'In case you'd been drinking.'

Kath said, 'I haven't. Been drinking.' She raised a hand to her breasts to test their fullness, but the stir of the wool gave her such a shock of desire that she couldn't press further.

'Well now you can, if you want to,' Kent said.

She sat just on the edge of the sofa, leaning forward, longing to ask him, did he come here by the front or the back way? That is, along the road or along the beach? If he had come along the beach he was almost bound to have seen the dancing. But there were quite a lot of people dancing on the dock now, so perhaps he would not have noticed individual dancers.

Nevertheless, the baby-sitter had spotted her. And he would have heard the baby-sitter calling her, calling her name. Then he would have looked to see where the baby-sitter was directing her call.

That is, if he came by the beach. If he came by the road and entered the house by the hall not the kitchen he wouldn't have seen the dancers at all.

'Did you hear her calling me?' Kath said. 'Is that why you went home and got the bottle?'

'I'd already thought about it,' he said. 'I thought it was time.' He held up the bottle to see how much Noelle had taken.

'Hungry,' he said.

She said, 'Yes.'

'So now's your opportunity. If you want to get sloshed.'

'Is that what you are? Sloshed?'

'I've taken on my fair share,' he said. 'Go on if you want to. Have yourself a time.'

She thought his cockiness sounded sad and faked. He must have seen her dancing. Or else he would have said, 'What have you done to your face?'

'I'd sooner wait for you,' she said.

He frowned at the baby, tipping up the bottle.

'Nearly finished,' he said. 'Okay if you want.'

'I just have to go to the bathroom,' Kath said. And in the bathroom, as she had expected in Monica's house, there was a good supply of Kleenex. She ran the water hot, and soaked and scrubbed, soaked and scrubbed, from time to time flushing a wad of black and purple tissues down the toilet.

IV

In the middle of the second drink, when Kent was talking about the astounding, really obscene prices of real estate these days in West Vancouver, Sonje said, 'You know, I have a theory.'

'Those places we used to live in,' he said. 'They went long ago. For a song, compared to now. Now I don't know what you'd get for them. Just for the property. Just for a teardown.'

What was her theory? About the price of real estate?

No. It was about Cottar. She did not believe that he was dead.

'Oh, I did at first,' she said. 'It never occurred to me to doubt it. And then suddenly I just woke up and saw it didn't necessarily have to be true. It didn't have to be true at all.'

Think of the circumstances, she said. A doctor had written to her. From Jakarta. That is, the person writing to her said that he was a doctor. He said that Cottar had died and he said what he had died of, he used the medical term which she forgot now. Anyway it was an infectious disease. But how did she know that this person really was a doctor? Or even, granted that he might be a doctor, how did she know that he was telling the truth? It would not be difficult for Cottar to have made the acquaintance of a doctor. To have become friends. Cottar had all sorts of friends.

'Or even to have paid him,' she said. 'That isn't outside the range of possibility either.'

Kent said, 'Why would he do that?'

'He wouldn't be the first doctor to do something like that. Maybe he needed the money to keep a clinic going for poor people, how do we know? Maybe he just wanted it for himself. Doctors aren't saints.'

'No,' said Kent. 'I meant Cottar. Why would Cottar do it? And did he have any money?'

'No. He didn't have any himself but – I don't know. It's only one hypothesis anyway. The money. And I was here, you know. I was here to take care of his mother. He really cared about his mother. He knew I'd never desert her. So that was all right.

'It really was all right,' she said. 'I was very fond of Delia. I didn't find it a burden. I might really have been better suited to taking care of her than to being married to Cottar. And you know, something strange. Delia thought the same as I did. About Cottar. She had the same suspicions. And she never mentioned them to me. I never mentioned mine to her. Each of us thought it would break the other's heart. Then one evening not that long before she – had to go, I was reading her a mystery story that was set in Hong Kong, and she said, "Maybe that's where Cottar is. Hong Kong."

'She said she hoped she hadn't upset me. Then I told her what I'd been thinking, and she laughed. We both laughed. You would expect an old mother would be grief-stricken talking about how her only child had run off and left her, but no. Maybe old people aren't like that. Really old people. They don't get grief-stricken anymore. They must figure it's not worth it.

'He knew I'd take care of her, though he probably didn't know how long that would last,' she said. 'I wish I could show you the doctor's letter, but I threw it out. That was very stupid, but I was distraught at the time. I didn't see how I was going to get through the rest of my life. I didn't think how I should follow up and find out what his credentials were or ask about a death certificate or anything. I thought of all that later and by then I didn't have an address. I couldn't write to the American embassy because they were the last people Cottar would have had anything to do with. And he wasn't a Canadian citizen. Maybe he even had another name. False identity he could slip into. False papers. He used to hint about things like that. That was part of the glamour about him, for me.'

'Some of that could have been along the lines of self-dramatizing,' Kent said. 'Don't you think?'

Sonje said, 'Of course I think.'

'There wasn't any insurance?'

'Don't be silly.'

'If there'd been insurance, they'd have found out the truth.'

'Yes but there wasn't,' Sonje said. 'So. That's what I intend to do.'

She said that this was one thing she had never

mentioned to her mother-in-law. That after she was on her own, she was going to go looking. She was going to find Cottar, or find the truth.

'I suppose you think that's some wild kind of fantasy?' she said.

Off her rocker, thought Kent with an unpleasant jolt. With every visit he had made on this trip, there had come a moment of severe disappointment. The moment when he realized that the person he was talking to, the person he had made a point of seeking out, was not going to give him whatever it was he had come for. The old friend he had visited in Arizona was obsessed with the dangers of life, in spite of his expensive residence in a protected community. His old friend's wife, who was over seventy, wanted to show him pictures of herself and some other old woman dressed up as Klondike dance-hall girls, for a musical show they had put on. And his grown-up children were caught up in their own lives. That was only natural and not a surprise to him. The surprise was that these lives, the lives his sons and daughter were living, seemed closed in now, somewhat predictable. Even the changes in them that he could foresee or was told were coming – Noelle was on the verge of leaving her second husband – were not very interesting. He had not made any admission of this to Deborah – hardly even to himself – but it was so. And now Sonje. Sonje whom he hadn't particularly liked, whom he'd been wary of in some way, but whom he'd respected, as a bit of a mystery – Sonje had turned into a talkative old woman with a secret screw loose.

And he'd had a reason for coming to see her that they were not getting any closer to, with this rant about Cottar.

'Well to be frank,' he said. 'It doesn't sound like such a sensible thing to do, to be frank about it.'

'A wild-goose chase,' said Sonje cheerfully.

'There's a probability he might be dead now anyway.'

'True.'

'And he could have gone anywhere and lived anywhere. That is if your theory is correct.'

'True.'

'So the only hope is if he really died then and your theory isn't correct, then you might find out about it and you wouldn't be any further ahead than you are now anyway.'

'Oh, I think I would.'

'You could do just as well then to stay here and write some letters.'

Sonje said she disagreed. She said you couldn't go through official channels regarding this sort of thing.

'You have to make yourself known in the streets.'

In the streets of Jakarta – that was where she meant to start. In places like Jakarta people don't shut themselves up. People live in the streets and things are known about them. Shopkeepers know, there's always somebody who knows somebody else and so forth. She would ask questions and word would get around that she was there. A man like Cottar could not have just slipped by. Even after all this time there'd be some memory. Information of one sort or another. Some of it expensive, not all of it truthful. Nevertheless.

Kent thought of asking her what she planned to use for money. Could she have inherited something from her parents? He seemed to remember that they'd cut her off at the time of her marriage. Perhaps she thought she could get a fat price for this property. A long shot, but maybe she was right.

Even so, she could fling it all away in a couple of months. Word would get around that she was there, all right.

'Those cities have changed a lot' was all he said.

'Not that I'd neglect the usual channels,' she said. 'I'd go after everybody I could. The embassy, the burial records, the medical registry if there is such a thing. In fact I've written letters already. But all you get is the runaround. You have to confront them in the flesh. You have to be there. Be there. Keep coming around and making a nuisance of yourself and finding out where their soft spots are and be prepared to pass something under the table if you have to. I don't have any illusions about its being easy.

'For instance I expect there'll be devastating heat. It doesn't sound as if it has a good location at all – Jakarta. There are swamps and lowlands all around. I'm not stupid. I'll get my shots and take all the precautions. I'll take my vitamins, and Jakarta being started by the Dutch there shouldn't be any shortage of gin. The Dutch East Indies. It's not a very old city, you know. It was built I think sometime in the 1600s. Just a minute. I have all sorts of – I'll show you – I have—'

She set down her glass which had been empty for some time, got up quickly, and after a couple of steps caught her foot in the torn sisal and lurched forward, but steadied herself by holding on to the door frame and didn't fall. 'Got to get rid of this old matting,' she said, and hurried into the house.

He heard a struggle with stiff drawers, then a sound as of a pile of papers falling, and all through this she kept talking to him, in that half-frantic reassuring way of people desperate not to lose your attention. He could not make out what she was saying, or didn't try to. He was taking the opportunity to swallow a pill – something he'd been thinking about doing for the last half hour. It was a small pill that didn't require him to take a drink – his glass was empty too – and he could probably have got it to his mouth without Sonje's noticing what he was doing. But something like shyness or superstition prevented him from trying. He did not mind Deborah's constant awareness of his condition, and his children of course had to know, but there seemed to be some sort of ban against revealing it to his contemporaries.

The pill was just in time. A tide of faintness, unfriendly heat, threatened disintegration, came crawling upwards and broke out in sweat drops on his temples. For a few minutes he felt this presence making headway, but by a controlled calm breathing and a casual rearrangement of his limbs he held his own against it. During this time Sonje reappeared with a batch of papers – maps and printed sheets that she must have copied from library books. Some of them slipped from her hands as she sat down. They lay scattered around on the sisal.

'Now, what they call old Batavia,' she said. 'That's very geometrically laid out. Very Dutch. There's a suburb called Weltevreden. It means "well contented." So wouldn't it be a joke if I found him living there? There's the Old Portuguese Church. Built in the late 1600s. It's a Muslim country of course. They have the biggest mosque there in Southeast Asia. Captain Cook put in to have his ships repaired, he was very complimentary about the shipyards. But he said the ditches out in the bogs were foul. They probably still are. Cottar never looked very strong, but he took better care of himself than you'd think. He wouldn't just go wandering round malarial bogs or buying drinks from a street vendor. Well of course now, if he's there, I expect he'll be completely acclimatized. I don't know what to expect. I can see him gone completely native or I can see him nicely set up with his little brown woman waiting on him. Eating

144

fruit beside a pool. Or he could be going around begging for the poor.'

As a matter of fact there was one thing Kent remembered. The night of the party on the beach, Cottar wearing nothing but an insufficient towel had come up to him and asked him what he knew, as a pharmacist, about tropical diseases.

But that had not seemed out of line. Anybody going where he was going might have done the same.

'You're thinking of India,' he said to Sonje.

He was stabilized now, the pill giving him back some reliability of his inner workings, halting what had felt like the runoff of bone marrow.

'You know one reason I know he's not dead?' said Sonje. 'I don't dream about him. I dream about dead people. I dream all the time about my mother-in-law.'

'I don't dream,' Kent said.

'Everybody dreams,' said Sonje. 'You just don't remember.'

He shook his head.

Kath was not dead. She lived in Ontario. In the Haliburton district, not so far from Toronto.

'Does your mother know I'm here?' he'd said to Noelle. And she'd said, 'Oh, I think so. Sure.'

But there came no knock on the door. When Deborah asked him if he wanted to make a detour he had said, 'Let's not go out of our way. It wouldn't be worth it.'

Kath lived alone beside a small lake. The man

145

she had lived with for a long time, and built the house with, was dead. But she had friends, said Noelle, she was all right.

When Sonje had mentioned Kath's name, earlier in the conversation, he had the warm and dangerous sense of these two women still being in touch with each other. There was the risk then of hearing something he didn't want to know but also the silly hope that Sonje might report to Kath how well he was looking (and he was, he believed so, with his weight fairly steady and the tan he'd picked up in the Southwest) and how satisfactorily he was married. Noelle might have said something of the kind, but somehow Sonje's word would count for more than Noelle's. He waited for Sonje to speak of Kath again.

But Sonje had not taken that tack. Instead it was all Cottar, and stupidity, and Jakarta.

The disturbance was outside now – not in him but outside the windows, where the wind that had been stirring the bushes, all this time, had risen to push hard at them. And these were not the sort of bushes that stream their long loose branches before such a wind. Their branches were tough and their leaves had enough weight so that each bush had to be rocked from its roots. Sunlight flashed off the oily greens. For the sun still shone, no clouds had arrived with the wind, it didn't mean rain.

'Another drink?' said Sonje. 'Easier on the gin?'

146

No. After the pill, he couldn't.

Everything was in a hurry. Except when every-thing was desperately slow. When they drove, he waited and waited, just for Deborah to get to the next town. And then what? Nothing. But once in a while came a moment when everything seemed to have something to say to you. The rocking bushes, the bleaching light. All in a flash, in a rush, when you couldn't concentrate. Just when you wanted summing up, you got a speedy, goofy view, as from a fun-ride. So you picked up the wrong idea, surely the wrong idea. That somebody dead might be alive and in Jakarta.

But when you knew somebody was alive, when you could drive to the very door, you let the opportunity pass.

What wouldn't be worth it? To see her a stranger that he couldn't believe he'd ever been married to, or to see that she could never be a stranger yet was unaccountably removed?

'They got away,' he said. 'Both of them.'

Sonje let the papers on her lap slide to the floor to lie with the others.

'Cottar and Kath,' he said.

'This happens almost every day,' she said. 'Almost every day this time of year, this wind in the late afternoon.'

The coin spots on her face picked up the light as she talked, like signals from a mirror.

'Your wife's been gone a long time,' she said. 'It's absurd, but young people seem unimportant to me. As if they could vanish off the earth and it wouldn't really matter.'

'Just the opposite,' Kent said. 'That's us you're talking about. That's us.'

Because of the pill his thoughts stretch out long and gauzy and lit up like vapor trails. He travels a thought that has to do with staying here, with listening to Sonje talk about Jakarta while the wind blows sand off the dunes.

A thought that has to do with not having to go on, to go home.

CORTES ISLAND

Little bride. I was twenty years old, five feet seven inches tall, weighing between a hundred and thirty-five and a hundred and forty pounds, but some people – Chess's boss's wife, and the older secretary in his office, and Mrs Gorrie upstairs, referred to me as a little bride. Our little bride, sometimes. Chess and I made a joke of it, but his public reaction was a look fond and cherishing. Mine was a pouty smile – bashful, acquiescent.

We lived in a basement in Vancouver. The house did not belong to the Gorries, as I had at first thought, but to Mrs. Gorrie's son Ray. He would come around to fix things. He entered by the basement door, as Chess and I did. He was a thin, narrow-chested man, perhaps in his thirties, always carrying a toolbox and wearing a workman's cap. He seemed to have a permanent stoop, which might have come from bending over most of the time, attending to plumbing jobs or wiring or carpentry. His face was waxy, and he coughed a good deal. Each cough was a discreet independent statement, defining his presence in the basement

149

as a necessary intrusion. He did not apologize for being there, but he did not move around in the place as if he owned it. The only times I spoke to him were when he knocked on the door to tell me that the water was going to be turned off for a little while, or the power. The rent was paid in cash every month to Mrs Gorrie. I don't know if she passed it all on to him or kept some of it out to help with expenses. Otherwise all she and Mr Gorrie had – she told me so – was Mr Gorrie's pension. Not hers. I'm not nearly old enough, she said.

Mrs Gorrie always called down the stairs to ask how Ray was and whether he would like a cup of tea. He always said he was okay and he didn't have time. She said that he worked too hard, just like herself. She tried to fob off on him some extra dessert she had made, some preserves or cookies or gingerbread – the same things she was always pushing at me. He would say no, he had just eaten, or that he had plenty of stuff at home. I always resisted, too, but on the seventh or eighth try I would give in. It was so embarrassing to go on refusing, in the face of her wheedling and disappointment. I admired the way Ray could keep saying no. He didn't even say, 'No, Mother.' Just no.

Then she tried to find some topic of conversation.

'So what's new and exciting with you?'

Not much. Don't know. Ray was never rude or irritable, but he never gave her an inch. His health was okay. His cold was okay. Mrs Cornish and Irene were always okay as well.

Mrs Cornish was a woman whose house he lived in, somewhere in East Vancouver. He always had jobs to do around Mrs Cornish's house as well as around this one – that was why he had to hurry away as soon as the work was done. He also helped with the care of her daughter Irene, who was in a wheelchair. Irene had cerebral palsy. 'The poor thing,' Mrs Gorrie said, after Ray told her that Irene was okay. She never reproached him to his face for the time he spent with the afflicted girl, the outings to Stanley Park or the evening jaunts to get ice cream. (She knew about these things because she sometimes talked on the phone to Mrs Cornish.) But to me she said, 'I can't help thinking what a sight she must be with the ice cream running down her face. I can't help it. People must have a good time gawking at them.'

She said that when she took Mr Gorrie out in his wheelchair people looked at them (Mr Gorrie had had a stroke), but it was different, because outside the house he didn't move or make a sound and she always made sure he was presentable. Whereas Irene lolled around and went *gaggledy-gaggledy-gaggledy*. The poor thing couldn't help it.

Mrs Cornish could have something in mind, Mrs Gorrie said. Who was going to look after that cripple girl when she was gone?

'There ought to be a law that healthy people

can't get married to someone like that, but so far there isn't.'

When Mrs Gorrie asked me to go up for coffee I never wanted to go. I was busy with my own life in the basement. Sometimes when she came knocking on my door I pretended not to be home. But in order to do that I had to get the lights out and the door locked the instant I heard her open the door at the top of the stairs, and then I had to stay absolutely still while she tapped her fingernails against the door and trilled my name. Also I had to be very quiet for at least an hour afterward and refrain from flushing the toilet. If I said that I couldn't spare the time, I had things to do, she would laugh and say, 'What things?'

'Letters I'm writing,' I said.

'Always writing letters,' she said. 'You must be homesick.'

Her eyebrows were pink – a variation of the pinkish red of her hair. I did not think the hair could be natural, but how could she have dyed her eyebrows? Her face was thin, rouged, vivacious, her teeth large and glistening. Her appetite for friendliness, for company, took no account of resistance. The very first morning that Chess brought me to this apartment, after meeting me at the train, she had knocked at our door with a plate of cookies and this wolfish smile. I still had my travelling hat on, and Chess had been interrupted in his pulling at my girdle. The cookies were dry and hard and covered with a bright-pink icing to celebrate my

152

bridal status. Chess spoke to her curtly. He had to get back to work within half an hour, and after he had got rid of her there was no time to go on with what he'd started. Instead, he ate the cookies one after another, complaining that they tasted like sawdust.

'Your hubby is so serious,' she would say to me. 'I have to laugh, he always gives me this serious, serious look when I see him coming and going. I want to tell him to take it easy, he hasn't got the world on his shoulders.'

Sometimes I had to follow her upstairs, torn away from my book or the paragraph I was writing. We sat at her dining-room table. There was a lace cloth on it, and an octagonal mirror reflecting a ceramic swan. We drank coffee out of china cups and ate off small matching plates (more of those cookies, or gluey raisin tarts or heavy scones) and touched tiny embroidered napkins to our lips to wipe away the crumbs. I sat facing the china cabinet in which were ranged all the good glasses, and the cream-and-sugar sets, the salt-and-peppers too dinky or ingenious for daily use, as well as bud vases, a teapot shaped like a thatched cottage, and candle-sticks shaped like lilies. Once every month Mrs Gorrie went through the china cabinet and washed everything. She told me so. She told me things that had to do with my future, the house and the future she assumed I would have, and the more she talked the more I felt an iron weight on my limbs, the more I wanted to yawn and yawn in the middle of the morning, to crawl away and hide and sleep. But out loud I admired everything. The contents of the china cabinet, the housekeeping routines of Mrs Gorrie's life, the matching outfits that she put on every morning. Skirts and sweaters in shades of mauve or coral, harmonizing scarves of artificial silk.

'Always get dressed first thing, just as if you're going out to work, and do your hair and get your makeup on' – she had caught me more than once in my dressing gown – 'and then you can always put an apron on if you have to do the washing or some baking. It's good for your morale.'

And always have some baking on hand for when people might drop in. (As far as I knew, she never had any visitors but me, and you could hardly say that I had dropped in.) And never serve coffee in mugs.

It wasn't put quite so baldly. It was 'I always—' or 'I always like to—' or 'I think it's nicer to—'

'Even when I lived away off in the wilds, I always liked to—' My need to yawn or scream subsided for a moment. Where had she lived in the wilds? And when?

'Oh, away up the coast,' she said. 'I was a bride, too, once upon a time. I lived up there for years. Union Bay. But that wasn't too wild. Cortes Island.'

I asked where that was, and she said, 'Oh, away up there.'

'That must have been interesting,' I said.

154

'Oh, interesting,' she said. 'If you call bears interesting. If you call cougars interesting. I'd rather have a little civilization myself.'

The dining room was separated from the living room by sliding oak doors. They were always open a little way so that Mrs Gorrie, sitting at the end of the table, could keep an eye on Mr Gorrie, sitting in his recliner in front of the living-room window. She spoke of him as 'my husband in the wheelchair,' but in fact he was only in the wheelchair when she took him out for his walk. They didn't have a television set – television was still almost a novelty at that time. Mr Gorrie sat and watched the street, and Kitsilano Park across the street and Burrard Inlet beyond that. He made his own way to the bathroom, with a cane in one hand and the other hand gripping chair backs or battering against the walls. Once inside he managed by himself, though it took him a long time. And Mrs Gorrie said that there was sometimes a bit of mopping up.

All I could usually see of Mr Gorrie was a trouser leg stretched out on the bright-green recliner. Once or twice he had to make this drag and lurch along to the bathroom when I was there. A large man – large head, wide shoulders, heavy bones.

I didn't look at his face. People who had been crippled by strokes or disease were bad omens to me, rude reminders. It wasn't the sight of useless limbs or the other physical marks of their horrid luck I had to avoid – it was their human eyes.

I don't believe he looked at me, either, though

Mrs Gorrie called out to him that here I was visiting from downstairs. He made a grunting noise that could have been the best he could do by way of a greeting, or dismissal.

There were two and a half rooms in our apartment. It was rented furnished, and in the way of such places it was half furnished, with things that would otherwise have been thrown away. I remember the floor of the living room, which was covered with leftover squares and rectangles of linoleum – all the different colors and patterns fitted together and stitched like a crazy quilt with strips of metal. And the gas stove in the kitchen, which was fed with quarters. Our bed was in an alcove off the kitchen – it fitted into the alcove so snugly that you had to climb into bed from the bottom. Chess had read that this was the way the harem girls had to enter the bed of the sultan, first adoring his feet, then crawling upward paying homage to his other parts. So we sometimes played this game.

A curtain was kept closed all the time across the foot of the bed, to divide the alcove from the kitchen. It was actually an old bedspread, a slippery fringed cloth that showed yellowy beige on one side, with a pattern of winy roses and green leaves, and on the other, bedward-side stripes of wine red and green with flowers and foliage appearing like ghosts in the beige color. This curtain is the thing I remember more vividly than anything else in the apartment. And no wonder. In the full spate of sex,

156

and during its achieved aftermath, that fabric was in front of my eyes and became a reminder of what I liked about being married – the reward for which I suffered the unforeseen insult of being a little bride and the peculiar threat of a china cabinet.

Chess and I both came from homes where unmarried sex was held to be disgusting and unforgivable, and married sex was apparently never mentioned and soon forgotten about. We were right at the end of the time of looking at things that way, though we didn't know it. When Chess's mother had found condoms in his suitcase, she went weeping to his father. (Chess said that they had been given out at the camp where he had taken his university military training – which was true – and that he had forgotten all about them, which was a lie.) So having a place of our own and a bed of our own where we could carry on as we liked seemed marvellous to us. We had made this bargain, but it never occurred to us that older people – our parents, our aunts and uncles – could have made the same bargain, for lust. It seemed as if their main itch had been for houses, property, power mowers, and home freezers and retaining walls. And, of course, as far as women were concerned, for babies. All those things were what we thought we might choose, or might not choose, in the future. We never thought any of that would come on us inexorably, like age or weather.

And now that I come to think of it honestly, it didn't. Nothing came without our choice. Not pregnancy, either. We risked it, just to see if we were really grown up, if it could really happen.

The other thing I did behind the curtain was read. I read books that I got from the Kitsilano Library a few blocks away. And when I looked up in that churned-up state of astonishment that a book could bring me to, a giddiness of gulped riches, the stripes were what I'd see. And not just the characters, the story, but the climate of the book became attached to the unnatural flowers and flowed along in the dark-wine stream or the gloomy green. I read the heavy books whose titles were already familiar and incantatory to me – I even tried to read *The Betrothed* – and in between these courses I read the novels of Aldous Huxley and Henry Green, and *To the Lighthouse* and *The Last of Chéri* and *The Death of the Heart*. I bolted them down one after the other without establishing any preferences, surrendering to each in turn just as I'd done to the books I read in my childhood. I was still in that stage of leaping appetite, of voracity close to anguish.

But one complication had been added since childhood – it seemed that I had to be a writer as well as a reader. I bought a school notebook and tried to write – did write, pages that started off authoritatively and then went dry, so that I had to tear them out and twist them up in hard punishment and put them in the garbage can. I did this over and over again until I had only the notebook cover left. Then I bought another notebook and started the whole process once more. The same cycle – excitement and despair, excitement and despair. It was like having a secret pregnancy and miscarriage every week.

Not entirely secret, either. Chess knew that I read a lot and that I was trying to write. He didn't discourage it at all. He thought that it was something reasonable that I might quite possibly learn to do. It would take hard practice but could be mastered, like bridge or tennis. This generous faith I did not thank him for. It just added to the farce of my disasters.

Chess worked for a wholesale grocery firm. He had thought of being a history teacher, but his father had persuaded him that teaching was no way to support a wife and get on in the world. His father had helped him get this job but told him that once he got in he was not to expect any favors. He didn't. He left the house before it was light, during this first winter of our marriage, and came home after dark. He worked hard, not asking that the work he did fit in with any interests he might have had or have any purpose to it that he might once have honored. No purpose except to carry us both toward that life of lawnmowers and freezers which we believed we had no mind for. I might marvel at his submission, if I thought about it. His cheerful, you might say gallant, submission.

But then, I thought, it's what men do.

★   ★   ★

159

I went out to look for work myself. If it wasn't raining too hard I went down to the drugstore and bought a paper and read the ads while I drank a cup of coffee. Then I set out, even in a drizzle, to walk to the places that had advertised for a waitress or a salesgirl or a factory worker – any job that didn't specifically require typing or experience. If the rain had come on heavily I would travel by bus. Chess said that I should always go by bus and not walk to save money. While I was saving money, he said, some other girl could have got the job.

That was in fact what I seemed to be hoping for. I was never altogether sorry to hear it. Sometimes I would get to my destination and stand on the sidewalk, looking at the Ladies' Dress Shop, with its mirrors and pale carpeting, or watch the girls tripping downstairs on their lunch break from the office that needed a filing clerk. I would not even go inside, knowing how my hair and fingernails and flat scuffed shoes would tell against me. And I was just as daunted by the factories – I could hear the noise of the machines going in the buildings where soft drinks were bottled or Christmas decorations put together, and I could see the bare lightbulbs hanging down from the barnlike ceilings. My fingernails and flat heels might not matter there, but my clumsiness and mechanical stupidity would get me sworn at, shouted at (I could also hear the shouted orders above the noise of the machines). I would be disgraced and fired. I didn't think myself capable even of learning to operate a cash register. I told the manager of a restaurant that, when he actually seemed to be thinking of hiring me. 'Do you think you could pick it up?' he said, and I said no. He looked as if he had never heard anybody admit to such a thing before. But I spoke the truth. I didn't think I could pick things up, not in a hurry and out in public. I would freeze. The only things that I could pick up easily were things like the convolutions of the Thirty Years' War.

The truth is, of course, that I didn't have to. Chess was supporting me, at our very basic level. I didn't have to push myself out into the world because he had done it. Men had to.

I thought that maybe I could manage the work in the library, so I asked there, though they hadn't advertised. A woman put my name on a list. She was polite but not encouraging. Then I went into bookstores, choosing the ones that looked as if they wouldn't have a cash register. The emptier and untidier the better. The owners would be smoking or dozing at the desk, and in the secondhand stores there was often a smell of cat.

'We're not busy enough in the winter,' they said.

One woman said I might come back in the spring.

'Though we're not usually very busy then, either.'

Winter in Vancouver was not like any winter I had ever known. No snow, not even anything much in the way of a cold wind. In the middle of the day, downtown, I could smell something like burned sugar – I think it had to do with the trolley wires. I walked along Hastings Street, where there wouldn't be another woman walking – just drunks, tramps, poor old men, shuffling Chinese. Nobody spoke an ill word to me. I walked past warehouses, weedy lots where there wouldn't be even a man in sight. Or through Kitsilano, with its high wooden houses crammed with people living tight, as we were, to the tidy Dunbar district, with its stucco bungalows and pollarded trees. And through Kerrisdale, where the classier trees appeared, birches on the lawns. Tudor beams, Georgian symmetry, Snow White fantasies with imitation thatched roofs. Or maybe real thatched roofs, how could I tell?

In all these places where people lived, the lights came on around four in the afternoon, and then the streetlights came on, the lights in the trolley buses came on, and often, too, the clouds broke apart in the west over the sea to show the red streaks of the sun's setting – and in the park, through which I circled home, the leaves of the winter shrubs glistened in the damp air of a faintly rosy twilight. People who had been shopping were going home, people at work were thinking about going home, people who had been in the houses all day came out to take a little walk that would make home more appealing. I met women with baby carriages and complaining toddlers and never

162

thought that so soon I'd be in the same shoes. I met old people with their dogs, and other old people, slow moving or in wheelchairs, being propelled by their mates or keepers. I met Mrs Gorrie pushing Mr Gorrie. She wore a cape and beret of soft purple wool (I knew by now that she made most of her own clothes) and a lot of rosy face coloring. Mr Gorrie wore a low cap and a thick scarf wrapped around his neck. Her greeting to me was shrill and proprietary, his nonexistent. He did not look as if he was enjoying the ride. But people in wheelchairs rarely did look anything more than resigned. Some looked affronted or downright mean.

'Now, when we saw you out in the park the other day,' Mrs Gorrie said, 'you weren't on your way back from looking for a job then, were you?'

'No,' I said, lying. My instinct was to lie to her about anything.

'Oh, good. Because I was just going to say, you know, that if you were out looking for a job you really should fix yourself up a little bit. Well, you know that.'

Yes, I said.

'I can't understand the way some women go out nowadays. I'd never go out in my flat shoes and no makeup on, even if I was just going to the grocery store. Let alone if I was going to ask somebody to give me a job.'

She knew I was lying. She knew I froze on the other side of the basement door, not answering her knock. I wouldn't have been surprised if she went through our garbage and discovered and read the messy, crumpled pages on which were spread out my prolix disasters. Why didn't she give up on me? She couldn't. I was a job set out for her – maybe my peculiarities, my ineptitude, were in a class with Mr Gorrie's damages, and what couldn't be righted had to be borne.

She came down the stairs one day when I was in the main part of the basement doing our washing. I was allowed to use her wringer-washer and laundry tubs every Tuesday.

'So is there any chance of a job yet?' she said, and on the spur of the moment I said that the library had told me they might have something for me in the future. I thought that I could pretend to be going to work there – I could go and sit there every day at one of the long tables, reading or even trying my writing, as I had done occasionally in the past. Of course, the cat would be out of the bag if Mrs Gorrie ever went into the library, but she wouldn't be able to push Mr Gorrie that far, uphill. Or if she ever mentioned my job to Chess – but I didn't think that would happen either. She said she was sometimes afraid to say hello to him, he looked so cross.

'Well, maybe in the meantime . . . ,' she said. 'It just occurred to me that maybe in the meantime you would like to have a little job sitting in the afternoons with Mr Gorrie.'

She said that she had been offered a job helping out in the gift shop at St Paul's Hospital three or four afternoons a week. 'It's not a paid job or I'd have sent you to ask about it,' she said. 'It's just volunteer work. But the doctor says it'd do me good to get out of the house. 'You'll wear yourself out,' he said. It's not that I need the money, Ray is so good to us, but just a little volunteer job, I thought—' She looked into the rinse tub and saw Chess's shirts in the same clear water as my flowered nightgown and our pale-blue sheets.

'Oh, dear,' she said. 'You didn't put the whites and the coloreds in together?'

'Just the light coloreds,' I said. 'They don't run.'

'Light coloreds are still coloreds,' she said. 'You might think the shirts are white that way, but they won't be as white as they could be.'

I said I would remember next time.

'It's just the way you take care of your man,' she said, with her little scandalized laugh.

'Chess doesn't mind,' I said, not realizing how this would become less and less true in the years ahead and how all these jobs that seemed incidental and almost playful, on the borders of my real life, were going to move front and center.

I took the job, sitting with Mr Gorrie in the afternoons. On one little table beside the green recliner there was spread a hand towel – to catch spills – and on top of it were his pill bottles and liquid medicines and a small clock to tell him the time. The table on the other side was stacked with reading material. The morning paper, last evening's paper, copies of *Life* and *Look* and *Maclean's*, which were all big floppy magazines then. On the lower shelf of this table was a pile of scrapbooks – the kind that children use at school, with heavy brownish paper and rough edges. There were bits of newsprint and photographs sticking out of them. These were scrapbooks that Mr Gorrie had kept over the years, until he had his stroke and couldn't cut things out anymore. There was a bookcase in the room, but all it held was more magazines and more scrapbooks and a half shelf of high-school textbooks, probably Ray's.

'I always read him the paper,' Mrs Gorrie said. 'He hasn't lost his ability, but he can't manage to hold it up with both hands, and his eyes get tired out.'

So I read to Mr Gorrie while Mrs Gorrie, under her flowered umbrella, stepped lightly off to the bus stop. I read him the sports page and the municipal news and the world news and all about murders and robberies and bad weather. I read the letters to the editor and the letters to a doctor who gave medical advice and the letters to Ann Landers, and her replies. It seemed that the sports news and Ann Landers roused his interest the most. I would sometimes mispronounce a player's name or mix up the terminology, so that what I read made no sense, and he would direct me with dissatisfied grunts to try again. When I read the sports page he was always on edge, intent and frowning. But when I read Ann Landers his face relaxed and

he made noises that I took to be appreciative –
a kind of gurgling and deep snorting. He made
these noises particularly when the letters touched
on some especially feminine or trivial concern (a
woman wrote that her sister-in-law always pretended that she had baked a cake herself, even
though the paper doily from the bakeshop was still
under it when it was served) or when they referred
– in the careful manner of that time – to sex.

During the reading of the editorial page or of
some long rigmarole about what the Russians said
and what the Americans said at the United Nations,
his eyelids would droop – or, rather, the eyelid over
his better eye would droop almost all the way and
the one over his bad, darkened eye would droop
slightly – and the movements of his chest would
become more noticeable, so that I might pause for
a moment to see if he had gone to sleep. And then
he would make another sort of noise – a curt and
reproving one. As I got used to him, and he got used
to me, this noise began to seem less like reproof and
more like reassurance. And the reassurance was not
just about his not being asleep but about the fact
that he was not at that moment dying.

His dying in front of my eyes had been at first
a horrible consideration. Why should he not die,
when he seemed at least half dead already? His bad
eye like a stone under dark water, and that side
of his mouth pulled open, showing his original,
wicked teeth (most old people then had false teeth)
with their dark fillings glowering through the damp

enamel. His being alive and in the world seemed to me an error that could be wiped out at any moment. But then, as I said, I got used to him. He was on a grand scale, with his big noble head and wide laboring chest and his powerless right hand lying on his long trousered thigh, invading my sight as I read. Like a relic, he was, an old warrior from barbarous times. Eric Blood-Axe. King Knut.

My strength is failing fast, said the sea king to
  his men.
I will never sail the seas, like a conqueror again.

That was what he was like. His half-wrecked hulk of a body endangering the furniture and battering the walls as he made his momentous progress to the bathroom. His smell, which was not rank but not reduced to infantile soap-and-talcum cleanliness, either – a smell of thick clothing with its residue of tobacco (though he didn't smoke anymore) and of the enclosed skin that I thought of as thick and leathery, with its lordly excretions and animal heat. A slight but persistent smell of urine, in fact, which would have disgusted me on a woman but which seemed in his case not just forgivable but somehow an expression of ancient privilege. When I went into the bathroom after he had been there, it was like the lair of some mangy, still powerful beast.

Chess said I was wasting my time baby-sitting Mr Gorrie. The weather was clearing now, and the days were getting longer. The shops were putting up new displays, stirring out of their winter torpor. Everybody was more apt to be thinking of hiring. So I ought to be out now, seriously looking for a job. Mrs Gorrie was paying me only forty cents an hour.

'But I promised her,' I said.

One day he said he had seen her getting off a bus. He saw her from his office window. And it wasn't anywhere near St Paul's Hospital.

I said, 'She might have been on a break.'

Chess said, 'I never saw her out in the full light of day before. Jesus.'

I suggested taking Mr. Gorrie for a walk in his wheelchair, now that the weather had improved. But he rejected the idea with some noises that made me certain there was something distasteful to him about being wheeled about in public – or maybe about being taken out by somebody like me, obviously hired to do the job.

I had interrupted my reading of the paper to ask him this, and when I tried to continue he made a gesture and another noise, telling me he was tired of listening. I laid the paper down. He waved the good hand toward the pile of scrapbooks on the lower shelf of the table beside him. He made more noises. I can only describe these noises as grunts, snorts, hawkings, barks, mumbles. But by this time they sounded to me almost like words. They did sound like words. I heard them not only as peremptory statements and demands ('Don't want to,' 'Help me up,' 'Let me see the time,' 'I need a drink')

169

but as more complicated pronouncements: 'Christ, why doesn't that dog shut up?' or 'Lot of hot air' (this after I'd read some speech or editorial in the paper).

What I heard now was 'Let's see if there's anything in here better than what's in the paper.'

I pulled the stack of scrapbooks off the shelf and settled with them on the floor by his feet. On the front covers were written, in large black crayoned letters, the dates of recent years. I flipped through 1952 and saw the cutout newspaper account of George VI's funeral. Above it the crayon lettering. 'Albert Frederick George. Born 1885. Died 1952.' The picture of the three queens in their mourning veils.

On the next page a story about the Alaska Highway.

'This is an interesting record,' I said. 'Do you want me to help you start another book? You could choose what things you want me to cut out and paste in, and I'd do it.'

His noise meant 'Too much trouble' or 'Why bother now?' or even 'What a stupid idea.' He brushed aside King George VI, wished to see the dates on the other books. They weren't what he wanted. He motioned toward the bookcase. I brought out another pile of scrapbooks. I understood that it was the book for one particular year that he was looking for, and I held each book up so that he could see the cover. Occasionally I flipped the pages open in spite of his rejection. I saw an article about the cougars on Vancouver Island and one about the death of a trapeze artist and another about a child who had lived though trapped in an avalanche. Back through the war years we went, back through the thirties, through the year I was born in, nearly a decade beyond that before he was satisfied. And gave the order. *Look at this one. 1923.*

I started going through that one from the beginning.

'January snowfall buries villages in—'

That's not it. Hurry up. Get on with it.

I began to flip the pages.

Slow down. Go easy. Slow down.

I lifted the pages one by one without stopping to read anything till we reached the one he wanted.

There. Read that.

There was no picture or headline. The crayoned letters said, '*Vancouver Sun*, April 17, 1923.'

'Cortes Island,' I read. 'Okay?'

Read it. Go on.

Cortes Island. Early Sunday morning or sometime late Saturday night the home of Anson James Wild at the south end of the island was totally destroyed by fire. The house was at a long distance from any other dwelling or habitation and as a result the flames were not noticed by anyone living on the island. There are reports that a fire was spotted early Sunday morning by a fishing boat going towards

171

Desolation Sound but those on board thought somebody was burning brush. Knowing that brush fire posed no danger due to the wet condition of the woods at present they proceeded on their way.

Mr Wild was the proprietor of Wildfruit Orchards and had been a resident on the island for about fifteen years. He was a solitary man whose previous history had been in the military service but he was cordial to those he met. He was married some time ago and had one son. It is believed he was born in the Atlantic Provinces.

The house was reduced to ruin by the blaze and the beams had fallen in. The body of Mr Wild was found amongst the charred remains burnt almost beyond recognition.

A blackened tin thought to have contained kerosene was discovered within the ruins.

Mr Wild's wife was away from home at the time, having on the previous Wednesday accepted a ride on a boat that was picking up a load of apples to be transported from her husband's orchard to Comox. She was intending to return the same day but remained away for three days and four nights due to engine trouble with the boat. On Sunday morning she returned with the friend who had offered her the ride and together they discovered the tragedy.

Fears were entertained for the Wilds' young son who was not in the house when it burned.

A search was started as soon as possible and before dark on Sunday evening the child was located in the woods less than a mile from his home. He was wet and cold from being in the underbrush for several hours but otherwise unharmed. It appears that he took some food with him when leaving the house as he had some pieces of bread with him when found.

An inquest will be held in Courtenay into the cause of the fire which destroyed the Wilds' home and resulted in the loss of Mr Wild's life.

'Did you know these people?' I said.
Turn the page.

August 4, 1923. An inquest held in Courtenay on Vancouver Island into the fire that caused the death of Anson James Wild of Cortes Island in April of this year found that suspicion of arson by the deceased man or by person or persons unknown cannot be substantiated. The presence of an empty kerosene can at the site of the fire has not been accepted as sufficient evidence. Mr Wild regularly purchased and made use of kerosene, according to Mr Percy Kemper, storekeeper, Manson's Landing, Cortes Island.

The seven-year-old son of the deceased man was not able to provide any evidence about the fire. He was found by a search party several hours later wandering in the woods not far from his home. In response to questioning he said that his father had given him some bread and apples and told him to walk to Manson's Landing but that he lost his way. But in later weeks he has said that he does not remember this being the case and does not know how he came to lose his way, the path having been travelled by him many times before. Dr Anthony Helwell of Victoria stated that he had examined the boy and believes that he may have run away at the first sight of the fire perhaps having time to lay hold of some food to take with him, which he has no recollection of now. Alternately he says the boy's story may be correct and recollection of it suppressed at a later date. He said that further questioning of the child would not be useful because he is probably unable to distinguish between fact and his imagination in this matter.

Mrs Wild was not at home at the time of the fire having gone to Vancouver Island on a boat belonging to James Thompson Gorrie of Union Bay.

The death of Mr Wild was ruled to be an accident due to misadventure, its cause being a fire of origins unknown.

Close up the book now.
Put it away. Put them all away.
No. No. Not like that. Put them away in order.
Year by year. That's better. Just the way they were.

Is she coming yet? Look out the window.
Good. But she will be coming soon.
There you are, what do you think of that?
I don't care. I don't care what you think of it.
Did you ever think that people's lives could be like
that and end up like this? Well, they can.

I did not tell Chess about this, though I usually told him anything I thought would interest or amuse him about my day. He had a way now of dismissing any mention of the Gorries. He had a word for them. It was 'grotesque.'

All the dingy-looking little trees in the park came out in bloom. Their flowers were a bright pink, like artificially colored popcorn.

And I began working at a real job.

The Kitsilano Library phoned and asked me to come in for a few hours on a Saturday afternoon. I found myself on the other side of the desk, stamping the due date in people's books. Some of these people were familiar to me, as fellow borrowers. And now I smiled at them, on behalf of the library. I said, 'See you in two weeks.'

Some laughed and said, 'Oh, a lot sooner,' being addicts like myself.

It turned out that this was a job I could handle. No cash register – when fines were paid you got the change out of a drawer. And I already knew where most of the books were on the shelves. When it came to filing cards, I knew the alphabet.

More hours were offered to me. Soon, a temporary full-time job. One of the steady workers had had a miscarriage. She stayed away for two months and at the end of that time she was pregnant again and her doctor advised her not to come back to work. So I joined the permanent staff and kept this job until I was halfway into my own first pregnancy. I worked with women I had known by sight for a long time. Mavis and Shirley, Mrs Carlson and Mrs Yost. They all remembered how I used to come in and mooch around – as they said – for hours in the library. I wished they hadn't noticed me so much. I wished I hadn't come in so often.

What a simple pleasure it was, to take up my station, to face people from behind the desk, to be capable and brisk and friendly with those who approached me. To be seen by them as a person who knew the ropes, who had a clear function in the world. To give up my lurking and wandering and dreaming and become the girl in the library.

Of course, I had less time for reading now, and sometimes I would hold a book in my hand for a moment, in my work at the desk – I would hold a book in my hand as an object, not as a vessel I had to drain immediately – and I would have a flick of fear, as in a dream when you find yourself in the wrong building or have forgotten the time for the exam and understand that this is only the tip of some shadowy cataclysm or lifelong mistake.

But this scare would vanish in a minute.

The women I worked with recalled the times they had seen me writing in the library.

I said I had been writing letters.

'You write your letters in a scribbler?'

'Sure,' I said. 'It's cheaper.'

The last notebook grew cold, hidden in the drawer with my tumbled socks and underwear. It grew cold, the sight of it filled me with misgiving and humiliation. I meant to get rid of it but didn't.

Mrs Gorrie had not congratulated me on getting this job.

'You didn't tell me you were still looking,' she said.

I said I'd had my name in at the library for a long time and that I'd told her so.

'That was before you started working for me,' she said. 'So what will happen now about Mr Gorrie?'

'I'm sorry,' I said.

'That doesn't do him much good, does it?'

She raised her pink eyebrows and spoke to me in the high-falutin' way I had heard her speak on the phone, to the butcher or the grocer who had made a mistake in her order.

'And what am I supposed to do?' she said. 'You've left me high and dry, haven't you? I hope you keep your promises to other people a little better than your promises to me.'

This was nonsense, of course. I had not promised her anything about how long I'd stay. Yet I felt a guilty unease, if not guilt itself. I hadn't promised her anything, but what about the times when I hadn't answered her knock, when I'd tried to sneak in and out of the house unnoticed, lowering my head as I passed under her kitchen window? What about the way I'd kept up a thin but sugary pretense of friendship in answer to her offers – surely – of the real thing?

'It's just as well, really,' she said. 'I wouldn't want anybody who wasn't dependable looking after Mr Gorrie. I wasn't entirely pleased with the way you were taking care of him, anyway, I can tell you that.'

Soon she had found another sitter – a little spider woman with black, netted hair. I never heard her speak. But I heard Mrs Gorrie speaking to her. The door at the top of the stairs was left open so that I should.

'She never even washed his teacup. Half the time she never even made his tea. I don't know what she was good for. Sit and read the paper.'

When I left the house nowadays the kitchen window was flung up and her voice rang out over my head, though she was ostensibly talking to Mr Gorrie.

'There she goes. On her way. She won't even bother to wave at us now. We gave her a job when nobody else would have her, but she won't bother. Oh, no.'

I didn't wave. I had to go past the front window where Mr Gorrie was sitting, but I had an idea that

178

if I waved now, even if I looked at him, he would be humiliated. Or angered. Anything I did might seem like a taunt.

Before I was half a block away I forgot about both of them. The mornings were bright, and I moved with a sense of release and purpose. At such times my immediate past could seem vaguely disgraceful. Hours behind the alcove curtain, hours at the kitchen table filling page after page with failure, hours in an overheated room with an old man. The shaggy rug and plush upholstery, the smell of his clothes and his body and of the dry pasted scrapbooks, the acres of newsprint I had to make my way through. The grisly story that he had saved and made me read. (I never understood for a moment that it was in the category of the human tragedies I honored, in books.) Recalling all that was like recalling a period of illness in childhood when I had been willingly trapped in cozy flannelette sheets with their odor of camphorated oil, trapped by my own lassitude and the feverish, not quite decipherable messages of the tree branches seen through my upstairs window. Such times were not regretted so much as naturally discarded. And it seemed to be a part of myself – a sickly part? – that was now going into the discard. You would think marriage would have worked this transformation, but it hadn't, for a while. I had hibernated and ruminated as my old self – mulish, unfeminine, irrationally secretive. Now I picked up my feet and acknowledged my luck at being transformed into a wife and an employee. Goodlooking and competent enough when I took the trouble. Not weird. I could pass.

Mrs Gorrie brought a pillowcase to my door. Showing her teeth in a hopeless, hostile smile, she asked if it might be mine. I said without hesitation that it wasn't. The two pillowcases that I owned were on the two pillows on our bed.

She said in a martyred tone, 'Well, it's certainly not mine.'

I said, 'How can you tell?'

Slowly, poisonously, her smile grew more confident.

'It's not the kind of material I'd ever put on Mr Gorrie's bed. Or on mine.'

Why not?

'Because – it – isn't – good – enough.'

So I had to go and take the pillowcases off the pillows on the alcove bed and bring them out to her, and it did turn out that they were not a pair, though they had looked it to me. One was made of 'good' fabric – that was hers – and the one in her hand was mine.

'I wouldn't believe you hadn't noticed,' she said, 'if it was anybody but you.'

Chess had heard of another apartment. A real apartment, not a 'suite' – it had a full bathroom and two bedrooms. A friend of his at work was leaving it, because he and his wife had bought a house. It was in a building at the corner of First Avenue and Macdonald Street. I could still walk to work, and he could take the same bus he took now. With two salaries, we could afford it. The friend and his wife were leaving some furniture behind, which they would sell cheaply. It would not suit their new house, but to us it seemed splendid in its respectability. We walked around the bright third-story rooms, admiring the cream-painted walls, the oak parquet, the roomy kitchen cupboards, and the tiled bathroom floor. There was even a tiny balcony looking out onto the leaves of Macdonald Park. We fell in love with each other in a new way, in love with our new status, our emergence into adult life from the basement that had been only a very temporary way station. It would be featured in our conversation as a joke, an endurance test, for years to come. Every move we made – the rented house, the first house we owned, the second house we owned, the first house in a different city – would produce this euphoric sense of progress and tighten our connection. Until the last and by far the grandest house, which I entered with inklings of disaster and the faintest premonitions of escape.

We gave our notice to Ray, without telling Mrs Gorrie. That raised her to a new level of hostility. In fact, she went a little crazy.

'Oh, she thinks she's so clever. She can't even keep two rooms clean. When she sweeps the floor all she does is sweep the dirt into a corner.'

When I had bought my first broom I had forgotten to buy a dustpan, and for a time I had done that. But she could have known about it only if she let herself into our rooms with a key of her own while I was out. Which it became apparent that she had done.

'She's a sneak, you know. I knew the first I saw of her what a sneak she was. And a liar. She isn't right in the head. She'd sit down there and say she's writing letters and she writes the same thing over and over again – it's not letters, it's the same thing over and over. She's not right in the head.'

Now I knew that she must have uncrumpled the pages in my wastebasket. I often tried to start the same story with the same words. As she said, over and over again.

The weather had turned quite warm, and I went to work without a jacket, wearing a snug sweater tucked into my skirt, and a belt pulled to its tightest notch.

She opened the front door and yelled after me.

'Slut. Look at the slut, the way she sticks her chest out and wobbles her rear end. You think you're Marilyn Monroe?'

And 'We don't need you in our house. The sooner you get out of here the better.'

She phoned up Ray and told him I was trying to steal her bed linen. She complained that I was telling stories about her up and down the street. She had opened the door to make sure I could hear, and she shouted into the phone, but this was hardly necessary, because we were on the same line and could listen in anytime we wanted to. I never did so – my instinct was to block my ears – but one evening when Chess was home he picked up the phone and spoke.

'Don't pay any attention to her, Ray, she's just a crazy old woman. I know she's your mother, but I have to tell you she's crazy.'

I asked him what Ray had said, whether he was angry at that.

'He just said, "Sure, okay."'

Mrs Gorrie had hung up and was shouting directly down the stairs, 'I'll tell you who's crazy. I'll tell you who's a crazy liar spreading lies about me and my husband—'

Chess said, 'We're not listening to you. You leave my wife alone.' Later he said to me, 'What does she mean about her and her husband?'

I said, 'I don't know.'

'She just has it in for you,' he said. 'Because you're young and nice-looking and she's an old hag.

'Forget it,' he said, and made a halfway joke to cheer me up.

'What is the point of old women anyway?'

We moved to the new apartment by taxi with just our suitcases. We waited out on the sidewalk with our backs to the house. I expected some final screaming then, but there was not a sound.

'What if she's got a gun and shoots me in the back?' I said.

'Don't talk like her,' Chess said.

'I'd like to wave to Mr Gorrie if he's there.'

'Better not.'

I didn't take a final look at the house, and I didn't walk down that street, that block of Arbutus Street that faces the park and the sea, ever again. I don't have a clear idea of what it looked like, though I remember a few things – the alcove curtain, the china cabinet, Mr Gorrie's green recliner – so well.

We got to know other young couples who had started out as we did, living in cheap spaces in other people's houses. We heard about rats, cockroaches, evil toilets, crazy landladies. And we would tell about our crazy landlady. Paranoia.

Otherwise, I didn't think of Mrs Gorrie.

But Mr Gorrie showed up in my dreams. In my dreams I seemed to know him before he knew her. He was agile and strong, but he wasn't young, and he didn't look any better than he did when I had read to him in the front room. Perhaps he could talk, but his talk was on the level of those noises I had learned to interpret – it was abrupt and peremptory, an essential but perhaps disdained footnote to the action. And the action was explosive, for these were erotic dreams. All the time that I was a young wife, and then, without undue delay, a young mother – busy, faithful, regularly satisfied – I kept having dreams now and then in which the attack, the response, the possibilities, went beyond anything life offered. And from which romance was banished. Decency as well. Our bed – Mr Gorrie's and mine – was the gravelly beach or the rough boat deck or the punishing coils of greasy rope. There was a relish of what you might call ugliness. His pungent smell, his jelly eye, his dog's teeth. I woke out of these pagan dreams drained even of astonishment, or shame, and fell asleep again and woke with a memory I got used to denying in the morning. For years and years and surely long after he was dead Mr Gorrie operated in my nightlife this way. Until I used him up, I suppose, the way we use up the dead. But it never seemed to be this way – that I was in charge, that I had brought him there. It seemed to be working both ways, as if he had brought me there, too, and it was his experience as much as it was mine.

And the boat and the dock and the gravel on the shore, the trees sky-pointed or crouching, leaning out over the water, the complicated profile of surrounding islands and dim yet distinct mountains, seemed to exist in a natural confusion, more extravagant and yet more ordinary than anything I could dream or invent. Like a place that will go on existing whether you are there or not, and that in fact is still there.

But I never saw the charred beams of the house fallen down on the body of the husband. That had happened a long time before and the forest had grown up all around it.

SAVE THE REAPER

The game they played was almost the same one that Eve had played with Sophie, on long dull car trips when Sophie was a little girl. Then it was spies – now it was aliens. Sophie's children, Philip and Daisy, were sitting in the backseat. Daisy was barely three and could not understand what was going on. Philip was seven, and in control. He was the one who picked the car they were to follow, in which there were newly arrived space travellers on their way to the secret headquarters, the invaders' lair. They got their directions from the signals offered by plausible-looking people in other cars or from somebody standing by a mailbox or even riding a tractor in a field. Many aliens had already arrived on earth and been translated – this was Philip's word – so that anybody might be one. Gas station attendants or women pushing baby carriages or even the babies riding in the carriages. They could be giving signals.

Usually Eve and Sophie had played this game on a busy highway where there was enough traffic that they wouldn't be detected. (Though once they had got carried away and ended up in a suburban drive.) On the country roads that Eve was taking today that wasn't so easy. She tried to solve the problem by saying that they might have to switch from following one vehicle to another because some were only decoys, not heading for the hideaway at all, but leading you astray.

'No, that isn't it,' said Philip. 'What they do, they suck the people out of one car into another car, just in case anybody is following. They can be like inside one body and then they go *schlup* through the air into another body in another car. They go into different people all the time and the people never know what was in them.'

'Really?' Eve said. 'So how do we know which car?'

'The code's on the license plate,' said Philip. 'It's changed by the electrical field they create in the car. So their trackers in space can follow them. It's just one simple little thing, but I can't tell you.'

'Well no,' said Eve. 'I suppose very few people know it.'

Philip said, 'I am the only one right now in Ontario.'

He sat as far forward as he could with his seat belt on, tapping his teeth sometimes in urgent concentration and making light whistling noises as he cautioned her.

'Unh-unh, watch out here,' he said. 'I think you're going to have to turn around. Yeah. Yeah. I think this may be it.'

They had been following a white Mazda, and were now, apparently, to follow an old green pickup truck, a Ford. Eve said, 'Are you sure?'

'Sure.'

'You felt them sucked through the air?'

'They're translated simultaneously,' Philip said. 'I might have said "sucked," but that's just to help people understand it.'

What Eve had originally planned was to have the headquarters turn out to be in the village store that sold ice cream, or in the playground. It could be revealed that all the aliens were congregated there in the form of children, seduced by the pleasures of ice cream or slides and swings, their powers temporarily in abeyance. No fear they could abduct you – or get into you – unless you chose the one wrong flavor of ice cream or swung the exact wrong number of times on the designated swing. (There would have to be some remaining danger, or else Philip would feel let down, humiliated.) But Philip had taken charge so thoroughly that now it was hard to manage the outcome. The pickup truck was turning from the paved county road onto a gravelled side road. It was a decrepit truck with no topper, its body eaten by rust – it would not be going far. Home to some farm, most likely. They might not meet another vehicle to switch to before the destination was reached.

'You're positive this is it?' said Eve. 'It's only one man by himself, you know. I thought they never travelled alone.'

'The dog,' said Philip.

For there was a dog riding in the open back of the truck, running back and forth from one side to the other as if there were events to be kept track of everywhere.

'The dog's one too,' Philip said.

That morning, when Sophie was leaving to meet Ian at the Toronto airport, Philip had kept Daisy occupied in the children's bedroom. Daisy had settled down pretty well in the strange house – except for wetting her bed every night of the holiday – but this was the first time that her mother had gone off and left her behind. So Sophie had asked Philip to distract her, and he did so with enthusiasm (happy at the new turn events had taken?). He shot the toy cars across the floor with angry engine noises to cover up the sound of Sophie's starting the real rented car and driving away. Shortly after that he shouted to Eve, 'Has the B.M. gone?'

Eve was in the kitchen, clearing up the remains of breakfast and disciplining herself. She walked into the living room. There was the boxed tape of the movie that she and Sophie had been watching last night.

The Bridges of Madison County.

'What does mean "B.M."?' said Daisy.

The children's room opened off the living room. This was a cramped little house, fixed up on the cheap for summer rental. Eve's idea had been to get a lakeside cottage for the holiday – Sophie's

189

and Philip's first visit with her in nearly five years and Daisy's first ever. She had picked this stretch of the Lake Huron shore because her parents used to bring her here with her brother when they were children. Things had changed – the cottages were all as substantial as suburban houses, and the rents were out of sight. This house half a mile inland from the rocky, unfavored north end of the usable beach had been the best she could manage. It stood in the middle of a cornfield. She had told the children what her father had once told her – that at night you could hear the corn growing.

Every day when Sophie took Daisy's hand-washed sheets off the line, she had to shake out the corn bugs.

'It means "bowel movement,"' said Philip with a look of sly challenge at Eve.

Eve halted in the doorway. Last night she and Sophie had watched Meryl Streep sitting in the husband's truck, in the rain, pressing down on the door handle, choking with longing, as her lover drove away. Then they had turned and had seen each other's eyes full of tears and shook their heads and started laughing.

'Also it means "Big Mama,"' Philip said in a more conciliatory tone. 'Sometimes that's what Dad calls her.'

'Well then,' said Eve. 'If that's your question, the answer to your question is yes.'

She wondered if he thought of Ian as his real father. She hadn't asked Sophie what they'd told

190

him. She wouldn't, of course. His real father had been an Irish boy who was travelling around North America trying to decide what to do now that he had decided not to be a priest. Eve had thought of him as a casual friend of Sophie's, and it seemed that Sophie had thought of him that way too, until she seduced him. ('He was so shy I never dreamed it would take,' she said.) It wasn't until Eve saw Philip that Eve could really picture what the boy had looked like. Then she saw him faithfully reproduced – the bright-eyed, pedantic, sensitive, scornful, fault-finding, blushing, shrinking, arguing young Irishman. Something like Samuel Beckett, she said, even to the wrinkles. Of course as the baby got older, the wrinkles tended to disappear.

Sophie was a full-time archaeology student then. Eve took care of Philip while she was off at her classes. Eve was an actress – she still was, when she could get work. Even in those days there were times when she wasn't working, or if she had daytime rehearsals she could take Philip along. For a couple of years they all lived together – Eve and Sophie and Philip – in Eve's apartment in Toronto. It was Eve who wheeled Philip in his baby carriage – and, later on, in his stroller – along all the streets between Queen and College and Spadina and Ossington, and during these walks she would sometimes discover a perfect, though neglected, little house for sale in a previously unknown to her two-block-long, tree-shaded, dead-end street.

She would send Sophie to look at it; they would go round with the real-estate agent, talk about a mortgage, discuss what renovations they would have to pay for, and which they could do themselves. Dithering and fantasizing until the house was sold to somebody else, or until Eve had one of her periodic but intense fits of financial prudence, or until somebody persuaded them that these charming little side streets were not half so safe for women and children as the bright, ugly, brash, and noisy street that they continued to live on.

Ian was a person Eve took even less note of than she had of the Irish boy. He was a friend; he never came to the apartment except with others. Then he went to a job in California – he was an urban geographer – and Sophie ran up a phone bill which Eve had to speak to her about, and there was a change altogether in the atmosphere of the apartment. (Should Eve not have mentioned the bill?) Soon a visit was planned, and Sophie took Philip along, because Eve was doing a summer play in a regional theater.

Not long afterwards came the news from California. Sophie and Ian were going to get married.

'Wouldn't it be smarter to try living together for a while?' said Eve on the phone from her boarding house, and Sophie said, 'Oh, no. He's weird. He doesn't believe in that.'

'But I can't get off for a wedding,' Eve said. 'We run till the middle of September.'

192

'That's okay,' said Sophie. 'It won't be a *wedding* wedding.'

And until this summer, Eve had not seen her again. There was the lack of money at both ends, in the beginning. When Eve was working she had a steady commitment, and when she wasn't working she couldn't afford anything extra. Soon Sophie had a job, too – she was a receptionist in a doctor's office. Once Eve was just about to book a flight, when Sophie phoned to say that Ian's father had died and that he was flying to England for the funeral and bringing his mother back with him.

'And we only have the one room,' she said.

'Perish the thought,' said Eve. 'Two mothers-in-law in one house, let alone in one room.'

'Maybe after she's gone?' said Sophie.

But that mother stayed till after Daisy was born, stayed till they moved into the new house, stayed eight months in all. By then Ian was starting to write his book, and it was difficult for him if there were visitors in the house. It was difficult enough anyway. The time passed during which Eve felt confident enough to invite herself. Sophie sent pictures of Daisy, the garden, all the rooms of the house.

Then she announced that they could come, she and Philip and Daisy could come back to Ontario this summer. They would spend three weeks with Eve while Ian worked alone in California. At the end of that time he would join them and they would fly from Toronto to England to spend a month with his mother.

'I'll get a cottage on the lake,' said Eve. 'Oh, it will be lovely.'

'It will,' said Sophie. 'It's crazy that it's been so long.'

And so it had been. Reasonably lovely, Eve had thought. Sophie hadn't seemed much bothered or surprised by Daisy's wetting the bed. Philip had been finicky and standoffish for a couple of days, responding coolly to Eve's report that she had known him as a baby, and whining about the mosquitoes that descended on them as they hurried through the shoreline woods to get to the beach. He wanted to be taken to Toronto to see the Science Centre. But then he settled down, swam in the lake without complaining that it was cold, and busied himself with solitary projects – such as boiling and scraping the meat off a dead turtle he'd lugged home, so he could keep its shell. The turtle's stomach contained an undigested crayfish, and its shell came off in strips, but none of this dismayed him.

Eve and Sophie, meanwhile, developed a pleasant, puttering routine of morning chores, afternoons on the beach, wine with supper, and late-evening movies. They were drawn into half-serious speculations about the house. What could be done about it? First strip off the living-room wallpaper, an imitation of imitation-wood panelling. Pull up the linoleum with its silly pattern of gold fleurs-de-lis turned brown by ground-in sand and dirty scrub

194

water. Sophie was so carried away that she loosened a bit of it that had rotted in front of the sink and discovered pine floorboards that surely could be sanded. They talked about the cost of renting a sander (supposing, that is, that the house was theirs) and what colors they would choose for the paint on the doors and woodwork, shutters on the windows, open shelves in the kitchen instead of the dingy plywood cupboards. What about a gas fireplace?

And who was going to live here? Eve. The snowmobilers who used the house for a winter clubhouse were building a place of their own, and the landlord might be happy to rent it year-round. Or maybe sell it very cheaply, considering its condition. It could be a retreat, if Eve got the job she was hoping for, next winter. And if she didn't, why not sublet the apartment and live here? There'd be the difference in the rents, and the old-age pension she started getting in October, and the money that still came in from a commercial she had made for a diet supplement. She could manage.

'And then if we came in the summers we could help with the rent,' said Sophie.

Philip heard them. He said, 'Every summer?'

'Well you like the lake now,' Sophie said. 'You like it here now.'

'And the mosquitoes, you know they're not as bad every year,' Eve said. 'Usually they're just bad in the early summer. June, before you'd even get here. In the spring there are all these boggy places full of water, and they breed there, and then the boggy places dry up, and they don't breed again. But this year there was so much rain earlier, those places didn't dry up, so the mosquitoes got a second chance, and there's a whole new generation.'

She had found out how much he respected information and preferred it to her opinions and reminiscences.

Sophie was not keen on reminiscence either. Whenever the past that she and Eve had shared was mentioned – even those months after Philip's birth that Eve thought of as some of the happiest, the hardest, the most purposeful and harmonious, in her life – Sophie's face took on a look of gravity and concealment, of patiently with-held judgments. The earlier time, Sophie's own childhood, was a positive minefield, as Eve discovered, when they were talking about Philip's school. Sophie thought it a little too rigorous, and Ian thought it just fine.

'What a switch from Blackbird,' Eve said, and Sophie said at once, almost viciously, 'Oh, Blackbird. What a farce. When I think that you paid for that. You *paid*.'

Blackbird was an ungraded alternative school that Sophie had gone to (the name came from 'Morning Has Broken'). It had cost Eve more than she could afford, but she thought it was better for a child whose mother was an actress and whose father was not in evidence. When Sophie was nine or ten, it had broken up because of disagreements among the parents.

'I learned Greek myths and I didn't know where Greece was,' said Sophie. 'I didn't know *what* it was. We had to spend art period making antinuke signs.'

Eve said, 'Oh, no, surely.'

'We did. And they literally badgered us – they badgered us – to talk about sex. It was verbal molestation. You *paid*.'

'I didn't know it was as bad as all that.'

'Oh well,' said Sophie. 'I survived.'

'That's the main thing,' Eve said shakily. 'Survival.'

Sophie's father was from Kerala, in the southern part of India. Eve had met him, and spent her whole time with him, on a train going from Vancouver to Toronto. He was a young doctor studying in Canada on a fellowship. He had a wife already, and a baby daughter, at home in India.

The train trip took three days. There was a half-hour stop in Calgary. Eve and the doctor ran around looking for a drugstore where they could buy condoms. They didn't find one. By the time they got to Winnipeg, where the train stopped for a full hour, it was too late. In fact – said Eve, when she told their story – by the time they got to the Calgary city limits, it was probably too late.

He was travelling in the day coach – the fellowship was not generous. But Eve had splurged and got herself a roomette. It was this extravagance – a last-minute decision – it was the convenience and privacy of the roomette that were responsible, Eve said, for the existence of Sophie and the greatest change in her, Eve's, life. That, and the fact that you couldn't get condoms anywhere around the Calgary station, not for love or money.

In Toronto she waved goodbye to her lover from Kerala, as you would wave to any train acquaintance, because she was met there by the man who was at that time the serious interest and main trouble in her life. The whole three days had been underscored by the swaying and rocking of the train – the lovers' motions were never just what they contrived themselves, and perhaps for that reason seemed guiltless, irresistible. Their feelings and conversations must have been affected, too. Eve remembered these as sweet and generous, never solemn or desperate. It would have been hard to be solemn when you were dealing with the dimensions and the projections of the roomette.

She told Sophie his Christian name – Thomas, after the saint. Until she met him, Eve had never heard about the ancient Christians in southern India. For a while when she was in her teens Sophie had taken an interest in Kerala. She brought home books from the library and took to going to parties in a sari. She talked about looking her father up, when she got older. The fact that she knew his first name and his special study – diseases of the blood – seemed to her possibly enough.

Eve stressed to her the size of the population of India and the chance that he had not even stayed there. What she could not bring herself to explain was how incidental, how nearly unimaginable, the existence of Sophie would be, necessarily, in her father's life. Fortunately the idea faded, and Sophie gave up wearing the sari when all those dramatic, ethnic costumes became too commonplace. The only time she mentioned her father, later on, was when she was carrying Philip, and making jokes about keeping up the family tradition of flyby fathers.

No jokes like that now. Sophie had grown stately, womanly, graceful, and reserved. There had been a moment – they were getting through the woods to the beach, and Sophie had bent to scoop up Daisy, so that they might move more quickly out of range of the mosquitoes – when Eve had been amazed at the new, late manifestation of her daughter's beauty. A full-bodied, tranquil, classic beauty, achieved not by care and vanity but by self-forgetfulness and duty. She looked more Indian now, her creamed-coffee skin had darkened in the California sun, and she bore under her eyes the lilac crescents of a permanent mild fatigue.

But she was still a strong swimmer. Swimming was the only sport she had ever cared for, and she swam as well as ever, heading it seemed for the middle of the lake. The first day she had done it she said, 'That was wonderful. I felt so free.' She didn't say that it was because Eve was watching the children that she had felt that way, but Eve understood that it didn't need to be said. 'I'm glad,' she said – though in fact she had been frightened. Several times she had thought, Turn around now, and Sophie had swum right on, disregarding this urgent telepathic message. Her dark head became a spot, then a speck, then an illusion tossed among the steady waves. What Eve feared, and could not think about, was not a failure of strength but of the desire to return. As if this new Sophie, this grown woman so tethered to life, could be actually more indifferent to it than the girl Eve used to know, the young Sophie with her plentiful risks and loves and dramas.

'We have to get that movie back to the store,' Eve said to Philip. 'Maybe we should do it before we go to the beach.'

Philip said, 'I'm sick of the beach.'

Eve didn't feel like arguing. With Sophie gone, with all plans altered, so that they were leaving, all of them leaving later in the day, she was sick of the beach, too. And sick of the house – all she could see now was the way this room would look tomorrow. The crayons, the toy cars, the large pieces of Daisy's simple jigsaw puzzle, all swept up and taken away. The storybooks gone that she knew by heart. No sheets drying outside the window. Eighteen more days to last, by herself, in this place.

'How about we go somewhere else today?' she said.

Philip said, 'Where is there?'

'Let it be a surprise.'

Eve had come home from the village the day before, laden with provisions. Fresh shrimp for Sophie – the village store was actually a classy supermarket these days, you could find almost anything – coffee, wine, rye bread without caraway seeds because Philip hated caraway, a ripe melon, the dark cherries they all loved, though Daisy had to be watched with the stones, a tub of mocha-fudge ice cream, and all the regular things to keep them going for another week.

Sophie was clearing up the children's lunch. 'Oh,' she cried. 'Oh, what'll we do with all that stuff?'

Ian had phoned, she said. Ian had phoned and said he was flying into Toronto tomorrow. Work on his book had progressed more quickly than he had expected; he had changed his plans. Instead of waiting for the three weeks to be up, he was coming tomorrow to collect Sophie and the children and take them on a little trip. He wanted to go to Quebec City. He had never been there, and he thought the children should see the part of Canada where people spoke French.

'He got lonesome,' Philip said.

Sophie laughed. She said, 'Yes. He got lonesome for us.'

Twelve days, Eve thought. Twelve days had passed of the three weeks. She had had to take the house for a month. She was letting her friend Dev use the apartment. He was another out-of-work actor, and was in such real or imagined financial peril that he answered the phone in various stage voices. She was fond of Dev, but she couldn't go back and share the apartment with him.

Sophie said that they would drive to Quebec in the rented car, then drive straight back to the Toronto airport, where the car was to be turned in. No mention of Eve's going along. There wasn't room in the rented car. But couldn't she have taken her own car? Philip riding with her, perhaps, for company. Or Sophie. Ian could take the children, if he was so lonesome for them, and give Sophie a rest. Eve and Sophie could ride together as they used to in the summer, travelling to some town they had never seen before, where Eve had got a job.

That was ridiculous. Eve's car was nine years old and in no condition to make a long trip. And it was Sophie Ian had got lonesome for – you could tell that by her warm averted face. Also, Eve hadn't been asked.

'Well that's wonderful,' said Eve. 'That he's got along so well with his book.'

'It is,' said Sophie. She always had an air of careful detachment when she spoke of Ian's book, and when Eve had asked what it was about she had said merely, 'Urban geography.' Perhaps this was the correct behavior for academic wives – Eve had never known any.

'Anyway you'll get some time by yourself,' Sophie said. 'After all this circus. You'll find out if you really would like to have a place in the country. A retreat.'

Eve had to start talking about something else, anything else, so that she wouldn't bleat out a question about whether Sophie still thought of coming next summer.

'I had a friend who went on one of those real retreats,' she said. 'He's a Buddhist. No, maybe a Hindu. Not a real Indian.' (At this mention of Indians Sophie smiled in a way that said this was another subject that need not be gone into.) 'Anyway, you could not speak on this retreat for three months. There were other people around all the time, but you could not speak to them. And he said that one of the things that often happened and that they were warned about was that you fell in love with one of these people you'd never spoken to. You felt you were communicating in a special way with them when you couldn't talk. Of course it was a kind of spiritual love, and you couldn't do anything about it. They were strict about that kind of thing. Or so he said.'

Sophie said, 'So? When you were finally allowed to speak what happened?'

'It was a big letdown. Usually the person you thought you'd been communicating with hadn't been communicating with you at all. Maybe they thought they'd been communicating that way with somebody else, and they thought—'

Sophie laughed with relief. She said, 'So it goes.' Glad that there was to be no show of disappointment, no hurt feelings.

Maybe they had a tiff, thought Eve. This whole visit might have been tactical. Sophie might have taken the children off to show him something. Spent time with her mother, just to show him something. Planning future holidays without him, to prove to herself that she could do it. A diversion.

And the burning question was, Who did the phoning?

'Why don't you leave the children here?' she said. 'Just while you drive to the airport? Then just drive back and pick them up and take off. You'd have a little time to yourself and a little time alone with Ian. It'll be hell with them in the airport.'

Sophie said, 'I'm tempted.'

So in the end that was what she did.

Now Eve had to wonder if she herself had engineered that little change just so she could get to talk to Philip.

(Wasn't it a big surprise when your dad phoned from California?

He didn't phone. My mom phoned him.

Did she? Oh I didn't know. What did she say?

She said, 'I can't stand it here, I'm sick of it, let's figure out some plan to get me away.')

★　　★　　★

204

Eve dropped her voice to a matter-of-fact level, to indicate an interruption of the game. She said, 'Philip. Philip, listen. I think we've got to stop this. That truck just belongs to some farmer and it's going to turn in someplace and we can't go on following.'

'Yes we can,' Philip said.

'No we can't. They'd want to know what we were doing. They might be very mad.'

'We'll call up our helicopters to come and shoot them.'

'Don't be silly. You know this is just a game.'

'They'll shoot them.'

'I don't think they have any weapons,' said Eve, trying another tack. 'They haven't developed any weapons to destroy aliens.'

Philip said, 'You're wrong,' and began a description of some kind of rockets, which she did not listen to.

When she was a child staying in the village with her brother and her parents, Eve had sometimes gone for drives in the country with her mother. They didn't have a car – it was wartime, they had come here on the train. The woman who ran the hotel was friends with Eve's mother, and they would be invited along when she drove to the country to buy corn or raspberries or tomatoes. Sometimes they would stop to have tea and look at the old dishes and bits of furniture for sale in some enterprising farm woman's front parlor. Eve's

205

father preferred to stay behind and play checkers with some other men on the beach. There was a big cement square with a checkerboard painted on it, a roof protecting it but no walls, and there, even in the rain, the men moved oversized checkers around in a deliberate way, with long poles. Eve's brother watched them or went swimming unsupervised – he was older. That was all gone now – the cement, even, was gone, or something had been built right on top of it. The hotel with its verandas extending over the sand was gone, and the railway station with its flower beds spelling out the name of the village. The railway tracks too. Instead there was a fake-old-fashioned mall with the satisfactory new supermarket and wineshop and boutiques for leisure wear and country crafts.

When she was quite small and wore a great hair bow on top of her head, Eve was fond of these country expeditions. She ate tiny jam tarts and cakes whose frosting was stiff on top and soft underneath, topped with a bleeding maraschino cherry. She was not allowed to touch the dishes or the lace-and-satin pincushions or the sallow-looking old dolls, and the women's conversations passed over her head with a temporary and mildly depressing effect, like the inevitable clouds. But she enjoyed riding in the backseat imagining herself on horseback or in a royal coach. Later on she refused to go. She began to hate trailing along with her mother and being identified as her mother's daughter. My daughter, Eve. How richly condescending, how mistakenly possessive, that voice sounded in her ears. (She was to use it, or some version of it, for years as a staple in some of her broadest, least accomplished acting.) She detested also her mother's habit of dressing up, wearing large hats and gloves in the country, and sheer dresses on which there were raised flowers, like warts. The oxford shoes, on the other hand – they were worn to favor her mother's corns – appeared embarrassingly stout and shabby.

'What did you hate most about your mother?' was a game that Eve would play with her friends in her first years free of home.

'Corsets,' one girl would say, and another would say, 'Wet aprons.'

Hair nets. Fat arms. Bible quotations. 'Danny Boy.'

Eve always said. 'Her corns.'

She had forgotten all about this game until recently. The thought of it now was like touching a bad tooth.

Ahead of them the truck slowed and without signalling turned into a long tree-lined lane. Eve said, 'I can't follow them any farther, Philip,' and drove on. But as she passed the lane she noticed the gateposts. They were unusual, being shaped something like crude minarets and decorated with whitewashed pebbles and bit of colored glass. Neither one of them was straight, and they were half hidden by goldenrod and wild carrot, so that they had lost all reality as gateposts and looked instead like lost stage props from some gaudy operetta. The minute she saw them Eve remembered something else – a whitewashed outdoor wall in which there were pictures set. The pictures were stiff, fantastic, childish scenes. Churches with spires, castles with towers, square houses with square, lopsided, yellow windows. Triangular Christmas trees and tropical-colored birds half as big as the trees, a fat horse with dinky legs and burning red eyes, curly blue rivers, like lengths of ribbon, a moon and drunken stars and fat sunflowers nodding over the roofs of houses. All of this made of pieces of colored glass set into cement or plaster. She had seen it, and it wasn't in any public place. It was out in the country, and she had been with her mother. The shape of her mother loomed in front of the wall – she was talking to an old farmer. He might only have been her mother's age, of course, and looked old to Eve.

Her mother and the hotel woman did go to look at odd things on those trips; they didn't just look at antiques. They had gone to see a shrub cut to resemble a bear, and an orchard of dwarf apple trees.

Eve didn't remember the gateposts at all, but it seemed to her that they could not have belonged to any other place. She backed the car and swung around into the narrow track beneath the trees. The trees were heavy old Scotch pines, probably dangerous – you could see dangling half-dead branches, and branches that had already blown down or fallen down were lying in the grass and weeds on either side of the track. The car rocked back and forth in the ruts, and it seemed that Daisy approved of this motion. She began to make an accompanying noise. *Whoppy. Whoppy. Whoppy.*

This was something Daisy might remember – all she might remember – of this day. The arched trees, the sudden shadow, the interesting motion of the car. Maybe the white faces of the wild carrot that brushed at the windows. The sense of Philip beside her – his incomprehensible serious excitement, the tingling of his childish voice brought under unnatural control. A much vaguer sense of Eve – bare, freckly, sun-wrinkled arms, gray-blond frizzy curls held back by a black hairband. Maybe a smell. Not of cigarettes anymore, or of the touted creams and cosmetics on which Eve once spent so much of her money. Old skin? Garlic? Wine? Mouthwash? Eve might be dead when Daisy remembered this. Daisy and Philip might be estranged. Eve had not spoken to her own brother for three years. Not since he said to her on the phone, 'You shouldn't have become an actress if you weren't equipped to make a better go of it.'

There wasn't any sign of a house ahead, but through a gap in the trees the skeleton of a barn rose up, walls gone, beams intact, roof whole but flopping to one side like a funny hat. There seemed to be pieces of machinery, old cars or trucks, scattered around it, in the sea of flowering weeds.

Eve had not much leisure to look – she was busy controlling the car on this rough track. The green truck had disappeared ahead of her – how far could it have gone? Then she saw that the lane curved. It curved; they left the shade of the pines and were out in the sunlight. The same sea foam of wild carrot, the same impression of rusting junk strewed about. A high wild hedge to one side, and there was the house, finally, behind it. A big house, two stories of yellowish-gray brick, an attic story of wood, its dormer windows stuffed with dirty foam rubber. One of the lower windows shone with aluminum foil covering it on the inside.

She had come to the wrong place. She had no memory of this house. There was no wall here around mown grass. Saplings grew up at random in the weeds.

The truck was parked ahead of her. And ahead of that she could see a patch of cleared ground where gravel had been spread and where she could have turned the car around. But she couldn't get past the truck to do that. She had to stop, too. She wondered if the man in the truck had stopped where he did on purpose, so that she would have to explain herself. He was now getting out of the truck in a leisurely way. Without looking at her, he released the dog, which had been running back and forth and barking with a great deal of angry spirit. Once on the ground, it continued to bark, but didn't leave the man's side. The man wore a cap that shaded his face, so that Eve could not see his expression. He stood by the truck looking at them, not yet deciding to come any closer.

Eve unbuckled her seat belt.

'Don't get out,' said Philip. 'Stay in the car. Turn around. Drive away.'

'I can't,' said Eve. 'It's all right. That dog's just a yapper, he won't hurt me.'

'Don't get out.'

She should never have let that game get so far out of control. A child of Philip's age could get too carried away. 'This isn't part of the game,' she said. 'He's just a man.'

'I know,' said Philip. 'But *don't get out.*'

'Stop that,' said Eve, and got out and shut the door.

'Hi,' she said. 'I'm sorry. I made a mistake. I thought this was somewhere else.'

The man said something like 'Hey.'

'I was actually looking for another place,' said Eve. 'It was a place where I came once when I was a little girl. There was a wall with pictures on it all made with pieces of broken glass. I think a cement wall, whitewashed. When I saw those pillars by the road, I thought this must be it. You must have thought we were following you. It sounds so silly.'

She heard the car door open. Philip got out, dragging Daisy behind him. Eve thought he had come to be close to her, and she put out her arm to welcome him. But he detached himself from Daisy and circled round Eve and spoke to the man. He had brought himself out of the alarm of a moment before and now he seemed steadier than Eve was.

'Is your dog friendly?' he said in a challenging way.

'She won't hurt you,' the man said. 'Long as I'm here, she's okay. She gets in a tear because she's not no more than a pup. She's still not no more than a pup.'

He was a small man, no taller than Eve. He was wearing jeans and one of those open vests of colorful weave, made in Peru or Guatemala. Gold chains and medallions sparkled on his hairless, tanned, and muscular chest. When he spoke he threw his head back and Eve could see that his face was older than his body. Some front teeth were missing.

'We won't bother you anymore,' she said. 'Philip, I was just telling this man we drove down this road looking for a place I came when I was a little girl, and there were pictures made of colored glass set in a wall. But I made a mistake, this isn't the place.'

'What's its name?' said Philip.

'Trixie,' the man said, and on hearing her name the dog jumped up and bumped his arm. He swatted her down. 'I don't know about no pictures. I don't live here. Harold, he's the one would know.'

'It's all right,' said Eve, and hoisted Daisy up on her hip. 'If you could just move the truck ahead, then I could turn around.'

'I don't know no pictures. See, if they was in the front part the house I never would've saw them because Harold, he's got the front part of the house shut off.'

'No, they were outside,' said Eve. 'It doesn't matter. This was years and years ago.'

'Yeah. Yeah. Yeah,' the man was saying, warming to the conversation. 'You come in and get Harold to tell you about it. You know Harold? He's who owns it here. Mary, she owns it, but Harold he put her in the Home, so now he does. It wasn't his fault, she had to go there.' He reached into the truck and took out two cases of beer. 'I just had to go to town, Harold sent me into town. You go on. You go in. Harold be glad to see you.'

'Here Trixie,' said Philip sternly.

The dog came yelping and bounding around them, Daisy squealed with fright and pleasure and somehow they were all on the route to the house, Eve carrying Daisy, and Philip and Trixie scrambling around her up some earthen bumps that had once been steps. The man came close behind them, smelling of the beer that he must have been drinking in the truck.

'Open it up, go ahead in,' he said. 'Make your way through. You don't mind it's got a little untidy here? Mary's in the Home, nobody to keep it tidied up like it used to be.'

Massive disorder was what they had to make their way through – the kind that takes years to accumulate. The bottom layer of it made up of chairs and tables and couches and perhaps a stove or two, with old bedclothes and newspapers and window shades and dead potted plants and ends of lumber and empty bottles and broken lighting fixtures and curtain rods piled on top of that, up to the ceiling in some places, blocking nearly all the light from outside. To make up for that, a light was burning by the inside door.

The man shifted the beer and got that door open, and shouted for Harold. It was hard to tell what sort of room they were in now – there were kitchen cupboards with the doors off the hinges, some cans on the shelves, but there were also a couple of cots with bare mattresses and rumpled blankets. The windows were so successfully covered up with furniture or hanging quilts that you could not tell where they were, and the smell was that of a junk store, a plugged sink, or maybe a plugged toilet, cooking and grease and cigarettes and human sweat and dog mess and unremoved garbage.

Nobody answered the shouts. Eve turned around – there was room to turn around here, as there hadn't been in the porch – and said, 'I don't think we should—' but Trixie got in her way and the man ducked round her to bang on another door.

'Here he is,' he said – still at the top of his voice, though the door had opened. 'Here's Harold in here.' At the same time Trixie rushed forward, and another man's voice said, 'Fuck. Get that dog out of here.'

'Lady here wants to see some pictures,' the little man said. Trixie whined in pain – somebody had kicked her. Eve had no choice but to go on into the room.

This was a dining room. There was the heavy old dining-room table and the substantial chairs. Three men were sitting down, playing cards. The fourth man had got up to kick the dog. The temperature in the room was about ninety degrees.

'Shut the door, there's a draft,' said one of the men at the table.

The little man hauled Trixie out from under the table and threw her into the outer room, then closed the door behind Eve and the children.

'Christ. Fuck,' said the man who had got up. His chest and arms were so heavily tattooed that he seemed to have purple or bluish skin. He shook one foot as if it hurt. Perhaps he had also kicked a table leg when he kicked Trixie.

Sitting with his back to the door was a young man with sharp narrow shoulders and a delicate neck. At least Eve assumed he was young, because he wore his hair in dyed golden spikes and had gold rings in his ears. He didn't turn around. The man across from him was as old as Eve herself, and had a shaved head, a tidy gray beard, and bloodshot blue eyes. He looked at Eve without any friendliness but with some intelligence or comprehension, and in this he was unlike the tattooed man, who had looked at her as if she was some kind of hallucination that he had decided to ignore.

215

At the end of the table, in the host's or the father's chair, sat the man who had given the order to close the door, but who hadn't looked up or otherwise paid any attention to the interruption. He was a large-boned, fat, pale man with sweaty brown curls, and as far as Eve could tell he was entirely naked. The tattooed man and the blond man were wearing jeans, and the gray-bearded man was wearing jeans and a checked shirt buttoned up to the neck and a string tie. There were glasses and bottles on the table. The man in the host's chair – he must be Harold – and the gray-bearded man were drinking whiskey. The other two were drinking beer.

'I told her maybe there was pictures in the front but she couldn't go in there you got that shut up,' the little man said.

Harold said, 'You shut up.'

Eve said, 'I'm really sorry.' There seemed to be nothing to do but go into her spiel, enlarging it to include staying at the village hotel as a little girl, drives with her mother, the pictures in the wall, her memory of them today, the gateposts, her obvious mistake, her apologies. She spoke directly to the graybeard, since he seemed the only one willing to listen or capable of understanding her. Her arm and shoulder ached from the weight of Daisy and from the tension which had got hold of her entire body. Yet she was thinking how she would describe this – she'd say it was like finding yourself in the middle of a Pinter play. Or like all her nightmares of a stolid, silent, hostile audience.

The graybeard spoke when she could not think of any further charming or apologetic thing to say. He said, 'I don't know. You'll have to ask Harold. Hey. Hey Harold. Do you know anything about some pictures made out of broken glass?'

'Tell her when she was riding around looking at pictures I wasn't even born yet,' said Harold, without looking up.

'You're out of luck, lady,' said the graybeard.

The tattooed man whistled. 'Hey you,' he said to Philip. 'Hey kid. Can you play the piano?'

There was a piano in the room behind Harold's chair. There was no stool or bench – Harold himself taking up most of the room between the piano and the table – and inappropriate things, such as plates and overcoats, were piled on top of it, as they were on every surface in the house.

'No,' said Eve quickly. 'No he can't.'

'I'm asking him,' the tattooed man said. 'Can you play a tune?'

The graybeard said, 'Let him alone.'

'Just asking if he can play a tune, what's the matter with that?'

'Let him alone.'

'You see I can't move until somebody moves the truck,' Eve said.

She thought, There is a smell of semen in this room.

Philip was mute, pressed against her side.

217

'If you could just move—' she said, turning and expecting to find the little man behind her. She stopped when she saw he wasn't there, he wasn't in the room at all, he had got out without her knowing when. What if he had locked the door?

She put her hand on the knob and it turned, the door opened with a little difficulty and a scramble on the other side of it. The little man had been crouched right there, listening.

Eve went out without speaking to him, out through the kitchen, Philip trotting along beside her like the most tractable little boy in the world. Along the narrow pathway on the porch, through the junk, and when they reached the open air she sucked it in, not having taken a real breath for a long time.

'You ought to go along down the road ask down at Harold's cousin's place,' the little man's voice came after her. 'They got a nice place. They got a new house, she keeps it beautiful. They'll show you pictures or anything you want, they'll make you welcome. They'll sit you down and feed you, they don't let nobody go away empty.'

He couldn't have been crouched against the door all the time, because he had moved the truck. Or somebody had. It had disappeared altogether, been driven away to some shed or parking spot out of sight.

Eve ignored him. She got Daisy buckled in. Philip was buckling himself in, without having to be reminded. Trixie appeared from somewhere and walked around the car in a disconsolate way, sniffing at the tires.

Eve got in and closed the door, put her sweating hand on the key. The car started, she pulled ahead onto the gravel – a space that was surrounded by thick bushes, berry bushes she supposed, and old lilacs, as well as weeds. In places these bushes had been flattened by piles of old tires and bottles and tin cans. It was hard to think that things had been thrown out of that house, considering all that was left in it, but apparently they had. And as Eve swung the car around she saw, revealed by this flattening, some fragment of a wall, to which bits of whitewash still clung.

She thought she could see pieces of glass embedded there, glinting.

She didn't slow down to look. She hoped Philip hadn't noticed – he might want to stop. She got the car pointed towards the lane and drove past the dirt steps to the house. The little man stood there with both arms waving and Trixie was wagging her tail, roused from her scared docility sufficiently to bark farewell and chase them partway down the lane. The chase was only a formality; she could have caught up with them if she wanted to. Eve had had to slow down at once when she hit the ruts.

She was driving so slowly that it was possible, it was easy, for a figure to rise up out of the tall weeds on the passenger side of the car and open the door – which Eve had not thought of locking – and jump in.

It was the blond man who had been sitting at the table, the one whose face she had never seen.

'Don't be scared. Don't be scared anybody. I just wondered if I could hitch a ride with you guys, okay?'

It wasn't a man or a boy; it was a girl. A girl now wearing a dirty sort of undershirt.

Eve said, 'Okay.' She had just managed to hold the car in the track.

'I couldn't ask you back in the house,' the girl said. 'I went in the bathroom and got out the window and run out here. They probably don't even know I'm gone yet. They're boiled.' She took hold of a handful of the undershirt which was much too large for her and sniffed at it. 'Stinks,' she said. 'I just grabbed this of Harold's, was in the bathroom. Stinks.'

Eve left the ruts, the darkness of the lane, and turned onto the ordinary road. 'Jesus I'm glad to get out of there,' the girl said. 'I didn't know nothing about what I was getting into. I didn't know even how I got there, it was night. It wasn't no place for me. You know what I mean?'

'They seemed pretty drunk all right,' said Eve.

'Yeah. Well. I'm sorry if I scared you.'

'That's okay.'

'If I hadn't've jumped in I thought you wouldn't stop for me. Would you?'

'I don't know,' said Eve. 'I guess I would have if it got through to me you were a girl. I didn't really get a look at you before.'

'Yeah. I don't look like much now. I look like shit now. I'm not saying I don't like to party. I like to party. But there's party and there's party, you know what I mean?'

She turned in the seat and looked at Eve so steadily that Eve had to take her eyes from the road for a moment and look back. And what she saw was that this girl was much more drunk than she sounded. Her dark-brown eyes were glazed but held wide open, rounded with effort, and they had the imploring yet distant expression that drunks' eyes get, a kind of last-ditch insistence on fooling you. Her skin was blotched in some places and ashy in others, her whole face crumpled with the effects of a mighty bingeing. She was a natural brunette – the gold spikes were intentionally and provocatively dark at the roots – and pretty enough, if you disregarded her present dinginess, to make you wonder how she had ever got mixed up with Harold and Harold's crew. Her way of living and the style of the times must have taken fifteen or twenty natural pounds off her – but she wasn't tall and she really wasn't boyish. Her true inclination was to be a cuddly chunky girl, a darling dumpling.

'Herb was crazy bringing you in there like that,' she said. 'He's got a screw loose, Herb.'

Eve said, 'I gathered that.'

'I don't know what he does around there, I guess he works for Harold. I don't think Harold uses him too good, neither.'

Eve had never believed herself to be attracted to

221

women in a sexual way. And this girl in her soiled and crumpled state seemed unlikely to appeal to anybody. But perhaps the girl did not believe this possible – she must be so used to appealing to people. At any rate she slid her hand along Eve's bare thigh, just getting a little way beyond the hem of her shorts. It was a practiced move, drunk as she was. To spread the fingers, to grasp flesh on the first try, would have been too much. A practiced, automatically hopeful move, yet so lacking in any true, strong, squirmy, comradely lust that Eve felt that the hand might easily have fallen short and caressed the car upholstery.

'I'm okay,' the girl said, and her voice, like the hand, struggled to put herself and Eve on a new level of intimacy. 'You know what I mean? You understand me. Okay?'

'Of course,' said Eve briskly, and the hand trailed away, its tired whore's courtesy done with. But it had not failed – not altogether. Blatant and halfhearted as it was, it had been enough to set some old wires twitching.

And the fact that it could be effective in any way at all filled Eve with misgiving, flung a shadow backwards from this moment over all the rowdy and impulsive as well as all the hopeful and serious, the more or less unrepented-of, couplings of her life. Not a real flare-up of shame, a sense of sin – just a dirty shadow. What a joke on her, if she started to hanker now after a purer past and a cleaner slate.

But it could be just that still, and always, she hankered after love.

She said, 'Where is it you want to go?'

The girl jerked backwards, faced the road. She said, 'Where you going? You live around here?' The blurred tone of seductiveness had changed, as no doubt it would change after sex, into a mean-sounding swagger.

'There's a bus goes through the village,' Eve said. 'It stops at the gas station. I've seen the sign.'

'Yeah but just one thing,' the girl said. 'I got no money. See, I got away from there in such a hurry I never got to collect my money. So what use would it be me getting on a bus without no money?'

The thing to do was not to recognize a threat. Tell her that she could hitchhike, if she had no money. It wasn't likely that she had a gun in her jeans. She just wanted to sound as if she might have one.

But a knife?

The girl turned for the first time to look into the backseat.

'You kids okay back there?' she said.

No answer.

'They're cute,' she said. 'They shy with strangers?'

How stupid of Eve to think about sex, when the reality, the danger, were elsewhere.

Eve's purse was on the floor of the car in front of the girl's feet. She didn't know how much money was in it. Sixty, seventy dollars. Hardly more. If she offered money for a ticket the girl would name an expensive destination. Montreal. Or at least Toronto. If she said, 'Just take what's there,' the girl would see capitulation. She would sense Eve's fear and might try to push further. What was the best she could do? Steal the car? If she left Eve and the children beside the road, the police would be after her in a hurry. If she left them dead in some thicket, she might get farther. Or if she took them along while she needed them, a knife against Eve's side or a child's throat.

Such things happen. But not as regularly as on television or in the movies. Such things don't often happen.

Eve turned onto the county road, which was fairly busy. Why did that make her feel better? Safety there was an illusion. She could be driving along the highway in the midst of the day's traffic taking herself and the children to their deaths.

The girl said, 'Where's this road go?'

'It goes out to the main highway.'

'Let's drive out there.'

'That's where I am driving,' Eve said.

'Which way's the highway go?'

'It goes north to Owen Sound or up to Tobermory where you get the boat. Or south to – I don't know. But it joins another highway, you can get to Sarnia. Or London. Or Detroit or Toronto if you keep going.'

Nothing more was said until they reached the

highway. Eve turned onto it and said, 'This is it.'

'Which way you heading now?'

'I'm heading north,' Eve said.

'That the way you live then?'

'I'm going to the village. I'm going to stop for gas.'

'You got gas,' the girl said. 'You got over half a tank.'

That was stupid. Eve should have said groceries.

Beside her the girl let out a long groan of decision, maybe of relinquishment.

'You know,' she said, 'you know. I might as well get out here if I'm going to hitch a ride. I could get a ride here as easy as anyplace.'

Eve pulled over onto the gravel. Relief was turning into something like shame. It was probably true that the girl had run away without collecting any money, that she had nothing. What was it like to be drunk, wasted, with no money, at the side of the road?

'Which way you said we're going?'

'North,' Eve told her again.

'Which way you said to Sarnia?'

'South. Just cross the road, the cars'll be headed south. Watch out for the traffic.'

'Sure,' the girl said. Her voice was already distant; she was calculating new chances. She was half out of the car as she said, 'See you.' And into the backseat, 'See you guys. Be good.'

'Wait,' said Eve. She leaned over and felt in her purse for her wallet, got out a twenty-dollar bill. She got out of the car and came round to where the girl was waiting. 'Here,' she said. 'This'll help you.'

'Yeah. Thanks,' the girl said, stuffing the bill in her pocket, her eyes on the road.

'Listen,' said Eve. 'If you're stranded I'll tell you where my house is. It's about two miles north of the village and the village is about half a mile north of here. North. This way. My family's there now, but they should be gone by evening, if that bothers you. It's got the name Ford on the mailbox. That's not my name, I don't know why it's there. It's all by itself in the middle of a field. It's got one ordinary window on one side of the front door and a funny-looking little window on the other. That's where they put in the bathroom.'

'Yeah,' the girl said.

'It's just that I thought, if you don't get a ride—'

'Okay,' the girl said. 'Sure.'

When they had started driving again, Philip said, 'Yuck. She smelled like vomit.'

A little farther on he said, 'She didn't even know you should look at the sun to tell directions. She was stupid. Wasn't she?'

'I guess so,' Eve said.

'Yuck. I never ever saw anybody so stupid.'

As they went through the village he asked if they could stop for ice-cream cones. Eve said no.

'There's so many people stopping for ice cream

226

it's hard to find a place to park,' she said. 'We've got enough ice cream at home.'

'You shouldn't say "home,"' said Philip. 'It's just where we're staying. You should say "the house."'

The big hay rolls in a field to the east of the highway were facing ends-on into the sun, so tightly packed they looked like shields or gongs or faces of Aztec metal. Past that was a field of pale soft gold tails or feathers.

'That's called barley, that gold stuff with the tails on it,' she said to Philip.

He said, 'I know.'

'The tails are called beards sometimes.' She began to recite, '"But the reapers, reaping early, in among the bearded barley—"'

Daisy said, 'What does mean "pearly"?'

Philip said, 'Bar-ley.'

'"Only reapers, reaping early,"' Eve said. She tried to remember. '"Save the reapers, reaping early—"' 'Save' was what sounded best. Save the reapers.

Sophie and Ian had bought corn at a roadside stand. It was for dinner. Plans had changed – they weren't leaving till morning. And they had bought a bottle of gin and some tonic and limes. Ian made the drinks while Eve and Sophie sat husking the corn. Eve said, 'Two dozen. That's crazy.'

'Wait and see,' said Sophie. 'Ian loves corn.'

Ian bowed when he presented Eve with her drink, and after she had tasted it she said, 'This is most heavenly.'

Ian wasn't much as she had remembered or pictured him. He was not tall, Teutonic, humorless. He was a slim fair-haired man of medium height, quick moving, companionable. Sophie was less assured, more tentative in all she said and did, than she had seemed since she'd been here. But happier, too.

Eve told her story. She began with the checkerboard on the beach, the vanished hotel, the drives into the country. It included her mother's city-lady outfits, her sheer dresses and matching slips, but not the young Eve's feelings of repugnance. Then the things they went to see – the dwarf orchard, the shelf of old dolls, the marvellous pictures made of colored glass.

'They were a little like Chagall?' Eve said.

Ian said, 'Yep. Even us urban geographers know about Chagall.'

Eve said, 'Sor-ry.' Both laughed.

Now the gateposts, the sudden memory, the dark lane and ruined barn and rusted machinery, the house a shambles.

'The owner was in there playing cards with his friends,' Eve said. 'He didn't know anything about it. Didn't know or didn't care. And my God, it could have been nearly sixty years ago I was there – think of that.'

Sophie said, 'Oh, Mom. What a shame.' She was

glowing with relief to see Ian and Eve getting on so well together.

'Are you sure it was even the right place?' she said.

'Maybe not,' said Eve. 'Maybe not.'

She would not mention the fragment of wall she had seen beyond the bushes. Why bother, when there were so many things she thought best not to mention? First, the game that she had got Philip playing, overexciting him. And nearly everything about Harold and his companions. Everything, every single thing about the girl who had jumped into the car.

There are people who carry decency and optimism around with them, who seem to cleanse every atmosphere they settle in, and you can't tell such people things, it is too disruptive. Ian struck Eve as being one of those people, in spite of his present graciousness, and Sophie as being someone who thanked her lucky stars that she had found him. It used to be older people who claimed this protection from you, but now it seemed more and more to be younger people, and someone like Eve had to try not to reveal how she was stranded in between. Her whole life liable to be seen as some sort of unseemly thrashing around, a radical mistake.

She could say that the house smelled vile, and that the owner and his friends looked altogether boozy and disreputable, but not that Harold was naked and never that she herself was afraid. And never what she was afraid of.

Philip was in charge of gathering up the corn husks and carrying them outside to throw them along the edge of the field. Occasionally Daisy picked up a few on her own, and took them off to be distributed around the house. Philip had added nothing to Eve's story and had not seemed to be concerned with the telling of it. But once it was told, and Ian (interested in bringing this local anecdote into line with his professional studies) was asking Eve what she knew about the breakup of older patterns of village and rural life, about the spread of what was called agribusiness, Philip did look up from his stooping and crawling work around the adults' feet. He looked at Eve. A flat look, a moment of conspiratorial blankness, a buried smile, that passed before there could be any need for recognition of it.

What did this mean? Only that he had begun the private work of storing and secreting, deciding on his own what should be preserved and how, and what these things were going to mean to him, in his unknown future.

If the girl came looking for her, they would all still be here. Then Eve's carefulness would go for nothing.

The girl wouldn't come. Much better offers would turn up before she'd stood ten minutes by the highway. More dangerous offers perhaps, but more interesting, likely to be more profitable.

The girl wouldn't come. Unless she found some

homeless, heartless wastrel of her own age. (*I know where there's a place we can stay, if we can get rid of the old lady.*)

Not tonight but tomorrow night Eve would lie down in this hollowed-out house, its board walls like a paper shell around her, willing herself to grow light, relieved of consequence, with nothing in her head but the rustle of the deep tall corn which might have stopped growing now but still made its live noise after dark.

THE CHILDREN STAY

Thirty years ago, a family was spending a holiday together on the east coast of Vancouver Island. A young father and mother, their two small daughters, and an older couple, the husband's parents.

What perfect weather. Every morning, every morning it's like this, the first pure sunlight falling through the high branches, burning away the mist over the still water of Georgia Strait. The tide out, a great empty stretch of sand still damp but easy to walk on, like cement in its very last stage of drying. The tide is actually less far out; every morning, the pavilion of sand is shrinking, but it still seems ample enough. The changes in the tide are a matter of great interest to the grandfather, not so much to anyone else.

Pauline, the young mother, doesn't really like the beach as well as she likes the road that runs behind the cottages for a mile or so north till it stops at the bank of the little river that runs into the sea.

If it wasn't for the tide, it would be hard to remember that this is the sea. You look across the water to the mountains on the mainland, the ranges that are the western wall of the continent of North America. These humps and peaks coming clear now through the mist and glimpsed here and there through the trees, by Pauline as she pushes her daughter's stroller along the road, are also of interest to the grandfather. And to his son Brian, who is Pauline's husband. The two men are continually trying to decide which is what. Which of these shapes are actual continental mountains and which are improbable heights of the islands that ride in front of the shore? It's hard to sort things out when the array is so complicated and parts of it shift their distance in the day's changing light.

But there is a map, set up under glass, between the cottages and the beach. You can stand there looking at the map, then looking at what's in front of you, looking back at the map again, until you get things sorted out. The grandfather and Brian do this every day, usually getting into an argument – though you'd think there would not be much room for disagreement with the map right there. Brian chooses to see the map as inexact. But his father will not hear a word of criticism about any aspect of this place, which was his choice for the holiday. The map, like the accommodation and the weather, is perfect.

Brian's mother won't look at the map. She says it boggles her mind. The men laugh at her, they accept that her mind is boggled. Her husband believes that this is because she is a female. Brian believes that it's because she's his mother. Her concern is always about whether anybody is hungry yet, or thirsty, whether the children have their sun hats on and have been rubbed with protective lotion. And what is the strange bite on Caitlin's arm that doesn't look like the bite of a mosquito? She makes her husband wear a floppy cotton hat and thinks that Brian should wear one too – she reminds him of how sick he got from the sun, that summer they went to the Okanagan, when he was a child. Sometimes Brian says to her, 'Oh, dry up, Mother.' His tone is mostly affectionate, but his father may ask him if that's the way he thinks he can talk to his mother nowadays.

'She doesn't mind,' says Brian.

'How do you know?' says his father.

'Oh for Pete's sake,' says his mother.

Pauline slides out of bed as soon as she's awake every morning, slides out of reach of Brian's long, sleepily searching arms and legs. What wakes her are the first squeaks and mutters of the baby, Mara, in the children's room, then the creak of the crib as Mara – sixteen months old now, getting to the end of babyhood – pulls herself up to stand hanging on to the railing. She continues her soft amiable talk as Pauline lifts her out – Caitlin, nearly five, shifting about but not waking, in her nearby bed – and as she is carried into the kitchen to be changed, on the floor. Then she is settled into her stroller, with a biscuit and a bottle of apple juice, while

Pauline gets into her sundress and sandals, goes to the bathroom, combs out her hair – all as quickly and quietly as possible. They leave the cottage; they head past some other cottages for the bumpy unpaved road that is still mostly in deep morning shadow, the floor of a tunnel under fir and cedar trees.

The grandfather, also an early riser, sees them from the porch of his cottage, and Pauline sees him. But all that is necessary is a wave. He and Pauline never have much to say to each other (though sometimes there's an affinity they feel, in the midst of some long-drawn-out antics of Brian's or some apologetic but insistent fuss made by the grandmother; there's an awareness of not looking at each other, lest their look should reveal a bleakness that would discredit others).

On this holiday Pauline steals time to be by herself – being with Mara is still almost the same thing as being by herself. Early morning walks, the late-morning hour when she washes and hangs out the diapers. She could have had another hour or so in the afternoons, while Mara is napping. But Brian has fixed up a shelter on the beach, and he carries the playpen down every day, so that Mara can nap there and Pauline won't have to absent herself. He says his parents may be offended if she's always sneaking off. He agrees though that she does need some time to go over her lines for the play she's going to be in, back in Victoria, this September.

Pauline is not an actress. This is an amateur production, but she is not even an amateur actress. She didn't try out for the role, though it happened that she had already read the play. *Eurydice* by Jean Anouilh. But then, Pauline has read all sorts of things.

She was asked if she would like to be in this play by a man she met at a barbecue, in June. The people at the barbecue were mostly teachers and their wives or husbands – it was held at the house of the principal of the high school where Brian teaches. The woman who taught French was a widow – she had brought her grown son who was staying for the summer with her and working as a night clerk in a downtown hotel. She told everybody that he had got a job teaching at a college in western Washington State and would be going there in the fall.

Jeffrey Toom was his name. 'Without the *B*,' he said, as if the staleness of the joke wounded him. It was a different name from his mother's, because she had been widowed twice, and he was the son of her first husband. About the job he said, 'No guarantee it'll last, it's a one-year appointment.'

What was he going to teach?

'Dram-ah,' he said, drawing the word out in a mocking way.

He spoke of his present job disparagingly, as well.

'It's a pretty sordid place,' he said. 'Maybe you

236

heard – a hooker was killed there last winter. And then we get the usual losers checking in to OD or bump themselves off.'

People did not quite know what to make of this way of talking and drifted away from him. Except for Pauline.

'I'm thinking about putting on a play,' he said. 'Would you like to be in it?' He asked her if she had ever heard of a play called *Eurydice*.

Pauline said, 'You mean Anouilh's?' and he was unflatteringly surprised. He immediately said he didn't know if it would ever work out. 'I just thought it might be interesting to see if you could do something different here in the land of Noël Coward.'

Pauline did not remember when there had been a play by Noël Coward put on in Victoria, though she supposed there had been several. She said, 'We saw *The Duchess of Malfi* last winter at the college. And the little theater did *A Resounding Tinkle*, but we didn't see it.'

'Yeah. Well,' he said, flushing. She had thought he was older than she was, at least as old as Brian (who was thirty, though people were apt to say he didn't act it), but as soon as he started talking to her, in this offhand, dismissive way, never quite meeting her eyes, she suspected that he was younger than he'd like to appear. Now with that flush she was sure of it.

As it turned out, he was a year younger than she was. Twenty-five.

She said that she couldn't be Eurydice; she couldn't act. But Brian came over to see what the conversation was about and said at once that she must try it.

'She just needs a kick in the behind,' Brian said to Jeffrey. 'She's like a little mule, it's hard to get her started. No, seriously, she's too self-effacing, I tell her that all the time. She's very smart. She's actually a lot smarter than I am.'

At that Jeffrey did look directly into Pauline's eyes – impertinently and searchingly – and she was the one who was flushing.

He had chosen her immediately as his Eurydice because of the way she looked. But it was not because she was beautiful. 'I'd never put a beautiful girl in that part,' he said. 'I don't know if I'd ever put a beautiful girl on stage in anything. It's too much. It's distracting.'

So what did he mean about the way she looked? He said it was her hair, which was long and dark and rather bushy (not in style at that time), and her pale skin ('Stay out of the sun this summer') and most of all her eyebrows.

'I never liked them,' said Pauline, not quite sincerely. Her eyebrows were level, dark, luxuriant. They dominated her face. Like her hair, they were not in style. But if she had really disliked them, wouldn't she have plucked them?

Jeffrey seemed not to have heard her. 'They give you a sulky look and that's disturbing,' he said. 'Also your jaw's a little heavy and that's sort of

238

Greek. It would be better in a movie where I could get you close up. The routine thing for Eurydice would be a girl who looked ethereal. I don't want ethereal.'

As she walked Mara along the road, Pauline did work at the lines. There was a speech at the end that was giving her trouble. She bumped the stroller along and repeated to herself, '"You are terrible, you know, you are terrible like the angels. You think everybody's going forward, as brave and bright as you are – oh, don't look at me, please, darling, don't look at me – perhaps I'm not what you wish I was, but I'm here, and I'm warm, I'm kind, and I love you. I'll give you all the happiness I can. Don't look at me. Don't look. Let me live."'

She had left something out. '"Perhaps I'm not what you wish I was, but you feel me here, don't you? I'm warm and I'm kind—"'

She had told Jeffrey that she thought the play was beautiful.

He said, 'Really?' What she'd said didn't please or surprise him – he seemed to feel it was predictable, superfluous. He would never describe a play in that way. He spoke of it more as a hurdle to be got over. Also a challenge to be flung at various enemies. At the academic snots – as he called them – who had done *The Duchess of Malfi*. And at the social twits – as he called them – in the little theater. He saw himself as an outsider heaving his weight against these people, putting on his play –

he called it his – in the teeth of their contempt and opposition. In the beginning Pauline thought that this must be all in his imagination and that it was more likely these people knew nothing about him. Then something would happen that could be, but might not be, a coincidence. Repairs had to be done on the church hall where the play was to be performed, making it unobtainable. There was an unexpected increase in the cost of printing advertising posters. She found herself seeing it his way. If you were going to be around him much, you almost had to see it his way – arguing was dangerous and exhausting.

'Sons of bitches,' said Jeffrey between his teeth, but with some satisfaction. 'I'm not surprised.'

The rehearsals were held upstairs in an old building on Fisgard Street. Sunday afternoon was the only time that everybody could get there, though there were fragmentary rehearsals during the week. The retired harbor pilot who played Monsieur Henri was able to attend every rehearsal, and got to have an irritating familiarity with everybody else's lines. But the hairdresser – who had experience only with Gilbert and Sullivan but now found herself playing Eurydice's mother – could not leave her shop for long at any other time. The bus driver who played her lover had his daily employment as well, and so had the waiter who played Orphée (he was the only one of them who hoped to be a real actor). Pauline had to depend on sometimes undependable high-school baby-sitters – for the first six weeks of the summer Brian was busy teaching summer school – and Jeffrey himself had to be at his hotel job by eight o'clock in the evenings. But on Sunday afternoons they were all there. While other people swam at Thetis Lake, or thronged Beacon Hill Park to walk under the trees and feed the ducks, or drove far out of town to the Pacific beaches, Jeffrey and his crew labored in the dusty high-ceilinged room on Fisgard Street. The windows were rounded at the top as in some plain and dignified church, and propped open in the heat with whatever objects could be found – ledger books from the 1920s belonging to the hat shop that had once operated downstairs, or pieces of wood left over from the picture frames made by the artist whose canvases were now stacked against one wall and apparently abandoned. The glass was grimy, but outside the sunlight bounced off the sidewalks, the empty gravelled parking lots, the low stuccoed buildings, with what seemed a special Sunday brightness. Hardly anybody moved through these downtown streets. Nothing was open except the occasional hole-in-the-wall coffee shop or fly-specked convenience store.

Pauline was the one who went out at the break to get soft drinks and coffee. She was the one who had the least to say about the play and the way it was going – even though she was the only one who had read it before – because she alone had never done any acting. So it seemed proper for her to volunteer. She enjoyed her short walk in the empty streets – she felt as if she had become an urban person, someone detached and solitary, who lived in the glare of an important dream. Sometimes she thought of Brian at home, working in the garden and keeping an eye on the children. Or perhaps he had taken them to Dallas Road – she recalled a promise – to sail boats on the pond. That life seemed ragged and tedious compared to what went on the rehearsal room – the hours of effort, the concentration, the sharp exchanges, the sweating and tension. Even the taste of the coffee, its scalding bitterness, and the fact that it was chosen by nearly everybody in preference to a fresher-tasting and maybe more healthful drink out of the cooler seemed satisfying to her. And she liked the look of the shop-windows. This was not one of the dolled-up streets near the harbor – it was a street of shoe- and bicycle-repair shops, discount linen and fabric stores, of clothes and furniture that had been so long in the windows that they looked secondhand even if they weren't. On some windows sheets of golden plastic as frail and crinkled as old cellophane were stretched inside the glass to protect the merchandise from the sun. All these enterprises had been left behind just for this one day, but they had a look of being fixed in time as much as cave paintings or relics under sand.

When she said that she had to go away for the two-week holiday Jeffrey looked thunderstruck, as if he had never imagined that things like holidays could come into her life. Then he turned grim and slightly satirical, as if this was just another blow that he might have expected. Pauline explained that she would miss only the one Sunday – the one in the middle of the two weeks – because she and Brian were driving up the island on a Monday and coming back on a Sunday morning. She promised to get back in time for rehearsal. Privately she wondered how she would do this – it always took so much longer than you expected to pack up and get away. She wondered if she could possibly come back by herself, on the morning bus. That would probably be too much to ask for. She didn't mention it.

She couldn't ask him if it was only the play he was thinking about, only her absence from a rehearsal that caused the thundercloud. At the moment, it very likely was. When he spoke to her at rehearsals there was never any suggestion that he ever spoke to her in any other way. The only difference in his treatment of her was that perhaps he expected less of her, of her acting, than he did of the others. And that would be understandable to anybody. She was the only one chosen out of the blue, for the way she looked – the others had all shown up at the audition he had advertised on the signs put up in cafés and bookstores around town. From her he appeared to want an immobility or awkwardness that he didn't want from the rest of them. Perhaps it was because, in the latter part of the play, she was supposed to be a person who had already died.

Yet she thought they all knew, the rest of the cast all knew, what was going on, in spite of Jeffrey's offhand and abrupt and none too civil ways. They knew that after every one of them had straggled off home, he would walk across the room and bolt the staircase door. (At first Pauline had pretended to leave with the rest and had even got into her car and circled the block, but later such a trick had come to seem insulting, not just to herself and Jeffrey, but to the others whom she was sure would never betray her, bound as they all were under the temporary but potent spell of the play.)

Jeffrey crossed the room and bolted the door. Every time, this was like a new decision, which he had to make. Until it was done, she wouldn't look at him. The sound of the bolt being pushed into place, the ominous or fatalistic sound of the metal hitting metal, gave her a localized shock of capitulation. But she didn't make a move, she waited for him to come back to her with the whole story of the afternoon's labor draining out of his face, the expression of matter-of-fact and customary disappointment cleared away, replaced by the live energy she always found surprising.

'So. Tell us what this play of yours is about,' Brian's father said. 'Is it one of those ones where they take their clothes off on the stage?'

'Now don't tease her,' said Brian's mother.

244

Brian and Pauline had put the children to bed and walked over to his parents' cottage for an evening drink. The sunset was behind them, behind the forests of Vancouver Island, but the mountains in front of them, all clear now and hard-cut against the sky, shone in its pink light. Some high inland mountains were capped with pink summer snow.

'Nobody takes their clothes off, Dad,' said Brian in his booming schoolroom voice. 'You know why? Because they haven't got any clothes on in the first place. It's the latest style. They're going to put on a bare-naked *Hamlet* next. Bare-naked *Romeo and Juliet*. Boy, that balcony scene where Romeo is climbing up the trellis and he gets stuck in the rosebushes—'

'Oh, Brian,' said his mother.

'The story of Orpheus and Eurydice is that Eurydice died,' Pauline said. 'And Orpheus goes down to the underworld to try to get her back. And his wish is granted, but only if he promises not to look at her. Not to look back at her. She's walking behind him—'

'Twelve paces,' said Brian. 'As is only right.'

'It's a Greek story, but it's set in modern times,' said Pauline. 'At least this version is. More or less modern. Orpheus is a musician travelling around with his father – they're both musicians – and Eurydice is an actress. This is in France.'

'Translated?' Brian's father said.

'No,' said Brian. 'But don't worry, it's not in French. It was written in Transylvanian.'

'It's so hard to make sense of anything,' Brian's mother said with a worried laugh. 'It's so hard, with Brian around.'

'It's in English,' Pauline said.

'And you're what's-her-name?'

She said, 'I'm Eurydice.'

'He get you back okay?'

'No,' she said. 'He looks back at me, and then I have to stay dead.'

'Oh, an unhappy ending,' Brian's mother said.

'You're so gorgeous?' said Brian's father skeptically. 'He can't stop himself from looking back?'

'It's not that,' said Pauline. But at this point she felt that something had been achieved by her father-in-law, he had done what he meant to do, which was the same thing that he nearly always meant to do, in any conversation she had with him. And that was to break through the structure of some explanation he had asked her for, and she had unwillingly but patiently given, and, with a seemingly negligent kick, knock it into rubble. He had been dangerous to her for a long time in this way, but he wasn't particularly so tonight.

But Brian did not know that. Brian was still figuring out how to come to her rescue.

'Pauline is gorgeous,' Brian said.

'Yes indeed,' said his mother.

'Maybe if she'd go to the hairdresser,' his father said. But Pauline's long hair was such an old objection of his that it had become a family joke. Even Pauline laughed. She said, 'I can't afford to till we get the veranda roof fixed.' And Brian laughed boisterously, full of relief that she was able to take all this as a joke. It was what he had always told her to do.

'Just kid him back,' he said. 'It's the only way to handle him.'

'Yeah, well, if you'd got yourselves a decent house,' said his father. But this like Pauline's hair was such a familiar sore point that it couldn't rouse anybody. Brian and Pauline had bought a handsome house in bad repair on a street in Victoria where old mansions were being turned into ill-used apartment buildings. The house, the street, the messy old Garry oaks, the fact that no basement had been blasted out under the house, were all a horror to Brian's father. Brian usually agreed with him and tried to go him one further. If his father pointed at the house next door all crisscrossed with black fire escapes, and asked what kind of neighbors they had, Brian said, 'Really poor people, Dad. Drug addicts.' And when his father wanted to know how it was heated, he'd said, 'Coal furnace. hardly any of them left these days, you can get coal really cheap. Of course it's dirty and it kind of stinks.'

So what his father said now about a decent house might be some kind of peace signal. Or could be taken so.

Brian was an only son. He was a math teacher. His father was a civil engineer and part owner of a contracting company. If he had hoped that

247

he would have a son who was an engineer and might come into the company, there was never any mention of it. Pauline had asked Brian whether he thought the carping about their house and her hair and the books she read might be a cover for this larger disappointment, but Brian had said, 'Nope. In our family we complain about just whatever we want to complain about. We ain't subtle, ma'am.'

Pauline still wondered, when she heard his mother talking about how teachers ought to be the most honored people in the world and they did not get half the credit they deserved and that she didn't know how Brian managed it, day after day. Then his father might say, 'That's right,' or, 'I sure wouldn't want to do it, I can tell you that. They couldn't pay me to do it.'

'Don't worry Dad,' Brian would say. 'They wouldn't pay you much.'

Brian in his everyday life was a much more dramatic person than Jeffrey. He dominated his classes by keeping up a parade of jokes and antics, extending the role that he had always played, Pauline believed, with his mother and father. He acted dumb, he bounced back from pretended humiliations, he traded insults. He was a bully in a good cause – a chivvying cheerful indestructible bully.

'Your boy has certainly made his mark with us,' the principal said to Pauline. 'He has not just survived, which is something in itself. He has made his mark.'

Your boy.

Brian called his students boneheads. His tone was affectionate, fatalistic. He said that his father was the King of the Philistines, a pure and natural barbarian. And that his mother was a dishrag, good-natured and worn out. But however he dismissed such people, he could not be long without them. He took his students on camping trips. And he could not imagine a summer without this shared holiday. He was mortally afraid, every year, that Pauline would refuse to go along. Or that, having agreed to go, she was going to be miserable, take offense at something his father said, complain about how much time she had to spend with his mother, sulk because there was no way they could do anything by themselves. She might decide to spend all day in their own cottage, reading and pretending to have a sunburn.

All those things had happened, on previous holidays. But this year she was easing up. He told her he could see that, and he was grateful to her.

'I know it's an effort,' he said. 'It's different for me. They're my parents and I'm used to not taking them seriously.'

Pauline came from a family that took things so seriously that her parents had got a divorce. Her mother was now dead. She had a distant, though cordial, relationship with her father and her two much older sisters. She said that they had nothing in common. She knew Brian could not understand how that could be a reason. She saw what comfort

249

it gave him, this year, to see things going so well. She had thought it was laziness or cowardice that kept him from breaking the arrangement, but now she saw that it was something far more positive. He needed to have his wife and his parents and his children bound together like this, he needed to involve Pauline in his life with his parents and to bring his parents to some recognition of her – though the recognition, from his father, would always be muffled and contrary, and from his mother too profuse, too easily come by, to mean much. Also he wanted Pauline to be connected, he wanted the children to be connected, to his own childhood – he wanted these holidays to be linked to holidays of his childhood with their lucky or unlucky weather, car troubles or driving records, boating scares, bee stings, marathon Monopoly games, to all the things that he told his mother he was bored to death hearing about. He wanted pictures from this summer to be taken, and fitted into his mother's album, a continuation of all the other pictures that he groaned at the mention of.

The only time they could talk to each other was in bed, late at night. But they did talk then, more than was usual with them at home, where Brian was so tired that often he fell immediately asleep. And in ordinary daylight it was often hard to talk to him because of his jokes. She could see the joke brightening his eyes (his coloring was very like hers – dark hair and pale skin and gray eyes, but her eyes were cloudy and his were light, like clear water over stones). She could see it pulling at the corners of his mouth, as he foraged among your words to catch a pun or the start of a rhyme – anything that could take the conversation away, into absurdity. His whole body, tall and loosely joined together and still almost as skinny as a teenager's, twitched with comic propensity. Before she married him, Pauline had a friend named Gracie, a rather grumpy-looking girl, subversive about men. Brian had thought her a girl whose spirits needed a boost, and so he made even more than the usual effort. And Gracie said to Pauline, 'How can you stand the nonstop show?'

'That's not the real Brian,' Pauline had said. 'He's different when we're alone.' But looking back, she wondered how true that had ever been. Had she said it simply to defend her choice, as you did when you had made up your mind to get married?

So talking in the dark had something to do with the fact that she could not see his face. And that he knew she couldn't see his face.

But even with the window open on the unfamiliar darkness and stillness of the night, he teased a little. He had to speak of Jeffrey as Monsieur le Directeur, which made the play or the fact that it was a French play slightly ridiculous. Or perhaps it was Jeffrey himself, Jeffrey's seriousness about the play, that had to be called in question.

Pauline didn't care. It was such a pleasure and a relief to her to mention Jeffrey's name.

251

Most of the time she didn't mention him; she circled around that pleasure. She described all the others, instead. The hairdresser and the harbor pilot and the waiter and the old man who claimed to have once acted on the radio. He played Orphée's father and gave Jeffrey the most trouble, because he had the stubbornest notions of his own, about acting.

The middle-aged impresario Monsieur Dulac was played by a twenty-four-year-old travel agent. And Mathias, who was Eurydice's former boyfriend, presumably around her own age, was played by the manager of a shoe store, who was married and a father of children.

Brian wanted to know why Monsieur le Directeur hadn't cast these two the other way round.

'That's the way he does things,' Pauline said. 'What he sees in us is something only he can see.'

For instance, she said, the waiter was a clumsy Orphée.

'He's only nineteen, he's so shy Jeffrey has to keep at him. He tells him not to act like he's making love to his grandmother. He has to tell him what to do. *Keep your arms around her a little longer, stroke her here a little*. I don't know how it's going to work – I just have to trust Jeffrey, that he knows what he's doing.'

'"Stroke her here a little"?' said Brian. 'Maybe I should come around and keep an eye on these rehearsals.'

252

When she had started to quote Jeffrey Pauline had felt a givingway in her womb or the bottom of her stomach, a shock that had travelled oddly upwards and hit her vocal cords. She had to cover up this quaking by growling in a way that was supposed to be an imitation (though Jeffrey never growled or ranted or carried on in any theatrical way at all).

'But there's a point about him being so inno-cent,' she said hurriedly. 'Being not so physical. Being awkward.' And she began to talk about Orphée in the play, not the waiter. Orphée has a problem with love or reality. Orphée will not put up with anything less than perfection. He wants a love that is outside of ordinary life. He wants a perfect Eurydice.

'Eurydice is more realistic. She's carried on with Mathias and with Monsieur Dulac. She's been around her mother and her mother's lover. She knows what people are like. But she loves Orphée. She loves him better in a way than he loves her. She loves him better because she's not such a fool. She loves him like a human person.'

'But she's slept with those other guys,' Brian said.

'Well with Mr Dulac she had to, she couldn't get out of it. She didn't want to, but probably after a while she enjoyed it, because after a certain point she couldn't help enjoying it.'

So Orphée is at fault, Pauline said decidedly. He looks at Eurydice on purpose, to kill her and get rid of her because she is not perfect. Because of him she has to die a second time.

Brian, on his back and with his eyes wide open (she knew that because of the tone of his voice) said, 'But doesn't he die too?'

'Yes. He chooses to.'

'So then they're together?'

'Yes. Like Romeo and Juliet. *Orphée is with Eurydice at last.* That's what Monsieur Henri says. That's the last line of the play. That's the end.' Pauline rolled over onto her side and touched her cheek to Brian's shoulder – not to start anything but to emphasize what she said next. 'It's a beautiful play in one way, but in another it's so silly. And it isn't really like *Romeo and Juliet* because it isn't bad luck or circumstances. It's on purpose. So they don't have to go on with life and get married and have kids and buy an old house and fix it up and—'

'And have affairs,' said Brian. 'After all, they're French.'

Then he said, 'Be like my parents.'

Pauline laughed. 'Do they have affairs? I can imagine.'

'Oh sure,' said Brian. 'I meant their life.

'Logically I can see killing yourself so you won't turn into your parents,' Brian said. 'I just don't believe anybody would do it.'

'Everybody has choices,' Pauline said dreamily. 'Her mother and his father are both despicable in a way, but Orphée and Eurydice don't have to be like them. They're not corrupt. Just because she's slept with those men doesn't mean she's corrupt. She wasn't in love then. She hadn't met Orphée. There's one speech where he tells her that everything she's done is sticking to her, and it's disgusting. Lies she's told him. The other men. It's all sticking to her forever. And then of course Monsieur Henri plays up to that. He tells Orphée that he'll be just as bad and that one day he'll walk down the street with Eurydice and he'll look like a man with a dog he's trying to lose.'

To her surprise, Brian laughed.

'No,' she said. 'That's what's stupid. It's not inevitable. It's not inevitable at all.'

They went on speculating, and comfortably arguing, in a way that was not usual, but not altogether unfamiliar to them. They had done this before, at long intervals in their married life – talked half the night about God or fear of death or how children should be educated or whether money was important. At last they admitted to being too tired to make sense any longer, and arranged themselves in a comradely position and went to sleep.

Finally a rainy day. Brian and his parents were driving into Campbell River to get groceries, and gin, and to take Brian's father's car to a garage, to see about a problem that had developed on the drive up from Nanaimo. This was a very slight problem, but there was the matter of the new-car warranty's being in effect at present, so Brian's father wanted to get it seen to as soon as possible. Brian had to go along, with his car, just in case his father's car had to be left in the garage. Pauline said that she had to stay home because of Mara's nap.

She persuaded Caitlin to lie down too – allowing her to take her music box to bed with her if she played it very softly. Then Pauline spread the script on the kitchen table and drank coffee and went over the scene in which Orphée says that it's intolerable, at last, to stay in two skins, two envelopes with their own blood and oxygen sealed up in their solitude, and Eurydice tells him to be quiet.

'Don't talk. Don't think. Just let your hand wander, let it be happy on its own.'

Your hand is my happiness, says Eurydice. Accept that. Accept your happiness.

Of course he says he cannot.

Caitlin called out frequently to ask what time it was. She turned up the sound of the music box. Pauline hurried to the bedroom door and hissed at her to turn it down, not to wake Mara.

'If you play it like that again I'll take it away from you. Okay?'

But Mara was already rustling around in her crib, and in the next few minutes there were sounds of soft, encouraging conversation from Caitlin, designed to get her sister wide awake. Also of the music being quickly turned up and then down. Then of Mara rattling the crib railing, pulling herself up, throwing her bottle out onto the floor, and starting the bird cries that would grow more and more desolate until they brought her mother.

'I didn't wake her,' Caitlin said. 'She was awake all by herself. It's not raining anymore. Can we go down to the beach?'

She was right. It wasn't raining. Pauline changed Mara, told Caitlin to get her bathing suit on and find her sand pail. She got into her own bathing suit and put her shorts over it, in case the rest of the family arrived home while she was down there. ('Dad doesn't like the way some women just go right out of their cottages in their bathing suits,' Brian's mother had said to her. 'I guess he and I just grew up in other times.') She picked up the script to take it along, then laid it down. She was afraid that she would get too absorbed in it and take her eyes off the children for a moment too long.

The thoughts that came to her, of Jeffrey, were not really thoughts at all – they were more like alterations in her body. This could happen when she was sitting on the beach (trying to stay in the half shade of a bush and so preserve her pallor, as Jeffrey had ordered) or when she was wringing out diapers or when she and Brian were visiting his parents. In the middle of Monopoly games, Scrabble games, card games. She went right on talking, listening, working, keeping track of the children, while some memory of her secret life disturbed her like a radiant explosion. Then a warm weight settled, reassurance filling up all her hollows. But it didn't last, this comfort leaked away, and she was like a miser whose windfall has vanished and who is convinced such luck can never strike again. Longing buckled her up and drove her to the discipline of counting days. Sometimes she even cut the days into fractions to figure out more exactly how much time had gone.

She thought of going into Campbell River, making some excuse, so that she could get to a phone booth and call him. The cottages had no phones – the only public phone was in the hall of the lodge. But she did not have the number of the hotel where Jeffrey worked. And besides that, she could never get away to Campbell River in the evening. She was afraid that if she called him at home in the daytime his mother the French teacher might answer. He said his mother hardly ever left the house in the summer. Just once, she had taken the ferry to Vancouver for the day. Jeffrey had phoned Pauline to ask her to come over. Brian was teaching, and Caitlin was at her play group.

Pauline said, 'I can't. I have Mara.'

Jeffrey said, 'Who? Oh. Sorry.' Then 'Couldn't you bring her along?'

She said no.

'Why not? Couldn't you bring some things for her to play with?'

No, said Pauline. 'I couldn't,' she said. 'I just couldn't.' It seemed too dangerous to her, to trundle her baby along on such a guilty expedition. To a house where cleaning fluids would not be bestowed on high shelves, and all pills and cough syrups and cigarettes and buttons put safely out of reach. And even if she escaped poisoning or choking, Mara might be storing up time bombs – memories of a strange house where she was strangely disregarded, of a closed door, noises on the other side of it.

'I just wanted you,' Jeffrey said. 'I just wanted you in my bed.'

She said again, weakly, 'No.'

Those words of his kept coming back to her. *I wanted you in my bed.* A half-joking urgency in his voice but also a determination, a practicality, as if 'in my bed' meant something more, the bed he spoke of taking on larger, less material dimensions.

Had she made a great mistake with that refusal? With that reminder of how fenced in she was, in what anybody would call her real life?

The beach was nearly empty – people had got used to its being a rainy day. The sand was too heavy for Caitlin to make a castle or dig an irrigation system – projects she would only undertake with her father, anyway, because she sensed that his interest in them was wholehearted, and Pauline's was not. She wandered a bit forlornly at the edge of the water. She probably missed the presence of other children, the nameless instant friends and occasional stone-throwing water-kicking enemies, the shrieking and splashing and falling about. A boy a little bigger than she was and apparently all by himself stood knee-deep in the water farther down the beach. If these two could get together it might be all right; the whole beach experience might be retrieved. Pauline couldn't tell whether Caitlin was now making little splashy runs into the water for his benefit or whether he was watching her with interest or scorn.

Mara didn't need company, at least for now. She stumbled towards the water, felt it touch her feet and changed her mind, stopped, looked around, and spotted Pauline. 'Paw. Paw,' she said, in happy recognition. 'Paw' was what she said for 'Pauline,' instead of 'Mother' or 'Mommy.' Looking around overbalanced her – she sat down half on the sand and half in the water, made a squawk of surprise that turned to an announcement, then by some determined ungraceful maneuvers that involved putting her weight on her hands, she rose to her feet, wavering and triumphant. She had been walking for half a year, but getting around on the sand was still a challenge. Now she came back towards Pauline, making some reasonable, casual remarks in her own language.

'Sand,' said Pauline, holding up a clot of it. 'Look. Mara. Sand.'

Mara corrected her, calling it something else – it sounded like 'whap.' Her thick diaper under her plastic pants and her terry-cloth playsuit gave her a fat bottom, and that, along with her plump cheeks and shoulders and her sidelong important expression, made her look like a roguish matron.

Pauline became aware of someone calling her

name. It had been called two or three times, but because the voice was unfamiliar she had not recognized it. She stood up and waved. It was the woman who worked in the store at the lodge. She was leaning over the balcony and calling, 'Mrs Keating. Mrs Keating? Telephone, Mrs Keating.'

Pauline hoisted Mara onto her hip and summoned Caitlin. She and the little boy were aware of each other now – they were both picking up stones from the bottom and flinging them out into the water. At first she didn't hear Pauline, or pretended not to.

'Store,' called Pauline. 'Caitlin. Store.' When she was sure Caitlin would follow – it was the word 'store' that had done it, the reminder of the tiny store in the lodge where you could buy ice cream and candy and cigarettes and mixer – she began the trek across the sand and up the flight of wooden steps above the sand and the salal bushes. Halfway up she stopped, said, 'Mara, you weigh a ton,' and shifted the baby to her other hip. Caitlin banged a stick against the railing.

'Can I have a Fudgsicle? Mother? Can I?'

'We'll see.'

'Can I please have a Fudgsicle?'

'Wait.'

The public phone was beside a bulletin board on the other side of the main hall and across from the door to the dining room. A bingo game had been set up in there, because of the rain.

'Hope he's still hanging on,' the woman who

worked in the store called out. She was unseen now behind her counter.

Pauline, still holding Mara, picked up the dangling receiver and said breathlessly, 'Hello?' She was expecting to hear Brian telling her about some delay in Campbell River or asking her what it was she had wanted him to get at the drugstore. It was just the one thing – calamine lotion – so he had not written it down.

'Pauline,' said Jeffrey. 'It's me.'

Mara was bumping and scrambling against Pauline's side, anxious to get down. Caitlin came along the hall and went into the store, leaving wet sandy footprints. Pauline said, 'Just a minute, just a minute.' She let Mara slide down and hurried to close the door that led to the steps. She did not remember telling Jeffrey the name of this place, though she had told him roughly where it was. She heard the woman in the store speaking to Caitlin in a sharper voice than she would use to children whose parents were beside them.

'Did you forget to put your feet under the tap?'

'I'm here,' said Jeffrey. 'I didn't get along well without you. I didn't get along at all.'

Mara made for the dining room, as if the male voice calling out 'Under the *N—*' was a direct invitation to her.

'Here. Where?' said Pauline.

She read the signs that were tacked up on the bulletin board beside the phone.

No Person under Fourteen Years of

Age Not Accompanied by Adult Allowed in Boats or Canoes.

Fishing Derby.

Bake and Craft Sale, St Bartholomew's Church.

Your Life Is in Your Hands. Palms and Cards Read. Reasonable and Accurate. Call Claire.

'In a motel. In Campbell River.'

Pauline knew where she was before she opened her eyes. Nothing surprised her. She had slept but not deeply enough to let go of anything.

She had waited for Brian in the parking area of the lodge, with the children, and had asked him for the keys. She had told him in front of his parents that there was something else she needed, from Campbell River. He asked, What was it? And did he have any money?

'Just something,' she said, so he would think that it was tampons or birth control supplies, that she didn't want to mention. 'Sure.'

'Okay but you'll have to put some gas in,' he said.

Later she had to speak to him on the phone. Jeffrey said she had to do it.

'Because he won't take it from me. He'll think I kidnapped you or something. He won't believe it.'

But the strangest thing of all the things that day was that Brian did seem, immediately, to believe

263

it. Standing where she had stood not so long before, in the public hallway of the lodge – the bingo game over now but people going past, she could hear them, people on their way out of the dining room after dinner – he said, 'Oh. Oh. Oh. Okay' in a voice that would have to be quickly controlled, but that seemed to draw on a supply of fatalism or foreknowledge that went far beyond that necessity.

As if he had known all along, all along, what could happen with her.

'Okay,' he said. 'What about the car?'

He said something else, something impossible, and hung up, and she came out of the phone booth beside some gas pumps in Campbell River.

'That was quick,' Jeffrey said. 'Easier than you expected.'

Pauline said, 'I don't know.'

'He may have known it subconsciously. People do know.'

She shook her head, to tell him not to say any more, and he said, 'Sorry.' They walked along the street not touching or talking.

They'd had to go out to find a phone booth because there was no phone in the motel room. Now in the early morning looking around at leisure – the first real leisure or freedom she'd had since she came into that room – Pauline saw that there wasn't much of anything in it. Just a junk dresser, the bed without a headboard, an armless upholstered chair, on the window a venetian blind with a broken slat and curtain of orange plastic that was supposed to look like net and that didn't have to be hemmed, just sliced off at the bottom. There was a noisy air conditioner – Jeffrey had turned it off in the night and left the door open on the chain, since the window was sealed. The door was shut now. He must have got up in the night and shut it.

This was all she had. Her connection with the cottage where Brian lay asleep or not asleep was broken, also her connection with the house that had been an expression of her life with Brian, of the way they wanted to live. She had no furniture anymore. She had cut herself off from all the large solid acquisitions like the washer and dryer and the oak table and the refinished wardrobe and the chandelier that was a copy of the one in a painting by Vermeer. And just as much from those things that were particularly hers – the pressed-glass tumblers that she had been collecting and the prayer rug which was of course not authentic, but beautiful. Especially from those things. Even her books, she might have lost. Even her clothes. The skirt and blouse and sandals she had put on for the trip to Campbell River might well be all she had now to her name. She would never go back to lay claim to anything. If Brian got in touch with her to ask what was to be done with things, she would tell him to do what he liked – throw everything into garbage bags and take it to the dump, if that was what he liked. (In fact she knew that he would probably pack up a trunk, which he did, sending on, scrupulously, not only her winter coat and boots but things like the waist cincher she had worn at her wedding and never since, with the prayer rug draped over the top of everything like a final statement of his generosity, either natural or calculated.)

She believed that she would never again care about what sort of rooms she lived in or what sort of clothes she put on. She would not be looking for that sort of help to give anybody an idea of who she was, what she was like. Not even to give herself an idea. What she had done would be enough, it would be the whole thing.

What she was doing would be what she had heard about and read about. It was what Anna Karenina had done and what Madame Bovary had wanted to do. It was what a teacher at Brian's school had done, with the school secretary. He had run off with her. That was what it was called. Running off with. Taking off with. It was spoken of disparagingly, humorously, enviously. It was adultery taken one step further. The people who did it had almost certainly been having an affair already, committing adultery for quite some time before they became desperate or courageous enough to take this step. Once in a long while a couple might claim their love was unconsummated and technically pure, but these people would be thought of – if anybody believed them – as being not only very serious and high-minded but almost devastatingly foolhardy, almost in a class with those who took a chance and gave up everything to go and work in some poor and dangerous country.

The others, the adulterers, were seen as irresponsible, immature, selfish, or even cruel. Also lucky. They were lucky because the sex they had been having in parked cars or the long grass or in each other's sullied marriage beds or most likely in motels like this one must surely have been splendid. Otherwise they would never have got such a yearning for each other's company at all costs or such a faith that their shared future would be altogether better and different in kind from what they had in the past.

Different in kind. That was what Pauline must believe now – that there was this major difference in lives or in marriages or unions between people. That some of them had a necessity, a fatefulness, about them that others did not have. Of course she would have said the same thing a year ago. People did say that, they seemed to believe that, and to believe that their own cases were all of the first, the special kind, even when anybody could see that they were not and that these people did not know what they were talking about. Pauline would not have known what she was talking about.

It was too warm in the room. Jeffrey's body was too warm. Conviction and contentiousness seemed to radiate from it, even in sleep. His torso was thicker than Brian's; he was pudgier around the waist. More flesh on the bones, yet not so slack to the touch. Not so good-looking in general – she was sure most people would say that. And not so fastidious. Brian in bed smelled of nothing. Jeffrey's skin, every time she'd been with him, had had a baked-in, slightly oily or nutty smell. He didn't wash last night – but then, neither did she. There wasn't time. Did he even have a toothbrush with him? She didn't. But she had not known she was staying.

When she met Jeffrey here it was still in the back of her mind that she had to concoct some colossal lie to serve her when she got home. And she – they – had to hurry. When Jeffrey said to her that he had decided that they must stay together, that she would come with him to Washington State, that they would have to drop the play because things would be too difficult for them in Victoria, she had looked at him just in the blank way you'd look at somebody the moment that an earthquake started. She was ready to tell him all the reasons why this was not possible, she still thought she was going to tell him that, but her life was coming adrift in that moment. To go back would be like tying a sack over her head.

All she said was 'Are you sure?'

He said, 'Sure.' He said sincerely, 'I'll never leave you.'

That did not seem the sort of thing that he would say. Then she realized he was quoting – maybe ironically – from the play. It was what Orphée says to Eurydice within a few moments of their first meeting in the station buffet.

So her life was falling forwards; she was becoming one of those people who ran away. A woman who shockingly and incomprehensibly gave everything up. For love, observers would say wryly. Meaning, for sex. None of this would happen if it wasn't for sex.

And yet what's the great difference there? It's not such a variable procedure, in spite of what you're told. Skins, motions, contact, results. Pauline isn't a woman from whom it's difficult to get results. Brian got them. Probably anybody would, who wasn't wildly inept or morally disgusting.

But nothing's the same, really. With Brian – especially with Brian, to whom she has dedicated a selfish sort of goodwill, with whom she's lived in married complicity – there can never be this stripping away, the inevitable flight, the feelings she doesn't have to strive for but only to give in to like breathing or dying. That she believes can only come when the skin is on Jeffrey, the motions made by Jeffrey, and the weight that bears down on her has Jeffrey's heart in it, also his habits, thoughts, peculiarities, his ambition and loneliness (that for all she knows may have mostly to do with his youth).

For all she knows. There's a lot she doesn't know. She hardly knows anything about what he likes to eat or what music he likes to listen to or what role his mother plays in his life (no doubt a mysterious but important one, like the role of Brian's parents). One thing she's pretty sure of –

whatever preferences or prohibitions he has will be definite.

She slides out from under Jeffrey's hand and from under the top sheet which has a harsh smell of bleach, she slips down to the floor where the bedspread is lying and wraps herself quickly in that rag of greenish-yellow chenille. She doesn't want him to open his eyes and see her from behind and note the droop of her buttocks. He's seen her naked before, but generally in a more forgiving moment.

She rinses her mouth and washes herself, using the bar of soap that is about the size of two thin squares of chocolate and firm as stone. She's hard-used between the legs, swollen and stinking. Urinating takes an effort, and it seems she's constipated. Last night when they went out and got hamburgers she found she could not eat. Presumably she'll learn to do all these things again, they'll resume their natural importance in her life. At the moment it's as if she can't quite spare the attention.

She has some money in her purse. She has to go out and buy a toothbrush, toothpaste, deodorant, shampoo. Also vaginal jelly. Last night they used condoms the first two times but nothing the third time.

She didn't bring her watch and Jeffrey doesn't wear one. There's no clock in the room, of course. She thinks it's early – there's still an early look to the light in spite of the heat. The stores probably won't be open, but there'll be someplace where she can get coffee.

Jeffrey has turned onto his other side. She must have wakened him, just for a moment.

They'll have a bedroom. A kitchen, an address. He'll go to work. She'll go to the Laundromat. Maybe she'll go to work too. Selling things, waiting on tables, tutoring students. She knows French and Latin – do they teach French and Latin in American high schools? Can you get a job if you're not an American? Jeffrey isn't.

She leaves him the key. She'll have to wake him to get back in. There's nothing to write a note with, or on.

It is early. The motel is on the highway at the north end of town, beside the bridge. There's no traffic yet. She scuffs along under the cottonwood trees for quite a while before a vehicle of any kind rumbles over the bridge – though the traffic on it shook their bed regularly late into the night.

Something is coming now. A truck. But not just a truck – there's a large bleak fact coming at her. And it has not arrived out of nowhere – it's been waiting, cruelly nudging at her ever since she woke up, or even all night.

Caitlin and Mara.

Last night on the phone, after speaking in such a flat and controlled and almost agreeable voice – as if he prided himself on not being shocked, not objecting or pleading – Brian cracked open. He said with contempt and fury and no concern for

271

whoever might hear him, 'Well then – what about the kids?'

The receiver began to shake against Pauline's ear.

She said, 'We'll talk—' but he did not seem to hear her.

'The children,' he said, in this same shivering and vindictive voice. Changing the word 'kids' to 'children' was like slamming a board down on her – a heavy, formal, righteous threat.

'The children stay,' Brian said. 'Pauline. Did you hear me?'

'No,' said Pauline. 'Yes. I heard you but—'

'All right. You heard me. Remember. The children stay.'

It was all he could do. To make her see what she was doing, what she was ending, and to punish her if she did so. Nobody would blame him. There might be finagling, there might be bargaining, there would certainly be humbling of herself, but there it was like a round cold stone in her gullet, like a cannonball. And it would remain there unless she changed her mind entirely. The children stay.

Their car – hers and Brian's – was still sitting in the motel parking lot. Brian would have to ask his father or his mother to drive him up here today to get it. She had the keys in her purse. There were spare keys – he would surely bring them. She unlocked the car door and threw her keys on the seat and locked the door on the inside and shut it.

Now she couldn't go back. She couldn't get into the car and drive back and say that she'd been insane. If she did that he would forgive her, but he'd never get over it and neither would she. They'd go on, though, as people did.

She walked out of the parking lot, she walked along the sidewalk, into town.

The weight of Mara on her hip, yesterday. The sight of Caitlin's footprints on the floor.

Paw. Paw.

She doesn't need the keys to get back to them, she doesn't need the car. She could beg a ride on the highway. Give in, give in, get back to them any way at all, how can she not do that?

A sack over her head.

A fluid choice, the choice of fantasy, is poured out on the ground and instantly hardens; it has taken its undeniable shape.

This is acute pain. It will become chronic. Chronic means that it will be permanent but perhaps not constant. It may also mean that you won't die of it. You won't get free of it, but you won't die of it. You won't feel it every minute, but you won't spend many days without it. And you'll learn some tricks to dull it or banish it, trying not to end up destroying what you incurred this pain to get. It isn't his fault. He's still an innocent or a savage, who doesn't know there's a pain so durable in the world. Say to yourself, You lose them anyway. They grow up. For a mother there's always waiting this private slightly ridiculous desolation. They'll forget this time, in one way or another they'll disown you. Or hang around till you don't know what to do about them, the way Brian has.

And still, what pain. To carry along and get used to until it's only the past she's grieving for and not any possible present.

Her children have grown up. They don't hate her. For going away or staying away. They don't forgive her, either. Perhaps they wouldn't have forgiven her anyway, but it would have been for something different.

Caitlin remembers a little about the summer at the lodge, Mara nothing. One day Caitlin mentions it to Pauline, calling it 'that place Grandma and Grandpa stayed at.'

'The place we were at when you went away,' she says. 'Only we didn't know till later you went away with Orphée.'

Pauline says, 'It wasn't Orphée.'

'It wasn't Orphée? Dad used to say it was. He'd say, "And then your mother ran away with Orphée."'

'Then he was joking,' says Pauline.

'I always thought it was Orphée. It was somebody else then.'

'It was somebody else connected with the play. That I lived with for a while.'

'Not Orphée.'

'No. Never him.'

RICH AS STINK

While the plane was pulling up to the gate on a summer evening in 1974, Karin reached down and got some things out of her backpack. A black beret which she pulled on so it slanted over one eye, a red lipstick which she was able to apply to her mouth by using the window as a mirror – it was dark in Toronto – and a long black cigarette holder which she held ready to clamp between her teeth at the right moment. The beret and the cigarette holder had been filched from the Irma la Douce outfit her stepmother had worn to a costume party, and the lipstick was something she had bought for herself.

She knew that she could hardly manage to look like a grown-up tart. But she would not look like the ten-year-old who had got on the plane at the end of last summer, either.

Nobody in the crowd looked at her twice, even when she stuck the cigarette holder in her mouth and put on a sullen leer. Everybody was too anxious, distraught, delighted, or bewildered. Lots of them seemed to be in costume themselves. Black men swished along in bright robes and little embroidered hats, and old women sat bowed on suitcases with shawls over their heads. Hippies were all in beads and tatters, and she found herself hedged in for a few moments by a group of somber-looking men who wore black hats and had little ringlets dangling down their cheeks.

People waiting to meet passengers were not supposed to get in here, but they did anyway, slipping through the automatic doors. In the crowd on the other side of the baggage carousel Karin spotted her mother, Rosemary, who had not yet seen her. Rosemary was wearing a long dark-blue dress with gold and orange moons on it and had her hair freshly dyed, very black, piled up in a toppling bird's nest on top of her head. She looked older than she did in Karin's memory, and a little forlorn. Karin's glance swept past her – looking for Derek. Derek was easy to find in a crowd because of his height and his shining forehead and his pale, wavy, shoulder-length hair. Also because of his bright steady eyes and satirical mouth, and his ability to stay still. Not like Rosemary, who was twitching and stretching and staring about now in a dazed, discouraged way.

Derek wasn't standing behind Rosemary, and he wasn't anywhere nearby. Unless he had gone to the men's room, he wasn't there.

Karin removed the cigarette holder and pushed the beret back on her head. If Derek wasn't there, the joke lost its point. Playing a joke like that on Rosemary would just turn into confusion – when

Rosemary looked confused enough, bereft enough, already.

'You're wearing *lip*-stick,' Rosemary said, wet eyed and dazzled. She wrapped Karin in her winglike sleeves and her smell of cocoa butter. 'Don't tell me your father lets you wear lipstick.'

'I was going to fool you,' Karin said. 'Where's Derek?'

'Not here,' said Rosemary.

Karin spotted her suitcase on the carousel; she ducked and eeled her way between bodies and dragged it off. Rosemary tried to help her carry it, but Karin said, 'Okay. Okay.' They pushed through to the exit doors and past all the waiting people who had not had the nerve or the patience to push inside. They did not speak until they were out in the hot night air and moving towards the parking lot. Then Karin said, 'What's the matter – you two having one of your squalls?'

'Squall' was the name Rosemary and Derek themselves used to describe their fights, which were blamed on the difficulties of working together on Derek's book.

Rosemary said with dire serenity, 'We aren't seeing each other anymore. We aren't working together.'

'Really?' said Karin. 'You mean you've broken up?'

'If people like us can break up,' Rosemary said.

* * *

The lights of cars were still pouring down every road into the city, and at the same time pouring out of it, around the big curving overpasses and in streams underneath them. There was no air-conditioning in Rosemary's car – not because she couldn't afford it, but because she did not believe in it – and so the windows had to be open, letting the traffic noise rush in like a river on the gassy air. Rosemary hated driving around Toronto. When she came to the city once a week to see the publisher she worked for, she made the trip on a bus, and at other times she usually had Derek drive her. Karin kept quiet while they got off the airport highway and drove east on 401, and turned, after eighty or so miles of her mother's jumpy concentration, onto the secondary highway that would take them nearly to where Rosemary lived.

'So has Derek gone away?' Karin said, then 'Has he gone off on a trip?'

'Not that I know of,' Rosemary said. 'But then I wouldn't know.'

'How about Ann? Is she still there?'

'Probably,' said Rosemary. 'She never goes any-where.'

'Did he take his stuff and all?'

Derek had brought more things to Rosemary's trailer than were strictly necessary for the work on his bundles of manuscripts. Books, of course – not just the books that had to be referred to but books and magazines to read during breaks in the work, when he might lie down on Rosemary's

278

bed. Records to listen to. Clothes, boots to wear if he decided to hike back into the bush, pills for stomach troubles or headaches, even the tools and lumber with which he built a gazebo. His shaving things were in the bathroom, also a toothbrush and his special toothpaste for sensitive gums. His coffee grinder was on the kitchen counter. (A newer, fancier one that Ann had bought sat on the counter of the kitchen in what was still his house.)

'All cleared out,' said Rosemary. She pulled into the lot of a doughnut shop that was still open, on the edge of the first town on this highway.

'Coffee to keep me alive,' she said.

Usually when they stopped at this place Karin stayed with Derek in the car. He wouldn't drink such coffee. 'Your mother is addicted to places like this because of her awful childhood,' he said. He didn't mean that Rosemary had been taken to places like this but that she had been forbidden to go into them, just as she had been forbidden all fried or sugary food, and kept to a diet of vegetables and slimy porridge. Not because her parents were poor – they were rich – but because they were food fanatics before their time. Derek had known Rosemary only a short while – compared, say, to the years that Karin's father, Ted, had known her – but he spoke more readily than Ted ever would about her early life and divulged details about it, such as the ritual of weekly enemas, that Rosemary's own stories left out.

Never, never, in her school-year life, her life with Ted and Grace, would Karin find herself in a place with this horrid smell of scorched sugar and grease and cigarette smoke and rank coffee. But Rosemary's eyes ranged with pleasure over the selection of doughnuts with cream (spelled 'crème') and jelly filling, with butterscotch and chocolate icing, the crullers and éclairs, and dutchies and filled croissants and monster cookies. She saw no reason for rejecting any of this, except perhaps the fear of getting fat, and she could never believe that such food was not just what everybody was craving.

At the counter – where you were not supposed to sit for more than twenty minutes, according to the sign – were two very fat women with massive curly hairdos, and between them a thin boyish-looking but wrinkled man, who was talking fast and seemed to be telling them jokes. While the women were shaking their heads and laughing, and Rosemary was picking out her almond croissant, he gave Karin a wink that was lewd and conspiratorial. It made her realize that she was still wearing lipstick. 'Can't resist, eh?' he said to Rosemary, and she laughed, taking this for country friendliness.

'Never can,' she said. 'You're sure?' she said to Karin. 'Not a thing?'

'Little girl watching her figure?' that wrinkled man said.

There was hardly any traffic north of this town. The air had turned cooler and smelled swampy.

The frogs were making such a loud noise in some places that you could hear them over the noise of the car. This two-lane highway wound past stands of black evergreens and the softer darkness of small juniper-spotted fields, farms going back to the bush. Then on a curve the headlights lit up the first jumble of rocks, some of them glittery pink and gray and some a dried-blood red. Soon this was happening more and more often, and in places the rocks, instead of being jumbled and jammed together, were laid as if by hand in thick or thin layers, and these were gray or greenish white. Limestone, Karin remembered. Limestone bedrock, alternating here with the rocks of the Precambrian Shield. Derek had taught her about that. Derek said that he wished he had been a geologist because he loved rocks. But he wouldn't have loved making money for mining companies. And history drew him too – it was an odd combination. History for the indoor man, geology for the outdoor man, he said, with a solemnity that told her he was making a joke of himself.

What Karin wanted to get rid of now – she wished it would just flow out of the car windows on the rush of midnight air – was her feeling of squeamishness and superiority. About the almond croissant, the bad coffee that Rosemary was sipping almost surreptitiously, and the man at the counter, and even about Rosemary's youthful hippielike dress and the messy heap of hair. Also she'd like to get rid of her own missing of Derek, the sense that there was space to fill, and a thinning out of possibility. She said out loud, 'I'm glad, I'm glad he's gone.'

Rosemary said, 'Are you really?'

'You'll be happier,' Karin said.

'Yes,' said Rosemary. 'I'm getting my self-respect back. You know you don't realize how much you've lost of your self-respect and how much you miss it till you start getting it back. I want you and me to have a really good summer. We could go on little trips, even. I don't mind driving where it isn't hairy. We could go hiking back in the bush where Derek took you. I'd like to do that.'

Karin said, 'Yeah,' though she wasn't at all sure that without Derek they wouldn't get lost. Her thoughts were not really on hiking but on a scene last summer. Rosemary on the bed, rolled up in a quilt, weeping, stuffing handfuls of the quilt and the pillow into her mouth, biting on them in a rage of grief, and Derek sitting at the table where they worked, reading a page of the manuscript. 'Can you do anything to quiet your mother?' he said.

Karin said, 'She wants you.'

'I can't cope with her when she's like this,' said Derek. He laid down the page he'd finished and picked up another. Between pages he looked up at Karin, with a long-suffering grimace. He looked worn out, old and haggard. He said, 'I can't stand it. I'm sorry.'

So Karin went into the bedroom and stroked

Rosemary's back, and Rosemary too said that she was sorry.

'What's Derek doing?' she said.

'Sitting in the kitchen,' said Karin. She didn't like to say 'reading.'

'What did he say?'

'He said I should go in and talk to you.'

'Oh, Karin. I'm so ashamed.'

What had happened to start such a row? Calmed down and cleaned up, Rosemary always said it was the work, disagreements they had about the work. 'Then why don't you quit working on his book?' Karin said. 'You've got all your other stuff to do.' Rosemary edited manuscripts – that was how she had met Derek. Not because he had submitted his book to the publisher she worked for – he hadn't done so yet – but because she knew a friend of his and the friend had said, 'I know a woman who could be a help to you.' And in a little while Rosemary had moved to the country and into the trailer that was not far from his house, so that she could be closer to him to do this work. At first she kept her apartment in Toronto, but then she let it go, because she was spending more and more time in the trailer. She still did other work but not so much of it, and she managed her one workday a week in Toronto by leaving at six o'clock in the morning and getting home after eleven at night.

'What's this book about?' Ted had said to Karin.

Karin said, 'It's sort of about the explorer La Salle and the Indians.'

'Is this guy a historian? Does he teach at a university?'

Karin didn't know. Derek had done a lot of things – he had worked as a photographer; he had worked in a mine and as a surveyor; but as far as his teaching went she thought it had been in a high school. Ann spoke of his work as being 'outside the system.'

Ted himself taught at a university. He was an economist.

She didn't, of course, tell Ted or Grace about the grief brought on, apparently, by disagreements about the book. Rosemary blamed herself. It's the tension, she said. Sometimes she said it was the menopause. Karin had heard her say to Derek, 'Forgive me,' and Derek had said, 'Nothing to forgive,' in a voice of cool satisfaction.

At this Rosemary had left the room. They did not hear her start to weep again, but they kept waiting for it. Derek looked hard into Karin's eyes – he made a comical face of distress and bewilderment.

So what did I do this time?

'She's very sensitive,' said Karin. Her voice was full of shame. Was this because of Rosemary's behavior? Or because Derek seemed to be including her – Karin – in some feeling of satisfaction, of despising, that went far beyond this moment. And because she could not help but feel honored.

Sometimes she just got out. She went up the road to see Ann, and Ann always seemed glad that she had come. She never asked Karin why, but if Karin said, 'They're having a stupid fight,' or – later on, when they'd come up with the special word – 'They're having one of their squalls,' she never seemed surprised or displeased. 'Derek is very exacting,' she might say, or 'Well, I expect they'll work it out.' But if Karin tried to go further, saying 'Rosemary's crying,' Ann would say, 'There's some things I just think it's better not to talk about, don't you?'

But there were other things she would listen to, though sometimes with a smile of reservation. Ann was a sweet-looking, rounded woman with light-gray hair cut in bangs and falling loose over her shoulders. When she talked she often blinked, and didn't quite meet your eyes (Rosemary said that this was nerves). Also her lips – Ann's lips – were so thin they almost disappeared when she smiled, always with her mouth closed, in a way of holding something back.

'You know how Rosemary met Ted?' said Karin. 'It was at the bus stop in the rain and she was putting on lipstick.' Then she had to backtrack and explain that Rosemary had to put on her lipstick at the bus stop because her parents didn't know she wore it – lipstick being forbidden by their religion, as well as movies, high heels, dancing, sugar, coffee, and alcohol and cigarettes, it goes without saying. Rosemary was in her first year of college and did not want to look like a religious geek. Ted was a teaching assistant.

'But they already knew who each other were,' Karin said, and explained about their living on the same street. Ted in the gatehouse of the biggest of the rich houses, his father being the chauffeur-gardener and his mother the housekeeper, and Rosemary in one of the more ordinary-rich houses across the street (though the life her parents led in it was not ordinary-rich at all, since they played no games and never went to parties or took a trip and for some reason used an icebox instead of a refrigerator, until the ice company went out of business).

Ted had a car he had bought for a hundred dollars, and he felt sorry for Rosemary and picked her up in the rain.

When Karin was telling this story she remembered her parents telling it, laughing and interrupting each other in their practiced way. Ted always mentioned the price of the car and its make and year (Studebaker, 1947) and Rosemary mentioned the fact that the passenger door would not open and Ted had to get out and let her climb in over the driver's seat. And he would tell how soon he took her to her first movie – in the afternoon – and the name of the movie was *Some Like It Hot*, and he came out in broad daylight with lipstick all over his face, because whatever it was that other girls did with lipstick, blot it or powder it or whatever, Rosemary had not learned to do. 'She was very enthusiastic,' he always said.

Then they got married. They went to a minister's

house; the minister's son was a friend of Ted's. Their parents didn't know what they were going to do. And right after the ceremony Rosemary started her period and the first thing Ted had to do as a married man was go out and buy a box of Kotex.

'Does your mother know you tell me these things, Karin?'

'She wouldn't mind. And then *her* mother had to go to bed when she found out, she felt so awful that they'd got married. If her parents had known she was going to marry an infidel they would have shut her up in this church school in Toronto.'

'Infidel?' said Ann. 'Really? What a pity.'

Maybe she meant that it was a pity, after all this trouble, that the marriage hadn't lasted.

Karin scrunched down in the seat. Her head bumped Rosemary's shoulder.

'Does this bother you?' she said.

'No,' said Rosemary.

Karin said, 'I'm not really going to sleep. I want to be awake when we turn up into the valley.'

Rosemary started to sing.

'Wake up, wake up, Darlin' Cory—'

She sang in a slow, deep voice, imitating Pete Seeger on the record, and the next thing Karin knew the car had stopped; they had climbed the short, rutted bit of road to the trailer and were sitting under the trees outside it. The light was on over the door. No Derek inside, though. None of Derek's stuff. Karin didn't want to move. She squirmed and protested in delicious crankiness, as she could not have done if anybody except Rosemary had been there.

'Out, out,' Rosemary said. 'You'll be in bed in a minute, come on,' she said, tugging and laughing. 'You think I can carry you?' When she had pulled Karin out, and got her stumbling towards the door, she said, 'Look at the stars. Look at the stars. They're wonderful.' Karin kept her head down, grumbling.

'Bed, bed,' said Rosemary. They were inside. A faint smell of Derek – marijuana, coffee beans, lumber. And the smell of the closed-up trailer, its carpets and cooking. Karin flopped fully dressed on her narrow bed, and Rosemary flung her last-year's pajamas at her. 'Get undressed or you'll feel awful when you wake up,' she said. 'We'll get your suitcase in the morning.'

Karin made what seemed to her the greatest effort that could be required in her life, heaved herself to a sitting position, and dragged off her clothes, then pulled on her pajamas. Rosemary was going around opening windows. The last thing Karin heard her say was 'That lipstick – what was the idea of that lipstick?' and the last thing she felt was a washcloth's motherly, ungentle attack on her face. She spat its taste out, revelling in this childishness and in the cool field of the bed beneath her, and her greed for sleep.

★   ★   ★

That was on Saturday night. Saturday night and early Sunday morning. On Monday morning Karin said, 'Okay if I go up the road and visit Ann?' and Rosemary said, 'Sure, go ahead.'

They had slept late on Sunday and had not left the trailer all day. Rosemary was dismayed that it was raining. 'The stars were out last night, the stars were out when we got home,' she said. 'Raining on the first day of your summer.' Karin had to tell her that it was okay, she felt so lazy she didn't want to go out anyway. Rosemary made her café au lait and cut up a melon, which wasn't quite ripe (Ann would have noticed, but Rosemary didn't). Then at four o'clock in the afternoon they made a big meal of bacon and waffles and strawberries and fake whipped cream. The sun came out around six, but they were still in their pajamas; the day was destroyed. 'At least we didn't watch television,' Rosemary said. 'We've got that to congratulate ourselves on.'

'Up till now,' said Karin, and switched it on.

They were sitting amid piles of old magazines that Rosemary had hauled out of the cupboard. These had been in the trailer when she moved in, and she said she was finally going to throw them out – after she had sorted through them to see if there was anything worth keeping. Not much sorting got done because she kept finding things to read aloud. Karin was bored at first but allowed herself to be drawn into this old time, with its quaint advertisements and unbecoming hairstyles.

She noticed the blanket folded and placed on top of the telephone. She said, 'Don't you know how to turn the phone off?'

Rosemary said, 'I don't really want it off. I want to hear it ring and not answer it. To be able to ignore it. I don't want it too loud, is all.'

But it didn't ring, all day.

Monday morning the blanket was still over the phone and the magazines were back in the closet, because Rosemary couldn't decide to throw them out after all. The sky was cloudy, but it wasn't raining. They got up very late again because they had watched a movie till two in the morning.

Rosemary spread some typed pages out over the kitchen table. Not Derek's manuscript – that big stack was gone. 'Was Derek's book really interesting?' Karin said.

She had never thought to talk to Rosemary about it before. The manuscript had been just like a big tangled roll of barbed wire that sat all the time on the table, with Derek and Rosemary trying to untangle it.

'Well, he kept changing it,' Rosemary said. 'It was interesting but it was confused. First La Salle was all that interested him and then he got onto Pontiac and he wanted to cover too much and he was never satisfied.'

'So you're glad that you're rid of it,' said Karin.

'Enormously glad. It was just unending complications.'

'But don't you miss Derek?'

'The friendship is played out,' said Rosemary in a preoccupied way, bending over a sheet of paper and making a mark on it.

'What about Ann?'

'That friendship, I guess it's played out too. In fact I've been thinking.' She put her pen down. 'I've been thinking of getting out of here. But I thought I'd wait for you. I didn't want you to come back and find everything dislocated. But the reason for being here was Derek's book. Well, it was Derek. You know that.'

Karin said, 'Derek and Ann.'

'Derek and Ann. Yes. And now that reason is gone.'

That was when Karin said, 'Okay if I go up the road and visit Ann?' And Rosemary said, 'Sure, go ahead. We don't have to make up our minds in a hurry, you know. It's just an idea I had.'

Karin walked up the gravel road and wondered what was different. Aside from the clouds, which were never there in her memories of the valley. Then she knew. There were no cattle pasturing in the fields, and because of this the grass had grown up, the juniper bushes had spread out, you could no longer see the water in the creek.

The valley was long and narrow, with Ann and Derek's white house at the far end of it. The valley floor was pasture that had been flat and tidy last year with the creek winding cleanly through it. (Ann had rented the land to a man who had Black

Angus cattle.) The wooded ridges rose steeply on either side and closed in at the far end, behind the house. The trailer Rosemary rented had originally been put in place for Ann's parents, who moved down there when the valley filled up with snow in the winter. They had wanted to be nearer to the store, which stood then at the corner of the township road. Now there was nothing but the cement platform with two holes in it where the gas tanks had been and an old bus with flags over the windows, where some hippies were living. They sometimes sat on the platform and waved back solemnly and eleborately to Rosemary as she drove past.

Derek said they had weed growing in the bushes. But he wouldn't buy from them, not trusting their security.

Rosemary refused to smoke with Derek.

'I'm too turbulent around you,' she said. 'I don't think it would be good.'

'Suit yourself,' said Derek. 'It might help.'

Neither would Ann smoke. She said she would feel silly. She had never smoked anything; she didn't even know how to inhale.

They didn't know that Derek had let Karin try once. She didn't know how to inhale either, and he had to teach her. She tried too hard; she inhaled too deeply and had to fight to keep from throwing up. They were out in the barn, where Derek kept all the rock samples he had collected up on the ridges. Derek tried to steady her by telling her to look at the rocks.

'Just look at them,' he said. 'Look into them. See the colors. Don't try too hard. Just look and wait.'

But what calmed her down eventually was the lettering on a cardboard box. There was a pile of cardboard boxes which Ann had packed things in when she and Derek had moved back here from Toronto, a couple of years ago. One of them had a silhouette of a toy battleship on the side, and the word DREADNOUGHT. The first part of the word – DREAD – was in red lettering. The letters shimmered as if written in neon tubing, and issued a command to Karin that had to do with more than the word's meaning. She had to dismember it and find the words inside.

'What are you laughing at?' Derek said, and she told him what she was doing. The words came tumbling out miraculously.

Read. Red. Dead. Dare. Era. Ear. Are. Add. Adder. 'Adder' was the best. It used up all the letters.

'Amazing,' said Derek. 'Amazing Karin. Dread the Red Adder.'

He never had to tell her not to mention any of this to her mother or to Ann. When Rosemary kissed her that night she sniffed her hair and laughed and said, 'God, the smell of it's everywhere, Derek's such a dedicated old pothead.'

This was one of the times when Rosemary was happy. They had been to Derek and Ann's house to eat supper on the closed-in sun porch. Ann had said, 'Come with me, Karin, see if you can help me get the mousse out of the mold.' Karin had followed her, but came back – pretending it was to get the mint sauce.

Rosemary and Derek were leaning across the table teasing each other, making kissing faces. They never saw her.

Maybe it was that same night, leaving, that Rosemary laughed at the two chairs set outside the back door. Two old dark-red metal-tube chairs, with cushions. They faced west, towards the last remnants of the sunset.

'Those old chairs,' said Ann. 'I know they're a sight. They belonged to my parents.'

'They're not even all that comfortable,' said Derek.

'No, no,' said Rosemary. 'They're beautiful, they're you. I love them. They just say Derek and Ann. Derek and Ann. Derek and Ann watching the sunset at the end of the day's labors.'

'If they can see it through the pea vines,' Derek said.

The next time Karin went out to pick vegetables for Ann, she noticed the chairs were gone. She didn't ask Ann what had become of them.

Ann's kitchen was in the basement of the house, just partly underground. You had to go down four steps. Karin did that, and pressed her face against the screen door. The kitchen was a dark room, with bushes growing against its high windows – Karin had never been there when the light was not on. But it wasn't on now, and at first she thought the room was empty. Then she saw somebody sitting at the table, and it was Ann, but her head was a different shape. She had her back to the door.

She had cut her hair. It was cut short and fluffed out like any gray-haired matron's. And she was doing something – her elbows moved. She was working in the dim light, but Karin couldn't see what the work was.

She tried the trick of making Ann turn around by staring at the back of her head. But it didn't work. She tried running her fingers lightly down the screen. Finally she made a noise.

'Woo-oo-ooo-woo.'

Ann got up and turned around so reluctantly that Karin had the swift unreasonable suspicion that she might have known who was there all the time – might have seen Karin coming, in fact, and arranged herself in this guarded position.

'It's me, it's me. It's your lost child,' said Karin.

'Why so it is,' said Ann, unhooking the door. She didn't greet Karin by hugging her – but then she and Derek never did that.

She had got fatter – or the short hair made her look that way – and her face had red blotches on it, as if bugs had been biting her. Her eyes looked sore.

'Do your eyes hurt?' Karin said. 'Is that why you're working in the dark?'

Ann said, 'Oh, I hadn't noticed. I hadn't noticed

the light wasn't on, I was just cleaning some silver and I thought I could see fine.' Then she seemed to make an effort to brighten up, speaking as if Karin was some much younger child. 'Cleaning silver is such a boring job, it must have put me in a trance. What a good thing you came along to help me.'

As a temporary tactic, Karin became this much younger child. She sprawled in a chair beside the table and said boisterously, 'So – where's old Derek?' She was thinking that this strange behavior of Ann's might mean that Derek had gone off on one of his expeditions over the ridges and not come back, leaving both Ann and Rosemary. Or that he was sick. Or depressed. Ann had once said, 'Derek wasn't depressed half so often once we left the city.' Karin had wondered if 'depressed' was the right word. Derek seemed to her critical, and sometimes fed up. Was that depression?

'I'm sure he's around somewhere,' Ann said.

'He and Rosemary had a big split-up, did you know that?'

'Oh yes, Karin. I knew that.'

'Do you feel sorry about it?'

Ann said, 'This is a new way I've got of cleaning silver. I'll show you. You just take a fork or spoon or whatever and you dip it in this solution here in the basin and leave it just a moment and then you take it out and dip it in the rinse water and wipe it dry. See? It shines just as well as ever it did when I used to do all that rubbing and polishing. I think

296

so. I think it's just as good a shine. I'll get us some fresh rinse water.'

Karin dipped a fork. She said, 'Yesterday Rosemary and I did what we wanted all day. We never even got dressed. We made waffles and we read stuff in these old magazines. Old *Ladies' Home Journals*.'

'Those were my mother's,' said Ann with a slight stiffness.

'She's lovely,' said Karin. 'She's engaged. She uses Pond's.'

Ann smiled – that was a relief – and said, 'I remember.'

'Can this marriage be saved?' said Karin, taking on a deep ominous tone. Then she changed to wheedling and whining.

'The problem is that my husband is really mean and I just don't know what to do about him. For one thing he has gone and eaten up all our children. It's not because I don't give him good meals to eat either because I do. I slave all day over a hot stove and make him a delicious dinner and then he comes home and the first thing he does is pull a leg off the baby—'

'Now stop,' said Ann, not smiling anymore. 'Just stop, Karin.'

'But I really want to know,' said Karin, in a subdued but stubborn voice. '*Can* this marriage be saved?'

All last year, when she thought of the place where she most wanted to be, Karin had thought of this kitchen. A big room whose corners stayed dim even when the light was on. The patterns of green leaves brushing the windows. All the things here and there that strictly speaking didn't belong in a kitchen. The treadle sewing machine and the big overstuffed armchair, its maroon covering oddly worn to gray-green on the armrests. The large painting of a waterfall done long ago by Ann's mother when she was just a bride and had the time, which she never had again.

('A lucky thing for all of us,' said Derek.)

There was the sound of a car in the yard and Karin thought, could it be Rosemary? Had Rosemary been the one to get depressed, left alone; had she followed Karin for company?

When she heard the boots on the kitchen steps she knew it was Derek.

She called out, 'Surprise, surprise. Look who's here!'

Derek came into the room and said, 'Hullo Karin,' without a trace of welcome. He set a couple of bags down on the table. Ann said politely, 'Did you get the right film?'

'Yes,' said Derek. 'What's this muck?'

'For cleaning the silver,' Ann said. To Karin, as if to apologize, she said, 'He's just been to town to get some film. To take pictures of his rocks.'

Karin bent over the knife she was drying. It would be the worst thing in the world if she should cry (last summer it would have been impossible). Ann asked about some other things – groceries –

that Derek had got, and Karin raised her eyes deliberately and fixed them on the front of the stove. It was a kind of stove no longer made, Ann had told her. A combination wood-and-electric stove with a sailing ship stamped on the door of the warming oven. Above the ship, the words CLIPPER STOVES.

That, too, she had remembered.

'I'd think Karin could be a help to you,' said Ann. 'She could help you set up the rocks.'

There was a slight pause during which they might have looked at each other. Then Derek said, 'Okay, Karin. Come on and help me take pictures.'

Many of the rocks were just sitting around on the barn floor – not yet sorted or labelled. Others sat on shelves, separately displayed, with printed cards to identify them. For some time Derek was silent, moving these around, then fiddling with the camera, trying to get the best angle and the proper light. When he started to take the pictures he gave brief orders to Karin, getting her to shift the rocks or tilt them, and pick up others from the floor, to be photographed even without labels. It didn't seem to her that he really needed – or wanted – her help at all. Several times he drew in his breath as if he was going to say this – or tell her something else that was important and unpleasant – but then all he said was 'Shift to the right a little,' or 'Give me a look at the other side.'

All last summer Karin had nagged in her brat

way and requested in a serious way to be taken along on one of Derek's forays, and finally he had said she could come. He made it as hard as he could, a test. They sprayed themselves with Off!, but it didn't entirely prevent the bugs from getting at them, burrowing into their hair and finding a way under neck bands and shirt cuffs. They had to squelch through boggy places where their boot prints immediately filled up with water, then climb up steep banks covered with berry canes and wild rosebushes and tough, tripping vines. Also clamber over smooth, tilted outcrops of bare rocks. They wore bells around their necks, so that they could locate each other if separated, and so any bears could hear them coming and stay clear.

They came on one big mound of bear scat, with a fresh glisten to it and an apple core only half digested.

Derek had told her that there were mines all through this country. Almost every known mineral was there but usually not enough to make them profitable, he said. He had visited all these abandoned, almost forgotten mines and hacked out his samples or simply picked them up off the ground. 'The first time I brought him home he just disappeared up the ridge and found a mine,' Ann said. 'I knew then that he'd probably marry me.'

The mines were a disappointment, though Karin would never have said so. She had been hoping for some Ali Baba cave with a gleam of glittery rocks in the darkness. Instead Derek showed her a narrow entryway, almost a natural split in the rock, blocked off now by a poplar tree that had taken root in that absurd place and grown up crooked. The other entry, that Derek said was the most feasible anywhere, was just a hole in the side of a hill, with rotted beams lying on the ground or still supporting part of the roof and bricks holding back some of the earth and rock rubble. Derek pointed out the faint tracks where the rails had run for the ore cart. Pieces of mica were lying around, and Karin collected some. They at least were beautiful and looked like authentic treasure. They were like flakes of smooth dark glass that turned to silver when you held them to the light.

Derek said she should take just one piece and that for a private keepsake, not to be shown to people. 'Keep it under your hat,' he said. 'I don't want talk about this place.'

Karin said, 'Do you want me to swear to God?'

He said, 'Just remember.' Then he asked her if she wanted to see the castle.

Another disappointment, and a joke. He led her to a cement-walled ruin that he said had probably been a storage place for ore. He showed her the break in the tall trees, filled up with saplings, where the rail line had run. The joke was that some of the hippies had got lost in here a couple of years ago and come out with the report of a castle. Derek hated people making mistakes like that, not seeing what was in front of their eyes or could be figured out with the right information.

301

Karin walked around the top of the crumbling wall and he did not tell her to watch her footing or be careful she didn't break her neck.

On the way home there was a thunderstorm and they had to stay inside a heavy thicket of cedars. Karin could not keep still – she couldn't tell if she was scared or elated. Elated, she decided, and she jumped up and ran in circles, throwing up her arms and shrieking in the brightness of the light that penetrated even this shelter. Derek told her to calm down, just to sit and count to fifteen after each flash and see if that didn't bring the thunder.

But she thought he was pleased with her. He didn't think she was scared.

It was the truth, that there were people whom you positively ached to please. Derek was one of them. If you failed with such people they would put you into a category in their minds where they could keep you and have contempt for you forever. Fear of the lightning, fear when she saw the bear scat, or the wish to believe the ruin was the ruin of a castle – even a failure to recognize the different qualities of mica, pyrite, quartz, silver, feldspar – any of that could make Derek decide to give up on her. As he had given up in different ways on Rosemary and Ann. Out here with Karin he was more seriously himself, he paid everything the honor of his serious attention. When he was with her and not with either of them.

★   ★   ★

'Notice some elements of doom and gloom around here today?' Derek said.

Karin slid her hands over a piece of quartz that looked like ice with a candle inside. She said, 'Is it because of Rosemary?'

'No,' said Derek. 'This is serious. Ann got an offer on this place. A shark from Stoco came out and told her some Japanese company wants to buy it. They want the mica. To build ceramic engine blocks for cars. She's thinking about it. She can sell it if she wants to. It's hers.'

Karin said, 'Why would she want to? Sell it?'

'Money,' said Derek. 'Try money.'

'Doesn't Rosemary pay her enough rent?'

'How long is that going to last? The pasture isn't rented this year, the land's too soggy. The house needs money spent or it'll fall down. I've worked four years on a book that isn't even finished. We're running low. You know what the real-estate guy said to her? He said, "This could be another Sudbury." He didn't say that for a joke.'

Karin didn't see why he would. She knew nothing about Sudbury. 'If I was rich I could buy it,' she said. 'Then you could go on like now.'

'Someday you will be rich,' Derek said matter-of-factly. 'But not soon enough.' He was putting the camera away in its case. 'Keep on the right side of your mother,' he said. 'She's rich as stink.'

Karin felt her face heat up, she felt the shock of

those words. It was something she'd never heard before. *Rich as stink*. It sounded hateful.

He said, 'Okay – into town to see when they'll develop this.' He didn't ask if she wanted to go along and she could hardly have answered him anyway; her eyes were filling up disastrously. She was struck and blinded by what he'd said.

She had to go to the bathroom, so she walked over to the house.

There was a good smell from the kitchen – the smell of some slow-cooking meat.

The only bathroom was upstairs. Karin could hear Ann up there, moving around in her room. She didn't call or look in at her. But when she started to go downstairs again, Ann called her.

She had put makeup on her face so it didn't look so blotchy.

There were piles of clothes lying around on the bed and on the floor.

'I'm trying to get things organized,' Ann said. 'There's clothes here I'd forgotten I had. I have to get rid of some of them once and for all.'

That meant she was serious about moving out. Getting rid of things before she moved out. When Rosemary was getting ready to move out she packed her trunk while Karin was at school. Karin never saw her choose the things that went into it. She just saw them turn up later, in the apartment in Toronto and now in the trailer. A cushion, a pair of candlesticks, a big platter – familiar but forever out of place. As far as Karin was concerned it would be better if she had not brought anything at all.

'You see that suitcase,' Ann said. 'Up there on top of the wardrobe? Do you think you could just climb up on a chair and tilt it over the edge so that I could catch it? I tried but I got dizzy. Just tilt it over and I'll catch it.'

Karin climbed up and pushed the suitcase over so that it teetered on the edge of the wardrobe, and Ann caught it. She thanked Karin breathlessly and plopped it down on the bed.

'I've got the key, I've got the key here,' she said.

The lock was stiff and the clasps hard to pry open. Karin helped. When the lid fell back a smell of mothballs rose from a heap of limp cloth. The smell was well known to Karin from the secondhand stores where Rosemary liked to shop.

'Are these your mom's old things?' she said.

'Karin! It's my wedding dress,' said Ann, half laughing. 'That's only the old sheet it's wrapped up in.' She picked the grayish cloth away and lifted out a bundle of lace and taffeta. Karin cleared a place for it on the bed. Then very carefully Ann began turning it right side out. The taffeta rustled like leaves.

'My veil, too,' Ann said, lifting a film that clung to the taffeta. 'Oh, I should have taken better care of it.'

There was a long fine slit in the skirt that looked as if it could have been made by a razor blade.

'I should have had it hanging up,' said Ann. 'I should have had it in one of those bags you get from the cleaner's. Taffeta is so fragile. That cut came from where it was folded. I knew that too. Never, never fold taffeta.'

Now she began to separate one piece of material from another, lifting it bit by bit with little private sounds of encouragement, until she was able to shake the whole thing into the shape of a dress. The veil was loose on the floor. Karin picked it up.

'Net,' she said. She talked to keep the sound of Derek's voice out of her head.

'Tulle,' said Ann. 'T-u-l-l-e. Lace and tulle. Shame on me for not taking better care. It's a wonder it lasted as well as it has. It's a wonder it lasted at all.'

'Tulle,' said Karin. 'I never heard of tulle. I don't think I ever heard of taffeta.'

'They used a lot of it,' Ann said. 'Once upon a time.'

'Do you have a picture of you in it? Do you have a picture of your wedding?'

'Mother and Dad had a picture, but I've no idea what became of it. Derek isn't one for wedding pictures. He wasn't even one for weddings. I don't know how I got away with it. I had it in the Stoco church, think of that. And I had my three girlfriends, Dorothy Smith and Muriel Lifton and Dawn Challeray. Dorothy played the organ and Dawn was my bridesmaid and Muriel sang.'

Karin said, 'What color did your bridesmaid wear?'

'Apple green. A lace dress with chiffon inserts. No, the other way round. Chiffon with lace.'

Ann said all this in a slightly skeptical voice, examining the seams of the dress.

'What did the one who sang sing?'

'Muriel. "O Perfect Love." *O, Perfect Love, all human love transcending* – but it's really a hymn. It's really talking about a divine kind of love. I don't know who picked it.'

Karin touched the taffeta. It felt dry and cool.

'Try it on,' she said.

'Me?' Ann said. 'It's made for somebody with a twenty-four-inch waist. Did Derek get away to town? With his film?'

She didn't listen to Karin say yes. She must of course have heard the car.

'He thinks he has to get a pictorial record,' she said. 'I don't know why all the hurry. Then he's going to get it all boxed and labelled. He seems to think he's never going to see it again. Did he give you the impression the place was sold?'

'Not yet,' said Karin.

'No. Not yet. And I wouldn't do it unless I had to. I won't do it unless I have to. Though I think I will have to. Sometimes things just become necessary. People don't have to make it all into a tragedy or some personal kind of punishment.'

'Can I try it?' Karin said.

Ann looked her over. She said, 'We have to be very careful.'

Karin stepped out of her shoes and her shorts and pulled off her shirt. Ann lowered the dress over her head, shutting her up for a moment in a white cloud. The lace sleeves had to be worked down delicately, until the points they ended in were lying on the backs of Karin's hands. They made her hands look brown, though she wasn't tanned yet. The hooks and eyes had to be done up all down the side of the waist, then there were more hooks and eyes at the back of the neck. They had to hold a band of lace tight around Karin's throat. Wearing nothing underneath the dress but her underpants, she felt her skin prickle at the touch of lace. Lace was more deliberate, in its here-and-there contact, than anything she was used to. She shrank from feeling it against her nipples, but fortunately it was looser there, pooked out where Ann's breasts had been. Karin's chest was still almost flat, but sometimes her nipples felt swollen, tender, as if they were going to burst.

The taffeta had to be pulled out from between her legs and arranged into a bell-like skirt. Then lace fell in loops over the skirt.

'You're taller than I thought,' Ann said. 'You could walk around in it if you just held it up a bit.'

She took a hairbrush from the dresser and began to brush Karin's hair down over her lace-covered shoulders.

'Nut-brown hair,' she said. 'I remember in books, girls used to be described as having nut-brown hair. And you know they did use nuts to color it. My mother remembered girls boiling walnuts to make a dye and then putting the dye on their hair. Of course if you got the stain on your hands it was a dead giveaway. It was so hard to get out.

'Hold still,' she said, and shook the veil down over the smooth hair, then stood in front of Karin to pin it on. 'The headdress to this has disappeared altogether,' she said. 'I must have used it for something else or given it away to somebody to wear at their wedding. I can't remember. Anyway it would look silly nowadays. It was a Mary Queen of Scots.'

She looked around and picked some silk flowers – a branch of apple blossoms – out of a vase on the dresser. This new idea meant she had to take the pins out and start again, bending the apple blossom stem to make a headdress. The stem was stiff, but at last she got it bent and pinned to her satisfaction. She moved out of the way and gently pushed Karin in front of the mirror.

Karin said, 'Oh. Can I have it for when I get married?'

She didn't mean that. She had never thought of getting married. She said it to please Ann, after all Ann's effort, and to cover her embarrassment when she looked into the mirror.

'They'll have something so different in style then,' Ann said. 'This isn't even in style now.'

Karin looked away from the mirror and looked into it again, better prepared. She saw a saint. The shining hair and the pale blossoms, the faint shadows of the falling lace on her cheeks, the storybook dedication, the kind of beauty so in earnest about itself that there is something fated about it, and something foolish. She made a face to crack that face open, but it didn't work – it seemed as if the bride, the girl born in the mirror, was now the one in control.

'I wonder what Derek would say if he saw you now,' Ann said. 'I wonder if he'd even know it was my wedding dress?' Her eyelids were fluttering in their shy troubled way. She stood close to take the blossoms and pins out. Karin smelled soap from under her arms, and garlic on her fingers.

'He'd say, What kind of a stupid outfit is that?' said Karin, doing a superior Derek voice, as Ann lifted the veil away.

They heard the car coming down the valley. 'Speak of the devil,' said Ann. Now she was in such a great hurry to undo the hooks and eyes her fingers were clumsy and trembling. When she tried to pull the dress over Karin's head something got caught.

'Curses,' Ann said.

'You go on,' said Karin, muffled up. 'You go on and let me. I've got it.'

When she emerged she saw Ann's face twisted in what looked like grief.

'I was just kidding about Derek,' she said.

But perhaps Ann's look was just one of alarm and concern about the dress.

'What do you mean?' Ann said. 'Oh. Hush. Forget it.'

Karin stood still on the stairs to hear their voices in the kitchen. Ann had run down ahead of her.

Derek said, 'Is that going to be good? Whatever you're making?'

'I hope so,' said Ann. 'It's osso buco.'

Derek's voice had changed. He wasn't mad anymore. He was eager to make friends. Ann's voice was relieved, out of breath, trying to match up with his new mood.

'Is there going to be enough for company?' he said.

'What company?'

'Just Rosemary. I hope there's enough, because I asked her.'

'Rosemary and Karin,' Ann said calmly. 'There's enough of this, but there isn't any wine.'

'There is now,' said Derek. 'I got some.'

Then there was some muttering or whispering from Derek to Ann. He must be standing very close to her and talking against her hair or her ear. He seemed to be teasing, pleading, comforting, promising to reward her, all at once. Karin was so afraid that words would surface out of this – words she would understand and never forget – that she went banging down the stairs and into the kitchen, calling, 'Who's this Rosemary? Did I hear "Rosemary"?'

'Don't sneak up on us like that, *enfant*,' said Derek. 'Make a little noise so we hear you coming.'

'Did I hear "Rosemary"?'

'Your mother's name,' he said. 'I swear to you, your mother's name.'

All the tight displeasure was gone. He was full of challenges and high spirits, as he'd been sometimes last summer.

Ann looked at the wine and said, 'That's lovely wine, Derek, that'll go beautifully. Let's see. Karin, you can help. We'll set the long table on the porch. We'll use the blue dishes and the good silver – isn't it lucky we just cleaned the silver. We'll put two sets of candles. The tall yellow ones in the middle, Karin, and a circle of little white ones around them.'

'Like a daisy,' Karin said.

'That's right,' said Ann. 'A celebration dinner. Because you're back for the summer.'

'What can I do?' said Derek.

'Let me think. Oh – you can go out and get me some things for the salad. Some lettuce and some sorrel, and do you think there's any cress in the creek?'

'There is,' said Derek. 'I saw some.'

'Get some of that too.'

Derek glided a hand round her shoulders. He said, 'All will be well.'

★ ★ ★

When they were almost ready Derek put on a record. This was one of the records he had taken to Rosemary's place and must have brought back here. It was called *Ancient Airs and Dances for Lute*, and it had a cover that showed a group of old-fashioned, exquisitely thin ladies, all wearing high-waisted dresses, with little curls down in front of their ears, and dancing in a circle. The music had often inspired Derek to do a stately and ridiculous dance, in which Karin and Rosemary would join him. Karin could match him in a dance, but Rosemary couldn't. Rosemary tried too hard, she moved a little late, she tried to imitate what could only be spontaneous.

Karin started dancing now, round the kitchen table where Ann was tearing salad and Derek was opening the wine. 'Ancient *airs* and *dances* for the *lute*,' she sang raptly. 'My *mom* is coming to supper, my mom is coming to *supper*.'

'I believe Karin's mom is coming to supper,' said Derek. He held up his hand. 'Quiet, quiet. Is that her car I hear?'

'Oh, dear. I should at least wash my face,' said Ann. She dropped the greens and hurried into the hall and up the stairs.

Derek went to stop the record. He took the needle back to the beginning. When he had it going again he went out to meet Rosemary – a thing he did not usually do. Karin had intended to run out herself. But when Derek did, she decided not to. Instead she followed Ann up the stairs. Not all the way, though. There was a small window on the landing where nobody ever halted or looked out. A net curtain over it, so that you were not likely to be seen.

She was quick enough to see Derek stepping across the lawn, going through the gap in the hedge. Long, eager, stealthy strides. He would be in time to bend and open the car door, to open it with a flourish and help Rosemary out. Karin had never seen him do that, but she knew he meant to do it now.

Ann was still in the bathroom – Karin could hear the shower. There would be a few minutes for her to watch undisturbed.

And now she heard the car door shut. But she did not hear their voices. She couldn't, with the music pouring through the house. And they hadn't come into sight in the gap in the hedge. Not yet. And not yet. And not yet.

Once after Rosemary left Ted she came back. Not to the house – she was not supposed to come to the house. Ted delivered Karin to a restaurant and there Rosemary was. The two of them had lunch in the restaurant. Karin had a Shirley Temple and chips. Rosemary told her that she was going to Toronto, that she had a job there with a publisher. Karin did not know what a publisher was.

Here they come. Pressing together through the gap in the hedge, where they should have gone single file. Rosemary is wearing her harem pants, made of thin, soft, raspberry-colored cotton. Her shadowy legs show through. Her top is of heavier cotton covered with embroidery and some tiny, sewn-on mirrors. She seems to be concerned about her piled-up hair – her hands fly up, in a gesture of charming nervousness, to loosen some more little wisps and curls that can flutter and dangle around her face. (Something the way those ladies' curls dangle over their ears, on the cover of *Ancient Airs and Dances*.) Her fingernails are painted to match her pants.

Derek is not putting his hands on Rosemary anywhere but looks as if he is always just about to do so.

'Yes, but will you *live* there?' said Karin in the restaurant.

Tall Derek bends close to Rosemary's wild pretty hair, as if that is a nest he is all but ready to drop into. He is so intent. Whether he touches her or not, whether he speaks to her or not. He is pulling her to him, studiously attending to the job. But being pulled himself, being tempted to delight. Karin can just recognize that lovely flirting feeling when you're saying, No, I'm not sleepy, no, I'm still awake—

Rosemary at this moment doesn't know what to do, but thinks she doesn't yet have to do anything. Look at her spinning around in her cage of rosy colors. Her cage of spun sugar. Look at Rosemary twittering and beguiling.

Rich as stink, he said.

Ann comes out of the bathroom, her gray hair dark and damp, pushed flat to her head, her face glowing from the shower.

'Karin. What are you doing here?'

'Watching.'

'Watching what?'

'A pair of lover-dovers.'

'Oh now Karin,' says Ann, going on down the stairs.

And soon come happy cries from the front door (special occasion) and from the hallway, 'What is that marvellous smell?' (Rosemary). 'Just some old bones Ann's simmering' (Derek).

'And that – it's beautiful,' says Rosemary as the sociable flurry moves into the living room. Speaking of the bunch of green leaves and June grass and early orange lilies Ann has stuck in the cream jug by the living-room door.

'Just some old weeds Ann hauled in,' says Derek, and Ann says, 'Oh well, I thought they looked nice,' and Rosemary says again, 'Beautiful.'

Rosemary said after lunch that she wanted to get Karin a present. Not for a birthday and not for Christmas – just a wonderful present.

They went to a department store. Every time Karin slowed down to look at something, Rosemary showed immediate enthusiasm and willingness to buy it. She would have bought a velvet coat with a fur collar and cuffs, an antique-style painted rocking horse, a pink plush elephant that looked about a quarter life-size. To put an end to this miserable wandering, Karin picked out a cheap ornament – the figure of a ballerina poised on a mirror. The ballerina did not twirl around, there was no music played for her – nothing that could justify the choice. You would think that Rosemary would understand that. She should have understood what such a choice said – that Karin was not to be made happy, amends were not possible, forgiveness was out of the question. But she didn't see that. Or she chose not to. She said, 'Yes. I like that. She's so graceful. She'll look pretty on your dresser. Oh, yes.'

Karin put the ballerina away in a drawer. When Grace found it, she explained that a friend at school had given it to her and that she couldn't hurt the friend's feelings by saying it wasn't the kind of thing she liked.

Grace wasn't so used to children then, or she might have questioned such a story.

'I can understand that,' she said. 'I'll just give it to the hospital sale – it's not likely she'll ever see it there. Anyway they must have made hundreds like it.'

Ice cubes cracked downstairs, as Derek dropped them into the drinks. Ann said, 'Karin's around somewhere, I'm sure she'll pop up in a minute.'

Karin went softly, softly up the remaining stairs and into Ann's room. There were the tumbled clothes on the bed, and the wedding dress, again wrapped up in its sheet, lying on top of them. She took off her shorts and her shirt and her shoes and began the desperate, difficult process of getting into this dress. Instead of trying to put it on over her head, she wriggled her way up into it, through the crackling skirt and lace bodice. She got her arms into the sleeves, being careful not to snag the lace with a fingernail. Her fingernails were mostly too short to be a problem, but she was careful anyway. She pulled the lace points over her hands. Then she did up all the hooks at the waist. The hardest thing was to do the hooks at the back of the neck. She bent her head and hunched her shoulders, trying to make those hooks easier to get at. Even so, she had a disaster – the lace ripping a little under one arm. That shocked her and even made her stop for a second. But it seemed she had gone too far to give up now, and she got the rest of the hooks fastened without mishap. She could sew up that tear when she got the dress off. Or she could lie, and claim she had noticed it before she had put the dress on. Ann might not see it anyway.

Now the veil. She had to be very careful with the veil. Any tear would show. She shook it all out and tried to secure it with the branch of apple blossoms, just as Ann had done. But she couldn't get the branch to bend properly or the slippery pins to hold it. She thought it might be better to tie the whole thing on with a ribbon or a sash. She went to Ann's closet to see if she could find something. And there hung a man's tie rack, a man's ties. Derek's ties, though she had never seen him wearing a tie.

She pulled a striped tie off the rack and tied it around her forehead, tying it at the back of her head, holding the veil firmly in place. She did this in front of the mirror and when it was done she saw that she had created a gypsy effect, a flaunting comic effect. An idea came to her which forced her to undo with strenuous effort all those hooks and eyes, then pad the front of the dress with tightly wadded-up clothing from Ann's bed. She filled and overfilled the lace that had hung limp, being fashioned for Ann's breasts. Better this way, better to make them laugh. She could not then get all the hooks done up afterwards, but she got enough to hold the clownish cloth bosom in place. She got the neck band fastened as well. She was sweating all over when she finished.

Ann didn't wear lipstick or eye makeup, but on the top of the dresser there was, surprisingly, a pot of hardened rouge. Karin spat in it and rubbed round splotches on her cheeks.

The front door led into the hall at the bottom of the stairs, and from this hall a side door led into the sunporch, and another door (on the same side) led into the living room. You could also go directly from the porch into the living room, through a door at the far end. The house was oddly planned or not planned at all, Ann said. Things had been altered or added on just as people thought of them. The long narrow glassed-in porch was no good for catching the sun, since it was on the east side of the house and shaded, in any case, by a stand of poplar saplings that had got out of hand and grown up quickly, as poplars do. In Ann's childhood the porch's main use was for storing apples, though she and her sister had loved the roundabout route provided by the three doors. And she liked the room now, for serving supper in during the summertime. When the table was pulled out there was hardly room to walk between the chairs and the inner wall. But if you seated people along one side, facing the windows, and at either end – that was the way the table was set tonight – there was room for a thin person, and certainly for Karin, to pass.

Karin came downstairs barefoot. Nobody could see her from the living room. And she chose not to go into that room by the usual door, but to enter the porch and go alongside the table and then appear, or burst in on them, from the porch where they would never have expected her to be.

The porch was already shadowy. Ann had lit the two tall yellow candles, though not the little white ones that were clustered round them. The yellow ones had a scent of lemons, which she was probably counting on to dispel any stuffiness in the room.

Also she had opened the window at one end of the table. On the stillest evening you could always get a breeze from the poplars.

Karin used both hands to hold her skirt as she went past the table. She had to hold it up slightly so that she could walk. And she did not want the taffeta to make a noise. She meant to start singing 'Here comes the bride' just as she appeared in the doorway.

> *Here comes the bride*
> *Fair, fat, and wide.*
> *See how she wobbles*
> *From side to side—*

The breeze came towards her with a little gust of energy and pulled her veil. But it was held to her head so tightly that she had no worries about losing it.

As she turned to go into the living room the whole veil rose and drifted through the flames of the candles. The people in the room no sooner saw her than they saw the fire that was chasing her. She herself had just time to smell the lace as it crumbled – a queer poisonous edge on the smell of the marrow bones cooking for dinner. Then a rush of nonsensical heat and screams, a brutal pitching into darkness.

Rosemary got to her first, pounding her head with a cushion. Ann ran for the crock in the hallway and threw water, lilies, grass, and all onto her fiery veil and hair. Derek tore the rug up off the floor, sending stools and tables and drinks crashing, and was able to wrap Karin tightly and suffocate the last flames. Some bits of lace stayed smoldering in her soaked hair, and Rosemary got her fingers burned, tearing them out.

The skin on her shoulders and on her upper back and on one side of her neck was marred by burning. Derek's tie had kept the veil back a little from her face and so saved her from the most telling traces. But even when her hair grew long again and she brushed it forward, it could not altogether hide the damage to her neck.

She had a series of skin grafts, and then she looked better. By the time she was in college she could wear a bathing suit.

When she first opened her eyes in the room in the Belleville hospital, she saw all sorts of daisies. White daisies, yellow and pink and purple daisies, even on the windowsill.

'Aren't they lovely?' Ann said. 'They keep sending them. They keep sending more, and the first ones are still fresh, or at least not ready to throw out. Everywhere they stop on their trip they send some. They ought to be in Cape Breton by now.'

Karin said, 'Did you sell the farm?'

Rosemary said, 'Karin.'

Karin closed her eyes and tried again.

'Did you think it was Ann?' said Rosemary.

'Ann and Derek are off on a trip. I was just telling you. Ann did sell the farm, or anyway she's going to. That's a funny thing for you to be thinking about.'

'They're on their honeymoon,' said Karin. This was a trick – to bring Ann back if it was really her – to make her say, reprovingly, 'Oh, Karin.'

'It's the wedding dress making you think of that,' Rosemary said. 'They're actually on a trip looking for where they want to live next.'

So it was really Rosemary. And Ann on the trip. Ann on the trip with Derek.

'It would have to be a second honeymoon,' Rosemary said. 'You never hear about anybody going on their third honeymoon, do you? Or their eighteenth honeymoon?'

It was all right, everybody was in the right place. Karin felt as if she might be the one who had brought this about, through some exhausting effort. She knew she should feel satisfaction. She did feel satisfaction. But it all seemed unimportant in some way. As if Ann and Derek and perhaps even Rosemary were behind a hedge that was too thick and troublesome to climb through.

'I'm here though,' said Rosemary. 'I've been here all the time. But they won't let me touch you.'

She said this last thing as if it was a matter for heartbreak.

She still says this once in a while.

323

'What I remember most is that I couldn't touch you and wondering if you understood.'

Karin says yes. She understood. What she doesn't bother to say is that back then she thought Rosemary's sorrow was absurd. It was as if she was complaining about not being able to reach across a continent. For that was what Karin felt she had become – something immense and shimmering and sufficient, ridged up in pain in some places and flattened out, otherwise, into long dull distances. Away off at the edge of this was Rosemary, and Karin could reduce her, any time she liked, into a configuration of noisy black dots. And she herself – Karin – could be stretched out like this and at the same time shrunk into the middle of her territory, as tidy as a bead or a ladybug.

She came out of that, of course, she came back to being a Karin. Everybody thought she was just the same except for her skin. Nobody knew how she had changed and how natural it seemed to her to be separate and polite and adroitly fending for herself. Nobody knew the sober, victorious feeling she had sometimes, when she knew how much she was on her own.

BEFORE THE CHANGE

Dear R. My father and I watched Kennedy debate Nixon. He's got a television since you were here. A small screen and rabbit ears. It sits out in front of the sideboard in the dining room so that there's no easy way now to get at the good silver or the table linen even if anybody wanted to. Why in the dining room where there's not one really comfortable chair? Because it's a while since they've remembered they have a living room. Or because Mrs Barrie wants to watch it at suppertime.

Do you remember this room? Nothing new in it but the television. Heavy side curtains with wine-colored leaves on a beige ground and the net curtains in between. Picture of Sir Galahad leading his horse and picture of Glencoe, red deer instead of the massacre. The old filing cabinet moved in years ago from my father's office but still no place found for it so it just sits there not even pushed back against the wall. And my mother's closed sewing machine (the only time he ever mentions her, when he says 'your mother's sewing machine') with the same array of plants, or what looks like the same, in clay pots or tin cans, not flourishing and not dying.

So I'm home now. Nobody has broached the question as to how long for. I just stuffed the Mini with all my books and papers and clothes and drove here from Ottawa in one day. I had told my father on the phone that I was finished with my thesis (I've actually given it up but I didn't bother telling him that) and that I thought I needed a break.

'Break?' he said, as if he'd never heard of such a thing. 'Well. As long as it isn't a nervous break.'

I said, What?

'Nervous breakdown,' he said with a warning cackle. That's the way he still refers to panic attacks and acute anxiety and depression and personal collapse. He probably tells his patients to buck up.

Unfair. He probably sends them away with some numbing pills and a few dry kind words. He can tolerate other people's shortcomings more easily than mine.

There wasn't any big welcome when I got here, but no consternation either. He walked around the Mini and grunted at what he saw and nudged the tires.

'Surprised you made it,' he said.

I'd thought of kissing him – more bravado than an upsurge of affection, more this-is-the-way-I-do-things-now. But by the time my shoes hit gravel I knew I couldn't. There was Mrs B. standing halfway between the drive and the kitchen door. So I went and threw my arms around her instead and nuzzled the bizarre black hair cut in a Chinese sort of bob around her small withered face. I could smell her stuffy cardigan and bleach on her apron and feel her old toothpick bones. She hardly comes up to my collarbone.

Flustered, I said, 'It's a beautiful day, it's been the most beautiful drive.' So it was. So it had been. The trees not turned yet, just rusting at the edges and the stubble fields like gold. So why does this benevolence of landscape fade, in my father's presence and in his territory (and don't forget it's in Mrs Barrie's presence and in her territory)? Why does my mentioning it – or the fact that I mentioned it in a heartfelt not perfunctory way – seem almost in a class with my embracing Mrs B.? One thing seems to be a piece of insolence and the other pretentious gush.

When the debate was over my father got up and turned off the television. He won't watch a commercial unless Mrs B. is there and speaks up in favor, saying she wants to see the cute kid with his front teeth out or the chicken chasing the thingamajig (she won't try to say 'ostrich,' or she can't remember). Then whatever she enjoys is permitted, even dancing cornflakes, and he may say, 'Well, in its own way it's clever.' This I think is a kind of warning to me.

What did he think about Kennedy and Nixon?

'Aw, they're just a couple of Americans.'

I tried to open the conversation up a bit.

'How do you mean?'

When you ask him to go into subjects that he thinks don't need to be talked about, or take up an argument that doesn't need proving, he has a way of lifting his upper lip at one side, showing a pair of big tobacco stained teeth.

'Just a couple of Americans,' he said, as if the words might have got by me the first time.

So we sit there not talking but not in silence because as you may recall he is a noisy breather. His breath gets dragged down stony alleys and through creaky gates. Then takes off into a bit of tweeting and gurgling as if there was some inhuman apparatus shut up in his chest. Plastic pipes and colored bubbles. You're not supposed to take any notice, and I'll soon be used to it. But it takes up a lot of space in a room. As he would anyway with his high hard stomach and long legs and his expression. What is that expression? It's as if he's got a list of offenses both remembered and anticipated and he's letting it be known how his patience can be tried by what you know you do wrong but also by what you don't even suspect. I think a lot of fathers and grandfathers strive for that look – even some who unlike him don't have any authority outside of their own houses – but he's the one who's got it exactly permanently right.

R. Lots for me to do here and no time to – as they say – mope. The waiting-room walls are scuffed all round where generations of patients have leaned their chairs back against them. The *Reader's Digests* are in rags on the table. The patients' files are in cardboard boxes under the examining table, and the wastebaskets – they're wicker – are mangled all around the top as if eaten by rats. And in the house it's no better. Cracks like brown hairs in the downstairs washbasin and a disconcerting spot of rust in the toilet. Well you must have noticed. It's silly but the most disturbing thing I think is all the coupons and advertising flyers. They're in drawers and stuck under saucers or lying around loose and the sales or discounts they're advertising are weeks or months or years past.

It isn't that they've abdicated or aren't trying. But everything is complicated. They send out the laundry, which is sensible, rather than having Mrs B. still do it, but then my father can't remember which day it's due back and there's this unholy fuss about will there be enough smocks etc. And Mrs B. actually believes the laundry is cheating her and taking the time to rip off the name tapes and sew them onto inferior articles. So she argues with the deliveryman and says he comes here last on purpose and he probably does.

Then the eaves need to be cleaned and Mrs B.'s nephew is supposed to come and clean them, but he has put his back out so his son is coming. But his son has had to take over so many jobs that he's behind etc., etc.

My father calls this nephew's son by the nephew's name. He does this with everybody. He refers to stores and businesses in town by the name of the previous owner or even the owner before that. This is more than a simple lapse of memory; it's something like arrogance. Putting himself beyond the need to keep such things straight. The need to notice changes. Or individuals.

I asked what color of paint he'd like on the waiting-room walls. Light green, I said, or light yellow? He said, Who's going to paint them?

'I am.'

'I never knew you were a painter.'

'I've painted places I've lived in.'

'Maybe so. But I haven't seen them. What are you going to do about my patients while you're painting?'

'I'll do it on a Sunday.'

'Some of them wouldn't care for that when they heard about it.'

'Are you kidding? In this day and age?'

'It may not be quite the same day and age you think it is. Not around here.'

Then I said I could do it at night, but he said the smell the next day would upset too many stomachs. All I was allowed to do in the end was throw out the *Reader's Digests* and put out some copies of *Maclean's* and *Chatelaine* and *Time* and *Saturday Night*. And then he mentioned there'd been complaints. People missed looking up the jokes they remembered in the *Reader's Digests*. And some of them didn't like modern writers. Like Pierre Berton.

'Too bad,' I said, and I couldn't believe that my voice was shaking.

Then I tackled the filing cabinet in the dining room. I thought it was probably full of the files of patients who were long dead and if I could clear those files out I could fill it up with the files from the cardboard boxes, and move the whole thing back to the office where it belonged.

Mrs B. saw what I was doing and went and got my father. Not a word to me.

He said, 'Who told you you could go poking around in there? I didn't.'

R. The days you were here Mrs B. was off for Christmas with her family. (She has a husband who has been sick with emphysema it seems for half his life, and no children, but a horde of nieces and nephews and connections.) I don't think you saw her at all. But she saw you. She said to me yesterday, 'Where's that Mr So-and-so you were supposed to be engaged to?' She'd seen of course that I wasn't wearing my ring.

'I imagine in Toronto,' I said.

'I was up at my niece's last Christmas and we seen you and him walking up by the standpipe and my niece said, "I wonder where them two are off to?"' This is exactly how she talks and it already sounds quite normal to me except when I write it down. I guess the implication is that we were going somewhere to carry on, but there was a deep freeze on, if you remember, and we were just walking to get away from the house. No. We were getting outside so we could continue our fight, which could only be bottled up for so long.

Mrs B. started to work for my father about the same time I went away to school. Before that we had some young women I liked, but they left to get married, or to work in war plants. When I was nine or ten and had been to some of my school friends' houses, I said to my father, 'Why does our maid have to eat with us? Other people's maids don't eat with them.'

My father said, 'You call Mrs Barrie Mrs Barrie. And if you don't like to eat with her you can go and eat in the woodshed.'

Then I took to hanging around and getting her to talk. Often she wouldn't. But when she did, it could be rewarding. I had a fine time imitating her at school.

(Me) Your hair is really black, Mrs Barrie.

(Mrs B.) Everyone in my family is got black hair. They all got black hair and it never ever gets gray. That's on my mother's side. It stays black in their coffin. When my grandpa died they kept him in the place in the cemetery all winter while the ground was froze and come spring they was going to put him in the ground and one or other us says, 'Let's take a look see how he made it through the winter.' So we got the fellow to lift the lid and there he was looking fine with his face not dark or caved in or anything and his hair was black. Black.

I could even do the little laughs she does, little

laughs or barks, not to indicate that anything is funny but as a kind of punctuation.

By the time I met you I'd got sick of myself doing this.

After Mrs B. told me all that about her hair I met her one day coming out of the upstairs bathroom. She was hurrying to answer the phone, which I wasn't allowed to answer. Her hair was bundled up in a towel and a dark trickle was running down the side of her face. A dark purplish trickle, and my thought was that she was bleeding.

As if her blood could be eccentric and dark with malevolence as her nature sometimes seemed to be.

'Your head's bleeding,' I said, and she said, 'Oh, get out of my road,' and scrambled past to get the phone. I went on into the bathroom and saw purple streaks in the basin and the hair dye on the shelf. Not a word was said about this, and she continued to talk about how everybody on her mother's side of the family had black hair in their coffins and she would, too.

My father had an odd way of noticing me in those years. He might be passing through a room where I was, and he'd say as if he hadn't seen me there,

> 'The chief defect of Henry King,
> Was chewing little bits of string—'

And sometimes he'd speak to me in a theatrically growly voice.

333

'Hello little girl. Would you like a piece of candy?'

I had learned to answer in a wheedling baby-girl voice. 'Oh yes sir.'

'Wahl.' Some fancy drawing out of the *a*. 'Wahl. You can't have one.'

And:

'"Solomon Grundy, born on Monday—"' He'd jab a finger at me to take it up.

'"Christened on Tuesday—"'

'"Married on Wednesday—"'

'"Sick on Thursday—"'

'"Worse on Friday—"'

'"Died on Saturday—"'

'"Buried on Sunday—"'

Then both together, thunderously. '"And that was the end of Solomon Grundy!"'

Never any introduction, no comment when these passages were over. For a joke I tried calling him Solomon Grundy. The fourth or fifth time he said, 'That's enough. That's not my name. I'm your father.'

After that we probably didn't do the rhyme anymore.

The first time I met you on the campus, and you were alone and I was alone, you looked as if you remembered me but weren't sure about acknowledging it. You had just taught that one class, filling in when our regular man was sick and you had to do the lecture on logical positivism. You joked about its being a funny thing to bring somebody over from the Theological College to do.

You seemed to hesitate about saying hello, so I said, 'The former King of France is bald.'

That was the example you'd given us, of a statement that makes no sense because the subject doesn't exist. But you gave me a truly startled and cornered look that you then covered up with a professional smile. What did you think of me?

A smart aleck.

R. My stomach is still a little puffy. There are no marks on it, but I can bunch it up in my hands. Otherwise I'm okay, my weight is back to normal or a little below. I think I look older, though. I think I look older than twenty-four. My hair is still long and unfashionable, in fact a mess. Is this a memorial to you because you never liked me to cut it? I wouldn't know.

Anyway I've started going on long walks around town, for exercise. I used to go off in the summers, anywhere I liked. I hadn't any sense of what rules there might be, or different grades of people. That could have been because of never going to school in town or because of our house being out of town here where it is, down the long lane. Not properly belonging. I went to the horse barns by the racetrack where the men were horse owners or paid horse trainers and the other kids were boys. I didn't know any names, but they all knew mine. They had to put up with me, in other words, because of whose daughter I was. We were allowed to put down feed and muck out behind the horses. It seemed adventurous. I wore an old golf hat of my father's and a pair of baggy shorts. We'd get up on the roof and they'd grapple and try to push each other off but me they left alone. The men would periodically tell us to get lost. They'd say to me, 'Does your dad know you're here?' Then the boys started teasing each other and the one teased would make a puking noise and I knew it was about me. So I quit going. I gave up the idea of being a Girl of the Golden West. I went down to the dock and looked at the lake boats, but I don't think I went so far as dreaming of being taken on as a deckhand. Also I didn't fool them into thinking I was anything but a girl. A man leaned over and yelled down to me:

'Hey. You got any hair on it yet?'

I almost said, 'Pardon?' I wasn't frightened or humiliated so much as mystified. That a grown-up man with responsible work should be interested in the patchy itchy sprouting in between my legs. Should bother to be disgusted by it, as his voice surely indicated that he was.

The horse barns have been torn down. The road down to the harbor is not so steep. There is a new grain elevator. And new suburbs that could be suburbs anywhere, which is what everybody likes about them. Nobody walks now; everybody drives. The suburbs don't have sidewalks, and the sidewalks along the old backstreets are unused and cracked and uptilted by frost and disappearing under earth and grass. The long dirt path under the pine trees along our lane is lost now under drifts of pine needles and rogue saplings and wild raspberry canes. People have walked up that path for decades to see the doctor. Out from town on a special short extension of sidewalk along the highway (the only other extension was to the cemetery) and then between the double row of pines on that side of the lane. Because there's been a doctor living in this house since the end of the last century.

All sorts of noisy grubby patients, children and mothers and old people, all afternoon, and quieter patients coming singly in the evenings. I used to sit out where there was a pear tree trapped in a clump of lilac bushes, and I'd spy on them, because young girls like to spy. That whole clump is gone now, cleaned out to make things easier for Mrs B.'s nephew's son on the power mower. I used to spy on ladies who got dressed up, at that time, for a visit to the doctor. I remember the clothes from soon after the war. Long full skirts and cinch belts and puffed-up blouses and sometimes short white gloves, for gloves were worn then in summer and not just to church. Hats not just to church either. Pastel straw hats that framed the face. A dress with light summer flounces, a ruffle on the shoulders like a little cape, a sash like a ribbon round the waist. The cape-ruffle could lift in the breeze, and the lady would raise her hand in a crocheted glove to brush it away from her face. This gesture was like a symbol to me of unattainable feminine loveliness. The wisp of cobweb cloth against the perfect velvet mouth. Not having a mother may have had something to do with how I felt. But I didn't know anybody who had a mother that looked the way they did. I'd crouch under the bushes eating the spotty yellow pears and worshipping.

One of our teachers had got us reading old ballads like 'Patrick Spens' and 'The Twa Corbies,' and there'd been a rash of ballad making at school.

> *I'm going down the corridor*
> *My good friend for to see*
> *I'm going to the lav-a-to-ry*
> *To have myself a pee—*

Ballads really tumbled you along into rhymes before you had a chance to think what anything meant. So with my mouth full of mushy pear I made them up.

> *A lady walks on a long long path*
> *She's left the town behind.*
> *She's left her home and her father's wrath*
> *Her destiny for to find—*

When the wasps started bothering me too much I went into the house. Mrs Barrie would be in the kitchen, smoking a cigarette and listening to the radio, until my father called her. She stayed till the last patient had left and the place had been tidied up. If there was a yelp from the office she might give her own little yelping laugh and say, 'Go ahead and holler.' I never bothered describing to her the clothes or the looks of the women I'd seen because I knew she'd never admire anybody for being beautiful or well dressed. Any more than she'd admire them for knowing something nobody needed to know, like a foreign language. Good card players she admired, and fast knitters – that was about all. Many people she had no use for. My father said that too. He had no use. That made me want to ask, If they did have a use, what would the use be? But I knew neither one would tell me. Instead they'd tell me not to be so smart.

> *His Uncle came on Frederick Hyde*
> *Carousing in the Dirt.*
> *He shook him Hard from Side to Side*
> *And Hit him where it Hurt—*

If I decided to send all this to you, where would I send it? When I think of writing the whole address on the envelope I am paralyzed. It's too painful to think of you in the same place with your life going on in the same way, minus me. And to think of you not there, you somewhere else but I don't know where, is worse.

Dear R., Dear Robin, How do you think I didn't know? It was right in front of my eyes all the time. If I had gone to school here, I'd surely have known. If I'd had friends. There's no way one of the high-school girls, one of the older girls, wouldn't have made sure I knew.

Even so, I had plenty of time in the holidays. If I hadn't been so bound up in myself, mooching around town and making up ballads, I could have figured it out. Now that I think of it, I knew that some of those evening patients, those ladies, came on the train. I associated them and their beautiful clothes with the evening train. And there was a late-night train they must have left on. Of course there could just as easily have been a car that dropped them off at the end of the lane.

And I was told – by Mrs B., I think, not by him – that they came to my father for vitamin shots. I know that, because I would think, Now she's getting her shot, whenever we heard a woman make a noise, and I would be a little surprised that women so sophisticated and self-controlled were not more stoical about needles.

Even now, it has taken me weeks. Through all this time of getting used to the ways of the house, to the point where I would never dream of picking up a paintbrush and would hesitate to straighten a drawer or throw out an old grocery receipt without consulting Mrs B. (who can never make up her mind about it anyway). To the point where I've given up trying to get them even to accept perked coffee. (They prefer instant because it always tastes the same.)

My father laid a check beside my plate. At lunch today, Sunday. Mrs Barrie is never here on Sundays. We have a cold lunch which I fix, of sliced meat and bread and tomatoes and pickles and cheese, when my father gets back from church. He never asks me to go to church with him – probably thinking that would just give me a chance to air some views he doesn't care to hear.

The check was for five thousand dollars.

'That's for you,' he said. 'So you'll have something. You can put it in the bank or invest it how you like. See how the rates are. I don't keep up. Of course you'll get the house too. All in the fullness of time, as they say.'

A bribe? I thought. Money to start a little business with, go on a trip with? Money for the down payment on a little house of my own, or to go back to university to get some more of what he has called my unnegotiable degrees.

Five thousand dollars to get rid of me.

I thanked him, and more or less for conversation's sake I asked him what he did with his money. He said that was neither here nor there.

'Ask Billy Snyder if you're looking for advice.' Then he remembered that Billy Snyder was no longer in the accounting business; he had retired.

'There's some new fellow there with a queer name,' he said. 'It's like Ypsilanti, but it's not Ypsilanti.'

'Ypsilanti is a town in Michigan,' I said.

'It's a town in Michigan, but it was a man's name

before it was a town in Michigan,' my father said. It seems it was the name of a Greek leader who fought against the Turks early in the 1800s.

I said, 'Oh. In Byron's war.'

'Byron's war?' said my father. 'What makes you call it that? Byron didn't fight in any war. He died of typhus. Then he's dead, he's the big hero, he died for the Greeks and so on.' He said this contentiously, as if I had been one of those responsible for this mistake, this big fuss over Byron. But then he calmed down and recounted for me or recalled for himself the progress of the war against the Ottoman Empire. He spoke of the Porte and I wanted to say that I've never been sure if that was an actual gate, or was it Constantinople, or the Sultan's court? But it's always best not to interrupt. When he starts to talk like this there's the sense of a truce, or a breathing spell, in an undeclared underground war. I was sitting facing the window, and I could see through the net curtains the heaps of yellow-brown leaves on the ground in the rich generous sunlight (maybe the last of those days we'll get for a long while by the sound of the wind tonight) and it brought to mind my relief as a child, my secret pleasure, whenever I could get him going, by a question or by accident, on a spiel like this.

Earthquakes, for instance. They happen in the volcanic ridges but one of the biggest was right in the middle of the continent, in New Madrid (pronounced 'New Mad-rid,' mind you) in Missouri, in 1811. I know that from him. Rift valleys. Instability that there is no sign of on the surface. Caverns formed in limestone, water under the earth, mountains that given enough time wear away to rubble.

Also numbers. I asked him about numbers once and he said, Well, they're called the arabic numerals, aren't they, any fool knows that. But the Greeks could have managed a good system, he went on to say, the Greeks could have done it, only they didn't have the concept of zero.

Concept of zero. I put that away in my mind like a package on a shelf, to open someday.

If Mrs B. was with us there was of course no hope of getting anything like this out of him.

Never mind, he would say, eat your meal.

As if any question I asked had an ulterior motive, and I suppose it did. I was angling to direct the conversation. And it wasn't polite to leave Mrs B. out. So it was her attitude to what caused earthquakes, or the history of numbers (an attitude not just of indifference but of contempt) that had to be deferred to, had to reign supreme.

So we come round to Mrs B. again. In the present, Mrs B.

I came in last night at about ten o'clock. I'd been out at a meeting of the Historical Society, or at least at a meeting to try and organize one. Five people showed up and two of them walked with canes. When I opened the kitchen door I saw Mrs B. framed in the doorway to the back hall – the hall that leads from the office to the washroom and the front part of the house. She had a covered basin in her hands. She was on her way to the washroom and she could have gone on, passing the kitchen as I came in. I would hardly have noticed her. But she stopped in her tracks and stood there, partly turned towards me; she made a grimace of dismay.

Oh-oh. Caught out.

Then she scurried away towards the toilet.

This was an act. The surprise, the dismay, the hurrying away. Even the way she held the basin out so that I had to notice it. That was all deliberate.

I could hear the rumble of my father's voice in the office, talking to a patient. I had seen the office lights on anyway, I had seen the patient's car parked outside. Nobody has to walk anymore.

I took off my coat and went on upstairs. All I seemed to be concerned about was not letting Mrs B. have it her way. No questions, no shocked realization. No *What is that you have in the basin, Mrs B., oh what have you and my daddy been up to?* (Not that I ever called him my daddy.) I got busy at once rooting around in one of the boxes of books I still hadn't unpacked. I was looking for the journals of Anna Jameson. I had promised them to the other person under seventy who had been at the meeting. A man who is a photographer and knows something about the history of Upper Canada. He would like to have been a history teacher but has a stammer which prevented him. He told me this in the half hour we stood out on the sidewalk talking instead of taking the more decisive step of going for coffee. As we said good night he told me that he'd like to have asked me for coffee, but he had to get home and spell his wife because the baby had colic.

I unpacked the whole box of books before I was through. It was like looking at relics from a bygone age. I looked through them till the patient was gone and my father had taken Mrs B. home and had come upstairs and used the bathroom and gone to bed. I read here and there till I was so groggy I almost fell asleep on the floor.

At lunch today, then, my father finally said, 'Who cares about the Turks anyway? Ancient history.'

And I had to say, 'I think I know what's going on here.'

His head reared up and he snorted. He really did, like an old horse.

'You do, do you? You think you know what?'

I said, 'I'm not accusing you. I don't disapprove.'

'Is that so?'

'I believe in abortion,' I said. 'I believe it should be legal.'

'I don't want you to use that word again in this house,' my father said.

'Why not?'

'Because I am the one who says what words are used in this house.'

'You don't understand what I'm saying.'

'I understand that you've got too loose a tongue.

You've got too loose a tongue and not enough sense. Too much education and not enough ordinary brains.'

I still did not shut up. I said, 'People must know.'

'Must they? There's a difference between knowing and yapping. Get that through your head once and for all.'

We have not spoken for the rest of the day. I cooked the usual roast for dinner and we ate it and did not speak. I don't think he finds this difficult at all. Neither do I so far because everything seems so stupid and outrageous and I'm angry, but I won't stay in this mood forever and I could find myself apologizing. (You may not be surprised to hear that.) It's so obviously time that I got out of here.

The young man last night told me that when he felt relaxed his stammer practically disappeared. Like when I'm talking to you, he said. I could probably make him fall in love with me, to a certain extent. I could do that just for recreation. That is the sort of life I could get into here.

Dear R. I haven't gone, the Mini wasn't fit for it. I took it in to be overhauled. Also the weather has changed, the wind has got into an autumn rampage scooping up the lake and battering the beach. It caught Mrs Barrie on her own front steps – the wind did – and knocked her sideways and shattered her elbow. It's her left elbow and she said she could work with her right arm, but my father told her it was a complicated fracture and he wanted her to rest for a month. He asked me if I would mind postponing my departure. Those were his words – 'postponing my departure.' He hasn't asked where I'm planning to go; he just knows about the car.

I don't know where I'm planning to go, either.

I said all right, I'd stay while I could be useful. So we're on decent speaking terms; in fact it's fairly comfortable. I try to do just about what Mrs B. would do, in the house. No tries now at reorganization, no discussion of repairs. (The eaves have been done – when the Mrs B. relation came I was astonished and grateful.) I hold the oven door shut the way Mrs B. did with a couple of heavy medical textbooks set on a stool pushed up against it. I cook the meat and the vegetables in her way and never think about bringing home an avocado or bottle of artichoke hearts or a garlic bulb, though I see all those things are now for sale in the supermarket. I make the coffee from the powder in the jar. I tried drinking that myself to see if I could get used to it and of course I could. I clean up the office at the end of every day and look after the laundry. The laundryman likes me because I don't accuse him of anything.

I'm allowed to answer the phone, but if it's a woman asking for my father and not volunteering details I'm supposed to take the number and say that the doctor will phone back. So I do, and sometimes the woman just hangs up. When I tell my father this he says, 'She'll likely call again.'

There aren't many of those patients – the ones he calls the specials. I don't know – maybe one a month. Mostly he's dealing with sore throats and cramped colons and bealing ears and so on. Jumpy hearts, kidney stones, sour digestions.

R. Tonight he knocked on my door. He knocked though it wasn't all the way closed. I was reading. He asked – not in a supplicating way of course, but I would say with a reasonable respect – if I could give him a hand in the office.

The first special since Mrs B. has been away.

I asked what he wanted me to do.

'Just more or less to keep her steady,' he said. 'She's young and she's not used to it yet. Give your hands a good scrub too, use the soap in the bottle in the toilet downstairs.'

The patient was lying flat on the examining table with a sheet over her from the waist down. The top part of her was fully dressed in a dark-blue buttoned-up cardigan and a white blouse with a lace-trimmed collar. These clothes lay loosely over her sharp collarbone and nearly flat chest. Her hair was black, pulled tightly back from her face and braided and pinned on top of her head. This prim and severe style made her neck look long and emphasized the regal bone structure of her white face, so that from a distance she could be taken

348

for a woman of forty-five. Close up you could see that she was quite young, probably around twenty. Her pleated skirt was hung up on the back of the door. The rim of white panties showed, that she had thoughtfully hung underneath it.

She was shivering hard though the office wasn't cold.

'Now Madeleine,' my father said. 'The first thing is we've got to get your knees up.'

I wondered if he knew her. Or did he just ask for a name and use whatever the woman gave him?

'Easy,' he said. 'Easy. Easy.' He got the stirrups in place and her feet into them. Her legs were bare and looked as if they'd never known a suntan. She was still wearing her loafers.

Her knees shook so much in this new position that they clapped together.

'You'll have to hold steadier than that,' my father said. 'You know, now, I can't do my job unless you do yours. Do you want a blanket over you?'

He said to me, 'Get her a blanket. Off the bottom shelf there.'

I arranged the blanket to cover the top part of Madeleine's body. She didn't look at me. Her teeth rattled against one another. She clenched her mouth shut.

'Now just slide down this way a bit,' my father said. And to me. 'Hold her knees. Get them apart. Just hold her easy.'

I put my hands on the knobs of the girl's knees

349

and moved them apart as gently as I could. My father's breathing filled the room with its busy unintelligible comments. I had to hold Madeleine's knees quite firmly to keep them from jerking together.

'Where's that old woman?' she said.

I said, 'She's at home. She had a fall. I'm here instead.'

So she had been here before.

'She's rough,' she said.

Her voice was matter-of-fact, almost a growl, not so nervous as I would have expected from the agitation of her body.

'I hope I'm not that rough,' I said.

She didn't answer. My father had picked up a thin rod like a knitting needle.

'Now. This is the hard part,' he said. He spoke in a conversational tone, milder I think than any I have ever heard from him. 'And the more you tighten up the harder it will be. So just – easy. There. Easy. Good girl. Good girl.'

I was trying to think of something to say that would ease her or distract her. I could see now what my father was doing. Laid out on a white cloth on the table beside him, he had a series of rods, all of the same length but of a graduated thickness. These were what he would use, one after the other, to open and stretch the cervix. From my station behind the sheeted barrier beyond the girl's knees, I could not see the actual, intimate progress of these instruments. But I could feel it, from the arriving waves of pain in her body that beat down the spasms of apprehension and actually made her quieter.

Where are you from? Where did you go to school? Do you have a job? (I had noticed a wedding ring, but quite possibly they all wore wedding rings.) Do you like your job? Do you have any brothers or sisters?

Why should she want to answer any of that, even if she wasn't in pain?

She sucked her breath back through her teeth and widened her eyes at the ceiling.

'I know,' I said. 'I know.'

'Getting there,' my father said. 'You're a good girl. Good quiet girl. Won't be long now.'

I said, 'I was going to paint this room, but I never got around to it. If you were going to paint it, what color would you choose?'

'Hoh,' said Madeleine. 'Hoh.' A sudden startled expulsion of breath. 'Hoh. Hoh.'

'Yellow,' I said. 'I thought a light yellow. Or a light green?'

By the time we got to the thickest rod Madeleine had thrust her head back into the flat cushion, stretching out her long neck and stretching her mouth too, lips wide and tight over her teeth.

'Think of your favorite movie. What is your favorite movie?'

A nurse said that to me, just as I reached the unbelievable interminable plateau of pain and was convinced that relief would not come, not this time.

How could movies exist anymore in the world? Now I'd said the same thing to Madeleine, and Madeleine's eyes flicked over me with the coldly distracted expression of someone who sees that a human being can be about as much use as a stopped clock.

I risked taking one hand off her knee and touched her hand. I was surprised at how quickly and fiercely she grabbed it and mashed the fingers together. Some use after all.

'Say some—' she hissed through her teeth. 'Reese. Right.'

'Now then,' my father said. 'Now we're some-place.'

Recite.

What was I supposed to recite? Hickory dickery dock?

What came into my head was what you used to say, 'The Song of Wandering Aengus.'

'"I went into a hazel wood, / Because a fire was in my head—"'

I didn't remember how it went on from there. I couldn't think. Then what should come into my head but the whole last verse.

> *'Though I am old from wandering*
> *Through hollow lands and hilly lands,*
> *I will find out where you have gone,*
> *And kiss your face and take your hands—'*

Imagine me saying a poem in front of my father.

What she thought of it I didn't know. She had closed her eyes.

I thought I was going to be afraid of dying because of my mother's dying that way, in childbirth. But once I got onto that plateau I found that dying and living were both irrelevant notions, like favorite movies. I was stretched to the limit and convinced that I couldn't do a thing to move what felt like a giant egg or a flaming planet not like a baby at all. It was stuck and I was stuck, in a space and time that could just go on forever – there was no reason why I should ever get out, and all my protests had already been annihilated.

'Now I need you,' my father said. 'I need you round here. Get the basin.'

I held in place the same basin that I had seen Mrs Barrie holding. I held it while he scraped out the girl's womb with a clever sort of kitchen instrument. (I don't mean that it was a kitchen instrument but that it had a slightly homely look to me.)

The lower parts of even a thin young girl can look large and meaty in this raw state. In the days after labor, in the maternity ward, women lay carelessly, even defiantly, with their fiery cuts or tears exposed, their black-stitch wounds and sorry flaps and big helpless haunches. It was a sight to see.

Out of the womb now came plops of wine jelly, and blood, and somewhere in there the fetus. Like the bauble in the cereal box or the prize in the popcorn. A tiny plastic doll as negligible as a fingernail. I didn't look for it. I held my head up, away from the smell of warm blood.

'Bathroom,' my father said. 'There's a cover.' He meant the folded cloth that lay beside the soiled rods. I did not like to say, 'Down the toilet?' and took it for granted that that was what he meant. I carried the basin along the hall to the downstairs toilet, dumped the contents, flushed twice, rinsed the basin, and brought it back. My father by this time was bandaging the girl and giving her some instructions. He's good at this – he does it well. But his face looked heavy, weary enough to drop off the bones. It occurred to me that he had wanted me here, all through the procedure, in case he should collapse. Mrs B., at least in the old days, apparently waited in the kitchen until the last moments. Maybe she stays with him all the way through now.

If he had collapsed I don't know what I'd have done.

He patted Madeleine's legs and told her she should lie flat.

'Don't try to get up for a few minutes,' he said. 'Have you got your ride arranged for?'

'He's supposed to've been out there all the time,' she said, in a weak but spiteful voice. 'He wasn't supposed to've gone anyplace.'

My father took off his smock and walked to the window of the waiting room.

'You bet,' he said. 'Right there.' He let out

a complicated groan, said, 'Where's the laundry basket?' remembered that it was back in the bright room where he'd been working, came back and deposited the smock and said to me, 'I'd be very obliged if you could tidy this up.' Tidy up meaning doing the sterilizing and mopping up in general.

I said I would.

'Good,' he said. 'I'll say good night now. My daughter will see you out when you're ready to go.' I was somewhat surprised to hear him say 'my daughter' instead of my name. Of course I'd heard him say that before. If he had to introduce me, for instance. Still, I was surprised.

Madeleine swung her legs off the table the minute he was out of the room. Then she staggered and I went to help her. She said, 'Okay, okay, just got off of the table too quick. Where'd I put my skirt? I don't want to stand around looking like this.'

I got her the skirt and panties off the back of the door and she put them on without help but very shakily.

I said, 'You could rest a minute. Your husband will wait.'

'My husband's working in the bush up near Kenora,' she said. 'I'm going up there next week. He's got a place I can stay.

'Now. I laid my coat down somewheres,' she said.

My favorite movie – as you ought to know and if I could have thought of it when the nurse asked me

355

– is *Wild Strawberries*. I remember the moldy little theater where we used to see all those Swedish and Japanese and Indian and Italian movies and I remember that it had recently switched over from showing *Carry On* movies, and Martin and Lewis, but the name of it I can't remember. Since you were teaching philosophy to future ministers, your favorite movie should have been *The Seventh Seal*, but was it? I think it was Japanese and I forget what it was about. Anyway we used to walk home from the theater, it was a couple of miles, and we used to have fervent conversations about human love and selfishness and God and faith and desperation. When we got to my rooming house we had to shut up. We had to go so softly up the stairs to my room.

Ahhh, you would say gratefully and wonderingly as you got in.

I would have been very nervous about bringing you here last Christmas if we hadn't already been deep into our fight. I would have felt too protective of you to expose you to my father.

'Robin? Is that a man's name?'

You said, Well yes, it was your name.

He pretended he'd never heard it before.

But in fact you got along pretty well together. You had a discussion about some great conflict between different orders of monks in the seventh century, wasn't that it? The row those monks had was about how they should shave their heads.

356

A curly-headed beanpole was what he called you. Coming from him that was almost complimentary.

When I told him on the phone that after all you and I would not be getting married, he said, 'Oh-oh. Do you think you'll ever manage to get another one?' If I'd objected to his saying that he would naturally have said it was a joke. And it was a joke. I have not managed to get another one but perhaps have not been in the best condition to try.

Mrs Barrie is back. She's back in less than three weeks though it was supposed to be a month. But she has to work shorter days than she did before. It takes her so long to get dressed and to do her own housework that she seldom gets here (delivered by her nephew or her nephew's wife) until around ten o'clock in the morning.

'Your father looks poorly' was the first thing she said to me. I think she's right.

'Maybe he should take a rest,' I said.

'Too many people bothering him,' she said.

The Mini is out of the garage and the money is in my bank account. What I should do is take off. But I think stupid things. I think, What if we get another special? How can Mrs B. help him? She can't use her left hand yet to hold any weight, and she could never hold on to the basin with just her right hand.

★   ★   ★

357

R. This day. This day was after the first big snowfall. It all happened overnight and in the morning the sky was clear, blue; there was no wind and the brightness was preposterous. I went for an early walk, under the pine trees. Snow was sifting through them, straight down, bright as the stuff on Christmas trees, or diamonds. The highway had already been plowed and so had our lane, so that my father could drive out to the hospital. Or I could drive out whenever I wanted to.

Some cars went by, in and out of town, as on any other morning.

Before I went back into the house I just wanted to see if the Mini would start, and it did. On the passenger seat I saw a package. It was a two-pound box of chocolates, the kind you buy at the drugstore. I couldn't think how it had got there – I wondered if it could possibly be a present from the young man at the Historical Society. That was a stupid thought. But who else?

I stomped my boots free of snow outside the back door and reminded myself that I must put a broom out. The kitchen had filled up with the day's blast of light.

I thought I knew what my father would say.

'Out contemplating nature?'

He was sitting at the table with his hat and coat on. Usually by this time he had left to see his patients in the hospital.

He said, 'Have they got the road plowed yet? What about the lane?'

I said that both were plowed and clear. He could have seen that the lane was plowed by looking out the window. I put the kettle on and asked if he would like another cup of coffee before he went out.

'All right,' he said. 'Just so long as it's plowed so I can get out.'

'What a day,' I said.

'All right if you don't have to shovel yourself out of it.'

I made the two cups of instant coffee and set them on the table. I sat down, facing the window and the incoming light. He sat at the end of the table, and had shifted his chair so that the light was at his back. I couldn't see what the expression on his face was, but his breathing kept me company as usual.

I started to tell my father about myself. I hadn't intended to do this at all. I had meant to say something about my going away. I opened my mouth and things began to come out of it that I heard with equal amounts of dismay and satisfaction, the way you hear the things you say when you are drunk.

'You never knew I had a baby,' I said. 'I had it on the seventeenth of July. In Ottawa. I've been thinking how ironic that was.'

I told him that the baby had been adopted right away and that I didn't know whether it had been a boy or a girl. That I had asked not to be told. And I had asked not to have to see it.

'I stayed with Josie,' I said. 'You remember me

359

speaking about my friend Josie. She's in England now but she was all alone then in her parents' house. Her parents had been posted to South Africa. That was a godsend.'

I told him who the father of the baby was. I said it was you, in case he wondered. And that since you and I were already engaged, even officially engaged, I had thought that all we had to do was get married.

But you thought differently. You said that we had to find a doctor. A doctor who would give me an abortion.

He did not remind me that I was never supposed to speak that word in his house.

I told him that you said we could not just go ahead and get married, because anybody who could count would know that I had been pregnant before the wedding. We could not get married until I was definitely not pregnant anymore.

Otherwise you might lose your job at the Theological College.

They could bring you up before a committee that might judge you were morally unfit. Morally unfit for the job of teaching young ministers. You could be judged to have a bad character. And even supposing this did not happen, that you did not lose your job but were only reprimanded, or were not even reprimanded, you would never be promoted; there would be a stain on your record. Even if nobody said anything to you, they would *have something* on you, and you could not stand that.

The new students coming in would hear about you from the older ones; there'd be jokes passed on, about you. Your colleagues would have a chance to look down on you. Or be understanding, which was just as bad. You would be a man quietly or not so quietly despised, and a failure.

Surely not, I said.

Oh yes. Never underestimate the meanness there is in people's souls. And for me too, it would be devastating. The wives controlled so much, the older professors' wives. They'd never let me forget. Even when they were being kind – *especially* when they were being kind.

But we could just pick up and go somewhere else, I said. Somewhere where nobody would know.

They'd know. There's always somebody who makes sure that people know.

Besides, that would mean you'd have to start at the bottom again. You'd have to start at a lower salary, a pitiful salary, and how could we manage with a baby, in that case?

I was astonished at these arguments which did not seem to be consistent with the ideas of the person I had loved. The books we had read, the movies we had seen, the things we had talked about – I asked if that meant nothing to you. You said yes, but this was life. I asked if you were somebody who could not stand the thought of someone laughing at him, who could cave in before a bunch of professors' wives.

You said, That's not it, that's not it at all.

I threw my diamond ring away and it rolled under a parked car. As we argued we were walking along a street near my rooming house. It was winter, like now. January or February. But the battle dragged on after that. I was supposed to find out about an abortion from a friend who had a friend who was rumored to have had one. I gave in; I said I'd do it. You couldn't even risk making inquiries. But then I lied, I said the doctor had moved away. Then I admitted lying. I can't do it, I said.

But was that because of the baby? Never. It was because I believed I was right, in the argument.

I had contempt. I had contempt when I saw you scrambling to get under the parked car, and the tails of your overcoat were flapping around your buttocks. You were clawing in the snow to find the ring and you were so relieved when you found it. You were ready to hug me and laugh at me, thinking I'd be relieved too and we'd make up on the spot. I told you you would never do anything admirable in your whole life.

Hypocrite, I said. Sniveller. Philosophy teacher.

Not that that was the end. For we did make up. But we didn't forgive each other. And we didn't take steps. And it got to be too late and we saw that each of us had invested too much in being in the right and we walked away and it was a relief. Yes, at that time I'm sure it was a relief for us both and a kind of victory.

'So isn't that ironic?' I said to my father. 'Considering?'

I could hear Mrs Barrie outside stomping her boots, so I said this in a hurry. My father had sat all the time rigid with embarrassment as I thought, or with profound distaste.

Mrs Barrie opened the door saying, 'Ought to get a broom out there—' Then she cried out, 'What are you doing sitting there? What's the matter with you? Can't you see the man's dead?'

He wasn't dead. He was in fact breathing as noisily as ever and perhaps more so. What she had seen and what I would have seen, even against the light, if I had not been avoiding looking at him whilst I told my tale, was that he had suffered a blinding and paralyzing stroke. He sat slightly tilted forward, the table pressing into the firm curve of his stomach. When we tried to move him from his chair, we managed only to jar him so that his head came down on the table, with a majestic reluctance. His hat stayed on. And his coffee cup stayed in place a couple of inches from his unseeing eye. It was still about half full.

I said we couldn't do anything with him; he was too heavy. I went to the phone and called the hospital, to get one of the other doctors to drive out. There's no ambulance yet in this town. Mrs B. paid no attention to what I said and kept pulling at my father's clothes, undoing buttons and yanking at the overcoat and grunting and whimpering with the exertion. I ran out to the lane, leaving the door open. I ran back, and got a broom, and set it outside by the door. I went and put a hand on Mrs B.'s arm and said, 'You can't—' or something like that, and she gave me the look of a spitting cat.

A doctor came. He and I together were able to pull my father out to the car and get him into the backseat. I got in beside him to hold on to him and keep him from toppling over. The sound of his breathing was more peremptory than ever and seemed to be criticizing whatever we did. But the fact was that you could take hold of him now, and shove him around, and manage his body as you had to, and this seemed very odd.

Mrs B. had fallen back and quieted down as soon as she saw the other doctor. She didn't even follow us out of the house to see my father loaded into the car.

This afternoon he died. At about five o'clock. I was told it was very lucky for all concerned.

I was full of other things to say, just when Mrs Barrie came in. I was going to say to my father, What if the law should change? The law might change soon, I was going to say. Maybe not, but it might. He'd be out of business then. Or out of one part of his business. Would that make a great difference to him?

What could I expect him to answer?

Speaking of business, that is none of yours.

Or, I'd still make a living.

No, I would say. I didn't mean the money. I meant the risk. The secrecy. The power.

Change the law, change what a person does, change what a person is?

Or would he find some other risk, some other knot to make in his life, some other underground and problematic act of mercy?

And if that law can change, other things can change. I'm thinking about you now, how it could happen that you wouldn't be ashamed to marry a pregnant woman. There'd be no shame to it. Move ahead a few years, just a few years, and it could be a celebration. The pregnant bride is garlanded and led to the altar, even in the chapel of the Theological College.

If that happened, though, there'd likely be something else to be ashamed or afraid of, there'd be other errors to be avoided.

So what about me? Would I always have to find a high horse? The moral relish, the rising above, the being in the right, which can make me flaunt my losses.

Change the person. We all say we hope it can be done.

Change the law, change the person. Yet we don't want everything – not the whole story – to be dictated from outside. We don't want what we are, all we are, to be concocted that way.

Who is this 'we' I'm talking about?

R. My father's lawyer says, 'It's very unusual.' I

realize that for him this is quite a strong, and sufficient, word.

There is enough money in my father's bank account to cover his funeral expenses. Enough to bury him, as they say. (Not the lawyer – he doesn't talk like that.) But there isn't much more. There are no stock certificates in his safety deposit box; there is no record of investments. Nothing. No bequest to the hospital, or to his church, or to the high school to establish a scholarship. Most shocking of all, there is no money left to Mrs Barrie. The house and its contents are mine. And that's all there is. I have my five thousand dollars.

The lawyer seems embarrassed, painfully embarrassed, and worried about this state of affairs. Perhaps he thinks I might suspect him of misconduct. Try to blacken his name. He wants to know if there's a safe in my (my father's) house, any hiding place at all for a large amount of cash. I say there isn't. He tries to suggest to me – in such a discreet and roundabout way that I don't know at first what he's talking about – that there might be reasons for my father's wanting to keep the amount of his earnings a secret. A large amount of cash holed away somewhere is therefore a possibility.

I tell him I'm not terribly concerned about the money.

What a thing to say. He can hardly look me in the eye.

'Perhaps you could go home and take a very good look,' he says. 'Don't neglect the obvious places. It could be in a cookie tin. Or in a box under the bed. Surprising the places people can pick. Even the most sensible and intelligent people.

'Or in a pillow slip,' he's saying as I go out the door.

A woman on the phone wants to speak to the doctor.

'I'm sorry. He's dead.'

'Dr Strachan. Have I got the right doctor?'

'Yes but I'm sorry, he's dead.'

'Is there anyone – does he by any chance have a partner I could talk to? Is there anybody else there?'

'No. No partner.'

'Could you give me any other number I could call? Isn't there some other doctor that can—'

'No. I haven't any number. There isn't anybody that I know of.'

'You must know what this is about. It's very crucial. There are very special circumstances—'

'I'm sorry.'

'There isn't any problem about money.'

'No.'

'Please try to think of somebody. If you do think of somebody later on, could you give me a call? I'll leave you my number.'

'You shouldn't do that.'

'I don't care. I trust you. Anyway it's not for myself. I know everybody must say that but really it's not. It's for my daughter who's in a very

bad condition. Mentally she's in a very bad condition.'

'I'm sorry.'

'If you knew what I went through to get this
number you would try to help me.'

'Sorry.'

'Please.'

'I'm sorry.'

Madeleine was the last one of his specials. I saw
her at the funeral. She hadn't got to Kenora. Or
else she'd come back. I didn't recognize her at first
because she was wearing a wide-brimmed black hat
with a horizontal feather. She must have borrowed
it – she wasn't used to the feather which came
drooping down over her eye. She spoke to me in
the lineup at the reception in the church hall. I said
to her just the same thing I said to everybody.

'So good of you to come.'

Then I realized what an odd thing she'd said to
me.

'I was just counting on you to have a sweet
tooth.'

'Perhaps he didn't always charge,' I say to the
lawyer. 'Perhaps he worked for nothing sometimes.
Some people do things out of charity.'

The lawyer is getting used to me now. He says,
'Perhaps.'

'Or possibly an actual charity,' I say. 'A charity
he supported without keeping any record of it.'

The lawyer holds my eyes for a moment.

'A charity,' he says.

'Well I haven't dug up the cellar floor yet,' I say, and he smiles wincingly at this levity.

Mrs Barrie hasn't given her notice. She just hasn't shown up. There was nothing in particular for her to do, since the funeral was in the church and the reception was in the church hall. She didn't come to the funeral. None of her family came. So many people were there that I would not have noticed that if someone hadn't said to me, 'I didn't see any of the Barrie connection, did you?'

I phoned her several days afterwards and she said, 'I never went to the church because I had too bad a cold.'

I said that that wasn't why I'd called. I said I could manage quite well but wondered what she planned to do.

'Oh I don't see no need for me to come back there now.'

I said that she should come and get something from the house, a keepsake. By this time I knew about the money and I wanted to tell her I felt bad about it. But I didn't know how to say that.

She said, 'I got some stuff I left there. I'll be out when I can.'

She came out the next morning. The things she had to collect were mops and pails and scrub brushes and a clothes basket. It was hard to believe she would care about retrieving articles like these.

And hard to believe she wanted them for senti-mental reasons, but maybe she did. They were things she had used for years – during all her years in this house, where she had spent more waking hours than she had spent at home.

'Isn't there anything else?' I said. 'For a keep-sake?'

She looked around the kitchen, chewing on her bottom lip. She might have been chewing back a smile.

'I don't think there's nothing here I'd have much use for,' she said.

I had a check ready for her. I just needed to write in the amount. I hadn't been able to decide how much of the five thousand dollars to share with her. A thousand? I had been thinking. Now that seemed shameful. I thought I'd better double it.

I got out the checks that I had hidden in a drawer. I found a pen. I made it out for four thousand dollars.

'This is for you,' I said. 'And thank you for everything.'

She took the check in her hand and glanced at it and stuffed it in her pocket. I thought maybe she hadn't been able to read how much it was for. Then I saw the darkening flush, the tide of embarrassment, the difficulty of being grateful.

She managed to pick up all the things she was taking, using her one good arm. I opened the door for her. I was so anxious for her to say something more that I almost said, Sorry that's all.

Instead I said, 'Your elbow's not better yet?'

'It'll never be better,' she said. She ducked her head as if she was afraid of another of my kisses. She said, 'Well-thanks-very-much-goodbye.'

I watched her making her way to the car. I had assumed her nephew's wife had driven her out here.

But it was not the usual car that the nephew's wife drove. The thought crossed my mind that she might have a new employer. Bad arm or not. A new and rich employer. That would account for her haste, her cranky embarrassment.

It was the nephew's wife, after all, who got out to help with the load. I waved, but she was too busy stowing the mops and pails.

'Gorgeous car,' I called out, because I thought that was a compliment both women would appreciate. I didn't know what make the car was, but it was shining new and large and glamorous. A silvery lilac color.

The nephew's wife called out, 'Oh yeah,' and Mrs Barrie ducked her head in acknowledgment.

Shivering in my indoor clothes, but compelled by my feelings of apology and bewilderment, I stood there and waved the car out of sight.

I couldn't settle down to do anything after that. I made myself coffee and sat in the kitchen. I got Madeleine's chocolates out of the drawer and ate a couple, though I really did not have enough of a sweet tooth for their chemically colored orange and yellow centers. I wished I had thanked her. I didn't see how I could now – I didn't even know her last name.

I decided to go out skiing. There are gravel pits that I believe I told you about at the back of our property. I put on the old wooden skis that my father used to wear in the days when the back roads were not plowed out in winter, and he might have to go across the fields to deliver a baby or take out an appendix. There were only cross straps to hold your feet in place.

I skied back to the gravel pits whose slopes have been padded with grass over the years and are now additionally covered with snow. There were dog tracks, bird tracks, the faint circles that the skittering voles make, but no sign of humans. I went up and down, up and down, first choosing a cautious diagonal and then going on to steeper descents. I fell now and then, but easily on the fresh plentiful snow, and between one moment of falling and the next of getting to my feet I found out that I knew something.

I knew where the money had gone.
Perhaps a charity.
Gorgeous car.
And four thousand dollars out of five.

Since that moment I have been happy.

I've been given the feeling of seeing money thrown over a bridge or high up into the air.

Money, hopes, love letters – all such things can be tossed off into the air and come down changed, come down all light and free of context.

The thing I can't imagine is my father caving in to blackmail. Particularly not to people who wouldn't be very credible or clever. Not when the whole town seems to be on his side, or at least on the side of silence.

What I can imagine, though, is a grand perverse gesture. To forestall demand, maybe, or just to show he didn't care. Looking forward to the lawyer's shock, and to my trying even harder to figure him out, now that he's dead.

No. I don't think he'd be thinking of that. I don't think I'd have come into his thoughts so much. Never so much as I'd like to believe.

What I've been shying away from is that it could have been done for love.

For love, then. Never rule that out.

I climbed out of the gravel pit and as soon as I came out on the fields the wind hit me. Wind was blowing snow over the dog tracks and the fine chain traces of the vole and the trail that will likely be the last ever to be broken by my father's skis.

Dear R., Robin – what should be the last thing I say to you?

Goodbye and good luck.

I send you my love.

(What if people really did that – sent their love through the mail to get rid of it? What would it be that they sent? A box of chocolates with centers like the yolks of turkeys' eggs. A mud doll with hollow eye sockets. A heap of roses slightly more fragrant than rotten. A package wrapped in bloody newspaper that nobody would want to open.)

Take care of yourself.

Remember – the present King of France is bald.

MY MOTHER'S DREAM

During the night – or during the time she had been asleep – there had been a heavy fall of snow.

My mother looked out from a big arched window such as you find in a mansion or an old-fashioned public building. She looked down on lawns and shrubs, hedges, flower gardens, trees, all covered by snow that lay in heaps and cushions, not levelled or disturbed by wind. The white of it did not hurt your eyes as it does in sunlight. The white was the white of snow under a clear sky just before dawn. Everything was still; it was like 'O Little Town of Bethlehem' except that the stars had gone out.

Yet something was wrong. There was a mistake in this scene. All the trees, all the shrubs and plants, were out in full summer leaf. The grass that showed underneath them, in spots sheltered from the snow, was fresh and green. Snow had settled overnight on the luxury of summer. A change of season unexplainable, unexpected. Also, everybody had gone away – though she couldn't think who 'everybody' was – and my mother was alone in the high spacious house amongst its rather formal trees and gardens.

She thought that whatever had happened would soon be made known to her. Nobody came, however. The telephone did not ring; the latch of the garden gate was not lifted. She could not hear any traffic, and she did not even know which way the street was – or the road, if she was out in the country. She had to get out of the house, where the air was so heavy and settled.

When she got outside she remembered. She remembered that she had left a baby out there somewhere, before the snow had fallen. Quite a while before the snow had fallen. This memory, this certainty, came over her with horror. It was as if she was awakening from a dream. Within her dream she awakened from a dream, to a knowledge of her responsibility and mistake. She had left her baby out overnight, she had forgotten about it. Left it exposed somewhere as if it was a doll she tired of. And perhaps it was not last night but a week or a month ago that she had done this. For a whole season or for many seasons she had left her baby out. She had been occupied in other ways. She might even have travelled away from here and just returned, forgetting what she was returning to.

She went around looking under hedges and broad-leaved plants. She foresaw how the baby would be shrivelled up. It would be dead, shrivelled and brown, its head like a nut, and on its tiny shut-up face there would be an expression not of distress but of bereavement, an old patient grief. There would not be any accusation of her, its mother – just the look of patience and helplessness with which it waited for its rescue or its fate.

The sorrow that came to my mother was the sorrow of the baby's waiting and not knowing it waited for her, its only hope, when she had forgotten all about it. So small and new a baby that could not even turn away from the snow. She could hardly breathe for her sorrow. There would never be any room in her for anything else. No room for anything but the realization of what she had done.

What a reprieve, then, to find her baby lying in its crib. Lying on its stomach, its head turned to one side, its skin pale and sweet as snowdrops and the down on its head reddish like the dawn. Red hair like her own, on her perfectly safe and unmistakable baby. The joy to find herself forgiven.

The snow and the leafy gardens and the strange house had all withdrawn. The only remnant of the whiteness was the blanket in the crib. A baby blanket of light white wool, crumpled halfway down the baby's back. In the heat, the real summer heat, the baby was wearing only a diaper and a pair of plastic pants to keep the sheet dry. The plastic pants had a pattern of butterflies.

My mother, still thinking no doubt about the snow and the cold that usually accompanies snow, pulled the blanket up to cover the baby's bare back and shoulders, its red-downed head.

★   ★   ★

It is early morning when this happens in the real world. The world of July 1945. At a time when, on any other morning, it would be demanding its first feeding of the day, the baby sleeps on. The mother, though standing on her feet and with her eyes open, is still too far deep in sleep in her head to wonder about this. Baby and mother are worn out by a long battle, and the mother has forgotten even that at the moment. Some circuits are closed down; the most unrelenting quiet has settled on her brain and her baby's. The mother – my mother – makes no sense of the daylight which is increasing every moment. She doesn't understand that the sun is coming up as she stands there. No memory of the day before, or of what happened around midnight, comes up to jolt her. She pulls the blanket up over her baby's head, over its mild, satisfied, sleeping profile. She pads back to her own room and falls down on the bed and is again, at once, unconscious.

The house in which this happens is nothing like the house in the dream. It is a one-and-a-half-story white wooden house, cramped but respectable, with a porch that comes to within a few feet of the sidewalk, and a bay window in the dining room looking out on a small hedged yard. It is on a backstreet in a small town that is indistinguishable – to an outsider – from a lot of other small towns to be found ten or fifteen miles apart in the once thickly populated farmland near Lake Huron. My father and his sisters grew up in this house, and the sisters and mother were still living here when my mother joined them – and I joined them too, being large and lively inside her – after my father was killed in the final weeks of the war in Europe.

My mother – Jill – is standing beside the dining-room table in the bright late afternoon. The house is full of people who have been invited back there after the memorial service in the church. They are drinking tea or coffee and managing to hold in their fingers the dinky sandwiches, or slices of banana bread, nut loaf, pound cake. The custard tarts or raisin tarts with their crumbly pastry are supposed to be eaten with a dessert fork off one of the small china plates that were painted with violets by Jill's mother-in-law when she was a bride. Jill picks everything up with her fingers. Pastry crumbs have fallen, a raisin has fallen, and been smeared into the green velvet of her dress. It's too hot a dress for the day, and it's not a maternity dress at all but a loose sort of robe made for recitals, occasions when she plays her violin in public. The hem rides up in front, due to me. But it's the only thing she owns that is large enough and good enough for her to wear at her husband's memorial service.

What is this eating all about? People can't help but notice. 'Eating for two,' Ailsa says to a group of her guests, so that they won't get the better of her by anything they say or don't say about her sister-in-law.

Jill has been queasy all day, until suddenly in the church, when she was thinking how bad the organ was, she realized that she was, all of a sudden, as hungry as a wolf. All through 'O Valiant Hearts' she was thinking of a fat hamburger dripping with meat juice and melted mayonnaise, and now she is trying to find what concoction of walnuts and raisins and brown sugar, what tooth-jabbing sweetness of coconut icing or soothing mouthful of banana bread or dollop of custard, will do as a substitute. Nothing will, of course, but she keeps on going. When her real hunger is satisfied her imaginary hunger is still working, and even more an irritability amounting almost to panic that makes her stuff into her mouth what she can hardly taste any longer. She couldn't describe this irritability except to say it has something to do with furriness and tightness. The barberry hedge outside the window, thick and bristling in the sunlight, the feel of the velvet dress clinging to her damp armpits, the nosegays of curls – the same color as the raisins in the tarts – bunched on her sister-in-law Ailsa's head, even the painted violets that look like scabs you could pick off the plate, all these things seem particularly horrid and oppressive to her though she knows they are quite ordinary. They seem to carry some message about her new and unexpected life.

Why unexpected? She has known for some time about me and she also knew that George Kirkham might be killed. He was in the air force, after all. (And around her in the Kirkhams' house this afternoon people are saying – though not to her,

380

his widow, or to his sisters – that he was just the sort you always knew would be killed. They mean because he was good-looking and high-spirited and the pride of his family, the one on whom all the hopes had been pinned.) She knew this, but she went ahead with her ordinary life, lugging her violin onto the streetcar on dark winter mornings, riding to the Conservatory where she practiced hour after hour within sound of others but alone in a dingy room with the radiator racket for company, the skin of her hands blotchy at first with the cold, then parched in the dry indoor heat. She went on living in a rented room with an ill-fitting window that let in flies in summer and a windowsill sprinkle of snow in winter, and dreaming – when she wasn't sick – of sausages and meat pies and dark chunks of chocolate. At the Conservatory people treated her pregnancy tactfully, as if it was a tumor. It didn't show for a long time anyway, as first pregnancies generally don't on a big girl with a broad pelvis. Even with me turning somersaults she played in public. Majestically thickened, with her long red hair lying in a bush around her shoulders, her face broad and glowing, her expression full of somber concentration, she played a solo in her most important recital so far. The Mendelssohn Violin Concerto.

She paid some attention to the world – she knew the war was ending. She thought that George might be back soon after I was born. She knew that she wouldn't be able to go on living in her room then – she'd have to live somewhere with him. And she knew that I'd be there, but she thought of my birth as bringing something to an end rather than starting something. It would bring an end to the kicking in the permanent sore spot on one side of her belly and the ache in her genitals when she stands up and the blood rushes into them (as if she'd had a burning poultice laid there). Her nipples will no longer be large and dark and nubbly, and she won't have to wind bandages around her legs with their swollen veins before she gets out of bed every morning. She won't have to urinate every half hour or so, and her feet will shrink back into their ordinary shoes. She thinks that once I'm out I won't give her so much trouble.

After she knew that George would not be coming back she thought about keeping me for a while in that same room. She got a book about babies. She bought the basic things that I would need. There was an old woman in the building who could look after me while she practiced. She would get a war widow's pension and in six more months she would graduate from the Conservatory.

Then Ailsa came down on the train and collected her. Ailsa said, 'We couldn't leave you stuck down here all by yourself. Everybody wonders why you didn't come up when George went overseas. It's time you came now.'

'My family's crackers,' George had told Jill. 'Iona's

a nervous wreck and Ailsa should have been a sergeant major. And my mother's senile.'

He also said, 'Ailsa got the brains, but she had to quit school and go and work in the Post Office when my dad died. I got the looks and there wasn't anything left for poor old Iona but the bad skin and the bad nerves.'

Jill met his sisters for the first time when they came to Toronto to see George off. They hadn't been at the wedding, which had taken place two weeks before. Nobody was there but George and Jill and the minister and the minister's wife and a neighbor called in to be the second witness. I was there as well, already tucked up inside Jill, but I was not the reason for the wedding and at the time nobody knew of my existence. Afterwards George insisted that he and Jill take some poker-faced wedding pictures of themselves in one of those do-it-yourself picture booths. He was in relentless high spirits. 'That'll fix them,' he said, when he looked at the pictures. Jill wondered if there was anybody special he meant to fix. Ailsa? Or the pretty girls, the cute and perky girls, who had run after him, writing him sentimental letters and knitting him argyle socks? He wore the socks when he could, he pocketed the presents, and he read the letters out in bars for a joke.

Jill had not had any breakfast before the wedding, and in the midst of it she was thinking of pancakes and bacon.

★　　★　　★

The two sisters were more normal-looking than she had expected. Though it was true about George getting the looks. He had a silky wave to his dark-blond hair and a hard gleeful glint in his eyes and a clean-cut enviable set of features. His only drawback was that he was not very tall. Just tall enough to look Jill in the eye. And to be an air force pilot.

'They don't want tall guys for pilots,' he said. 'I beat them out there. The beanpole bastards. Lots of guys in the movies are short. They stand on boxes for the kissing.'

(At the movies, George could be boisterous. He might hiss the kissing. He didn't go in for it much in real life either. Let's get to the action, he said.)

The sisters were short, too. They were named after places in Scotland, where their parents had gone on their honeymoon before the family lost its money. Ailsa was twelve years older than George, and Iona was nine years older. In the crowd at Union Station they looked dumpy and bewildered. Both of them wore new hats and suits, as if they were the ones who had recently been married. And both were upset because Iona had left her good gloves on the train. It was true that Iona had bad skin, though it wasn't broken out at present and perhaps her acne days were over. It was lumpy with old scars and dingy under the pink powder. Her hair slipped out in droopy tendrils from under her hat and her eyes were teary, either because of Ailsa's scolding or because her brother was going away to war. Ailsa's hair was arranged in bunches of tight permanented curls, with her hat riding on top. She had shrewd pale eyes behind sparkle-rimmed glasses, and round pink cheeks, and a dimpled chin. Both she and Iona had tidy figures – high breasts and small waists and flaring hips – but on Iona this figure looked like something she had picked up by mistake and was trying to hide by stooping her shoulders and crossing her arms. Ailsa managed her curves assertively not provocatively, as if she was made of some sturdy ceramic. And both of them had George's dark-blond coloring, but without his gleam. They didn't seem to share his sense of humor either.

'Well I'm off,' George said. 'I'm off to die a hero on the field at Passchendaele.' And Iona said, 'Oh don't say that. Don't talk like that.' Ailsa twitched her raspberry mouth.

'I can see the lost-and-found sign from here,' she said. 'But I don't know if that's just for things you lose in the station or is it for things that they find in the trains? Passchendaele was in the First World War.'

'Was it? You sure? I'm too late?' said George, beating his hand on his chest.

And he was burned up a few months later in a training flight over the Irish Sea.

Ailsa smiles all the time. She says, 'Well of course I am proud. I am. But I'm not the only one to lose somebody. He did what he had to do.' Some people find her briskness a bit shocking. But others say, 'Poor Ailsa.' All that concentrating on George, and saving to send him to law school, and then he flouted her – he signed up; he went off and got himself killed. He couldn't wait.

His sisters sacrificed their own schooling. Even getting their teeth straightened – they sacrificed that. Iona did go to nursing school, but as it turned out getting her teeth fixed would have served her better. Now she and Ailsa have ended up with a hero. Everybody grants it – a hero. The younger people present think it's something to have a hero in the family. They think the importance of this moment will last, that it will stay with Ailsa and Iona forever. 'O Valiant Hearts' will soar around them forever. Older people, those who remember the previous war, know that all they've ended up with is a name on the cenotaph. Because the widow, the girl feeding her face, will get the pension.

Ailsa is in a hectic mood partly because she has been up two nights in a row, cleaning. Not that the house wasn't decently clean before. Nevertheless she felt the need to wash every dish, pot, and ornament, polish the glass on every picture, pull out the fridge and scrub behind it, wash the cellar steps off, and pour bleach in the garbage can. The very lighting fixture overhead, over the dining-room table, had to be taken apart, and every piece on it dunked in soapy water, rinsed, and rubbed dry and reassembled. And because of her work at the Post Office Ailsa couldn't start this till after supper. She is the postmistress now, she could have given herself a day off, but being Ailsa she would never do that.

Now she's hot under her rouge, twitchy in her dark-blue lace-collared crepe dress. She can't stay still. She refills the serving plates and passes them around, deplores the fact that people's tea may have got cold, hurries to make a fresh pot. Mindful of her guests' comfort, asking after their rheumatism or minor ailments, smiling in the face of her tragedy, repeating over and over again that hers is a common loss, that she must not complain when so many others are in the same boat, that George would not want his friends to grieve but to be thankful that all together we have ended the war. All in a high and emphatic voice of cheerful reproof that people are used to from the Post Office. So that they are left with an uncertain feeling of perhaps having said the wrong thing, just as in the Post Office they may be made to understand that their handwriting cannot help but be a trial or their packages are done up sloppily.

Ailsa is aware that her voice is too high and that she is smiling too much and that she has poured out tea for people who said they didn't want any more. In the kitchen, while warming the teapot, she says, 'I don't know what's the matter with me. I'm all wound up.'

The person she says this to is Dr Shantz, her neighbor across the backyard.

'It'll soon be over,' he says. 'Would you like a bromide?'

His voice undergoes a change as the door from the dining room opens. The word 'bromide' comes out firm and professional.

Ailsa's voice changes too, from forlorn to valiant. She says, 'Oh, no thank you. I'll just try and keep going on my own.'

Iona's job is supposed to be to watch over their mother, to see that she doesn't spill her tea – which she may do not out of clumsiness but forgetfulness – and that she is taken away if she starts to sniffle and cry. But in fact Mrs Kirkham's manners are gracious most of the time and she puts people at ease more readily than Ailsa does. For a quarter of an hour at a time she understands the situation – or she seems to – and she speaks bravely and cogently about how she will always miss her son but is grateful she still has her daughters: Ailsa so efficient and reliable, a wonder as she's always been, and Iona the soul of kindness. She even remembers to speak of her new daughter-in-law but perhaps gives a hint of being out of line when she mentions what most women of her age don't mention at a social gathering, and with men listening. Looking at Jill and me, she says, 'And we all have a comfort to come.'

Then passing from room to room or guest to guest, she forgets entirely, she looks around her own house and says, 'Why are we here? What a lot

388

of people – what are we celebrating?' And catching on to the fact that it all has something to do with George, she says, 'Is it George's wedding?' Along with her up-to-date information she has lost some of her mild discretion. 'It's not your wedding, is it?' she says to Iona. 'No. I didn't think so. You never had a boyfriend, did you?' A let's-face-facts, devil-take-the-hindmost note has come into her voice. When she spots Jill she laughs.

'That's not the bride, is it? Oh-oh. Now we understand.'

But the truth comes back to her as suddenly as it went away.

'Is there news?' she says. 'News about George?' And it's then that the weeping starts that Ailsa was afraid of.

'Get her out of the way if she starts making a spectacle,' Ailsa had said.

Iona isn't able to get her mother out of the way – she has never been able to exert authority over anybody in her life – but Dr Shantz's wife catches the old woman's arm.

'George is dead?' says Mrs Kirkham fearfully, and Mrs Shantz says, 'Yes he is. But you know his wife is having a baby.'

Mrs Kirkham leans against her; she crumples and says softly, 'Could I have my tea?'

Everywhere my mother turns in that house, it seems she sees a picture of my father. The last and official one, of him in his uniform, sits on an embroidered runner on the closed sewing machine in the bay of the dining-room window. Iona puts flowers around it, but Ailsa took them away. She said it made him look too much like a Catholic saint. Hanging above the stairs there is one of him at six years old, out on the sidewalk, with his knee in his wagon, and in the room where Jill sleeps there's one of him beside his bicycle, with his *Free Press* newspaper sack. Mrs Kirkham's room has the one of him dressed for the grade-eight operetta, with a gold cardboard crown on his head. Being unable to carry a tune, he couldn't have a leading role, but he was of course picked for the best background role, that of the king.

The hand-tinted studio photo over the buffet shows him at the age of three, a blurred blond tot dragging a rag doll by one leg. Ailsa thought of taking that down because it might seem tear-jerking, but she left it up rather than show a bright patch on the wallpaper. And no one said anything about it but Mrs Shantz, who paused and said what she had said sometimes before, and not tearfully but with a faintly amused appreciation.

'Ah – Christopher Robin.'

People were used to not paying much attention to what Mrs Shantz said.

In all of his pictures George looks bright as a dollar. There's always a sunny dip of hair over his brow, unless he's wearing his officer's hat or his crown. And even when he was little more than an infant he looked as if he knew himself to be a capering, calculating, charming sort of fellow. The sort who never let people alone, who whipped them up to laugh. At his own expense occasionally, but usually at other people's. Jill recalls when she looks at him how he drank but never seemed drunk and how he occupied himself getting other drunk people to confess to him their fears, prevarications, virginity, or two-timing, which he would then turn into jokes or humiliating nicknames that his victims pretended to enjoy. For he had legions of followers and friends, who maybe latched on to him out of fear – or maybe just because, as was always said of him, he livened things up. Wherever he was was the center of the room, and the air around him crackled with risk and merriment.

What was Jill to make of such a lover? She was nineteen when she met him, and nobody had ever claimed her before. She couldn't understand what attracted him, and she could see that nobody else could understand it, either. She was a puzzle to most people of her own age, but a dull puzzle. A girl whose life was given over to the study of the violin and who had no other interests.

That was not quite true. She would snuggle under her shabby quilts and imagine a lover. But he was never a shining cutup like George. She thought of some warm and bearlike fellow, or of a musician a decade older than herself and already legendary, with a fierce potency. Her notions of love were operatic, though that was not the sort of music she most admired. But George made jokes when he made love; he pranced around her room when he had finished; he made rude and infantile noises. His brisk performances brought her little of the pleasure she knew from her assaults on herself, but she was not exactly disappointed.

Dazed at the speed of things was more like it. And expecting to be happy – grateful and happy – when her mind caught up with physical and social reality. George's attentions, and her marriage – those were all like a brilliant extension of her life. Lighted rooms showing up full of a bewildering sort of splendor. Then came the bomb or the hurricane, the not unlikely stroke of disaster, and the whole extension was gone. Blown up and vanished, leaving her with the same space and options she'd had before. She had lost something, certainly. But not something she had really got hold of, or understood as more than a hypothetical layout of the future.

She has had enough to eat, now. Her legs ache from standing so long. Mrs Shantz is beside her, saying, 'Have you had a chance to meet any of George's local friends?'

She means the young people keeping to themselves in the hall doorway. A couple of nice-looking girls, a young man still wearing a naval uniform, others. Looking at them, Jill thinks clearly that no one is really sorry. Ailsa perhaps, but Ailsa has her own reasons. No one is really sorry George is dead. Not even the girl who was crying in church and looks as if she will cry some more. Now that girl can remember that she was in love with George

392

and think that he was in love with her – in spite of all – and never be afraid of what he may do or say to prove her wrong. And none of them will have to wonder, when a group of people clustered around George has started laughing, whom they are laughing at or what George is telling them. Nobody will have to strain to keep up with him or figure out how to stay in his good graces anymore.

It doesn't occur to her that if he had lived George might have become a different person, because she doesn't think of becoming a different person herself.

She says, 'No,' with a lack of enthusiasm that causes Mrs Shantz to say, 'I know. It's hard meeting new people. Particularly – if I was you I would rather go and lie down.'

Jill was almost sure she was going to say 'go and have a drink.' But there's nothing being offered here, only tea and coffee. Jill hardly drinks anyway. She can recognize the smell on someone's breath, though, and she thought she smelled it on Mrs Shantz.

'Why don't you?' says Mrs Shantz. 'These things are a great strain. I'll tell Ailsa. Go on now.'

Mrs Shantz is a small woman with fine gray hair, bright eyes, and a wrinkled, pointed face. Every winter she spends a month by herself in Florida. She has money. The house that she and her husband built for themselves, behind the Kirkhams' house, is long and low and blindingly white, with curved corners and expanses of glass bricks. Dr Shantz is twenty or twenty-five years younger than she is – a thickset, fresh, and amiable-looking man with a high smooth forehead and fair curly hair. They have no children. It is believed that she has some, from a first marriage, but they don't come to visit her. In fact the story is that Dr Shantz was her son's friend, brought home from college, and that he fell in love with his friend's mother, she fell in love with her son's friend, there was a divorce, and here they are married, living in luxurious, closemouthed exile.

Jill did smell whiskey. Mrs Shantz carries a flask whenever she goes to a gathering of which – as she says – she can have no reasonable hopes. Drink does not make her fall about or garble her words or pick fights or throw her arms about people. The truth may be that she's always a little bit drunk but never really drunk. She is used to letting the alcohol enter her body in a reasonable, reassuring way, so that her brain cells never get soaked or quite dried out. The only giveaway is the smell (which many people in this dry town attribute to some medicine she has to take or even to an ointment that she has to rub on her chest). That, and perhaps a deliberateness about her speech, the way she seems to clear a space around each word. She says things of course which a woman brought up around here would not say. She tells things on herself. She tells about being mistaken every once in a while for her husband's mother. She says most people go into a tailspin when they discover their mistake, they're so embarrassed. But some women – a waitress, maybe – will fasten on Mrs Shantz quite a dirty look, as if to say, What's he doing wasted on you?

And Mrs Shantz just says to them, 'I know. It isn't fair. But life isn't fair and you might as well get used to it.'

There isn't any way this afternoon that she can space her sips properly. The kitchen and even the poky pantry behind it are places where women can be coming and going at any time. She has to go upstairs to the bathroom, and that not too often. When she does that late in the afternoon, a little while after Jill has disappeared, she finds the bathroom door locked. She thinks of nipping into one of the bedrooms and is wondering which one is empty, which occupied by Jill. Then she hears Jill's voice coming from the bathroom, saying, 'Just a minute,' or something like that. Something quite ordinary, but the tone of voice is strained and frightened.

Mrs Shantz takes a quick swallow right there in the hall, seizing the excuse of emergency.

'Jill? Are you all right? Can you let me in?'

Jill is on her hands and knees, trying to mop up the puddle on the bathroom floor. She has read about the water breaking – just as she has read about contractions, show, transition stage, placenta – but just the same the escape of warm fluid surprised her. She has to use toilet paper, because Ailsa took all the regular towels away and put out the smooth scraps of embroidered linen called guest towels.

She holds on to the rim of the tub to pull herself up. She unbolts the door and that's when the first pain astonishes her. She is not to have a single mild pain, or any harbingers or orchestrated first stage of labor; it's all to be an unsparing onslaught and ripping headlong delivery.

'Easy,' says Mrs Shantz, supporting her as well as she can. 'Just tell me which room is yours, we'll get you lying down.'

Before they even reach the bed Jill's fingers dig into Mrs Shantz's thin arm to leave it black and blue.

'Oh, this is fast,' Mrs Shantz says. 'This is a real mover and shaker for a first baby. I'm going to get my husband.'

In that way I was born right in the house, about ten days early if Jill's calculations were to be relied on. Ailsa had barely time to get the company cleared out before the place was filled with Jill's noise, her disbelieving cries and the great shameless grunts that followed.

Even if a mother had been taken by surprise and had given birth at home, it was usual by that time to move her and the baby into the hospital afterwards. But there was some sort of summer flu in town, and the hospital had filled up with the worst cases, so Dr Shantz decided that Jill and I would be better off at home. Iona after all had finished part of her nurse's training, and she could take her two-week holiday now, to look after us.

Jill really knew nothing about living in a family. She had grown up in an orphanage. From the age of six to sixteen she had slept in a dormitory. Lights turned on and off at a specified time, furnace never operating before or beyond a specified date. A long oilcloth-covered table where they ate and did their homework, a factory across the street. George had liked the sound of that. It would make a girl tough, he said. It would make her self-possessed, hard and solitary. It would make her the sort who would not expect any romantic nonsense. But the place had not been run in such a heartless way as perhaps he thought, and the people who ran it had not been ungenerous. Jill was taken to a concert, with some others, when she was twelve years old, and there she decided that she must learn to play the violin. She had already fooled around with the piano at the orphanage. Somebody took enough interest to get her a secondhand, very second-rate violin, and a few lessons, and this led, finally, to a scholarship at the Conservatory. There was a recital for patrons and directors, a party with best dresses, fruit punch, speeches, and cakes. Jill had to make a little speech herself, expressing gratitude, but the truth was that she took all this pretty much for granted. She was sure that she and some violin were naturally, fatefully connected, and would have come together without human help.

In the dormitory she had friends, but they went off early to factories and offices and she forgot about them. At the high school that the orphans were sent to, a teacher had a talk with her. The words 'normal' and 'well rounded' came up in the talk. The teacher seemed to think that music was an escape from something or a substitute for something. For sisters and brothers and friends and dates. She suggested that Jill spread her energy around instead of concentrating on one thing. Loosen up, play volleyball, join the school orchestra if music was what she wanted.

Jill started to avoid that particular teacher, climbing the stairs or going round the block so as not to have to speak to her. Just as she stopped reading any page from which the words 'well rounded' or the word 'popular' leapt out at her.

At the Conservatory it was easier. There she met people quite as un – well rounded, as hard driven, as herself. She formed a few rather absentminded and competitive friendships. One of her friends had an older brother who was in the air force, and this brother happened to be a victim and worshipper of George Kirkham's. He and George dropped in on a family Sunday-night supper, at which Jill was a guest. They were on their way to get drunk somewhere else. And that was how George met Jill. My father met my mother.

There had to be somebody at home all the time, to watch Mrs Kirkham. So Iona worked the night shift at the bakery. She decorated cakes – even the fanciest wedding cakes – and she got the first round of bread loaves in the oven at five o'clock. Her hands, which shook so badly that she could not serve anybody a teacup, were strong and clever and patient, even inspired, at any solitary job.

One morning after Ailsa had gone off to work – this was during the short time that Jill was in the house before I was born – Iona hissed from the bedroom as Jill was going by. As if there was a secret. But who was there now in the house to keep a secret from? It couldn't be Mrs Kirkham.

Iona had to struggle to get a stuck drawer of her bureau open. 'Darn,' she said, and giggled. 'Darn it. There.'

The drawer was full of baby clothes – not plain necessary shirts and nightgowns such as Jill had bought at a shop that sold seconds, factory rejects, in Toronto, but knitted bonnets, sweaters and bootees and soakers, handmade tiny gowns. All possible pastel colors or combinations of colors – no blue or pink prejudice – with crocheted trimming and minute embroidered flowers and birds and lambs. The sort of stuff that Jill had barely known existed. She would have known, if she had done any thorough research in baby departments or peering into baby carriages, but she hadn't.

'Of course I don't know what you've got,' Iona said. 'You may have got so many things already, or maybe you don't like homemade, I don't know—' Her giggling was a kind of punctuation of speech and it was also an extension of her tone of apology. Everything she said, every look and gesture, seemed to be clogged up, overlaid with a sticky honey or snuffled mucus of apology, and Jill did not know how to deal with this.

'It's really nice,' she said flatly.

'Oh no, I didn't know if you'd even want it. I didn't know if you'd like it at all.'

'It's lovely.'

'I didn't do it all, I bought some of it. I went to the church bazaar and the Hospital Auxiliary, their bazaar, I just thought it would be nice, but if you don't like it or maybe you don't need it I can just put it in the Missionary Bale.'

'I do need it,' Jill said. 'I haven't got anything like this at all.'

'Haven't you really? What I did isn't so good, but maybe what the church ladies did or the Auxiliary, maybe you'd think that was all right.'

Was this what George had meant about Iona's being a nervous wreck? (According to Ailsa, her breakdown at the nursing school had been caused by her being a bit too thin-skinned and the supervisor's being a bit too hard on her.) You might think she was clamoring for reassurance, but whatever reassurance you tried seemed to be not enough, or not to get through to her. Jill felt as if Iona's words and giggles and sniffles and damp looks (no doubt she had damp hands as well) were things crawling on her – on Jill – mites trying to get under her skin.

But this was something she got used to, in time. Or Iona toned it down. Both she and Iona felt relief – it was as if a teacher had gone out of the room – when the door closed behind Ailsa in the morning. They took to having a second cup of coffee, while Mrs Kirkham washed the dishes. She did this job very slowly – looking around for the drawer or shelf where each item should go – and with some lapses. But with rituals, too, which she never omitted, such as scattering the coffee grounds on a bush by the kitchen door.

'She thinks the coffee makes it grow,' Iona whispered. 'Even if she puts it on the leaves not the ground. Every day we have to take the hose and rinse it off.'

Jill thought that Iona sounded like the girls who were most picked on at the orphanage. They were always eager to pick on somebody else. But once you got Iona past her strung-out apologies or barricades of humble accusations ('Of course I'm the last person they'd consult about anything down at the shop,' 'Of course Ailsa wouldn't listen to my opinion,' 'Of course George never made any secret about how he despised me') you might get her to talk about fairly interesting things. She told Jill about the house that had been their grandfather's and was now the center wing of the hospital, about the specific shady deals that had lost their father his job, and about a romance that was going on between two married people at the bakery. She also mentioned the supposed previous history of the Shantzes, and even the fact that Ailsa was soft on Dr Shantz. The shock treatment Iona had had after her nervous breakdown seemed perhaps to have blown a hole in her discretion, and the voice that came through this hole – once the disguising rubbish had been cleared away – was baleful and sly.

And Jill might as well spend her time chatting – her fingers had got too puffy now to try to play the violin.

And then I was born and everything changed, especially for Iona.

Jill had to stay in bed for a week, and even after she got up she moved like a stiff old woman and breathed warily each time she lowered herself into a chair. She was all painfully stitched together, and her stomach and breasts were bound tight as a mummy's – that was the custom then. Her milk came in plentifully; it was leaking through the binding and onto the sheets. Iona loosened the binding and tried to connect the nipple to my mouth. But I would not take it. I refused to take my mother's breast. I screamed blue murder. The big stiff breast might just as well have been a snouted beast rummaging in my face. Iona held me, she gave me a little warm boiled water, and I quieted down. I was losing weight, though. I couldn't live on water. So Iona mixed up a formula and took me out of Jill's arms where I stiffened and wailed. Iona rocked and soothed me and touched my cheek with the rubber nipple and that turned out to be what I preferred. I drank the formula greedily and kept it down. Iona's arms and the nipple that she was in charge of became my chosen home. Jill's breasts had to be bound even tighter, and she had to forgo liquids (remember, this was in the hot weather) and endure the ache until her milk dried up.

'What a monkey, what a monkey,' crooned Iona. 'You are a monkey, you don't want your mommy's good milk.'

I soon got fatter and stronger. I could cry louder. I cried if anybody but Iona tried to hold me. I rejected Ailsa and Dr Shantz with his thoughtfully warmed hands, but of course it was my aversion to Jill that got the most attention.

Once Jill was out of bed Iona got her sitting in the chair where she herself usually sat to feed me; she put her own blouse around Jill's shoulders and the bottle in Jill's hand.

No use, I was not fooled. I batted my cheek against the bottle and straightened my legs and hardened my abdomen into a ball. I would not accept the substitution. I cried. I would not give in.

My cries were still thin new-baby cries, but they were a disturbance in the house, and Iona was the only person who had the power to stop them. Touched or spoken to by a non-Iona, I cried. Put down to sleep, not rocked by Iona, I cried myself into exhaustion and slept for ten minutes and woke ready to go at it again. I had no good times or fussy times. I had the Iona-times and the Iona-desertion-times, which might become – oh, worse and worse – the other-people-times, mostly Jill-times.

How could Iona go back to work, then, once her two weeks were up? She couldn't. There wasn't any question of it. The bakery had to get someone else. Iona had gone from being the most negligible to being the most important person in the house; she was the one who stood between those who lived there and constant discordance, unanswerable complaint. She had to be up at all hours to keep the household in any sort of ease. Dr Shantz was concerned; even Ailsa was concerned.

'Iona, don't wear yourself out.'

And yet a wonderful change had taken place. Iona was pale but her skin glowed, as if she had finally passed out of adolescence. She could look anybody in the eye. And there was no more trembling, hardly any giggling, no sly cringing in her voice, which had grown as bossy as Ailsa's and more joyful. (Never more joyful than when she was scolding me for my attitude to Jill.)

'Iona's in seventh heaven – she just adores that baby,' Ailsa told people. But in fact Iona's behavior seemed too brisk for adoration. She did not care how much noise she made, quelling mine. She tore up the stairs calling breathlessly, 'I'm coming, I'm coming, hold your horses.' She would walk around with me carelessly plastered to her shoulder, held with one hand, while the other hand accomplished some task connected with my maintenance. She ruled in the kitchen, commandeering the stove for the sterilizer, the table for the mixing of the formula, the sink for the baby wash. She swore cheerfully, even in Ailsa's presence, when she had misplaced or spilled something.

She knew herself to be the only person who didn't wince, who didn't feel the distant threat of annihilation, when I sent up my first signal wail. Instead, she was the one whose heart jumped into double time, who felt like dancing, just from the sense of power she had, and gratitude.

Once her bindings were off and she'd seen the flatness of her stomach, Jill took a look at her hands. The puffiness seemed to be all gone. She went downstairs and got her violin out of the closet and took off its cover. She was ready to try some scales.

This was on a Sunday afternoon. Iona had lain down for a nap, one ear always open to hear my cry. Mrs Kirkham too was lying down. Ailsa was painting her fingernails in the kitchen. Jill began to tune the violin.

My father and my father's family had no real interest in music. They didn't quite know this. They thought that the intolerance or even hostility they felt towards a certain type of music (this showed even in the way they pronounced the word 'classical') was based on a simple strength of character, an integrity and a determination not to be fooled. As if music that departed from a simple tune was trying to put something over on you, and everybody knew this, deep down, but some people – out of pretentiousness, from want of simplicity and honesty – would never admit that it was so. And out of this artificiality and spineless tolerance came the whole world of symphony orchestras, opera, and ballet, concerts that put people to sleep.

Most of the people in this town felt the same way. But because she hadn't grown up here Jill did not understand the depth of this feeling, the taken-for-granted extent of it. My father had never made a parade of it, or a virtue of it, because he didn't go in for virtues. He had liked the idea of Jill's being a musician – not because of the music but because it made her an odd choice, as did her clothes and her way of living and her wild hair. Choosing her, he showed people what he thought of them. Showed those girls who had hoped to get their hooks in him. Showed Ailsa.

Jill had closed the curtained glass doors of the living room and she tuned up quite softly. Perhaps no sound escaped. Or if Ailsa heard something in the kitchen, she might have thought it was a sound from outdoors, a radio in the neighborhood.

Now Jill began to play her scales. It was true that her fingers were no longer puffy, but they felt stiff. Her whole body felt stiff, her stance was not quite natural, she felt the instrument clamped onto her in a distrustful way. But no matter, she would get into her scales. She was sure that she had felt this

406

way before, after she'd had flu, or when she was very tired, having overstrained herself practicing, or even for no reason at all.

I woke without a whimper of discontent. No warning, no buildup. Just a shriek, a waterfall of shrieks descended on the house, a cry unlike any cry I'd managed before. The letting loose of a new flood of unsuspected anguish, a grief that punished the world with its waves full of stones, the volley of woe sent down from the windows of the torture chamber.

Iona was up at once, alarmed for the first time at any noise made by me, crying, 'What is it, what is it?'

And Ailsa, rushing around to shut the windows, was calling out, 'It's the fiddle, it's the fiddle.' She threw open the doors of the living room.

'Jill. Jill. This is awful. This is just awful. Don't you hear your baby?'

She had to wrench out the screen under the living-room window, so that she could get it down. She had been sitting in her kimono to do her nails, and now a boy going by on a bicycle looked in and saw her kimono open over her slip.

'My God,' she said. She hardly ever lost control of herself to this extent. 'Will you put that thing away.'

Jill set her violin down.

Ailsa ran out into the hall and called up to Iona.

'It's Sunday. Can't you get it to stop?'

Jill walked speechlessly and deliberately out to

the kitchen, and there was Mrs Kirkham in her stocking feet, clinging to the counter.

'What's the matter with Ailsa?' she said. 'What did Iona do?'

Jill went out and sat down on the back step. She looked across at the glaring, sunlit back wall of the Shantzes' white house. All around were other hot backyards and hot walls of other houses. Inside them people well known to each other by sight and by name and by history. And if you walked three blocks east from here or five blocks west, six blocks south or ten blocks north, you would come to walls of summer crops already sprung high out of the earth, fenced fields of hay and wheat and corn. The fullness of the country. Nowhere to breathe for the reek of thrusting crops and barnyards and jostling munching animals. Woodlots at a distance beckoning like pools of shade, of peace and shelter, but in reality they were boiling up with bugs.

How can I describe what music is to Jill? Forget about landscapes and visions and dialogues. It is more of a problem, I would say, that she has to work out strictly and daringly, and that she has taken on as her responsibility in life. Suppose then that the tools that serve her for working on this problem are taken away. The problem is still there in its grandeur and other people sustain it, but it is removed from her. For her, just the back step and the glaring wall and my crying. My crying is a knife to cut out of her life all that isn't useful. To me.

'Come in,' says Ailsa through the screen door.

'Come on in. I shouldn't have yelled at you. Come in, people will see.'

By evening the whole episode could be passed off lightly. 'You must've heard the caterwauling over here today,' said Ailsa to the Shantzes. They had asked her over to sit on their patio, while Iona settled me to sleep.

'Baby isn't a fan of the fiddle apparently. Doesn't take after Mommy.'

Even Mrs Shantz laughed.

'An acquired taste.'

Jill heard them. At least she heard the laughing, and guessed what it was about. She was lying on her bed reading *The Bridge of San Luis Rey*, which she had helped herself to from the bookcase, without understanding that she should ask Ailsa's permission. Every so often the story blanked out on her and she heard those laughing voices over in the Shantzes' yard, then the next door patter of Iona's adoration, and she broke out in a sullen sweat. In a fairy tale she would have risen off the bed with the strength of a young giantess and gone through the house breaking furniture and necks.

When I was almost six weeks old, Ailsa and Iona were supposed to take their mother on an annual overnight visit to Guelph, to stay with some cousins. Iona wanted to take me along. But Ailsa brought in Dr Shantz to convince her that it was not a good idea to take a small baby on such a trip in hot weather. Then Iona wanted to stay at home.

'I can't drive and look after Mother both,' said Ailsa.

She said that Iona was getting too wrapped up in me, and that a day and a half looking after her own baby was not going to be too much for Jill.

'Is it, Jill?'

Jill said no.

Iona tried to pretend it wasn't that she wanted to stay with me. She said that driving on a hot day made her carsick.

'You don't drive, you just have to sit there,' Ailsa said. 'What about me? I'm not doing it for fun. I'm doing it because they expect us.'

Iona had to sit in the back, which she said made her carsickness worse. Ailsa said it wouldn't look right to put their mother there. Mrs Kirkham said she didn't mind. Ailsa said no. Iona rolled down the window as Ailsa started the car. She fixed her eyes on the window of the upstairs room where she had put me down to sleep after my morning bath and bottle. Ailsa waved to Jill, who stood at the front door.

'Goodbye little mother,' she called, in a cheerful, challenging voice that reminded Jill somehow of George. The prospect of getting away from the house and the new threat of disruption that was lodged in it seemed to have lifted Ailsa's spirits. And perhaps it also felt good to her – felt reassuring – to have Iona back in her proper place.

It was about ten o'clock in the morning when they

left, and the day ahead was to be the longest and the worst in Jill's experience. Not even the day of my birth, her nightmare labor, could compare to it. Before the car could have reached the next town, I woke in distress, as if I could feel Iona's being removed from me. Iona had fed me such a short time before that Jill did not think I could possibly be hungry. But she discovered that I was wet, and though she had read that babies did not need to be changed every time they were found wet and that wasn't usually what made them cry, she decided to change me. It wasn't the first time she had done this, but she had never done it easily, and in fact Iona had taken over more often than not and got the job finished. I made it as hard as I could – I flailed my arms and legs, arched my back, tried my best to turn over, and of course kept up my noise. Jill's hands shook, she had trouble driving the pins through the cloth. She pretended to be calm, she tried talking to me, trying to imitate Iona's baby talk and fond cajoling, but it was no use, such stumbling insincerity enraged me further. She picked me up once she had my diaper pinned, she tried to mold me to her chest and shoulder, but I stiffened as if her body was made of red-hot needles. She sat down, she rocked me. She stood up, she bounced me. She sang to me the sweet words of a lullaby that were filled and trembling with her exasperation, her anger, and something that could readily define itself as loathing.

We were monsters to each other, Jill and I.

At last she put me down, more gently than she would have liked to do, and I quieted, in my relief it seemed at getting away from her. She tiptoed from the room. And it wasn't long before I started up again.

So it continued. I didn't cry nonstop. I would take breaks of two or five or ten or twenty minutes. When the time came for her to offer me the bottle I accepted it, I lay in her arm stiffly and snuffled warningly as I drank. Once half the milk was down I returned to the assault. I finished the bottle eventually, almost absent-mindedly, between wails. I dropped off to sleep and she put me down. She crept down the stairs; she stood in the hall as if she had to judge a safe way to go. She was sweating from her ordeal and from the heat of the day. She moved through the precious brittle silence into the kitchen and dared to put the coffeepot on the stove.

Before the coffee was perked I sent a meat cleaver cry down on her head.

She realized that she had forgotten something. She hadn't burped me after the bottle. She went determinedly upstairs and picked me up and walked with me patting and rubbing my angry back, and in a while I burped, but I didn't stop crying and she gave up; she laid me down.

What is it about an infant's crying that makes it so powerful, able to break down the order you depend on, inside and outside of yourself? It is like a storm – insistent, theatrical, yet in a way pure and uncontrived. It is reproachful rather than supplicating – it comes out of a rage that can't be dealt with, a birthright rage free of love and pity, ready to crush your brains inside your skull.

All Jill can do is walk around. Up and down the living-room rug, round and round the dining-room table, out to the kitchen where the clock tells her how slowly, slowly time is passing. She can't stay still to take more than a sip of her coffee. When she gets hungry she can't stop to make a sandwich but eats cornflakes out of her hands, leaving a trail all over the house. Eating and drinking, doing any ordinary thing at all, seem as risky as doing such things in a little boat out in the middle of a tempest or in a house whose beams are buckling in an awful wind. You can't take your attention from the tempest or it will rip open your last defenses. You try for sanity's sake to fix on some calm detail of your surroundings, but the wind's cries – my cries – are able to inhabit a cushion or a figure in the rug or a tiny whirlpool in the window glass. I don't allow escape.

The house is shut up like a box. Some of Ailsa's sense of shame has rubbed off on Jill, or else she's been able to manufacture some shame of her own. A mother who can't appease her own baby – what is more shameful? She keeps the doors and windows shut. And she doesn't turn the portable floor fan on because in fact she's forgotten about it. She doesn't think anymore in terms of practical relief. She doesn't think that this Sunday is one of the hottest days of the summer

413

and maybe that is what is the matter with me. An experienced or instinctive mother would surely have given me an airing instead of granting me the powers of a demon. Prickly heat would have been what came to her mind, instead of rank despair.

Sometime in the afternoon, Jill makes a stupid or just desperate decision. She doesn't walk out of the house and leave me. Stuck in the prison of my making, she thinks of a space of her own, an escape within. She gets out her violin, which she has not touched since the day of the scales, the attempt that Ailsa and Iona have turned into a family joke. Her playing can't wake me up because I'm wide awake already, and how can it make me any angrier than I am?

In a way she does me honor. No more counterfeit soothing, no more pretend lullabies or concern for tummy-ache, no petsy-wetsy whatsamatter. Instead she will play Mendelssohn's Violin Concerto, the piece she played at her recital and must play again at her examination to get her graduating diploma.

The Mendelssohn is her choice – rather than the Beethoven Violin Concerto which she more passionately admires – because she believes the Mendelssohn will get her higher marks. She thinks she can master – has mastered – it more fully; she is confident that she can show off and impress the examiners without the least fear of catastrophe. This is not a work that will trouble her all her

414

life, she has decided; it is not something she will struggle with and try to prove herself at forever.

She will just play it.

She tunes up, she does a few scales, she attempts to banish me from her hearing. She knows she's stiff, but this time she's prepared for that. She expects her problems to lessen as she gets into the music.

She starts to play it, she goes on playing, she goes on and on, she plays right through to the end. And her playing is terrible. It's a torment. She hangs on, she thinks this must change, she can change it, but she can't. Everything is off, she plays as badly as Jack Benny does in one of his resolute parodies. The violin is bewitched, it hates her. It gives her back a stubborn distortion of everything she intends. Nothing could be worse than this – it's worse than if she looked in the mirror and saw her reliable face caved in, sick and leering. A trick played on her that she couldn't believe, and would try to disprove by looking away and looking back, away and back, over and over again. That is how she goes on playing, trying to undo the trick. But not succeeding. She gets worse, if anything; sweat pours down her face and arms and the sides of her body, and her hand slips – there is simply no bottom to how badly she can play.

Finished. She is finished altogether. The piece that she mastered months ago and perfected since, so that nothing in it remained formidable or even tricky, has completely defeated her. It has shown her to herself as somebody emptied out, vandalized. Robbed overnight.

She doesn't give up. She does the worst thing. In this state of desperation she starts in again; she will try the Beethoven. And of course it's no good, it's worse and worse, and she seems to be howling, heaving inside. She sets the bow and the violin down on the living-room sofa, then picks them up and shoves them underneath it, getting them out of sight because she has a picture of herself smashing and wrecking them against a chair back, in a sickening dramatic display.

I haven't given up in all this time. Naturally I wouldn't, against such competition.

Jill lies down on the hard sky-blue brocade sofa where nobody ever lies or even sits, unless there's company, and she actually falls asleep. She wakes up after who knows how long with her hot face pushed down into the brocade, its pattern marked on her cheek, her mouth drooling a little and staining the sky-blue material. My racket still or again going on rising and falling like a hammering headache. And she has got a headache, too. She gets up and pushes her way – that's what it feels like – through the hot air to the kitchen cupboard where Ailsa keeps the 222's. The thick air makes her think of sewage. And why not? While she slept I dirtied my diaper, and its ripe smell has had time to fill the house.

222's. Warm another bottle. Climb the stairs. She changes the diaper without lifting me from the crib. The sheet as well as the diaper is a mess. The 222's are not working yet and her headache increases in fierceness as she bends over. Haul the mess out, wash off my scalded parts, pin on a clean diaper, and take the dirty diaper and sheet into the bathroom to be scrubbed off in the toilet. Put them in the pail of disinfectant which is already full to the brim because the usual baby wash has not been done today. Then get to me with the bottle. I quiet again enough to suck. It's a wonder I have the energy left to do that, but I do. The feeding is more than an hour late, and I have real hunger to add to – but maybe also subvert – my store of grievance. I suck away, I finish the bottle, and then worn out I go to sleep, and this time actually stay asleep.

Jill's headache dulls. Groggily she washes out my diapers and shirts and gowns and sheets. Scrubs them and rinses them and even boils the diapers to defeat the diaper rash to which I am prone. She wrings them all out by hand. She hangs them up indoors because the next day is Sunday, and Ailsa, when she returns, will not want to see anything hanging outdoors on Sunday. Jill would just as soon not have to appear outside, anyway, especially now with evening thickening and people sitting out, taking advantage of the cool. She dreads being seen by the neighbors – even being greeted by the friendly Shantzes – after what they must have listened to today.

And such a long time it takes for today to be

417

over. For the long reach of sunlight and stretched shadows to give out and the monumental heat to stir a little, opening sweet cool cracks. Then all of a sudden the stars are out in clusters and the trees are enlarging themselves like clouds, shaking down peace. But not for long and not for Jill. Well before midnight comes a thin cry – you could not call it tentative, but thin at least, experimental, as if in spite of the day's practice I have lost the knack. Or as if I actually wonder if it's worth it. A little rest then, a false respite or giving up. But after that a thoroughgoing, an anguished, unforgiving resumption. Just when Jill had started to make more coffee, to deal with the remnants of her headache. Thinking that this time she might sit by the table and drink it.

Now she turns the burner off.

It's almost time for the last bottle of the day. If the feeding before had not been delayed, I'd be ready now. Perhaps I am ready? While it's warming, Jill thinks she'll dose herself with a couple more 222's. Then she thinks maybe that won't do; she needs something stronger. In the bathroom cupboard she finds only Pepto-Bismol, laxatives, foot powder, prescriptions she wouldn't touch. But she knows that Ailsa takes something strong for her menstrual cramps, and she goes into Ailsa's room and looks through her bureau drawers until she finds a bottle of pain pills lying, logically, on top of a pile of sanitary pads. These are prescriptions pills, too, but the label says clearly what they're for. She removes two of them and goes back to the kitchen and finds the water in the pan around the milk boiling, the milk too hot.

She holds the bottle under the tap to cool it – my cries coming down at her like the clamor of birds of prey over a gurgling river – and she looks at the pills waiting on the counter and she thinks, *Yes*. She gets out a knife and shaves a few grains off one of the pills, takes the nipple off the bottle, picks up the shaved grains on the blade of the knife, and sprinkles them – just a sprinkle of white dust – over the milk. Then she swallows one and seven-eighths or maybe one and eleven-twelfths or even one and fifteen-sixteenths of a pill herself, and takes the bottle upstairs. She lifts up my immediately rigid body and gets the nipple into my accusing mouth. The milk is still a little too warm for my liking and at first I spit it back at her. Then in a while I decide that it will do, and I swallow it all down.

Iona is screaming. Jill wakes up to a house full of hurtful sunlight and Iona's screaming.

The plan was that Ailsa and Iona and their mother would visit with their relatives in Guelph until the late afternoon, avoiding driving during the hot part of the day. But after breakfast Iona began to make a fuss. She wanted to get home to the baby, she said she had hardly slept all night for worrying. It was embarrassing to keep on arguing with her in front of the relatives, so Ailsa gave in and they arrived home late in the morning and opened the door of the still house.

Ailsa said, 'Phew. Is this what it always smells like in here, only we're so used to it we don't notice?'

Iona ducked past her and ran up the stairs.

Now she's screaming.

Dead. Dead. Murderer.

She knows nothing about the pills. So why does she scream 'Murderer'? It's the blanket. She sees the blanket pulled up right over my head. Suffocation. Not poison. It has not taken her any time, not half a second, to get from 'dead' to 'murderer.' It's an immediate flying leap. She grabs me from the crib, with the death blanket twisted round me, and holding the blanketed bundle squeezed against her body she runs screaming out of the room and into Jill's room.

Jill is struggling up, dopily, after twelve or thirteen hours of sleep.

'You've killed my baby,' Iona is screaming at her.

Jill doesn't correct her – she doesn't say, *Mine.* Iona holds me out accusingly to show me to Jill, but before Jill can get any kind of a look at me I have been snatched back. Iona groans and doubles up as if she's been shot in the stomach. Still holding on to me she stumbles down the stairs, bumping into Ailsa who is on her way up. Ailsa is almost knocked off her feet; she hangs on to the banister and Iona takes no notice; she seems to be trying to squeeze the bundle of me into a new terrifying hole in the middle of her body. Words come out of her between fresh groans of recognition.

Baby. Love my. Darling. Ooh. Oh. Get the. Suffocated. Blanket. Baby. Police.

Jill has slept with no covers over her and without changing into a nightdress. She is still in yesterday's shorts and halter, and she's not sure if she's waking from a night's sleep or a nap. She isn't sure where she is or what day it is. And what did Iona say? Groping her way up out of a vat of warm wool, Jill sees rather than hears Iona's cries, and they're like red flashes, hot veins in the inside of her eyelids. She clings to the luxury of not having to understand, but then she knows she has understood. She knows it's about me.

But Jill thinks that Iona has made a mistake. Iona has got into the wrong part of the dream. That part is all over.

The baby is all right. Jill took care of the baby. She went out and found the baby and covered it up. All right.

In the downstairs hall, Iona makes an effort and shouts some words all together. 'She pulled the blanket all the way over its head, she smothered it.'

Ailsa comes downstairs hanging on to the banister.

'Put it down,' she says. 'Put it down.'

Iona squeezes me and groans. Then she holds me out to Ailsa and says, 'Look. Look.'

Ailsa whips her head aside. 'I won't,' she says. 'I won't look.' Iona comes close to push me into her face – I am still all wrapped up in my blanket, but Ailsa doesn't know that and Iona doesn't notice or doesn't care.

Now it's Ailsa screaming. She runs to the other side of the dining-room table screaming, 'Put it down. Put it down. I'm not going to look at a corpse.'

Mrs Kirkham comes in from the kitchen, saying, 'Girls. Oh, girls. What's the trouble between you? I can't have this, you know.'

'Look,' says Iona, forgetting Ailsa and coming around the table to show me to her mother.

Ailsa gets to the hall phone and gives the operator Dr Shantz's number.

'Oh, a baby,' says Mrs Kirkham, twitching the blanket aside.

'She smothered it,' Iona says.

'Oh, no,' says Mrs Kirkham.

Ailsa is talking to Dr Shantz on the phone, telling him in a shaky voice to get over here at once. She turns from the phone and looks at Iona, gulps to steady herself, and says, 'Now you. You pipe down.'

Iona gives a high-pitched defiant yelp and runs away from her, across the hall into the living room. She is still hanging on to me.

Jill has come to the top of the stairs. Ailsa spots her.

She says, 'Come on down here.'

She has no idea what she's going to do to Jill, or say to her, once she gets her down. She looks as if she wants to slap her. 'It's no good now getting hysterical,' she says.

Jill's halter is twisted partway round so that most of one breast has got loose.

'Fix yourself up,' says Ailsa. 'Did you sleep in your clothes? You look drunk.'

Jill seems to herself to be walking still in the snowy light of her dream. But the dream has been invaded by these frantic people.

Ailsa is able to think now about some things that have to be done. Whatever has happened, there has got to be no question of such a thing as a murder. Babies do die, for no reason, in their sleep. She has heard of that. No question of the police. No autopsy – a sad quiet little funeral. The obstacle to this is Iona. Dr Shantz can give Iona a needle now; the needle will put her to sleep. But he can't go on giving her a needle every day.

The thing is to get Iona into Morrisville. This is the Hospital for the Insane, which used to be called the Asylum and in the future will be called the Psychiatric Hospital, then the Mental Health Unit. But most people just call it Morrisville, after the village nearby.

Going to Morrisville, they say. They took her off to Morrisville. Carry on like that and you're going to end up in Morrisville.

Iona has been there before and she can go there again. Dr Shantz can get her in and keep her in

423

until it's judged she's ready to come out. Affected by the baby's death. Delusions. Once that is established she won't pose a threat. Nobody will pay any attention to what she says. She will have had a breakdown. In fact it looks as if that may be the truth – it looks as if she might be halfway to a breakdown already, with that yelping and running around. It might be permanent. But probably not. There's all kinds of treatment nowadays. Drugs to calm her down, and shock if it's better to blot out some memories, and an operation they do, if they have to, on people who are obstinately confused and miserable. They don't do that at Morrisville – they have to send you to the city.

For all this – which has gone through her mind in an instant – Ailsa will have to count on Dr Shantz. Some obliging lack of curiosity on his part and a willingness to see things her way. But that should not be hard for anybody who knows what she has been through. The investment she has made in this family's respectability and the blows she's had to take, from her father's shabby career and her mother's mixed-up wits to Iona's collapse at nursing school and George's going off to get killed. Does Ailsa deserve a public scandal on top of this – a story in the papers, a trial, maybe even a sister-in-law in jail?

Dr Shantz would not think so. And not just because he can tote up these reasons from what he has observed as a friendly neighbor. Not just because he can appreciate that people who have

424

to do without respectability must sooner or later feel the cold.

The reasons he has for helping Ailsa are all in his voice as he comes running in the back door now, through the kitchen, calling her name.

Jill at the bottom of the stairs has just said, 'The baby's all right.'

And Ailsa has said, 'You keep quiet until I tell you what to say.'

Mrs Kirkham stands in the doorway between the kitchen and the hall, square in Dr Shantz's path.

'Oh, I'm glad to see you,' she says. 'Ailsa and Iona are all upset with each other. Iona found a baby at the door and now she says it's dead.'

Dr Shantz picks Mrs Kirkham up and puts her aside. He says again, 'Ailsa?' and reaches out his arms, but ends up just setting his hands down hard on her shoulders.

Iona comes out of the living room empty-handed.

Jill says, 'What did you do with the baby?'

'Hid it,' Iona says saucily, and makes a face at her – the kind of face a terminally frightened person can make, pretending to be vicious.

'Dr Shantz is going to give you a needle,' Ailsa says. 'That'll put paid to you.'

Now there is an absurd scene of Iona running around, throwing herself at the front door – Ailsa jumps to block her – and then at the stairs, which is where Dr Shantz gets hold of her and straddles her, pinning her arms and saying, 'Now, now, now, Iona. Take it easy. You'll be okay in a little while.' And Iona yells and whimpers and subsides. The noises she makes, and her darting about, her efforts at escape, all seem like playacting. As if – in spite of being quite literally at her wit's end – she finds the effort of standing up to Ailsa and Dr Shantz so nearly impossible that she can only try to manage it by this sort of parody. Which makes it clear – and maybe this is what she really intends – that she is not standing up to them at all but falling apart. Falling apart as embarrassingly and inconveniently as possible with Ailsa shouting at her, 'You ought to be disgusted with yourself.'

Administering the needle, Dr Shantz says, 'That-a-girl Iona. There now.'

Over his shoulder he says to Ailsa, 'Look after your mother. Get her to sit down.'

Mrs Kirkham is wiping tears with her fingers. 'I'm all right dear,' she says to Ailsa. 'I just wish you girls wouldn't fight. You should have told me Iona had a baby. You should have let her keep it.'

Mrs Shantz, wearing a Japanese kimono over her summer pajamas, comes into the house by the kitchen door.

'Is everybody all right?' she calls.

She sees the knife lying on the kitchen counter and thinks it prudent to pick it up and put it in a drawer. When people are making a scene the last thing you want is a knife ready to hand.

In the midst of this Jill thinks she has heard a faint cry. She has climbed clumsily over the banister to get around Iona and Dr Shantz – she ran partway

426

up the stairs again when Iona came running in that direction – and has lowered herself to the floor. She goes through the double doors into the living room where at first she sees no sign of me. But the faint cry comes again and she follows the sound to the sofa and looks underneath it.

That's where I am, pushed in beside the violin.

During that short trip from the hall to the living room, Jill has remembered everything, and it seems as if her breath stops and horror crowds in at her mouth, then a flash of joy sets her life going again, when just as in the dream she comes upon a live baby, not a little desiccated nutmeg-headed corpse. She holds me. I don't stiffen or kick or arch my back. I am still pretty sleepy from the sedative in my milk which knocked me out for the night and half a day and which, in a larger quantity – maybe not so much larger, at that – would have really finished me off.

It wasn't the blanket at all. Anybody who took a serious look at that blanket could see that it was so light and loosely woven that it could not prevent my getting all the air I needed. You could breathe through it just as easily as through a fishnet.

Exhaustion might have played a part. A whole day's howling, such a furious feat of self-expression, might have worn me out. That, and the white dust that fell on my milk, had knocked me into a deep and steadfast sleep with breathing so slight that Iona had not been able to detect it. You would think she would notice that I was not cold and you would think that all that moaning and crying out and running around would have brought me up to consciousness in a hurry. I don't know why that didn't happen. I think she didn't notice because of her panic and the state she was in even before she found me, but I don't know why I didn't cry sooner. Or maybe I did cry and in the commotion nobody heard me. Or maybe Iona did hear me and took a look at me and stuffed me under the sofa because by that time everything had been spoiled.

Then Jill heard. Jill was the one.

Iona was carried to that same sofa. Ailsa slipped off her shoes to save the brocade, and Mrs Shantz went upstairs to get a light quilt to put over her.

'I know she doesn't need it for warmth,' she said. 'But I think when she wakes up she'll feel better to have a quilt over her.'

Before this, of course, everybody had gathered round to take note of my being alive. Ailsa was blaming herself for not having discovered that right away. She hated to admit that she had been afraid to look at a dead baby.

'Iona's nerves must be contagious,' she said. 'I absolutely should have known.'

She looked at Jill as if she was going to tell her to go and put a blouse on over her halter. Then she recalled how roughly she had spoken to her, and for no reason as it turned out, so she didn't say anything. She did not even try to convince her mother that Iona had not had a baby, though she said in an undertone, to Mrs Shantz, 'Well, that could start the rumor of the century.'

'I'm so glad nothing terrible happened,' Mrs Kirkham said. 'I thought for a minute Iona had done away with it. Ailsa, you must try not to blame your sister.'

'No Momma,' said Ailsa. 'Let's go sit down in the kitchen.'

There was one bottle of formula made up that by rights I should have demanded and drunk earlier that morning. Jill put it on to warm, holding me in the crook of her arm all the time.

She had looked at once for the knife, when she came into the kitchen, and seen in wonderment that it wasn't there. But she could make out the faintest dust on the counter – or she thought she could. She wiped it with her free hand before she turned the tap on to get the water to heat the bottle.

Mrs Shantz busied herself making coffee. While it was perking she put the sterilizer on the stove and washed out yesterday's bottles. She was being tactful and competent, just managing to hide the fact that there was something about this whole debacle and disarray of feelings that buoyed her up.

'I guess Iona did have an obsession about the baby,' she said. 'Something like this was bound to happen.'

Turning from the stove to address the last of these words to her husband and Ailsa, she saw that Dr Shantz was pulling Ailsa's hands down from where she held them, on either side of her head. Too speedily and guiltily he took his own hands away. If he had not done that, it would have looked like ordinary comfort he was administering. As a doctor is certainly entitled to do.

'You know Ailsa, I think your mother ought to lie down too,' said Mrs. Shantz thoughtfully and without a break. 'I think I'll go and per-suade her. If she can get to sleep this may all pass right out of her head. Out of Iona's too, if we're lucky.'

Mrs Kirkham had wandered out of the kitchen almost as soon as she got there. Mrs Shantz found her in the living room looking at Iona, and fid-dling with the quilt to make sure she was well covered. Mrs Kirkham did not really want to lie down. She wanted to have things explained to her – she knew that her own explanations were somehow out of kilter. And she wanted to have people talk to her as they used to do, not in the peculiarly gentle and self-satisfied way they did now. But because of her customary politeness and her knowledge that the power she had in the household was negligible, she allowed Mrs Shantz to take her upstairs.

Jill was reading the instructions for making baby formula. They were printed on the side of the corn syrup tin. When she heard the footsteps going up the stairs she thought that there was something she had better do while she had the chance. She carried me into the living room and laid me down on a chair.

'There now,' she whispered confidentially. 'You stay still.'

She knelt down and nudged and gently tugged the violin out of its hiding place. She found its cover and case and got it properly stowed away. I stayed still – not yet being quite able to turn over – and I stayed quiet.

Left alone by themselves, alone in the kitchen, Dr Shantz and Ailsa probably did not seize this chance to embrace, but only looked at each other. With their knowledge, and without promises or despair.

Iona admitted that she hadn't felt for a pulse. And she never claimed that I was cold. She said I felt stiff. Then she said not stiff but heavy. So heavy, she said, she instantly thought I could not be alive. A lump, a dead weight.

I think there is something to this. I don't believe that I was dead, or that I came back from the dead, but I do think that I was at a distance, from which I might or might not have come back. I think that the outcome was not certain and that will was involved. It was up to me, I mean, to go one way or the other.

And Iona's love, which was certainly the most wholehearted love I will ever receive, didn't decide me. Her cries and her crushing me into her body didn't work, were not finally persuasive. Because it

431

wasn't Iona I had to settle for. (Could I have known that – could I even have known that it wasn't Iona, in the end, who would do me the most good?) It was Jill. I had to settle for Jill and for what I could get from her, even if it might look like half a loaf.

To me it seems that it was only then that I became female. I know that the matter was decided long before I was born and was plain to everybody else since the beginning of my life, but I believe that it was only at the moment when I decided to come back, when I gave up the fight against my mother (which must have been a fight for something like her total surrender) and when in fact I chose survival over victory (death would have been victory), that I took on my female nature.

And to some extent Jill took on hers. Sobered and grateful, not even able to risk thinking about what she'd just escaped, she took on loving me, because the alternative to loving was disaster.

Dr Shantz suspected something, but he let it go. He asked Jill how I had been the day before. Fussy? She said yes, very fussy. He said that premature babies, even slightly premature babies, were susceptible to shocks and you had to be careful with them. He recommended that I always be put to sleep on my back.

Iona did not have to have shock treatment. Dr Shantz gave her pills. He said that she had overstrained herself looking after me. The woman who had taken over her job at the bakery wanted to give it up – she did not like working nights. So Iona went back there.

That's what I remember best about my summer visits to my aunts, when I was six or seven years old. Being taken down to the bakery at the strange, usually forbidden hour of midnight and watching Iona put on her white hat and apron, watching her knead the great white mass of dough that shifted and bubbled like something alive. Then cutting out cookies and feeding me the leftover bits and on special occasions sculpting a wedding cake. How bright and white that big kitchen was, with night filling every window. I scraped the wedding icing from the bowl – the melting stabbing irresistible sugar.

Ailsa thought I should not be up so late, or eat so much sweet stuff. But she didn't do anything about it. She said she wondered what my mother would say – as if Jill was the person who swung the weight, not herself. Ailsa had some rules that I didn't have to observe at home – hang up that jacket, rinse that glass before you dry it, else it'll have spots – but I never saw the harsh, hounding person Jill remembered.

Nothing slighting was ever said then, about Jill's music. After all, she made our living at it. She had not been finally defeated by the Mendelssohn. She got her diploma; she graduated from the Conservatory. She cut her hair and got thin. She was able to rent a duplex near High Park in Toronto, and hire a woman to look after me part of the time, because she had her war widow's pension. And then she found a job with a radio orchestra. She was to be proud that all her working life she was employed as a musician and never had to fall back on teaching. She said that she knew that she was not a great violinist, she had no marvellous gift or destiny, but at least she could make her living doing what she wanted to do. Even after she married my stepfather, after we moved with him to Edmonton (he was a geologist), she went on playing in the symphony orchestra there. She played up until a week before each of my half sisters was born. She was lucky, she said – her husband never objected.

Iona did have a couple of further setbacks, the more serious one when I was about twelve. She was taken to Morrisville for several weeks. I think she was given insulin there – she returned fat and loquacious. I came back to visit while she was away, and Jill came with me, bringing my first little sister who had been born shortly before. I understood from the talk between my mother and Ailsa that it would not have been advisable to bring a baby into the house if Iona was there; it might have 'set her off.' I don't know if the episode that sent her to Morrisville had anything to do with a baby.

I felt left out of things on that visit. Both Jill and Ailsa had taken up smoking, and they would sit up late at night, drinking coffee and smoking cigarettes at the kitchen table, while they waited for the baby's one o'clock feeding. (My mother fed this baby from her breasts – I was glad to hear that no such intimate body-heated meals had been served to me.) I remember coming downstairs sulkily because I couldn't sleep, then turning talkative, full of giddy bravado, trying to break into their conversation. I understood that they were talking over things they didn't want me to hear about. They had become, unaccountably, good friends.

I grabbed for a cigarette, and my mother said, 'Go on now, leave those alone. We're talking.' Ailsa told me to get something to drink out of the fridge, a Coke or a ginger ale. So I did, and instead of taking it upstairs I went outside.

I sat on the back step, but the women's voices immediately went too low for me to make out any of their soft regretting or reassuring. So I went prowling around the backyard, beyond the patch of light thrown through the screen door.

The long white house with the glass-brick corners was occupied by new people now. The Shantzes had moved away, to live year-round in Florida. They sent my aunts oranges, which Ailsa said would make you forever disgusted with the kind of oranges you could buy in Canada. The new people had put in a swimming pool, which was used mostly by the two pretty teenage daughters – girls who would look right through me when they met me on the street – and by the daughters' boyfriends. Some bushes had grown up fairly high between my aunts' yard and theirs, but it was still possible for me to watch them running around the pool and pushing each other in, with great shrieks and splashes. I despised their antics because I took life seriously and had a much more lofty and tender notion of romance. But I would have liked to get their attention just the same. I would have liked for one of them to see my pale pajamas moving in the dark, and to scream out in earnest, thinking that I was a ghost.